ABOUT THE EDITORS

STEPHEN J. DUBNER is the author of *Confessions of a Hero Worshiper* and *Turbulent Souls*, and is a former writer and editor at the *New York Times Magazine*, where in 2003 he wrote the cover story about Steven Levitt that launched *Freakonomics*. He lives in New York City with his family.

OTTO PENZLER is the proprietor of the Mysterious Bookshop, the founder of the Mysterious Press, the creator of Otto Penzler Books, and the editor of many books and anthologies.

THOMAS H. COOK is the author of twenty-two books, including *The Chatham School Affair*, which won the Edgar Allan Poe award for Best Novel, and, most recently, *The Last Talk with Lola Faye*.

The Best American CRIME REPORTING
2010

The Best American Crime Reporting

Editors

2002: Nicholas Pileggi

2003: John Berendt

2004: Joseph Wambaugh

2005: James Ellroy

2006: Mark Bowden

2007: Linda Fairstein

2008: Jonathan Kellerman

2009: Jeffrey Toobin

The Best American
CRIME REPORTING
2010

Guest Editor
STEPHEN J. DUBNER

Series Editors
OTTO PENZLER AND
THOMAS H. COOK

An Imprint of HarperCollins*Publishers*

FIRST EDITION

Library of Congress Cataloging-in-Publication Data has been applied for.

ISBN: 978-0-06-149086-6

10 11 12 13 14 WBC/RRD 10 9 8 7 6 5 4 3

Contents

Preface

CRIME IS ARGUABLY CHIEF among our tragedies because it is not encoded within the human experience in the way that death is encoded in every living cell. We are not genetically fated either to commit or to suffer crime. In the vast majority of cases, it is an act first grimly willed, then either meticulously or haphazardly plotted, then finally, in the absence of an outwardly staying hand or an inwardly reasoning thought, cold-bloodedly carried out. Crime is seldom a response to a fleeting itch, but rather the product of an insistent urge, say, to make money without working for it or to eliminate a rival by killing rather than outthinking him. For the most part, crime doesn't strike impersonally, like a virus, nor in response to any actual physical appetite, as a leopard kills a deer. For that reason, it often victimizes people because they possess otherwise desirable qualities. It is beauty that catches the eye of the sex-enslaver. It is the wallet of an honest worker that attracts the mugger's hand.

The hungers that cause crime are rarely biological. Who robs a bank in order to buy a sandwich or murders a prostitute for lack of sex? There is little doubt that crime is sometimes the product of mental disease, of course, but mental disorder can no less easily drive men to acts of nobility and courage. Who can doubt, for example, that the man who killed John Wilkes Booth was completely out of his mind?

A criminal act almost always resides at some point on the spectrum of personal selfishness. Responding to a selfish urge, an esteemed financial advisor decides upon a course that will create a monster of mendacity, and the likes of Bernie Madoff suddenly sprouts among us. On a quiet street in Greenwich Village, a man sees a little boy on his way to school and decides that his own momentary sexual release is worth the whole life of a child. A Russian housing development becomes a killing field when a nondescript neighbor repeatedly follows an appetite whose satisfaction neither feeds nor clothes him, but whose dark allure seems almost as irresistible.

As a form of selfishness, crime is marked by a peculiar incapacity to delay gratification. In a luxurious house with a sparkling pool, a famous man chooses a route that will lead him to public infamy and lifelong exile because he cannot deny himself the fleeting ecstasy of a spasm. In a world so far from this it seems hardly possible that it occupies the same planet, a teenage girl plots the slaughter of her family because she cannot delay an independence that would but shortly have been hers. On an isolated train bridge, a young man cannot bear another moment without asserting himself, and finds the most immediate tool of that assertion in a loaded gun.

Because most crime is simply one form or another of selfish human action, its sources are generally quite clear. Criminals are known for many things, but subtlety and nuance are not among them. When a gang of bunglers steals a rack of buffalo bones, one does not assume an irrepressible interest in the physiology of mammoths. But the very same motive can lead very different men to breed killer dogs or turn a few squalid rooms into a South of the Border torture chamber. It is not the nature of the motive but the extremity with which it is pursued that makes all the difference, and it is in that difference that the mystery of motivation actually resides. For why, in response to the same need to be noticed, does one young man create havoc with a gun while another does it with a computer? Why does one man seek only to steal the skeleton of a buffalo, while another (say, Vladimir Putin) wishes to steal the freedom of an entire people?

Crime, in the end, is human frailty writ large. But even in response to crime, that frailty presides. For how can any legal code deal with the passionate need of a parent to reclaim a kidnapped child? How can juries fail to be swayed by myth when it is clothed as expertise?

Such are the issues confronted and the questions raised in this year's *Best American Crime Reporting*, a collection whose range and depth once again demonstrate the extraordinary contribution American crime reporting makes to our country's contemporary literature, as well as to our ongoing concern for and analysis of man's deepest needs and darkest acts. As a collection, and as a series, it continues to take man as man; neither less nor more than what his acts reveal, man for better and for worse, in sickness and in health, from this day forward and for evermore.

Thomas H. Cook
Otto Penzler
March 2010

Stephen J. Dubner

Introduction

I WILL NOT WASTE much of your time describing the stories you will read in this collection. They are told so well, with such perverse attention to detail, that simply summarizing them would constitute a crime in itself.

I will, however, ask you to consider a few questions that came to mind while reading them. Such as: *What causes crime in the first place?*

As the Great Recession of 2008 blasted into view, doleful prognosticators warned us that crime would surely spike. But it hasn't. For a society that is rather obsessive about crime, it turns out we don't know much about it. We assume that a bad economy inevitably leads to more crime, but in fact that is not so, especially for violent crime. The economy did quite well during stretches of the 1960s, when crime was rising fast, and once again during the late 1980s, which saw a crippling rise in crime.

So if a bad economy doesn't cause crime, what does?

Unwantedness, for one. That's right: unwanted children are more likely to turn into criminals than children whose parents want them badly. That's why, as jarring as this may sound, the legalization of abortion in 1973 led to a lagged decrease in crime—because it afforded many women the opportunity to terminate unwanted pregnancies, resulting in a generation of children that came of age without some of its most vulnerable citizens.

Lax prosecution and sentencing also encourage crime. Many of us preserve a useful fiction that criminals are unlike you and me in every way, but they aren't as different as we may wish—most centrally so in that they, like us, respond fiercely to incentives. When there is a weak incentive to not commit crimes, therefore, more crimes are committed. We saw this in much of the 1960s and 1970s, when judicial and civil rights reforms led to lower arrest rates, lower imprisonment rates, and shorter prison sentences. *Voila!* The perfect recipe for more crime. But this recipe was more recently reversed—and then some, with historically high rates of imprisonment. As a result: *voila!* again; crime fell.

As it happens, television also leads to crime. This is perhaps an even more controversial theory than the abortion theory, but the data strongly suggest it is true: children who grow up watching a lot of TV are more likely than other children to become criminals. The content itself, however, does not seem to be the culprit. Some people have long argued that violent TV shows lead to violent behavior, but that doesn't seem to be the case. Rather, it seems that children who take in a lot of TV from birth through age four—even the most innocuous, family-friendly fare—are more likely to engage in crime when they grow up. Why? It's hard to say. Maybe kids who watch a lot of TV don't get properly socialized, or never learn to entertain themselves. Perhaps TV makes the have-nots want the things the haves have, even if it means committing a crime to get them. Or maybe it has nothing to do with the kids at all; maybe it's a case of Mom and Dad becoming derelict when they realize that watching TV is a lot more entertaining than taking care of the kids.

So now we know a bit about why the modern world is so drenched in crime.

Or *is* it?

The next time you're at a bar or a dinner party, or wherever you convene with people who are willing to wager, try this one: *If you look at the homicide rate in, say, western Europe over the past six centuries, which century has the highest rate and which has the lowest?* You, dear reader, will likely win this bet, for the homicide rate in Europe was far higher in the fifteenth century than in the twentieth century—more than 40 times greater in Scandinavia and more than 15 times greater in Germany. Italy has seen the most amazing decline: there were 73 homicides per 100,000 people in the fifteenth century and fewer than 3 per 100,000 in the twentieth.

So perhaps we've been asking the wrong question all along. Rather than wonder why there's so much crime in the world, perhaps we should ask why there's so *little*. Isn't it remarkable? Consider how many of us share this increasingly crowded and competitive planet—in the aftermath of a calamitous financial meltdown, no less—and then look at the numberless opportunities we forego daily to steal, cheat, lie, and even kill.

Why?

Alas, that is a question for philosophers, or someone with more advanced degrees than mine.

But here is what I find particularly interesting: we collectively seem unwilling, or unable, to fully accept the fact that there is less crime today than there used to be. A dramatic decrease in crime began in this country nearly twenty years ago. It is hard to remember just how welcome—and startling—this crime drop was. At the time, violent crime drove the public discourse; it led the nightly news and it dominated political conversations. The smart money said the problem would get only worse. And then, instead, the problem went into reverse. In 1991, the rate of violent crime was 758 per 100,000 people; by 2001, it had plunged to 507, a 33 percent decrease. (Property crime also fell, from 5,140 per 100,000 people to 3,568, a 30 percent drop.)

Crime has continued to fall in recent years, albeit not as extravagantly as during the 1990s—a decrease of about 10 percent over the past decade. The decline has continued even during the recession. But do you know what the pollsters tell us? They say that Americans are convinced that crime is on the rise once again. Data be damned, that's what we think: the world is dangerous and getting more so, and we cannot be convinced otherwise.

Why on earth is this the case?

Perhaps we are still shaken up from those terrible high-crime decades and can't believe those shadows are gone for good. Perhaps we have come to distrust the data the police cite. Or maybe the recession has been so depressing that we've lost the ability to see straight.

I have one more possibility: TV shows. Have you noticed how many crime shows are on TV these days? Here are the top twenty shows from the fall/winter 2008 season, with the crime shows bolded:

1. *Dancing with the Stars*
2. *Dancing with the Stars Results*
3. ***CSI***
4. ***NCIS***
5. *NBC Sunday Night Football*
6. ***The Mentalist***
7. *Desperate Housewives*
8. *60 Minutes*
9. ***Criminal Minds***
10. *Grey's Anatomy*
11. ***CSI: NY***
12. *Two and a Half Men*
13. ***CSI: Miami***

14. ***Without a Trace***
15. *Survivor: Gabon*
16. ***Cold Case***
17. ***Eleventh Hour***
18. *Biggest Loser 7*
19. ***24********
20. *The OT*

And here are the top twenty shows from the 1991–1992 TV season,† when actual crime was at its worst:

1. *60 Minutes*
2. *Roseanne*
3. *Murphy Brown*
4. *Cheers*
5. *Home Improvement*
6. *Designing Women*
7. *Coach*
8. *Full House*
9. ***Unsolved Mysteries***
10. ***Murder, She Wrote***
11. *Major Dad*
12. *NFL Monday Night Football*
13. *Evening Shade*
14. *Northern Exposure*
15. *A Different World*
16. *The Cosby Show*

---

*   The criminals of *24* are primarily terrorists, but they are criminals nonetheless.

†   It is worth noting that *Unsolved Mysteries* was not exclusively about crime, and that *Murder, She Wrote* was a rather mellow program about a female mystery writer and amateur detective in coastal Maine—hardly a reflection of the era's gruesome carjackings and crack murders.

So there appears to be an inverse relationship between the amount of real crime in the U.S. and the number of popular TV shows about crime. And at this moment, crime seems to collectively captivate us well beyond the degree to which it actually exists. Why?

It may be that TV shows about murder and mayhem are more fun to watch when you're not so worried about actually getting murdered. Our relative safety lets us appreciate horrific TV murders for what they are: fictional exaggerations of real-life anomalies. Like a shark attack or a $100 million lottery winner, a murder is far more unlikely than the media would have us believe.

The stories in this fine book similarly represent the anomalies—and that is why we love them. They represent the rare moments when the human psyche, despite all encouragement to the contrary, plows through the barrier of accepted behavior and becomes a killer or a con man or a remorseless brute. A few of these criminals are very well-known (Bernie Madoff and Roman Polanski), but most of them would have never gained our attention at all had they not done something so very rare.

The writing you will encounter is simply spectacular. Weird and mesmerizing and chilling and bold. Kevin Gray profiles Helg Sgarbi, a Swiss swindler who to Gray's eyes (and, therefore, ours) doesn't appear at all capable of seducing even one wealthy woman, much less a string of them. And yet, in one of the most delicious kickers I have ever read, Sgarbi even seems to get his hooks into Christine, "the thirtysomething German translator I've brought to facilitate dealings with the prison guards." Upon leaving the prison, Christine admits as much to Gray: "Yes, it's strange, I know. I shouldn't feel sorry for him, but I do."

Of course we should never forget how cruel these crimes can be, nor how damaging and unfair for their victims. We might find ourselves wishing that criminals, even those as interesting as Sgarbi, would disappear, that crime itself might cease. But that of course is impossible. Wrongdoing is baked into the human condition. And we wouldn't quite want that anyway, would we? What would writers like Kevin Gray and Charles Bowden and David Grann do with themselves?

On the other hand: if crime disappeared entirely, there would probably be even more crime shows on TV to employ them.

The Best American CRIME REPORTING

2010

Calvin Trillin

WHAT WHOOPI GOLDBERG ("NOT A RAPE-RAPE"), HARVEY WEINSTEIN ("SO-CALLED CRIME"), ET AL. ARE SAYING IN THEIR OUTRAGE OVER THE ARREST OF ROMAN POLANSKI

FROM *The Nation*

A youthful error? Yes, perhaps.
But he's been punished for this lapse—
For decades exiled from LA
He knows, as he wakes up each day,
He'll miss the movers and the shakers.
He'll never get to see the Lakers.
For just one old and small mischance,
He has to live in Paris, France.

He's suffered slurs and other stuff.
Has he not suffered quite enough?
How can these people get so riled?
He only raped a single child.

Why make him into some Darth Vader
For sodomizing one eighth grader?
This man is brilliant, that's for sure—
Authentically, a film auteur.
He gets awards that are his due.
He knows important people, too—
Important people just like us.
And we know how to make a fuss.
Celebrities would just be fools
To play by little people's rules.
So Roman's banner we unfurl.
He only raped one little girl.

AT THE TRAIN BRIDGE

FROM *The New Yorker*

SCOTT JOHNSON SEES HIMSELF as one of those guys who never caught a break. "Seems like whatever I did was never enough," he told the police in one interview. "It seems like whenever I was almost at the point of obtaining something or getting somewhere, seems like something would happen and take it away. You know, it seems like it's been like that way through my whole life." The people who were affected by the crimes he committed see things differently. One of them has said, "Scott Johnson wanted to blame everyone and everything for his pathetic life." At the time of the crimes, the summer of 2008, Johnson's life would have indeed struck many people as pathetic. At thirty-eight—a healthy and fit and presentable thirty-eight—he was living with his mother in Kingsford, Michigan, having retreated in 2001 from an increasingly unsuccessful decade in Louisiana. Kingsford is just across the Menominee River from northern Wisconsin, at the mainland edge of what people in Michigan call the Upper Peninsula, or the U.P.—a vast, underpopulated, heavily wooded landmass that extends into the

Great Lakes. In growing up in Kingsford and in the contiguous city of Iron Mountain, Johnson could claim to have been short-changed when it came to fathers—his biological father left when Scott was an infant and his stepfather could apparently be a violent drunk—but his mother seemed devoted to him. Years later, after the crimes, she still talked about his smile and the twinkle in his eye. "I thought I was the luckiest mom alive to have a son like Scott," she said. Johnson actually had some pleasant memories of his childhood, particularly of hunting in the woods and target shooting. "He said that by the age of nine he received his first weapon, a single shot 20 gauge as a gift from his mother," one of the court-appointed psychologists who examined Johnson reported. "Later, he received from her a 30/30 rifle. He described these gifts as not inconsistent or unusual among his peer group or within the rural culture of upper Michigan."

Johnson got to Louisiana through the Army. Shortly after graduating from Kingsford High School, where he'd finished in the top half of his class, he left for basic training, and he was eventually assigned to Fort Polk. At a Baptist church, he met a young woman named Theresa, whose father was also in the Army, and in 1991 they were married. "That appears to be when everything started to go bad," the judge in Johnson's case later said. You could indeed see Johnson's marriage as the beginning of his problems or you could see it as a sort of canvas on which his problems became visible. The first year or so was fine, his wife later said, but he became controlling and abusive, particularly after he finished his Army hitch and they moved to Shreveport. By 1994, he'd begun to threaten to kill her. "Mrs. Johnson related that the defendant would constantly remind her of how stupid and worthless that he thought she was," the pre-sentence report on Scott Johnson said. When Theresa Johnson was five months pregnant with their daughter—their first child, a boy, had been born five years before—he pushed her down because she had failed to mail some Christmas cards when he wanted them mailed. The last straw came in 1999, when she confronted him about leaving their daughter in the back yard alone. According to the report, he got so angry that he threw the family cat against the wall hard enough to render it unconscious. When Theresa Johnson returned from the back yard with the daughter in her arms, he was pointing a rifle at her chest from approximately eight feet away. Although her memory of the incident is almost blank after that moment—she has surmised that she must have been in shock—she remembers one remark by her husband: "Look what you made me do." She and the children left for Ohio, where she had family, and she filed for divorce.

After his discharge, Johnson had held a succession of jobs. He worked in a V.A. hospital. He worked in a center for troubled adolescents. He worked as a shuttle driver for a Ramada Inn. He worked at a convenience store. His stories about how his various types of employment came to an end tend to involve some sort of altercation brought about by the unfairness of his employer. According to one psychologist, Johnson's stories in general tended to involve "the ways in which he has been mistreated by others and about his own superior assets and virtues." That was true of what he said about the National Guard, which he had joined after his active-duty Army service was over. He'd enrolled in Officer Candidate School, but eventually washed out. By his account, he'd taken two days off to attend his grandmother's funeral and "they got pissed off and fucked with me a lot after that. It was very unprofessional." When his wife divorced him, he was in the final year of a five-year apprentice plumbing program, but he dropped out without getting a plumbing license.

After 2001, he no longer saw his children. By the next year, he had begun skipping child-support payments. Theresa Johnson reported some phone calls threatening violence. He had passed some bad checks at a gun-and-knife show—one of them as payment for a .308 semi-automatic rifle. "I was depressed and drinking a lot and smoking pot," he told one of the psychologists. "I was self-destructing. I quit my job, wrote some bad checks, and ran before they could catch me. . . . I got a passport and planned to leave the country but then I went up to Kingsford to see my mom before I left and then it just got easy to stay in Michigan. . . . I couldn't work because they'd catch me, so I did a couple of little jobs or got money from my mom and brother. I just leeched off of them."

That arrangement lasted for six or seven years. Jobs were not as easy to find as they had once been in the part of the U.P. which borders Wisconsin—the iron ore that left names like Iron Mountain and Iron River and Vulcan played out decades ago; the forest-products industry has not been in a boom—but Johnson didn't try. In his view, the way to avoid the burden of child support and the threat of arrest for check-kiting was to "go off the grid." His only form of work was maintenance on his mother's house, a modest bungalow not far from the Menominee River. He stuck to himself, gradually not even eating meals with his mother and an older half brother, who also lived there. He did a lot of exercising. By his estimation, he ran eight to ten miles a day and rode his bicycle thirty miles a day. Sometimes he swam in the Menominee, at a swimming hole known locally as the train bridge.

Less than a mile from Johnson's mother's house, Skidmore Drive begins as a regular street but then turns into a gravel road. At the end of the gravel road, a footpath continues through the woods. After half a mile or so, the path veers sharply toward some railroad tracks that lead to a railroad bridge crossing high over the Menominee River. Side paths lead down to the riverbank. The Menominee is wide and slow there. Tall trees grow on either side, so that someone on the river's bank has a feeling of total isolation. Even by the standards of the U.P., where no one lives far from sylvan beauty, it's a gorgeous spot. For generations, people from the Iron Mountain and Kingsford area, particularly young people, have come to the train bridge to swim and to drop into the river from a rope that hangs from the bridge's superstructure and to drink beer in a place where there is nobody asking for your proof of age. On the Wisconsin side, there's another mile or so of woods between the river and the town of Niagara. It was in those woods that, around 2004, Scott Johnson secreted some supplies—a sleeping bag, clothes, a knife. In the fissure of a rock, he hid the rifle he'd bought at the Louisiana gun-and-knife show. To police detectives, he later explained this preparation with a maxim: "If you fail to plan, you can plan on failure."

JOHNSON'S ROUTINE WAS not the sort of routine that led to a lot of contact with women. Shortly after his return, he had lived with a woman briefly, but by the summer of 2008 he had not been with a woman in six years. The previous winter, at the Family Dollar store in Kingsford, he'd met a young woman who lived near him, and they had been in each other's company for several months in a platonic way. ("He knew that I don't even like being touched," she later said.) He stopped at her place now and then to chat or to help her with her garden. They sometimes took walks or bike rides—including a couple to the train bridge, which she had somehow never visited before. Then, on July 30, 2008, he asked her if she wanted to go for a bike ride. They went to the train bridge. "We went for a bike ride together in the evening," the young woman later wrote in a statement to the authorities. "We walked into the woods in East Kingsford and crossed the train bridge into Wisconsin. We were alone. He led me into the woods that was off of one of the trails and that's when he put his hands under my tank top and shoved me to the ground and pulled my pants and underpants off and he forced himself into me. I begged him to stop, but he wouldn't. I said 'NO' several times as he was on me but he wouldn't listen."

Johnson later offered another version of the event—in his version, he did not manage to complete the act—but he didn't deny that a sexual assault had taken place. He has said that, particularly because he didn't consider the young woman in question nearly as attractive as some of the women he'd known when he had a job and money, he became enraged when she rejected his advance. Apparently, he pleaded with her not to phone the police. He said that she could punish him anyway that she wanted, including beating him with a baseball bat. As he saw it, if she went to the police he'd be wanted in Louisiana for passing bad checks and in Ohio for failure to provide child support and in Wisconsin for sexual assault. He dreaded the thought of being sent to jail as a sex offender. That night, he stayed in the woods. When he went by his mother's house the next day, she told him that the police had been by and wanted to speak to him. He said he would straighten everything out after he had something to eat, and asked for ten dollars to go to Subway. "I went and got something to eat so I could sit down and think about it," he later said. "What am I gonna do? Am I gonna turn myself in or do the shoot 'em up thing? What am I gonna do?" By late that afternoon, he was walking over the train bridge, noticing the teenagers who had taken advantage of a beautiful summer day to go swimming in the river below. He walked to his camp, on the Wisconsin side of the river. According to a sentencing memo prepared by Assistant Attorney General Gary Freyberg, the lead prosecutor in Johnson's case, "He put on camouflage pants, a camouflage shirt, and a camouflage floppy-brimmed hat. He exchanged the tennis shoes he was wearing for boots, and placed camouflage field bandages in the pockets of his shirt. He retrieved his disassembled .308 caliber semi-automatic rifle from a gun case stashed in a jagged rock outcropping, put the pieces together, and cleaned the rifle."

Johnson has offered several versions of what was going on in his mind as he settled into a spot that gave him a good view of the teenagers on the Michigan bank of the river. "I'm thinking, do I go out with a bang, you know," he said in one police interview. "I got nothing to lose . . . the only power I have in this life is to take." At times, he seemed to imply that his plan was to shoot people at the train bridge in order to attract police and first responders so that he could kill as many of them as possible. ("My initial plan was to use those people as bait.") At times, he has implied that what he was planning was what is sometimes known as "suicide by cop," by putting "police in a position where they had to put me down." At times, he's said that what he contemplated doing was "balancing the scales," so that people could understand the pain he'd been through. At times, also, he has said that he had doubts that he could "really go through with this," and that he was about to dismantle his weapon when he heard people approaching.

"Tiffany Pohlson, 17, Anthony Spigarelli, 18, Katrina Coates, 17, and Derek Barnes, 18, swam across the river to Wisconsin in order to jump off of a large rock overhanging the river located west of the defendant's firing position," Freyberg's sentencing memo says. "In swimsuits and shorts, they walked barefoot in a staggered line on a rough trail through the woods toward the rock face where the defendant waited with his assault rifle. Anthony Spigarelli was in front chatting with his best friend Derek Barnes. Tiffany Pohlson and her best friend, Katrina Coates, followed closely behind. As he waited in ambush, the defendant heard the teenagers coming toward his position. He could tell by their voices that there were two males and two females. The defendant became afraid that he was 'trapped,' that he would be discovered, and that someone would have a cell phone and he would be 'busted.' When the group was about 15 to 20 feet away, the defendant jumped up from his position. The teenagers were startled and confused by the sight of a man in camouflage and they stopped on the trail. When the defendant raised his rifle and advanced toward them, all four teenagers turned to run. As they fled, the defendant opened fire. Anthony Spigarelli was shot in the back of the head and died instantly. His body rolled down the hill toward the river until its descent was stopped by a small tree. Tiffany Pohlson was holding the hand of Katrina Coates when she was struck by a bullet to the back of her head, killing her instantly."

Johnson fired some shots at the other two teenagers, who were fleeing through the woods. Then he turned his attention to the swimming hole and sprayed bullets at the people who were on the Michigan bank. Bryan Mort, nineteen, was seriously wounded. A teenager who had taken cover at the base of the bridge phoned 911 on his cell phone; as sirens approached, Johnson faded back into the woods. He had fired at least two dozen rounds.

No one knew the identity or the precise whereabouts of the shooter. Soon there were a hundred law-enforcement officers in the vicinity of the train bridge. A perimeter was formed around the woods on either side of the Menominee. Nearby houses were evacuated. It wasn't until eight in the evening·that officers were able to reach the bodies of Anthony Spigarelli and Tiffany Pohlson. By then, Bryan Mort had been moved by boat to a ramp that was accessible to an ambulance, but he was pronounced dead at the hospital. Scott Johnson spent the night in the woods. The next morning, he dismantled his rifle, walked out of the woods near Niagara, and surrendered.

SEVERAL MONTHS LATER, Lisa Hoffman, of the Iron Mountain *Daily News*, wrote a series of articles recalling the teenagers Johnson had killed. Tony Spigarelli, an outgoing young man from Iron Mountain who played soccer and hoped to study aeronautics someday, had been three weeks away from entering college.

Tiffany Pohlson, who was from Vulcan, about ten miles from Iron Mountain, had been due to start her senior year in high school in the fall; her goal was to become a surgical technician. Bryan Mort, who dreamed of opening an auto shop with his brothers someday, had dropped out of school at seventeen but, after working for a while, had gone back to get his diploma. On the summer day when he happened to go to the train bridge to swim, he was two weeks away from becoming the first member of his family to go to college. The shock caused in the community by the murders of three innocent teenagers—the mixture of disbelief and grief and rage—was intensified by the contrast between the horrific act and the tranquillity of the setting. Almost a year later, Terri Bianco-Spigarelli, as if still finding the events at the train bridge hard to believe, said of her son, "He was just going swimming."

That statement was made during Scott Johnson's sentencing hearing, this spring. Johnson had never expressed any interest in an insanity defense—what he called, in a letter from jail to his mother, "playing the coo-coo card." In one interview with a court-appointed psychologist, he said, "You don't have to be crazy to do what I did, just angry." The specialists who examined him agreed. They were unanimous in believing that he did not lack the capacity to understand the wrongfulness of his actions. In March, 2009, Johnson had changed his plea from not guilty to nolo contendere, which has the effect of a guilty plea, and the circuit-court judge, Tim Duket, had scheduled a hearing at which victims as well as Johnson would have an opportunity to speak before a sentence was imposed. No matter what was said, Johnson was expected to be sentenced to life in prison without the possibility of parole, the most severe penalty the state of Wisconsin has to offer.

For the family of Bryan Mort, that wasn't enough. Through a petition signed by local residents and the support of their congressman, the Morts pressed for a federal prosecution of Scott

Johnson. Under a federal law passed after 9/11, acts of violence on railroad property—which is where Mort was, since the railroad's right-of-way extends fifty feet on either side of the train bridge— can be prosecuted as acts of terrorism, with sentences that include the death penalty. Four days before the sentencing hearing, friends and family of Bryan Mort gathered at the Iron Mountain cemetery on what would have been his twentieth birthday. In the Iron Mountain *Daily News* coverage of the event, the quote from Bryan's father was succinct: "The Bible says 'an eye for an eye.'"

THE SENTENCING HEARING was held in the county seat of Marinette County, a city that is also called Marinette, about an hour and a half from the scene of the crimes. The audience sat in a large, panelled room that is ordinarily used for meetings of the county board. In the earlier days of the courthouse, before an annex was built, it had been used for trials—"Equal Justice for All" is still carved over the door—and it had been temporarily changed back into a courtroom to accommodate those who had a personal stake in the outcome of *Wisconsin v. Scott J. Johnson*. Except for lawyers, just about everyone was dressed informally, even those who were there to speak. Two people were wearing T-shirts that said "Spigarelli Excavating." Five women in one row, including Bryan Mort's mother, Sylvia, were wearing T-shirts that said on the back "Bryan W. Mort 1989–2008" and on the front, under Bryan's picture, "Always in our hearts." Judge Duket began by reminding people that they were, in fact, in a courtroom, temporary or not, and that outbursts would not be tolerated. To back that up, more than a dozen officers from the sheriff's office were stationed around the room. Before the judge began the proceedings, another employee of Marinette County—a woman responsible for the care of crime victims and their families—had handed out boxes of Kleenex and packages of hard candy.

Nine months had passed since the events at the train bridge, but there was no expectation that the anger felt by the families of those killed by Johnson had dissipated. From the release of documents like police interviews, it had become clear that he was not inclined to express remorse or to beg their forgiveness. ("What do other guys in my position tell 'em? They're sorry? What does that do for them?") In fact, in a jailhouse interview with the Associated Press, Johnson had said that being upset over the death of the teenagers was like being upset over spilled milk.

Given the anger at Johnson, who sat at the defense table in an orange prison jumpsuit, it was not surprising that a lot of what was said in the Marinette County courtroom seemed designed to wound him rather than to describe the loss and suffering that his crimes had caused. Tiffany Pohlson's uncle called him a "useless piece of garbage." Johnson was regularly reminded that he had failed at everything he'd ever attempted—including even his horrific crime, since he'd apparently intended to kill even more people than he had managed to kill. David Spigarelli, Tony's father, concluded his statement by saying that prison would give Johnson "a chance to finally achieve something for the first time in his life, when his cellmate, Bubba, says 'bend over, I'm ready to lay this pipe.' He will finally have achieved his master plumber's status. . . . Me and Tony will be laughing our asses off, Scott Johnson." Most of what Terri Bianco-Spigarelli said, through tears, seemed designed to memorialize her son rather than to excoriate the defendant, but she said that Johnson would burn in hell, because God forgives only the remorseful. "I never hated anybody," she said. "I'm a people lover. I get along with everybody. I hate him, and I could kill him."

Scott Johnson read a prepared speech. At the start, he said that

the points he would make were based on a maxim that he'd de-
vised when he was twelve: "The truth of the matter at hand is
that the truth doesn't count anymore. It is the quality of the lie
that endures." He had any number of complaints to make about
police-interrogation quotes being taken out of context or psychologists being biased or the press getting the facts wrong,
particularly about whether he had planned the shooting in advance. He reiterated his belief that no purpose would be served
by saying that he was sorry for what he'd done. ("If I showed a
hint of remorse, what would people say then? 'Oh, he's lying.
Oh, he's faking.' ") He said what he did regret was that he had
to live among people who were liars, gullible, arrogant, and
brainwashed. The audience controlled itself through most of
the speech, but, when Johnson implied that money donated to the
victims' families for funeral expenses exceeded the costs of the
funerals, there was shouting in the courtroom. Sylvia Mort stood
up and, before the judge could react, said, "Let me out of here!"
As she stormed out, she said, loudly enough to be heard throughout the room, "Fuckin' piece of shit!" When order had been restored, Johnson finished his remarks, closing by quoting two
verses of the Louis Armstrong standard "What a Wonderful
World."

   "These families have you pegged perfectly," Judge Duket said
to Johnson, when it came time to impose a sentence. He portrayed the defendant as someone who blamed others for his constant failures, who thought that he was smarter than everyone
else, who craved attention, and who responded to his own problems by murdering innocent children. In addition to the harm
Johnson had done to his victims and their families, the judge
said, he'd brought great suffering to his own family. Johnson's
mother had said, "The pain is so bad I wanted to die. This is like
a living death," and the daughter he professed to love, now twelve,
was, according to Theresa Johnson, terrified that Scott Johnson
would get out of jail and come to Ohio to kill her. "If ever there

was a constellation of criminal activities that called out for maximum consecutive sentences, this would be the case," Judge
Duket said. What the prosecutor had asked for, after enumerat-
ing the cases of murder, attempted murder, and sexual assault,
was three life sentences without the possibility of parole, to be
served consecutively, plus two hundred and ninety-five years—a
sentence that sounded as if it required something beyond lon-
gevity, in the direction of reincarnation. On the subject of sentences that can obviously not be fulfilled, Judge Duket quoted a
Wisconsin Court of Appeals decision holding that such sentences
can, among other things, "properly express the community's out-
rage." The judge imposed everything that the prosecutor had
asked for. Outside the courtroom, Sylvia Mort, who vowed to
keep pursuing the death penalty, said of the sentence, "It's a beginning."

Near where the path through the woods to the train
bridge begins, there is now a memorial to the three teenagers
killed in what the inscription calls "a senseless act of violence."
A small section of ground has been bricked over, and on it two
benches face each other, on either side of a rectangular granite
monument that has pictures of Tony Spigarelli and Tiffany
Pohlson and Bryan Mort on it. The monument is also inscribed
with the first verse of a William Cowper hymn, "God Moves in
a Mysterious Way." Other than the memorial, the train-bridge
swimming hole is unchanged from the time the three teenagers
pictured on the monument went there to swim a year ago. It
remains idyllic—a scene that could be a calendar painting depicting lazy summer days in some bucolic patch of the upper
Midwest.

The young woman who was assaulted by Scott Johnson had
mentioned the beauty of the spot when, to the surprise of everyone involved, she showed up at the sentencing hearing to deliver

a victim's statement about how Johnson had betrayed her with an act that still haunts her every day. The train bridge was also mentioned in the speech that Johnson made before he was sentenced. "The train bridge has been washed in the blood that I spilled," he said. "The beauty of that place has been cursed by my actions. My memorial is made of iron and concrete."

CALVIN TRILLIN *has been a staff writer for* The New Yorker *since 1963. For fifteen years, he did a* New Yorker *series called "U.S. Journal"—a three-thousand-word article from somewhere in the United States every three weeks. He is the author of twenty-six books, including* Killings *and* American Stories.

Coda

During the years I traveled around the country for a series of articles I was doing for *The New Yorker*, my wife used to joke that I'd go anywhere a transcript was available. There was a kernel of truth in that. Magazine reporters are, of course, attracted to stories that have the potential for, say, a strong narrative line or moments of great drama—such as the awful drama at the train bridge on that lovely summer day. But they are also attracted by the availability of raw material that can help tell the story—an official report, a trove of documents, or, yes, a transcript.

I learned of the incidents at the train bridge shortly before Scott Johnson's trial was scheduled to begin, when I read in a brief newspaper item that he had changed his plea from guilty to nolo contendere. The sort of crime Scott Johnson had committed normally ends in the death of the perpetrator—killed by the police or by his own hand. Because Johnson survived, psychologist reports and police interrogations would be available.

He and the families of his victims would be speaking at his sentencing hearing. As it turned out, the judge permitted tape recorders at the sentencing hearing—meaning that I was able to leave Wisconsin carrying, among other things, the rough equivalent of a transcript.

Rick Anderson

SMOOTH JAILING

FROM *Seattle Weekly*

SMOOTH IS ON THE PHONE. "I've been charging $750," he tells his customer one day in 2007. "You know, I just give you a deal . . . my prices [between] me and you don't be the same prices to everybody else."

Jersey, his customer, listens. "I've been getting $250 a quarter [ounce]," Smooth says over his cell. "Two a quarter, you know." Jersey, a police informant, agrees to meet up, handing the phone back to a Seattle vice detective.

And Smooth is busted for drugs again.

In a word, busted is the life story of Stacy Earl Stith, street name Smooth. He's been caught a lot, often stumbling into the hands of police. In 1996, when a prostitute at Seventh and Bell asked what he was doing, Smooth said, "Selling, man!"—and pulled a cache of rocks from his pants pocket. "I sell to everyone!" The undercover police hooker beckoned her backup team, and Smooth went to jail.

In 2006, plainclothes cops were nabbing another dealer when Smooth and his girlfriend made two drug sales practically in front of them in City Hall Park, next to the King County Courthouse, where he'd already been convicted of nine felonies. He was arrested and went to jail only hours after he had been released from prison that same day.

According to court records and interviews, catching him wasn't complicated. He was mostly a street dealer—a cop's easy quota—distributing his stones, as he calls crack cocaine, hand to hand from Belltown to SoDo or by vehicle to home-delivery customers in the 'burbs. At times he stowed the tiny bags of stones in his car's or van's engine compartment, from where, an informant told police, the bags would occasionally drop onto the street, requiring Smooth to hop out and run back through traffic to retrieve them. Other times he'd spread the stash around: In a 2004 bust, cops found more than 15 grams of marijuana separated into 16 different bags in Smooth's pants pocket, 27 grams of marijuana and nine grams of crack in the trunk of his vehicle, 11 grams of crack in bags tucked into his waistband, and 49 grams of bagged crack in his underwear.

A 230-pound black man, his braided hair often dangling from under a sideways ball cap, Smooth has been relentlessly, if ineptly, selling and using drugs in Seattle for more than 25 years. Along the way, he's compiled a criminal record that's something of a record itself, authorities say: Adding up misdemeanors and felonies since the mid-1980s, he has 112 convictions. Not arrests, convictions: 94 misdemeanors and 18 felonies, revolving through the doors of juvenile court to municipal court to district court to superior court to federal court, from traffic and theft offenses and weapons and assault charges to burglary and crack sales. His first day in court was at age 13; his most recent, in January, at age 39.

"I have never seen anyone with this number of convictions around here," says 12-year King County deputy prosecutor Andy Colasurdo, who couldn't think of another violator who even came close. Some had a similar number of felonies, but "most of them only had 20 to 40 misdemeanors."

For all those convictions, Smooth has served an aggregate 14 years behind bars in local jails and state prisons, by Colasurdo's count. He had been sentenced to considerably more time, but his terms typically ran concurrently and he was usually released early. So he's had to work fast, scoring those 112 convictions in just 11 years of freedom. That's an average of 10 guilty verdicts per year.

"He," by the way, could mean Stacy Stith—or James Howard or Cal Beaver or Eric Smith, among others. Smooth has used 18 aliases, five dates of birth, and four Social Security numbers. It's possible, given that older court documents are often incomplete and crimes could be recorded under some of those aliases, Smooth's record may be even longer.

On the street, beat cops would recognize him on sight and assume he was in violation of something—parole, work release, curfew, loitering; most likely there was an arrest warrant somewhere with his name on it. (Court records show he had been sought on 52 warrants over two decades for a variety of crimes and failures to appear in court.)

Smooth was a sometimes hapless lawbreaker. One early morning call brought officers to a smashed display window at the downtown Bon Marché, where they found him standing nearby with a pile of stolen clothes at his feet, department store tags flapping in the wind. But he was no comic figure. In 1999, he sped away from a police stop and careened around Central District corners in his '85 Buick. The chase ended when he slid sideways to a stop, tossed a loaded 40-caliber Glock out a window, and bailed. An officer pinned him down, but needed backup help to get him into handcuffs. Smooth was later convicted of being an armed felon.

He also has six convictions for resisting or obstructing police officers. In South King County in 2004, holding $1,300 in powder and rock cocaine, Smooth had to be Tasered four times before two cops could cuff him. Court records describe him as "a high-risk offender who presents a significant threat to the community."

Smooth has been found guilty so often that the word may be meaningless to him. Once he'd reached 50 convictions—as he did by age 19, for one of 31 theft offenses in his career—what was another 50?

Colasurdo, who is on loan as a special assistant prosecutor in gun and drug cases for the office of U.S. Attorney Jeff Sullivan in Seattle, thinks Smooth "is either incapable of changing his criminal ways or unwilling to do so." So today the law has finally come down on Smooth. Except it landed so hard his defenders think the system might have gone too far the other way. Seattle attorney John Crowley, who has represented Smooth, says, "He has a dope problem. Like many of these guys when they're young, he couldn't figure out how to market himself, and found the best thing he could market was drugs."

Another attorney, public defender Lynn Hartfield, thinks some compassion is in order. Smooth's criminal career, she says, is "a testament as much to his being a victim of crack cocaine as it is to his being a perpetrator of its harms."

But after 112 convictions, can Smooth possibly make a case for leniency?

STACY STITH WAS FIVE DAYS SHY of his 13th birthday when he was first arrested, for third-degree theft. He was convicted a week later in King County Juvenile Court, but given no time. Smooth was convicted of the same crime 15 more times in the following three years, with sentences ranging from a few days to a few months.

He later informed a drug counselor that he began using marijuana at age 12, and has continued to smoke it through adulthood. He also started drinking as a juvenile, and as an adult could down a fifth of liquor daily. Additionally, Smooth first used cocaine at age 16, a habit that grew to more than 10 rocks a day, he said.

Smooth has told counselors, attorneys, and judges that he just can't beat his addiction, and that's what led to his life of crime, which includes convictions for felony theft, forgery, and burglary. Court records show he's done time in juvenile hall for possession of marijuana and cocaine, and has 11 felony convictions for possession or distribution of crack cocaine, not counting two charges that were dropped.

He was at least occasionally drugged up when he broke the law. In 2004, a Seattle police officer stopped Smooth in a '72 Pontiac for erratic driving and displaying license plates that had expired four years earlier. He was driving without a license, something he'd already been convicted of 20 times, along with a DUI and a dozen other traffic offenses. He was worried the cop might see a baggie of rocks on his floorboard, so he confessed to having just smoked weed. Really, he said, "if I had stones, I would have run or something." The cop found the drugs anyway.

Born in St. Louis and raised in the Seattle area, Smooth dropped out of high school at 15. His mother and father divorced when he was young, and his mom remarried and ran a day care. Family members couldn't be reached, but prosecutor Colasurdo says Smooth "had parents at home who loved him, provided for him, and served as good role models."

Smooth worked at times in the construction industry, but court records state his drug use had a "negative impact on his employment . . . such as being late for work, diminished productivity, absences, and using [drugs] at work, and termination."

For much of his adult life, when not in jail, prison, or a halfway house, Smooth has lived in apartments in South King County or has been homeless. He recently suffered a minor heart attack from cocaine use, he told a drug counselor, who noted in his report that Smooth "enjoys playing basketball, fishing, and dancing with his girlfriend," who was also busted for drugs.

Smooth married a Tacoma woman in 1998. She did not respond to phone calls for this story, but court papers show they have a child and she filed for divorce in 2004. It did not seem a happy union. Smooth, she said in her divorce filing, "resided in the penitentiary for the duration of the marriage."

He was out for a while in 2004. That September—the month he and his wife officially separated—Smooth was arrested for possession of crack and marijuana, and was booked and released. Twelve days later he was arrested for selling crack, and again booked and released. Less than a month later he was arrested again for possession. He awaited trial in jail, and in 2005 was convicted of all three charges.

Smooth faced a maximum of 120 months. He got 24, and ultimately did 12, gaining his release on Sept. 2, 2006. "Amazingly," Colasurdo says in court papers, "Stith was arrested on drug charges that same day after officers observed him selling drugs in a Seattle park [the City Hall Park incident]. Then, after being booked and released on that charge, he was arrested 11 days later, on September 13, 2006, after he was found in possession of both crack cocaine and marijuana."

Smooth had repeat opportunities to escape his drug cycle, but always wound up in court again, records show. He was first told by a judge 20 years ago to undergo drug-diversion counseling, an order repeated with every drug conviction thereafter. Awaiting trial on the pair of 2006 busts, he asked again for treatment.

"I've been to prison several times," he told a drug counselor, and received some drug counseling while going cold turkey. "I always come home and use drugs and alcohol. I've been a drug addict for 25 years. Please, for once, can you give me a chance to get sober and stay clean by going through with the recommendation [for drug counseling]? Thank you."

He was allowed to enroll as an outpatient at a Renton treatment center in early 2007. After attending 25 two-hour sessions, completing about a third of an 18-month program, he bailed.

Then came the call from Jersey.

On June 29, 2007, still facing his two latest King County drug felonies, Smooth met with Jersey, the police informant, at a First Hill parking lot and sold him an ounce of crack for $700. Seattle police detectives watched and took pictures.

In July, outside a convenience store in Tukwila, Smooth sold Jersey another ounce, also under surveillance. A week later, after another buy was set up, plainclothes cops moved in on Smooth's Dodge Caravan at a Denny's parking lot in Tukwila. They found 11 ounces of crack and three ounces of powder cocaine hidden in the engine compartment. Another quarter-ounce rock was discovered under the gas cap. Police began typing up four charges—two for possession and two for distribution of cocaine—potentially his 109th through 112th convictions.

Prosecutor Colasurdo isn't sure how, exactly, the case came to him. He's been on assignment from the county to the U.S. Attorney's Office since 2004, and coordinates with local agencies on extraordinary cases. "It was SPD detectives or someone from the local task force, or maybe the [King County] prosecutor" who were concerned about the amount of drugs Smooth was selling, says Colasurdo. Only later did the breadth of his record emerge.

"Unfortunately, it is not uncommon to find a defendant who has been convicted of 10-plus felony offenses, or even close to 20 if juvenile felonies are included," says Colasurdo. "What really distinguished Stith from others was the total amount of convictions."

Statutes allow five-year sentences for cocaine convictions in state court, but Smooth's offender level—a scoring system, based on past offenses, used to determine sentence ranges—mandated lower and concurrent terms, and judges are reluctant to hand down exceptional sentences to drug users. "We tried to get the maximum or near the maximum on him," says Ian Goodhew, deputy chief of staff to King County Prosecutor Dan Satterberg. "And yet Mr. Stith just kept committing crimes." What's more, his mostly nonviolent felonies also did not qualify him for a "three strikes" prosecution. "I don't see what else we could have done to lock him up longer," Goodhew says.

But under federal law, as a career offender Smooth could be prosecuted not only for his recent offenses, but in a sense for all of them. And he easily passed the test—a convicted federal offender needs only two prior felonies to receive an enhanced sentence as a career criminal.

"The fact that he has continued to re-offend so quickly after his last two stints in prison is extremely concerning, as is the fact that he has re-offended every time he has been released from jail and while charges have been pending," wrote Colasurdo and fellow prosecutor Kit Dimke in court papers. "Not once did he repay the mercy shown to him by the prosecutors and/or the courts with law-abiding behavior. Each time he fell back into his old patterns, each time he made the same bad decisions, and each time he re-offended. Clearly, these prior sentences have not had the desired effect on him or his behavior. A sentence of 360 months surely will."

That's what prosecutors sought: 30 years in federal prison. If Smooth was convicted and survived incarceration, he would be almost 70 upon release.

PROSECUTORS OFFERED SMOOTH a plea deal, but he chose to go to trial, claiming the informant, whom he met in his drug-counseling classes, talked him into getting back into drugs before entrapping him into selling again.

The feds conceded that Jersey made other drug deals with

Smooth out of the circle of their sting. Smooth claimed that it was Jersey who was the drug dealer, and that the informant wasn't prosecuted for a separate felony drug deal. But a federal jury found it hard to overlook the nearly one pound of crack and powder cocaine in Smooth's van. And by using the entrapment defense, Smooth opened the door for prosecutors to introduce his prior bad acts to show the jury he was predisposed to sell drugs. The June 2008 trial lasted three days, swiftly followed by a guilty verdict.

"The thing with Stacy is you look at his record, there's a bunch of felony convictions, but they're extremely low-level types of deals," says his attorney, Crowley. "And it's his priors, not rocks, that got him."

Crowley, a onetime federal prosecutor who has been a criminal defense attorney for 11 years, says his client deserved some tough love early on that he never got. "The longest he served, I think, was six years, and he needed about 12 to see if the system could shake some sense into him. Damn, it hurts to watch [Smooth go down]. There's a little boy in every one of these guys I represent."

Smooth's other attorney, Hartfield, a federal public defender who argued on his behalf at sentencing, said that her client didn't deserve the three-decade term sought by prosecutors, instead asking for 20 years. Though she doesn't want to discuss the case while it's on appeal, she notes in court papers that her client was trying to turn his life around. She calls him an "addict, one whose craving for a drug is so strong that he continues to sell to support his habit, heedless of the consequences."

Hartfield also pointed to the disparity between crack and powder cocaine sentences, arguing that the laws discriminate against African-Americans such as Stith, who, while he's used and sold powder in the past, was federally charged with holding and distributing crack. The Anti-Drug Abuse Act of 1986 set longer penalties for trafficking in crack than in powder, a disparity that critics say comes down hardest on blacks. (A U.S. Sentencing Commission study found that 82 percent of convicted crack offenders are African-American, while 72 percent of more lightly punished powder-cocaine offenders were white or Hispanic.)

On that issue, prosecutor Colasurdo agrees. "Is there a disparity? Yes," he says. (In 2007 the U.S. Supreme Court ruled that judges can consider the unevenness of the laws when passing sentences; there are also reform efforts in Congress to balance crack and powder penalties.) But the longer potential sentence had as much to do with Smooth's criminal history and attitude, says Colasurdo. "The case involved more than 50 grams, and he had more than two priors. By law, that allowed us to go forward with the penalty enhancement. He was never willing to cooperate, never settle, or accept what he did was wrong. Our responsibility is to protect the community."

Colasurdo says prosecutors could have gone for additional time—a mandatory life term, in fact—but chose not to. The U.S. actually threatened to seek life as part of its plea-bargaining with Smooth, but later withdrew the motion.

On January 12, U.S. District Court Judge James L. Robart sentenced Smooth to federal prison for 24 years, with 10 years supervised release if and when he gets out. On the bench, Robart called Smooth's record "remarkable."

Still, notching his 112th conviction, Smooth got a couple final breaks. The two pending county drug charges from 2006 have been dropped now that's he's off to a federal pen. The federal court also gave him credit for the time he served awaiting trial. And his case isn't over yet: His public defender is pursuing a reversal or a reduced sentence through the appellate courts.

Colasurdo hopes Smooth gets drug-abuse treatment in prison, if he's amenable. "If not," Colasurdo says, "those services should be reserved for those that are ready and willing to put forth the effort."

Counting time for good behavior Smooth could earn while locked up, the Federal Bureau of Prisons projects his release date to be July 30, 2028, a month before his 59th birthday. That may not be life, but it will be a late start on having one.

RICK ANDERSON *is a staff writer at* Seattle Weekly *and former news columnist for the* The Seattle Post-Intelligencer *and* The Seattle Times, *where he won the Haywood Broun award for columns about the underdog. He is the author of* Seattle Vice *and* Home Front: The Government's War on Soldiers. *His work has appeared in* Mother Jones, The Village Voice, *and* Salon.

Coda

I had just completed a story about a career criminal and frequent cop shooter who had twenty-six felonies to his credit when I began wondering if that was some kind of record. It wasn't. As I learned reading through the tomelike court files of Stacy Stith, some fellow lawbreakers might aspire to the throne with 50 or even 100 arrests, but none could come close to Smooth's 112 *convictions.* I am now writing about a local crime boss who notched his first felony, a sex-related charge, when Truman was president, and today faces his ninth felony, a sex-related charge, in the age of Obama. The boss is ninety-two and claims to get laid, or tries to, every day. That's how it is with the pros. They persevere.

Lisa R. Cohen

WHAT HAPPENED TO ETAN PATZ?

FROM *New York*

IT WILL BE 30 YEARS this Memorial Day weekend since reporters swarmed the Soho loft of Stan and Julie Patz, along with hundreds of policemen, as the grimfaced parents spelled their son's name over and over again: "E-T-A-N . . . *ay-TAHN.*"

The Patzes' story was already front-page fodder. That Friday, May 25, 1979, 6-year-old Etan, wearing his favorite Eastern Air Lines Future Flight Captain hat, had vanished somewhere in the two short blocks between his Prince Street home and the West Broadway school-bus stop. It was the first time his parents had let him walk the route alone, a decision they'd agonized over. (*Other kids are allowed*, Etan had said. *Why not me?*) His school never alerted the Patzes to Etan's absence, and it wasn't until 3:30 P.M., when he hadn't returned, that Julie called their neighbors, wondering if he might be with a friend. Twenty minutes later she called the police.

Now journalists gathered in the hushed, sun-washed front area of the loft, where Julie normally ran an in-home day-care center and Stan, a commercial photographer, often sat immersed in photo editing. Most of the reporters were respectful if awkward; there is no painless way to ask a parent *How do you feel?* at such a time. But then there was the tabloid photographer whose question they would never forget.

"Would you mind working up a few tears for me now," the man asked Julie, "so I don't have to come back and bother you again when they find the body?"

The photographer never had to come back. Etan's body has never been found. And although an entire network for tracking missing children emerged from his disappearance—pictures on milk cartons and Amber alerts and National Missing Children's Day—that's small comfort for Stan and Julie Patz, both of whom fought very hard for such things so others wouldn't have to. After 30 years, Etan's case remains officially open in New York, the mysterious, enduring symbol of a parent's worst nightmare.

For a whole generation of parents, and children, the words *Etan Patz* are unforgettable, haunting. A woman who grew up in the city, playing with other 8-year-olds on the Great Lawn in Central Park until they drifted home at dinnertime, still remembers her reaction to the news as a young mother in 1979. "It all changed after Etan," she says. "We all looked at each other and said, 'Well, that world is gone.'"

Yet despite the blanket coverage and widely trumpeted false leads—authorities flew to Israel to look for Etan once—only a small part of the story is known to the public. Law enforcement usually responds with a terse "No comment." Stan and Julie recognized at some indefinable moment that their son was never coming home, no matter what they said, so they stopped saying anything, turning away from the spotlight. Although their loft housed terrible memories, the Patzes stayed on Prince Street, partly because *My God, what if we moved and he somehow found his way back?* And partly because they refused to be driven away: "We had other, better memories here before Etan disappeared," Stan says, "a whole history of happier times. We've raised our other children here"—their daughter, who was 8 in 1979, and another son, who was 2. "I was never prepared to cede all that to some faceless villain along with my son."

But for years now, Stan has had a face to concentrate on; twice a year, in fact, on Etan's birthday and on the anniversary of his disappearance, Stan sends one of the old LOST CHILD posters to a man who's already in prison. He won't be there much longer, however, unless the successor to Manhattan district attorney Robert Morgenthau can keep him in jail. In the meantime, Stan's packages serve notice that someone is still paying close attention. On the back of the poster, he always writes the same thing: "What did you do to my little boy?"

STAN AND JULIE never changed their phone number either; Etan knew it by heart. And in spiral-bound notebooks they kept detailed logs of every call, no matter how crazy or obscene. Tips came in from around the world. A man said he'd picked up a 21-year-old hitching upstate with a kid he was "almost positive" was Etan. A psychic claimed Etan was alive "in a province of Italy." Closer to home, the police interviewed scores of people connected to the family—even grilling the Patzes themselves— yet one link would go unseen.

In 1979, Jose Antonio Ramos was a 35-year-old bearded drifter with flat, dark eyes and an unexpectedly soft voice who collected junk to sell around lower Manhattan. He lived in Alphabet City, at 234 East 4th Street, a building that today is coveted real estate but was then a quasi-shooting gallery, home to tough characters and struggling artists. (Madonna would live there briefly.) One former resident recalls an encounter with Ramos from his childhood. Playing with his sister in their bedroom the boy saw a row of toy soldiers and an old Barbie magically appear outside the window, suspended by invisible wire. Opening the window, he reached toward a toy. The line was yanked up a few inches. Leaning out, he spotted Ramos up on the fire escape gesturing for him to climb the rusty metal stairs. Instead, he slammed the window shut and told his sister not to say a word about what had happened.

By 1982, Ramos was living in a drainpipe in the Bronx. Two boys told their parents he'd stolen their bookbags and tried to coax them inside. Once there, cops found toys and photographs of boys, many of whom were blond, they noticed, like Etan. When an assistant D.A. asked Ramos about the pictures, he said they were just friends—in between talking about violent voices he'd once heard and struggled to control. Then the assistant D.A. asked the question on everyone's mind: Did Ramos ever know Etan Patz?

"No, no," he said quickly, though he remembered reading about him in the papers. Moments later, however, he offered up a connection, unprompted, that stunned his questioner.

"Sandy used to take care of him."

Ramos, it turned out, had been a boyfriend of sorts to Sandy Harmon,* a woman hired to walk Etan home from school during a school-bus strike in the weeks before the boy disappeared. She had a young son as well, one of the boys whose picture showed up in Ramos's stash. She would later swear to police that she never imagined Ramos might be molesting him.

The Patzes learned through media reports about the drainpipe arrest and Ramos's connection to what reporters called a Patz "babysitter," the first real link ever made between a possible suspect and their case. It was the second worst weekend of Stan's life. For three years, there had always been two basic scenarios he could choose to believe. In one, evil, unthinkable forces had abducted his son. In the other, a deranged but well-intentioned motherly type was loving Etan somewhere in a parallel life. With

*   Some names have been changed.

WHAT HAPPENED TO ETAN PATZ? 35

great skepticism, Stan had worked hard to ignore the first image and nurture the second. It helped him get through each day. Now he began to wander fearfully down that other path. A pedophile? In a filthy drainage tunnel?

Except the Bronx D.A. would soon declare that Ramos wasn't connected to the Patz case. Investigators couldn't make the Sandy revelation pay off—even though Stan would complain to a *People* reporter that he and Julie were very unhappy about the way the "drainpipe case" was being pursued. When the Bronx parents declined to press charges, Ramos was released, and he eventually left town.

It wasn't until after Stuart GraBois, a federal prosecutor in then–U.S. Attorney Rudolph Giuliani's office, was assigned the Patz case that Ramos would become a prime suspect. GraBois, a six-foot, steel-haired, steely-eyed product of Bensonhurst, took on the investigation with prosecutorial zeal—no file would go unread—and he became very interested in this suspected pedophile. The only problem was that no one knew where Ramos was. He'd gone to ground years before.

So when a colleague of GraBois's ran Ramos's name one more time, in 1988, he couldn't contain his excitement: Ramos had popped up in prison in Pennsylvania. It turned out he'd been traveling around in an old school bus, and had made the mistake of targeting his victims at annual gatherings of the loose hippie community, the Rainbow Family of Living Light. It didn't take too long for the guy handing out toys to arouse suspicion, and by 1987, Ramos had been sentenced to three and a half to seven years for corruption of a minor and indecent assault—on a 5-year-old.

GraBois arranged for the inmate to be brought to New York for questioning. When he arrived, Ramos was in visibly high spirits. He thought they'd called him in because he'd neglected to pay taxes on his street vending. GraBois let Ramos continue to think that was the purpose of this visit—until he abruptly changed his tone.

"How many times did you try to have sex with Etan Patz?"

Ramos went white. "I guess you have a witness," he said. "I'll tell you everything," he sobbed, admitting that, yes, he'd taken a little boy to his apartment for sex on the day Etan disappeared. Yes, he was "90 percent sure" it was the same boy he later saw on TV. But no, he let him go when the boy refused his advances, even walked him to a subway station and waved good-bye there.

"That's bullshit, Jose!"

"No, it's true. Look, I want to tell you everything," Ramos said. But then he asked for a lawyer. A few days later, he came in wearing a yarmulke—to signal his newfound, self-proclaimed Jewish roots—with a legal-aid attorney, who advised him to remain silent. The statute of limitations on a nine-year-old molestation crime had run out. GraBois had to find another way to get more.

THUS BEGAN A LENGTHY GAME of prosecutor and mouse. If GraBois couldn't get Ramos on the Patz case, he warned him, he'd go to Warren, Pennsylvania, hard by the Ohio border, and resurrect another old case there, involving the sodomy of a different Rainbow child. "Do you know where that place is?" GraBois recalls Ramos scoffing. "It's some backwoods little hole out in the middle of nowhere. You're never going to go all the way down there."

"Just watch me," GraBois replied. It took over two years, and unprecedented legal maneuvering, but in November 1990, he sent Ramos away for a maximum of twenty years. That, however, wasn't GraBois's ultimate goal. It was merely the next step in a plan whose details have never been fully revealed. Ramos has long been the prime suspect in Etan's disappearance, written about in New York papers and *Vanity Fair* (clippings Ramos eagerly collected in jail), and then featured on an ABC News *PrimeTime Live* piece (called "The Prime Suspect") I produced in 1991. But what has not been told is how GraBois was subsequently able to make the case against Ramos even stronger.

In prison, Ramos, seething over the prosecutor he called his persecutor, was soon asking a jailhouse acquaintance specific questions about where GraBois lived. So, GraBois decided to turn the tables on Ramos—he recruited the man, Jon Morgan, as part of an undercover operation.

In 1991, together with FBI special agent Mary Galligan, Gra-Bois spent months orchestrating the delicate logistics of having Ramos transferred to a federal prison, then getting Morgan into Ramos's cell. Since Ramos was being held in a protective segregation unit, that meant lockdown 23 hours a day with a known sex offender in a space not much bigger than a bathroom. No promises on payback, GraBois told his plant, but we'll certainly be willing to put in a good word.

Morgan was an unassuming-looking former international chemical-waste salesman whose questionable business practices had landed him in federal custody. When he signed on to GraBois's plan in the winter of 1991, he passed a lie-detector test, then headed upstate to the Federal Correctional Institution at Otisville.

A few days after arriving in the Special Housing Unit, Morgan crossed paths with Ramos outside its tiny law library. As usual, Ramos was carrying a thick pile of paperwork: court transcripts, subpoenas, press clippings. "What's happening with that address you were going to get me?" he asked Morgan. "I'm still interested."

"Why do you want GraBois's address?" Morgan asked.

"I know a guy on the outside. He's a demolitions expert, and he owes me a big favor."

It seemed unlikely Ramos could pull off such a plan. Nevertheless, an order was placed in prison files that GraBois be notified of Ramos's release, and the prosecutor soon began to use a remote-control key chain that started his car from yards away.

GraBois's own plan progressed just days later, when Ramos's cellmate moved out and the inmate asked for Morgan to replace him. Lying on their bunk beds, the two men would talk, and as Morgan relayed information to GraBois and Galligan, it solidified his own credibility. When Ramos spoke about his days in the Navy, military records confirmed it. When Morgan reported that he'd bought the school bus in Florida for $2,500, that also checked out.

Finally, Morgan delivered information that interested the Feds even more. "He knows Etan's school-bus route," he told Gra-Bois. "He knows all the stops the bus made back in 1979, and he says Etan's was the third stop in Soho."

Perched on his top bunk while Ramos read a Stephen King novel below, Morgan scribbled secret notes on the conversations. At one point, he told GraBois about a woman whose name he could know only from Ramos: "He doesn't know for sure where Harmon is," Morgan said. "She's probably in the same dump on 13th Street." Morgan was struck by Ramos's ill will toward his former girlfriend. "She is a 'bitch cunt.' Every woman Ramos talks about is a bitch, a cunt, or some other derogatory name. He apparently does not like women."

One week turned into two, and Morgan's stamina was waning. No confession had come, and Ramos would often say one thing only to seemingly contradict himself. *They would never be able to charge him for Etan's murder because there was no body.* And then: *Etan would turn up one day alive.* Morgan began to feel the insanity might be infectious, and he wanted out.

Unbeknownst to Morgan, his relief was warming up in a nearby cell. Jeremy Fischer had arrived in the SHU. He was

GraBois's phase two. Fischer had met Ramos up at Otisville on a previous stint and had approached authorities after overhearing Ramos outside of Jewish services one day. "Eaten, Eaten," Fischer said Ramos cried out, "I never meant to hurt you." GraBois himself knew, as few others did, that Ramos pronounced Etan's name that way.

With his slicked-back hair and thin, sly features, Fischer was a more sophisticated con man than Morgan, which made him harder to trust. But his accounts of conversations with Ramos resonated with details no one else could know. Fischer approached the job methodically. He flattered Ramos by telling him Socrates had liked boys too. He played therapist, which yielded graphic confessions of how Ramos had targeted other victims, including one with Down syndrome . . . and Etan Patz.

Fischer said Ramos told him about violating the boy—not just attempting to—and even described picking him up on Prince Street.

"Why would he ever go with you? Fischer asked.

"I just walked up to him and said, 'Hi, remember me? I'm Sandy's friend.'"

But like others before him, Fischer couldn't get Ramos to finish his story. It's a misnomer to call Ramos lucky since he's been behind bars for almost 23 years, but before Fischer was able to get a full confession, Ramos stumbled upon his new cellmate's true mission.

"Get him out of the cell," screamed Ramos. "He's a goddamn snitch."

"If I'm a snitch," Fischer said, "then you'd better watch out. If I want to get you, I have enough on you to turn you in for murder." Inmates along the tier were treated to the sounds of an emergency rescue, as guards were forced to separate the two men.

"GraBois knows I did it," Fischer later quoted Ramos as saying. "And it's killing him because he can't get it out of me."

TYPICAL RAMOS HYPERBOLE, GraBois says today, but the now-former prosecutor does concede his frustration. The informant accounts, along with other evidence, were turned over to the New York County district attorney's office, after the case was ultimately deemed outside GraBois's federal jurisdiction. But while Ramos has been serving out his Pennsylvania sentence, the D.A.'s office, under Robert Morgenthau, has yet to charge him on the Patz case. Admittedly, it's a tough one to prosecute, particularly with no body. (In 2000, NYPD forensic teams re-searched the 234 East 4th Street basement using updated DNA technology, but found only the remains of dead animals.) When GraBois and Galligan handed their evidence over in 1991, the FBI briefed the Patzes on their case against Ramos. The Feds believed that he had killed Etan. The Patzes said nothing in response, but silent tears wet Julie's face, and Stan struggled to hold his in. He reached over to soothe his wife, gently placing his hand on her shoulder.

Based on what he learned that day, and in subsequent years, Stan has come to the same conclusion: Ramos killed his son. And both Stan and GraBois, who now runs the Carpenters Union Benefits Fund, have long been unhappy that the D.A.'s office hasn't moved forward. "All we've ever wanted is for the D.A. to take the next step," Stan says. "Let someone else look at the evidence—show it to a grand jury."

Troubled by the D.A.'s inaction, in 2001 Stan filed a wrongful-death suit against Ramos, which necessitated the painful step of having Etan declared legally dead. When Stan first arrived home from a lunch in 2000 with GraBois and Brian O'Dwyer, the lawyer who'd pledged his pro-bono services, he already knew what Julie's reaction would be to the suit. "It won't bring Etan back," she said. It would only make her life—and her family's—even harder. Julie didn't work in the cocoon of a home office, where Stan largely conducted his business. Every morning she caught the uptown subway to her job at a bustling public school. She was the one, not Stan, who dealt with well-meaning, but heart-stopping, comments from people who thought they'd seen Etan back in 1982 or yesterday. Any new jolt of press would raise her profile yet again, and she'd spent over a third of her life in this hell already. "You do what you have to do," she finally said to her husband, "but I can't have any part of it." Stan signed the papers without her.

Three years later, a civil judge found Ramos responsible for Etan's death and awarded the family a symbolic $2 million in monetary damages, money they will never see and wouldn't want anyway. The lawsuit was merely a means to an end.

"Don't get me wrong," says Stan. "I'm not sitting around doing nothing but mourning and thinking of revenge. But I've also waited 30 years to get justice for Etan. I'll wait as long as it takes."

Still, both he and GraBois worry about the next few years. Last month, that note in Ramos's file kicked in, and the prison called GraBois: Ramos had shaved sixteen months off his sentence and will now be released in 2012, not 2014, as previously expected. "So all those wonderful things we are planning on," Stan says, "the increased publicity from the 30th anniversary, the new D.A. election—all those things are going to have to work faster."

Two months ago, the 89-year-old Morgenthau announced he was finally stepping down as D.A. One would-be successor is Leslie Crocker Snyder. When she ran against Morgenthau in 2005, she stood on the steps of City Hall with Stan and declared that if elected, she'd have a grand jury look at all the evidence. At the time, Morgenthau responded that the case was "a priority" but couldn't be prosecuted without sufficient evidence.

"Priority?" says Snyder now. "You can see how much priority it got!" She's especially dismayed that even though Stan met with the D.A.'s office, Morgenthau himself didn't sit down with the Patzes as requested. (The D.A.'s office has declined to comment.)

Snyder goes back a long way with GraBois; they used to face off in court, he as a young public defender, she an assistant D.A. So she listens carefully to his judgment.

"I've always been convinced of the two informants' credibility and of the viability of the other evidence," says GraBois. "That evidence points squarely at Jose Ramos. I think he destroyed the body, and in fact has stated that they'll never be able to get him because they'll never have a body. I think it's time for another push. Time is running out."

When I last reached out to her, Sandy Harmon was still living in New York. As for Ramos, he's not talking much these days. I produced his only television interview eighteen years ago, but when I was working on my book, he refused to meet. A few months ago, however, he began writing me, decrying the injustice of his case and asking for a few thousand dollars to replace his typewriter, art supplies, and television. Ramos also wrote that he was mentally and physically abused, starting from the age of 5. "There was no one to complaint [sic] about the treatment I was forced to endure as a child."

In prison, according to Fischer, Ramos would say of Etan, "I honor him every day." Perhaps one day his honor will win out.

LISA R. COHEN *is an Emmy award–winning television producer with over twenty years in network news, including* ABC News' PrimeTime Live *and* CBS News' 60 Minutes. *Her first book,* After Etan: The Missing Child Case That Held America Captive, *is the only book ever written on the culture-shifting mystery of the disappearance of six-year-old Etan Patz.*

Cohen is also producer-director of a long-term vérité documentary set in Louisiana's maximum security Angola Prison about a unique hospice program where killers care for their dying fellow inmates, and she's an adjunct professor at Columbia University's Graduate School of Journalism.

Coda

In my work as a TV news producer, I've always been drawn to the little guy that no one hears about but whose hidden story amazes and inspires. *After Etan*, the book from which this piece was adapted, is about the quiet heroes who persisted no matter how long it took. It's about Etan's family, who fought to get their lives back with dignity and grace; who fought for other missing children as they helped create a movement. It's about a small band of faithful searchers who never, ever, ever gave up until they'd solved the twisting decades-long mystery.

The story is not over, as Etan's killer has won back a year on his prison term and is now set for release in 2012. He's never been charged with Etan's disappearance and murder, but the statute of limitations will run forever. It's just a question of how fast and how far Jose Ramos will run the minute he's free. Cy Vance Jr., the first new Manhattan District Attorney in three decades, pledged as he took office to take a fresh look at the case. Stan Patz, Etan's father, remains hopeful that Ramos will finally be held accountable, and that the serial pedophile can be kept off the streets forever.

Kevin Gray

Sex, Lies, & Videotape

from *Details*

THE GIGOLO IS not an attractive man. Thin-lipped and angular, Helg Sgarbi appears more bookish than rakish, and his blue eyes seem to telegraph a constant message: *vulnerability and need.* When I enter the visiting room at Munich's Stadelheim prison, he is slouched behind a long wooden table, sandwiched between two other inmates. A little girl plays on the floor while two brothers argue in low tones. Dressed in blue prison jeans and a collared jersey, arms folded high, Sgarbi looks bored, accustomed as he is to the salons of Monte Carlo, the spa resorts of Austria, and the company of sad, doting rich women.

When he sees me approach, followed by a translator, he appears startled. Sgarbi is expecting his lawyer, not a complete stranger. Perhaps I am a hit man, sent by a cuckolded husband. A former Credit Suisse banker, the 44-year-old Sgarbi used to make his living preying on lonely women of means, seducing them, videotaping them having sex with him, and blackmailing them. That is, until the summer of 2007, when he took on three for-profit affairs simultaneously, including the one with his prize catch—Susanne Klatten, the married heiress to the BMW fortune and the richest woman in Germany, worth $12 billion—who became his downfall. Tabloids called him the "Swiss Gigolo," and he ranks as the most notorious con-man Lothario in the world today, a grifter accused of swindling a half-dozen women (though one eventually dropped the charges) out of more than $38 million in the course of his career.

I assure Sgarbi I am not here to hurt him, that I have met with his lawyer. He cuts me off: "You spoke to *my* lawyer about *my* case?" he says in English. "I did not give permission." In fact, Sgarbi's attorney offered to broker an interview—for a few hundred euros—and is looking to cut a deal for the film rights to Sgarbi's life story. You can see Sgarbi struggling to keep up with who is selling what to whom. "I am sorry you have come all this way," he says, sounding quite genteel, as he stands. "But there is nothing that I can tell you."

There is plenty Sgarbi could say but hasn't. In March, he averted what would surely have been a long and sensational trial by delivering a bombshell five-line confession on his first day in court. It conveniently saved him and the powerful Klatten, or "Lady BMW," as the press calls her, from having to air in public the lurid details of their affair—which included a videotaped sex romp at a Holiday Inn. Although prosecutors asked that Sgarbi serve nine years in prison for fraud and blackmail, the judges sentenced him to only six after he confessed. Sgarbi, who is fluent in six languages, got to keep his mouth shut—and his ill-gotten millions hidden.

But now comes a noisy sideshow that could threaten Sgarbi's fortune. This month, Italian prosecutors will put Sgarbi's alleged puppet-master, a 64-year-old former mechanic, on trial for "criminal association." Police say Ernano Barretta, an Italian religious-sect leader who claims to be a faith healer and allegedly has used female followers for sex, controlled Sgarbi, helping him target women, videotape them, and spend their money—conveniently enough, by buying resort properties in Egypt and splurging on Ferraris and Lamborghinis. What Barretta couldn't spend, Italian prosecutors say, he buried on his estate, near a 13th-century village close to the Adriatic coast.

When police raided the compound after Sgarbi's arrest in early 2008, they found €1.5 million in cash stuffed in vases, a suit of armor, and moldy tin cans buried in the yard. Among seven people arrested that day were Barretta's wife, his adult son and daughter, several waitresses from a wedding hall Barretta runs, and Sgarbi's wife, Franziska, who lives in the village with their 3-year-old daughter.

With his wife and friends charged as co-conspirators, Sgarbi receives no visitors. Out of loneliness or curiosity, or perhaps just to practice his gamesmanship, he finally invites me to sit, but he remains suspicious. "There are two stories," Sgarbi says, "the lies they tell about me and my family and the person who I am. I feel very sorry for me and my friends involved in this case." The legendary ladies' man, who bragged he could "read women like a map" and noted that in the female "everything is signposted," is absorbed in self-pity.

Soon, though, he is peppering me with personal queries (how long have I been a journalist? How was my flight? Do I read the *Economist*?). He shows interest in my responses, what appears to be genuine empathy—a trait that must have helped him gain victims' trust. "He seemed," one woman told investigators, "very unthreatening."

HELG SGARBI WAS BORN Helg Russak in Zurich, the son of the deputy director of a machine and diesel-engine factory in the Swiss industrial center of Winterthur. He spent several years of his childhood in Brazil, after his father got work there as an engineer. At 22, he joined the Swiss Army. He later attended law school in Zurich, graduating in 1992 and going to work at

Credit Suisse. These are facts Sgarbi is willing to discuss. Other details are murkier.

Sgarbi liked to gain sympathy from women by spinning his middle-class upbringing into a hard-luck story of lost wealth—he had a falling-out with his father over an inheritance, he would tell them, and had raised himself since he was a teen. He would also claim he had the ears of prominent businessmen like Josef Ackermann, the head of Deutsche Bank. There were elements of truth in his tales. Ackermann had served as president of Credit Suisse's executive board during the four years that Sgarbi worked at the bank, in mergers and acquisitions. "Afterwards," admits Sgarbi's lawyer, Egon Geis, "his life is not so well-known." Sgarbi tells me, with great enthusiasm, that after leaving Credit Suisse he became a corporate consultant, "taking tech companies public." But he refuses to name any of them. He also boasts of having opened a translation company with 300 employees worldwide, called Technology Business Development. "It no longer exists," he says.

We're now sitting across from each other. After 30 minutes, he is more relaxed—and voluble. "I always try to find a niche," he tells me, "some new element to exploit."

It's unclear what Sgarbi was up to after leaving Credit Suisse in 1996, but much of what is known comes from court records. In 2001, he drew the attention of Swiss authorities when his new fiancée, 83-year-old Countess Verena du Pasquier-Guebels, reported that 20 million Swiss francs ($19 million) had gone missing from her bank accounts. Police arrested Sgarbi that September and charged him with extortion and theft. Sgarbi returned the 20 million francs to his dowager bride-to-be. Feeling sorry for him, the countess dropped the charges. She died the next year; by then Sgarbi had sponged from her or otherwise cost her 7 million francs, for which he was never charged.

How many more affairs he had over the next three or four years is unclear. But in 2005, he seduced the 64-year-old wife of a German furniture-maker. By this point his grift had evolved from simple transfers of money into a brilliant two-phase scam. In this case, he told the woman he had struck a child with his car in the United States; if he did not pay €1.2 million, he would face jail time. He persuaded her to put up half the money in cash. Then he turned the screw, saying he had secretly photographed the two of them having sex ("to have something to occupy myself with in between our rendezvous," he told her) and that his laptop had been stolen. The Mafia had gotten hold of it and was threatening to make the images public unless he paid €1.2 million. The woman borrowed the money from a bank and brought it to Sgarbi, who simply took the bundle of cash from her hands and sped off in a van. She told police, "He didn't even say thank you."

But this was only a test run for the con he would work at one of Europe's toniest spa resorts.

THE HOTEL LANSERHOF is a luxury spa near the Habsburgs' summer palace in Innsbruck, Austria, the type of retreat bored wealthy women seek out when they want to pay more than $300 for a "deep liver detox" and sip herbal tea in white robes while gazing out on the Alps. In short, it is the perfect hunting ground for a gigolo.

Sgarbi arrived, in the summer of 2007, with a sad story: His wife had run off with a Spaniard and he had come here to heal his soul. He quickly ingratiated himself with the well-heeled matrons: He displayed impeccable manners and an apparent pedigree. They loved that Sgarbi listened, he *understood*—unlike their busy husbands. He was an expert flirt, "more or less the 'flame' of women a certain age," one of his victims that summer later told police. "Women absolutely wanted to know more about him."

For his first big score, he seduced Monika Sandler, a 49-year-old German divorcée and owner of a textile empire.

Within days of meeting her, Sgarbi was staying at her home in the Austrian ski resort of Kitzbühel. "I realized he had a rather spiritual vein," Sandler told police. And a physical one—there was lots of sex, "in several hotels, several times, in various cities," she said, "in Rome, Munich, and my home in Kitzbühel."

On July 4, 12 days after they met, Sgarbi made his move. He called Sandler in a panic, telling her that his car had struck a motorcyclist in Bologna and had left a child injured. He turned up at her home later with a neck brace, scratches, and a harrowing tale: The Mafia was threatening him over the child and blackmailing him for nearly €3 million. He had been able to raise all but the last €300,000, he told Sandler. "He did not ask me directly for the money," she said. "But I decided with hesitation to help him."

Soon he had dropped out of sight, claiming he had been forced into hiding because the Mafia was still threatening him. In fact, he had returned to the Hotel Lanserhof and landed the biggest mark of his life.

SUSANNE KLATTEN IS TALL, shy, and discreet. At 47 years old, she has pretty blue eyes and the short blond hair favored by executive working moms. Despite her wealth, she has maintained a low public profile. For good reason. She is a member of the ultra-guarded and prudent Quandt dynasty, Germany's wealthiest and most powerful family and one of its most controversial. Her great-grandfather, Gunther Quandt, made equipment for U-boats and for V2 rockets for the Nazis, reportedly with slave labor from concentration camps.

Klatten had been the target of a kidnapping plot when she was 16 years old. She is so protective of her identity that when she met her future husband, Jan, she did not tell him she was heir to an industrial fortune. As she built her career at places like Young & Rubicam, she worked under assumed names. She has an M.B.A., with an emphasis in advertising, and sits on the boards of BMW and the multi-billion-dollar chemical giant Altana, in which she owns an 88 percent stake.

Klatten arrived at the Lanserhof on July 9 for a two-week holiday. According to Sgarbi, he checked in three days later. He sidled up to her as she was reading *The Alchemist*, the inspirational tale of a young shepherd pursuing his dreams. "My favorite book," he said. Soon they were taking walks in the mountains and having tea together. Klatten told police she found Sgarbi "charming, attentive, and at the same time kind of sad. That stirred a feeling in me that we had something in common."

After they both left the Lanserhof, Sgarbi continued seducing her with a constant stream of text messages. In August, he turned up at her vacation home in the south of France, proclaiming his love for her. His words apparently touched a nerve: The pair consummated the affair a few days later, on August 21, in a Munich Holiday Inn. Sgarbi chose Room 629—a few steps from the elevator, which led directly to the underground garage— because it offered the most privacy.

But Klatten proved to be a tougher nut than his previous conquests. About a week later, he summoned her to an urgent meeting at a Munich airport hotel, where he told his now well-rehearsed accident story: a little girl left paraplegic. "I said, 'Stop it now. The responsibility is yours. You have to confront this situation by yourself,'" Klatten told police. "I immediately had the feeling he would ask me for money."

But Sgarbi did not ask—then or ever. No seasoned con man would be so direct; it made more sense to let Klatten come around on her own—and she did. "I thought he was asking for help from me in an emergency. I reflected again on these facts, feeling bad about how I had treated this man," she said. "I refused to help a person that really needed it." Sgarbi had appealed to her noblesse oblige as he surgically set his hook. "You see things much too materialistically," he said to her. "At the basis of this we are dealing with love. It's a matter of love."

Sgarbi told Klatten he had raised €3 million but needed to come up with another €7 million, or $10 million—a third of the total each for the girl's family, the lawyers, and a fund to help the girl in the future. This last gesture had been Sgarbi's idea, he told Klatten, who was clearly touched. "I am helping somebody out," she told an associate. And she came up with a phrase to use when discussing the €7 million. As it was going "for a higher cause," helping the girl, they would call it "7-Up."

On September 11, Klatten pulled into the Holiday Inn's underground garage with a moving box stuffed with €7 million in plastic-wrapped €200 notes. It's hard to imagine what was going through her mind. "She was in love," says Thomas Steinkraus-Koch, a German prosecutor who interrogated Klatten. "And Sgarbi is a professional. This is not his first time in this." Sgarbi checked that the money was inside the box and then drove off.

"AFTER THE EXCHANGE OF MONEY, he told me he wanted to have a fixed relationship with me," Klatten told police, according to a transcript of her interrogation. Sgarbi had rented an apartment near the Holiday Inn. On September 29, Klatten met him there. It was in an ugly building, facing an office complex. "As soon as I entered I was scared, because one could see very well the workers in the offices," Klatten said. Meaning the workers could see into the apartment too. Also, curiously, there was no furniture (Sgarbi had the gumption to tell Germany's richest woman that he could pick some up at IKEA.)

But Klatten had other reasons to worry. Her husband, Jan, had opened her phone bills and spotted the numerous calls to Sgarbi's Swiss cell phone. When she told Sgarbi about the escalating tensions with Jan, rather than sympathy he offered an ultimatum: "You will have to tell your husband you are leaving him for me," he said. Sgarbi admitted he had nothing to offer financially, but suggested she bring along €290 million, which he could invest in a fund to get them started.

It was then Klatten sensed things had turned ugly. "I had the impression this situation had become a real danger for all of the family," she told police. A few days later, she called Sgarbi and ended the affair. Furious, he asked her, "Do you have a gun pointed to your head?"

At this point, Sgarbi could have slunk away with his €7 million in 7-Up money. Instead, he upped the ante: On October 16 Klatten received a letter from him that read, "Do you remember, my love, when we met in broad daylight in a Munich hotel room after your holidays?" It was signed, "Your gentle warrior." Accompanying the letter were several video stills. It was clear to Klatten they were from a video that must have been taken the first time she and Sgarbi had had sex. "I realized," she later told police, "Mr. Sgarbi had evidently met me only for this reason."

Klatten broke the news of the affair to her husband and then brought the details of her indiscretion to the police. By then, Sgarbi had laid out his demands. Getting rid of him, he said, would cost "seven times 7-Up." When Klatten refused to pay, he sent 38 minutes of video footage of them having sex to prove he meant business. He also dropped his demands to "two times 7-Up," and gave her till January 15, 2008, to deliver the money.

On January 14, on his way to Munich and the biggest windfall of his criminal career, Sgarbi pulled his Mercedes 300SD into a highway rest stop in Austria. As he sat in his car, three Swiss detectives who had been following him appeared at his door and arrested him. That might have been it for the convoluted case of the Swiss gigolo. But Sgarbi wasn't traveling alone.

One car over, in an Audi Q7 that Italian police say was purchased with €100,000 of Klatten's money, sat the religious-sect leader Ernano Barretta, a 63-year-old former auto mechanic with dyed-black hair and a fashion sense that favors T-shirts, warm-up jackets, and distressed Diesel jeans. After the detectives approached him, Barretta reportedly persuaded them to let him finish his food before they took him in. Police, alerted to Sgarbi's grift by Klatten, had been wiretapping Barretta and had recorded him talking about the BMW heiress; they believe he was directing Sgarbi's frauds or, at the least, helping plot them. After three days, Barretta was released to return home to Italy.

ERNANO BARRETTA HAD MOVED to Switzerland to work as a mechanic in the sixties. By the early nineties, he'd remade himself into a *sensitivo*, claiming he could help with spiritual troubles. (He was once convicted of dealing stolen cars.) As Barretta's flock grew, so did his mythology, which took on an intensely Christian character. He would appear bearing stigmata and would perform faith healings, receiving in return generous offerings from devotees, allegedly their entire life savings in some cases.

Barretta needed someone to look after that money. He met Sgarbi just as the young law-school grad was entering the banking world. Sgarbi, former sect members say, became a devoted follower, playing the roles of accountant and right-hand apostle. Sgarbi often referred to Barretta as "the father who protecteth me" and considered him "the maestro of my life."

Barretta and his followers became a family to Sgarbi, especially after his first wife left him in 1994, disturbed by his involvement in the sect. Through Barretta, he met Gabriele Franziska Sgarbi, whom he married in 2001 while romancing the Countess du Pasquier-Guebels. After his arrest for defrauding the countess, he took his new bride's last name, presumably to cover his tracks.

Several of Barretta's former followers have told the media that Barretta exerted sexual control over the women in his flock. One told the Zurich *Tages-Anzeiger*, "Whenever we had sex, he always told me it was to heal me. He said his sperm was the blood of Jesus Christ, it purifies the soul." Barretta reportedly convinced Sgarbi that his cons also had the power to purify. "Ernano told Helg that money is a sin," one former member tells me, "and it was Helg's duty to relieve rich women of their fortunes and direct the money for good works."

Sgarbi's "good works," say police, funded Barretta as he made a fiefdom of his native village, amassing up to 60 cars, the Rifugio Valle Grande banquet hall, and 40 houses, which he quietly put in the names of sect members. The money came in so fast, police say, Barretta had trouble spending it all. "A cubic meter of money!" he bragged in one wiretapped call after the Klatten score.

In March, 80 Italian police officers raided Barretta's compound, blew up a safe, and found a hand-scrawled map listing the locations of "good wine" buried on the property. (In a wiretapped call, Barretta had complained that €300,000 buried in a tin can had become moldy.) Using the map, police turned up €1.5 million in crisp bills, at least €1 million of it believed to be money Klatten had given Sgarbi.

When I arrive at his compound in early summer, Barretta announces he is happy to discuss "my love for Helg Sgarbi." According to police, when Sgarbi and Klatten were carrying on their affair in Room 629 of the Holiday Inn, Barretta was staying in Room 630 next door, possibly taping their liaisons. Barretta does not deny being in the hotel.

"Sgarbi is my friend and will always be my friend," says Barretta, standing on a back porch overlooking the Gran Sasso mountains in central Italy's Abruzzo region. "If I travel with him and he has a woman in his room, why am I supposed to know this?" Anyway, he adds, "what kind of woman is Klatten? If she was a real woman, she would be home with her children, not parading around with young men." At that, Barretta does a pantomime, effeminately prancing across the floor.

Barretta, his wife, and his children face up to 20 years in prison each if convicted. So does Franziska Sgarbi. Gerardo Valone, the Italian prosecutor, maintains that she was integrally involved. After her husband's arrest, she is heard on a wiretap saying, "If Klatten does not drop her accusations, we must send to the media all the pictures and video to make a problem for her."

Barretta's defense attorney, Sabatino Cipriette, says he plans to call Klatten, Monica Sandler, and the wife of the furniture-maker to the stand. "Mr. Sgarbi did not ask for money," he tells me. "Mrs. Klatten offered it to him because she felt guilty." Clearly he's hoping for a plea bargain for his client. "I think Mrs. Klatten is a powerful woman, a strong woman, a nice woman," he says. "Too much theater is not good for Klatten. Klatten has a story with one man, but too many questions about that story is not good."

"IF YOU WANT TO KNOW about me, my life is all over the Internet. I will never have another company," Sgarbi tells me at the prison. As he speaks, he looks over at Cristine, the thirty-something German translator I've brought to facilitate dealings with the prison guards. Sgarbi starts to ask her mundane personal questions: She worked in Paris? At Microsoft—in what department? What languages does she speak? Where in Germany did she grow up? Oh, her elderly mother is ailing. That's sad. Has she considered such and such treatment?

It's striking to see how he works, how all con artists work—digging for information and for intimacy, creating a connection, genuine on one end and dead on the other. His methods are shrewd and calculated, and hardly limited to separating rich women from their fortunes. When Sgarbi and Egon Geis, his attorney, decided he should plead guilty on his first day in court, it was yet another bit of Sgarbi theater and manipulation, meant to elicit sympathy—and leniency.

"We discussed it and weighed it," Geis tells me in his Frankfurt office. "The judge could have said 'No, I will hear evidence and Mrs. Klatten will tell her story.' But this was our strategy—that Mrs. Klatten would be happy not to testify and Mr. Sgarbi would get a lower judgment. He worked with me 100 percent on this. It was a risk, but we said to each other, 'It just might work.'"

It worked so well that the sentencing panel of three judges and two jurors took only four hours to hand Sgarbi a lenient punishment that allowed him to keep the location of his millions secret. Also hidden are the Klatten sex videos. When I ask Sgarbi about the recordings, he offers a thin, tight smile and shrugs. It's not inconceivable that, as Franziska indicated on the wiretap, they could surface in Barretta's and Sgarbi's wife's cases.

But Sgarbi is more concerned with telling Cristine of his hardships in prison. "It's difficult for me here," he says. "I had business all over the world. I handled technology mergers and a 300-person translation company. Now I have nothing at all."

Cristine notices Sgarbi playing with his wedding band. "I miss my 3-year-old daughter," he tells her. "She does not know where I am and cannot see me for six years." Sgarbi offers a pained wave to another visitor's young daughter, who is playing on the floor nearby. As Cristine and I prepare to leave she asks Sgarbi if he needs anything. "A few magazines, maybe, and a newspaper," he says. Cristine says that certainly, she will send him the subscriptions. When we say goodbye, he takes her by the hand and asks her to please write him.

Outside, it's clear that Cristine is still struck by Sgarbi's charms. In a sense, being in prison has been good for him—although he's had to admit to working his con on Klatten, whose reputation has been irreparably tainted, confinement has made him even more unthreatening. "Yes, it's strange, I know," Cristine says. "I shouldn't feel sorry for him, but I do."

KEVIN GRAY *writes about crime, politics, and foreign affairs. His work has taken him around the globe and into some of the weirder corners of American life. He has written about war in the Congo; sex slave traffickers in Romania; the Hezbollah uprising in Lebanon; and Chiquita-financed death squads in Colombia; as well as American serial killers, white suprema-cists, suburban swingers, and lesbians under siege in Mississippi. His work has appeared in* The New York Times Magazine, New York, 'News-week, Details, USA Today, *and* The Washington Post. *He is a for-mer producer at CNN, where he covered business news.*

Coda

There are three ways to land the jailhouse interview. Besiege the inmate with cloying letters appealing to his sense of injustice (because everyone in prison is innocent); besiege his lawyer with flattering phone calls (because every lawyer wants to preen in print); or do the prison pop-in. This last is the least palatable and, with some convicts, the most dangerous. I did this once with Kenny Kimes, a ruthless mama's boy doing life in prison for help-ing his mother kill an elderly Manhattan woman to gain control of her townhouse, and facing death row in another slaying. Kenny was not happy with me when I appeared uninvited in his visiting area. But like many pent-up men, he needed to talk. He talked for several hours over two visits. He then tried to con-vince me to come back for a third. Sensing something creepier than usual in his tone, I balked. Besides, I already had the goods. So instead, Kenny invited a young TV reporter to visit him, then grabbed her around the neck and held her own pencil to her eye, threatening to kill her unless the prison let him see his mommy. The stand-off lasted hours before Kenny finally gave up.

I had never done the pop-in in a foreign country and didn't know what I risked with the inmate or with the guards. So it was with some hair standing up on the back of my neck that I walked into Munich's Stadleheim prison for the first and only time to talk to Helg Sgarbi, completely uninvited. I had sent Sgarbi the cloying letters, but had no answer. I had done the J-School write-around reporting and had great material. But my editor didn't want a great write-around. He wanted Sgarbi. I made sure to visit Sgarbi's lawyer in Frankfurt first. He offered to sell me an interview with his client, a journalistic no-no. But I managed to take his business card—and used it at the prison to open the gates. Once inside, I didn't know if they'd shut for good behind me if Sgarbi freaked out. Sgarbi, it turned out, was upset, but more upset that his attorney had spoken to me. That little conflict became a conversational gambit, opening Sgarbi up to dialogue on a point of mutual interest. That visit also educated me on the fine points of his case and turned me into an unlikely insider. And like many imprisoned men, his talk began to flow after a bit.

Sgarbi continues biding his time in Stadleheim. Though he has no contact with his infant daughter or with his wife (whom Italian prosecutors have charged as a coconspirator in his crimes), he has reason to be content. Sgarbi has never revealed the whereabouts of the $10 million he received from scamming Susanne Klatten, the BMW heiress. His reputation may be in tatters, but if he has access to the money, he can start over nicely.

David Grann

TRIAL BY FIRE

FROM *The New Yorker*

I

THE FIRE MOVED QUICKLY through the house, a one-story wood-frame structure in a working-class neighborhood of Corsicana, in northeast Texas. Flames spread along the walls, bursting through doorways, blistering paint and tiles and furniture. Smoke pressed against the ceiling, then banked downward, seeping into each room and through crevices in the windows, staining the morning sky.

Buffie Barbee, who was eleven years old and lived two houses down, was playing in her back yard when she smelled the smoke. She ran inside and told her mother, Diane, and they hurried up the street; that's when they saw the smoldering house and Cameron Todd Willingham standing on the front porch, wearing only a pair of jeans, his chest blackened with soot, his hair and eyelids singed. He was screaming, "My babies are burning up!" His children—Karmon and Kameron, who were one-year-old twin girls, and two-year-old Amber—were trapped inside.

Willingham told the Barbees to call the fire department, and while Diane raced down the street to get help he found a stick and broke the children's bedroom window. Fire lashed through the hole. He broke another window; flames burst through it, too, and he retreated into the yard, kneeling in front of the house. A neighbor later told police that Willingham intermittently cried, "My babies!" then fell silent, as if he had "blocked the fire out of his mind."

Diane Barbee, returning to the scene, could feel intense heat radiating off the house. Moments later, the five windows of the children's room exploded and flames "blew out," as Barbee put it. Within minutes, the first firemen had arrived, and Willingham approached them, shouting that his children were in their bedroom, where the flames were thickest. A fireman sent word over his radio for rescue teams to "step on it."

More men showed up, uncoiling hoses and aiming water at the blaze. One fireman, who had an air tank strapped to his back and a mask covering his face, slipped through a window but was hit by water from a hose and had to retreat. He then charged through the front door, into a swirl of smoke and fire. Heading down the main corridor, he reached the kitchen, where he saw a refrigerator blocking the back door.

Todd Willingham, looking on, appeared to grow more hysterical, and a police chaplain named George Monaghan led him to the back of a fire truck and tried to calm him down. Willingham explained that his wife, Stacy, had gone out earlier that morning, and that he had been jolted from sleep by Amber screaming, "Daddy! Daddy!"

"My little girl was trying to wake me up and tell me about the fire," he said, adding, "I couldn't get my babies out."

While he was talking, a fireman emerged from the house, cradling Amber. As she was given CPR, Willingham, who was twenty-three years old and powerfully built, ran to see her, then suddenly headed toward the babies' room. Monaghan and another man restrained him. "We had to wrestle with him and then handcuff him, for his and our protection," Monaghan later told police. "I received a black eye." One of the first firemen at the scene told investigators that, at an earlier point, he had also held Willingham back. "Based on what I saw on how the fire was burning, it would have been crazy for anyone to try and go into the house," he said.

Willingham was taken to a hospital, where he was told that Amber—who had actually been found in the master bedroom— had died of smoke inhalation. Kameron and Karmon had been lying on the floor of the children's bedroom, their bodies severely burned. According to the medical examiner, they, too, died from smoke inhalation.

News of the tragedy, which took place on December 23, 1991, spread through Corsicana. A small city fifty-five miles northeast of Waco, it had once been the center of Texas's first oil boom, but many of the wells had since dried up, and more than a quarter of the city's twenty thousand inhabitants had fallen into poverty. Several stores along the main street were shuttered, giving the place the feel of an abandoned outpost.

Willingham and his wife, who was twenty-two years old, had virtually no money. Stacy worked in her brother's bar, called Some Other Place, and Willingham, an unemployed auto mechanic, had been caring for the kids. The community took up a collection to help the Willinghams pay for funeral arrangements.

Fire investigators, meanwhile, tried to determine the cause of the blaze. (Willingham gave authorities permission to search the house: "I know we might not ever know all the answers, but I'd just like to know why my babies were taken from me.") Douglas Fogg, who was then the assistant fire chief in Corsicana, conducted the initial inspection. He was tall, with a crew cut, and his voice was raspy from years of inhaling smoke from fires and cigarettes. He had grown up in Corsicana and, after graduating from high school, in 1963, he had joined the Navy, serving as a medic in Vietnam, where he was wounded on four occasions. He was awarded a Purple Heart each time. After he returned from Vietnam, he became a firefighter, and by the time of the Willingham blaze he had been battling fire—or what he calls "the beast"—for more than twenty years, and had become a certified arson investigator. "You learn that fire talks to you," he told me.

He was soon joined on the case by one of the state's leading arson sleuths, a deputy fire marshal named Manuel Vasquez, who has since died. Short, with a paunch, Vasquez had investigated more than twelve hundred fires. Arson investigators have always been considered a special breed of detective. In the 1991 movie "Backdraft," a heroic arson investigator says of fire, "It breathes, it eats, and it hates. The only way to beat it is to think like it. To know that this flame will spread this way across the door and up across the ceiling." Vasquez, who had previously worked in Army intelligence, had several maxims of his own. One was "Fire does not destroy evidence—it creates it." Another was "The fire tells the story. I am just the interpreter." He cultivated a Sherlock Holmes–like aura of invincibility. Once, he was asked under oath whether he had ever been mistaken in a case. "If I have, sir, I don't know," he responded. "It's never been pointed out."

Vasquez and Fogg visited the Willinghams' house four days after the blaze. Following protocol, they moved from the least burned areas toward the most damaged ones. "It is a systematic method," Vasquez later testified, adding, "I'm just collecting information. . . . I have not made any determination. I don't have any preconceived idea."

The men slowly toured the perimeter of the house, taking notes and photographs, like archeologists mapping out a ruin. Upon opening the back door, Vasquez observed that there was just enough space to squeeze past the refrigerator blocking the exit. The air smelled of burned rubber and melted wires; a damp ash covered the ground, sticking to their boots. In the kitchen, Vasquez and Fogg discerned only smoke and heat damage—a sign that the fire had not originated there—and so they pushed deeper into the nine-hundred-and-seventy-five-square-foot building. A central corridor led past a utility room and the master bedroom, then past a small living room, on the left, and the children's bedroom, on the right, ending at the front door, which opened onto the porch. Vasquez tried to take in everything, a process that he compared to entering one's mother-in-law's house for the first time: "I have the same curiosity."

In the utility room, he noticed on the wall pictures of skulls and what he later described as an image of "the Grim Reaper." Then he turned into the master bedroom, where Amber's body had been found. Most of the damage there was also from smoke and heat, suggesting that the fire had started farther down the hallway, and he headed that way, stepping over debris and ducking under insulation and wiring that hung down from the exposed ceiling.

As he and Fogg removed some of the clutter, they noticed deep charring along the base of the walls. Because gases become buoyant when heated, flames ordinarily burn upward. But Vasquez and Fogg observed that the fire had burned extremely low down, and that there were peculiar char patterns on the floor, shaped like puddles.

Vasquez's mood darkened. He followed the "burn trailer"— the path etched by the fire—which led from the hallway into the children's bedroom. Sunlight filtering through the broken windows illuminated more of the irregularly shaped char patterns. A flammable or combustible liquid doused on a floor will cause a fire to concentrate in these kinds of pockets, which is why investigators refer to them as "pour patterns" or "puddle configurations."

The fire had burned through layers of carpeting and tile and plywood flooring. Moreover, the metal springs under the children's beds had turned white—a sign that intense heat had radiated beneath them. Seeing that the floor had some of the deepest burns, Vasquez deduced that it had been hotter than the ceiling, which, given that heat rises, was, in his words, "not normal."

Fogg examined a piece of glass from one of the broken windows. It contained a spiderweb-like pattern—what fire investigators call "crazed glass." Forensic textbooks had long described the effect as a key indicator that a fire had burned "fast and hot," meaning that it had been fuelled by a liquid accelerant, causing the glass to fracture.

The men looked again at what appeared to be a distinct burn trailer through the house: it went from the children's bedroom into the corridor, then turned sharply to the right and proceeded out the front door. To the investigators' surprise, even the wood under the door's aluminum threshold was charred. On the concrete floor of the porch, just outside the front door, Vasquez and Fogg noticed another unusual thing: brown stains, which, they reported, were consistent with the presence of an accelerant.

The men scanned the walls for soot marks that resembled a "V." When an object catches on fire, it creates such a pattern, as heat and smoke radiate outward; the bottom of the "V" can therefore point to where a fire began. In the Willingham house, there was a distinct "V" in the main corridor. Examining it and other burn patterns, Vasquez identified three places where fire had originated: in the hallway, in the children's bedroom, and at the front door. Vasquez later testified that multiple origins pointed to one conclusion: the fire was "intentionally set by human hands."

By now, both investigators had a clear vision of what had happened. Someone had poured liquid accelerant throughout the children's room, even under their beds, then poured some more along the adjoining hallway and out the front door, creating a "fire barrier" that prevented anyone from escaping; similarly, a prosecutor later suggested, the refrigerator in the kitchen had been moved to block the back-door exit. The house, in short, had been deliberately transformed into a death trap.

The investigators collected samples of burned materials from the house and sent them to a laboratory that could detect the presence of a liquid accelerant. The lab's chemist reported that one of the samples contained evidence of "mineral spirits," a substance that is often found in charcoal-lighter fluid. The sample had been taken by the threshold of the front door.

The fire was now considered a triple homicide, and Todd Willingham—the only person, besides the victims, known to have been in the house at the time of the blaze—became the prime suspect.

POLICE AND FIRE INVESTIGATORS canvassed the neighborhood, interviewing witnesses. Several, like Father Monaghan, initially portrayed Willingham as devastated by the fire. Yet, over time, an increasing number of witnesses offered damning statements. Diane Barbee said that she had not seen Willingham try to enter the house until after the authorities arrived, as if he were putting on a show. And when the children's room exploded with flames, she added, he seemed more preoccupied with his car, which he moved down the driveway. Another neighbor reported that when Willingham cried out for his babies he "did not appear to be excited or concerned." Even Father Monaghan wrote in a statement that, upon further reflection, "things were not as they seemed. I had the feeling that [Willingham] was in complete control."

The police began to piece together a disturbing profile of Willingham. Born in Ardmore, Oklahoma, in 1968, he had been abandoned by his mother when he was a baby. His father, Gene, who had divorced his mother, eventually raised him with his stepmother, Eugenia. Gene, a former U.S. Marine, worked in a salvage yard, and the family lived in a cramped house; at night, they could hear freight trains rattling past on a nearby track. Willingham, who had what the family called the "classic

Willingham look"—a handsome face, thick black hair, and dark eyes—struggled in school, and as a teenager began to sniff paint. When he was seventeen, Oklahoma's Department of Human Services evaluated him, and reported, "He likes 'girls,' music, fast cars, sharp trucks, swimming, and hunting, in that order." Willingham dropped out of high school, and over time was arrested for, among other things, driving under the influence, stealing a bicycle, and shoplifting.

In 1988, he met Stacy, a senior in high school, who also came from a troubled background: when she was four years old, her stepfather had strangled her mother to death during a fight. Stacy and Willingham had a turbulent relationship. Willingham, who was unfaithful, drank too much Jack Daniel's and sometimes hit Stacy—even when she was pregnant. A neighbor said that he once heard Willingham yell at her, "Get up, bitch, and I'll hit you again."

On December 31st, the authorities brought Willingham in for questioning. Fogg and Vasquez were present for the interrogation, along with Jimmie Hensley, a police officer who was working his first arson case. Willingham said that Stacy had left the house around 9 a.m. to pick up a Christmas present for the kids, at the Salvation Army. "After she got out of the driveway, I heard the twins cry, so I got up and gave them a bottle," he said. The children's room had a safety gate across the doorway, which Amber could climb over but not the twins, and he and Stacy often let the twins nap on the floor after they drank their bottles. Amber was still in bed, Willingham said, so he went back into his room to sleep. "The next thing I remember is hearing 'Daddy, Daddy,'" he recalled. "The house was already full of smoke." He said that he got up, felt around the floor for a pair of pants, and put them on. He could no longer hear his daughter's voice ("I heard that last 'Daddy, Daddy' and never heard her again"), and he hollered, "Oh God—Amber, get out of the house! Get out of the house!"

He never sensed that Amber was in his room, he said. Perhaps she had already passed out by the time he stood up, or perhaps she came in after he left, through a second doorway, from the living room. He said that he went down the corridor and tried to reach the children's bedroom. In the hallway, he said, "you couldn't see nothing but black." The air smelled the way it had when their microwave had blown up, three weeks earlier—like "wire and stuff like that." He could hear sockets and light switches popping, and he crouched down, almost crawling. When he made it to the children's bedroom, he said, he stood and his hair caught on fire. "Oh God, I never felt anything that hot before," he said of the heat radiating out of the room.

After he patted out the fire on his hair, he said, he got down on the floor and groped in the dark. "I thought I found one of them once," he said, "but it was a doll." He couldn't bear the heat any longer. "I felt myself passing out," he said. Finally, he stumbled down the corridor and out the front door, trying to catch his breath. He saw Diane Barbee and yelled for her to call the fire department. After she left, he insisted, he tried without success to get back inside.

The investigators asked him if he had any idea how the fire had started. He said that he wasn't sure, though it must have originated in the children's room, since that was where he first saw flames; they were glowing like "bright lights." He and Stacy used three space heaters to keep the house warm, and one of them was in the children's room. "I taught Amber not to play with it," he said, adding that she got "whuppings every once in a while for messing with it." He said that he didn't know if the heater, which had an internal flame, was turned on. (Vasquez later testified that when he had checked the heater, four days after the fire, it was in the "Off" position.) Willingham speculated that the fire might have been started by something electrical: he had heard all that popping and crackling.

When pressed whether someone might have a motive to hurt

his family, he said that he couldn't think of anyone that "cold-blooded." He said of his children, "I just don't understand why anybody would take them, you know? We had three of the most pretty babies anybody could have ever asked for." He went on, "Me and Stacy's been together for four years, but off and on we get into a fight and split up for a while and I think those babies is what brought us so close together . . . neither one of us . . . could live without them kids." Thinking of Amber, he said, "To tell you the honest-to-God's truth, I wish she hadn't woke me up."

During the interrogation, Vasquez let Fogg take the lead. Finally, Vasquez turned to Willingham and asked a seemingly random question: had he put on shoes before he fled the house?

"No, sir," Willingham replied.

A map of the house was on a table between the men, and Vasquez pointed to it. "You walked out this way?" he said.

Willingham said yes.

Vasquez was now convinced that Willingham had killed his children. If the floor had been soaked with a liquid accelerant and the fire had burned low, as the evidence suggested, Willingham could not have run out of the house the way he had described without badly burning his feet. A medical report indicated that his feet had been unscathed.

Willingham insisted that, when he left the house, the fire was still around the top of the walls and not on the floor. "I didn't have to jump through any flames," he said. Vasquez believed that this was impossible, and that Willingham had lit the fire as he was retreating—first, torching the children's room, then the hallway, and then, from the porch, the front door. Vasquez later said of Willingham, "He told me a story of pure fabrication. . . . He just talked and he talked and all he did was lie."

Still, there was no clear motive. The children had life-insurance policies, but they amounted to only fifteen thousand dollars, and Stacy's grandfather, who had paid for them, was listed as the primary beneficiary. Stacy told investigators that even though

Willingham hit her he had never abused the children—"Our kids were spoiled rotten," she said—and she did not believe that Willingham could have killed them.

Ultimately, the authorities concluded that Willingham was a man without a conscience whose serial crimes had climaxed, almost inexorably, in murder. John Jackson, who was then the assistant district attorney in Corsicana, was assigned to prosecute Willingham's case. He later told the Dallas *Morning News* that he considered Willingham to be "an utterly sociopathic individual" who deemed his children "an impediment to his lifestyle." Or, as the local district attorney, Pat Batchelor, put it, "The children were interfering with his beer drinking and dart throwing."

On the night of January 8, 1992, two weeks after the fire, Willingham was riding in a car with Stacy when SWAT teams surrounded them, forcing them to the side of the road. "They pulled guns out like we had just robbed ten banks," Stacy later recalled. "All we heard was 'click, click.' . . . Then they arrested him."

Willingham was charged with murder. Because there were multiple victims, he was eligible for the death penalty, under Texas law. Unlike many other prosecutors in the state, Jackson, who had ambitions of becoming a judge, was personally opposed to capital punishment. "I don't think it's effective in deterring criminals," he told me. "I just don't think it works." He also considered it wasteful: because of the expense of litigation and the appeals process, it costs, on average, $2.3 million to execute a prisoner in Texas—about three times the cost of incarcerating someone for forty years. Plus, Jackson said, "What's the recourse if you make a mistake?" Yet his boss, Batchelor, believed that, as he once put it, "certain people who commit bad enough crimes give up the right to live," and Jackson came to agree that the heinous nature of the crime in the Willingham case—"one of the worst in terms of body count" that he had ever tried—mandated death.

Willingham couldn't afford to hire lawyers, and was assigned two by the state: David Martin, a former state trooper, and Robert Dunn, a local defense attorney who represented everyone from alleged murderers to spouses in divorce cases—a "Jack-of-all-trades," as he calls himself. ("In a small town, you can't say 'I'm a so-and-so lawyer,' because you'll starve to death," he told me.)

Not long after Willingham's arrest, authorities received a message from a prison inmate named Johnny Webb, who was in the same jail as Willingham. Webb alleged that Willingham had confessed to him that he took "some kind of lighter fluid, squirting [it] around the walls and the floor, and set a fire." The case against Willingham was considered airtight.

Even so, several of Stacy's relatives—who, unlike her, believed that Willingham was guilty—told Jackson that they preferred to avoid the anguish of a trial. And so, shortly before jury selection, Jackson approached Willingham's attorneys with an extraordinary offer: if their client pleaded guilty, the state would give him a life sentence. "I was really happy when I thought we might have a deal to avoid the death penalty," Jackson recalls.

Willingham's lawyers were equally pleased. They had little doubt that he had committed the murders and that, if the case went before a jury, he would be found guilty, and, subsequently, executed. "Everyone thinks defense lawyers must believe their clients are innocent, but that's seldom true," Martin told me. "Most of the time, they're guilty as sin." He added of Willingham, "All the evidence showed that he was one hundred percent guilty. He poured accelerant all over the house and put lighter fluid under the kids' beds." It was, he said, "a classic arson case": there were "puddle patterns all over the place—no disputing those."

Martin and Dunn advised Willingham that he should accept the offer, but he refused. The lawyers asked his father and stepmother to speak to him. According to Eugenia, Martin showed them photographs of the burned children and said,

"Look what your son did. You got to talk him into pleading, or he's going to be executed."

His parents went to see their son in jail. Though his father did not believe that he should plead guilty if he was innocent, his stepmother beseeched him to take the deal. "I just wanted to keep my boy alive," she told me.

Willingham was implacable. "I ain't gonna plead to something I didn't do, especially killing my own kids," he said. It was his final decision. Martin says, "I thought it was nuts at the time—and I think it's nuts now."

Willingham's refusal to accept the deal confirmed the view of the prosecution, and even that of his defense lawyers, that he was an unrepentant killer.

In August, 1992, the trial commenced in the old stone courthouse in downtown Corsicana. Jackson and a team of prosecutors summoned a procession of witnesses, including Johnny Webb and the Barbees. The crux of the state's case, though, remained the scientific evidence gathered by Vasquez and Fogg. On the stand, Vasquez detailed what he called more than "twenty indicators" of arson.

"Do you have an opinion as to who started the fire?" one of the prosecutors asked.

"Yes, sir," Vasquez said. "Mr. Willingham."

The prosecutor asked Vasquez what he thought Willingham's intent was in lighting the fire. "To kill the little girls," he said.

The defense had tried to find a fire expert to counter Vasquez and Fogg's testimony, but the one they contacted concurred with the prosecution. Ultimately, the defense presented only one witness to the jury: the Willinghams' babysitter, who said she could not believe that Willingham could have killed his children. (Dunn told me that Willingham had wanted to testify, but Martin and Dunn thought that he would make a bad witness.) The trial ended after two days.

During his closing arguments, Jackson said that the puddle

configurations and pour patterns were Willingham's inadvertent "confession," burned into the floor. Showing a Bible that had been salvaged from the fire, Jackson paraphrased the words of Jesus from the Gospel of Matthew: "Whomsoever shall harm one of my children, it's better for a millstone to be hung around his neck and for him to be cast in the sea."

The jury was out for barely an hour before returning with a unanimous guilty verdict. As Vasquez put it, "The fire does not lie."

II

When Elizabeth Gilbert approached the prison guard, on a spring day in 1999, and said Cameron Todd Willingham's name, she was uncertain about what she was doing. A forty-seven-year-old French teacher and playwright from Houston, Gilbert was divorced with two children. She had never visited a prison before. Several weeks earlier, a friend, who worked at an organization that opposed the death penalty, had encouraged her to volunteer as a pen pal for an inmate on death row, and Gilbert had offered her name and address. Not long after, a short letter, written with unsteady penmanship, arrived from Willingham. "If you wish to write back, I would be honored to correspond with you," he said. He also asked if she might visit him. Perhaps out of a writer's curiosity, or perhaps because she didn't feel quite herself (she had just been upset by news that her ex-husband was dying of cancer), she agreed. Now she was standing in front of the decrepit penitentiary in Huntsville, Texas—a place that inmates referred to as "the death pit."

She filed past a razor-wire fence, a series of floodlights, and a checkpoint, where she was patted down, until she entered a small chamber. Only a few feet in front of her was a man convicted of multiple infanticide. He was wearing a white jumpsuit with

"DR"—for death row—printed on the back, in large black letters. He had a tattoo of a serpent and a skull on his left biceps. He stood nearly six feet tall and was muscular, though his legs had atrophied after years of confinement.

A Plexiglas window separated Willingham from her; still, Gilbert, who had short brown hair and a bookish manner, stared at him uneasily. Willingham had once fought another prisoner who called him a "baby killer," and since he had been incarcerated, seven years earlier, he had committed a series of disciplinary infractions that had periodically landed him in the segregation unit, which was known as "the dungeon."

Willingham greeted her politely. He seemed grateful that she had come. After his conviction, Stacy had campaigned for his release. She wrote to Ann Richards, then the governor of Texas, saying, "I know him in ways that no one else does when it comes to our children. Therefore, I believe that there is no way he could have possibly committed this crime." But within a year Stacy had filed for divorce, and Willingham had few visitors except for his parents, who drove from Oklahoma to see him once a month. "I really have no one outside my parents to remind me that I am a human being, not the animal the state professes I am," he told Gilbert at one point.

He didn't want to talk about death row. "Hell, I live here," he later wrote her. "When I have a visit, I want to escape from here." He asked her questions about her teaching and art. He expressed fear that, as a playwright, she might find him a "one-dimensional character," and apologized for lacking social graces; he now had trouble separating the mores in prison from those of the outside world.

When Gilbert asked him if he wanted something to eat or drink from the vending machines, he declined. "I hope I did not offend you by not accepting any snacks," he later wrote her. "I didn't want you to feel I was there just for something like that."

She had been warned that prisoners often tried to con visitors.

He appeared to realize this, subsequently telling her, "I am just a simple man. Nothing else. And to most other people a convicted killer looking for someone to manipulate."

Their visit lasted for two hours, and afterward they continued to correspond. She was struck by his letters, which seemed introspective, and were not at all what she had expected. "I am a very honest person with my feelings," he wrote her. "I will not bullshit you on how I feel or what I think." He said that he used to be stoic, like his father. But, he added, "losing my three daughters . . . my home, wife and my life, you tend to wake up a little. I have learned to open myself."

She agreed to visit him again, and when she returned, several weeks later, he was visibly moved. "Here I am this person who nobody on the outside is ever going to know as a human, who has lost so much, but still trying to hold on," he wrote her afterward. "But you came back! I don't think you will ever know of what importance that visit was in my existence."

They kept exchanging letters, and she began asking him about the fire. He insisted that he was innocent and that, if someone had poured accelerant through the house and lit it, then the killer remained free.

Gilbert wasn't naïve—she assumed that he was guilty. She did not mind giving him solace, but she was not there to absolve him.

Still, she had become curious about the case, and one day that fall she drove down to the courthouse in Corsicana to review the trial records. Many people in the community remembered the tragedy, and a clerk expressed bewilderment that anyone would be interested in a man who had burned his children alive.

Gilbert took the files and sat down at a small table. As she examined the eyewitness accounts, she noticed several contradictions. Diane Barbee had reported that, before the authorities arrived at the fire, Willingham never tried to get back into the house—yet she had been absent for some time while calling the fire department. Meanwhile, her daughter Buffie had reported witnessing Willingham on the porch breaking a window, in an apparent effort to reach his children. And the firemen and police on the scene had described Willingham frantically trying to get into the house.

The witnesses' testimony also grew more damning after authorities had concluded, in the beginning of January, 1992, that Willingham was likely guilty of murder. In Diane Barbee's initial statement to authorities, she had portrayed Willingham as "hysterical," and described the front of the house exploding. But on January 4th, after arson investigators began suspecting Willingham of murder, Barbee suggested that he could have gone back inside to rescue his children, for at the outset she had seen only "smoke coming from out of the front of the house"—smoke that was not "real thick."

An even starker shift occurred with Father Monaghan's testimony. In his first statement, he had depicted Willingham as a devastated father who had to be repeatedly restrained from risking his life. Yet, as investigators were preparing to arrest Willingham, he concluded that Willingham had been *too* emotional ("He seemed to have the type of distress that a woman who had given birth would have upon seeing her children die"); and he expressed a "gut feeling" that Willingham had "something to do with the setting of the fire."

Dozens of studies have shown that witnesses' memories of events often change when they are supplied with new contextual information. Itiel Dror, a cognitive psychologist who has done extensive research on eyewitness and expert testimony in criminal investigations, told me, "The mind is not a passive machine. Once you believe in something—once you expect something—it changes the way you perceive information and the way your memory recalls it."

After Gilbert's visit to the courthouse, she kept wondering about Willingham's motive, and she pressed him on the matter.

In response, he wrote, of the death of his children, "I do not talk about it much anymore and it is still a very powerfully emotional pain inside my being." He admitted that he had been a "sorry-ass husband" who had hit Stacy—something he deeply regretted. But he said that he had loved his children and would never have hurt them. Fatherhood, he said, had changed him; he stopped being a hoodlum and "settled down" and "became a man." Nearly three months before the fire, he and Stacy, who had never married, wed at a small ceremony in his home town of Ardmore. He said that the prosecution had seized upon incidents from his past and from the day of the fire to create a portrait of a "demon," as Jackson, the prosecutor, referred to him. For instance, Willingham said, he had moved the car during the fire simply because he didn't want it to explode by the house, further threatening the children.

Gilbert was unsure what to make of his story, and she began to approach people who were involved in the case, asking them questions. "My friends thought I was crazy," Gilbert recalls. "I'd never done anything like this in my life."

One morning, when Willingham's parents came to visit him, Gilbert arranged to see them first, at a coffee shop near the prison. Gene, who was in his seventies, had the Willingham look, though his black hair had gray streaks and his dark eyes were magnified by glasses. Eugenia, who was in her fifties, with silvery hair, was as sweet and talkative as her husband was stern and reserved. The drive from Oklahoma to Texas took six hours, and they had woken at three in the morning; because they could not afford a motel, they would have to return home later that day. "I feel like a real burden to them," Willingham had written Gilbert.

As Gene and Eugenia sipped coffee, they told Gilbert how grateful they were that someone had finally taken an interest in Todd's case. Gene said that his son, though he had flaws, was no killer.

The evening before the fire, Eugenia said, she had spoken on the phone with Todd. She and Gene were planning to visit two days later, on Christmas Eve, and Todd told her that he and Stacy and the kids had just picked up family photographs. "He said, 'We got your pictures for Christmas,'" she recalled. "He put Amber on the phone, and she was tattling on one of the twins. Todd didn't seem upset. If something was bothering him, I would have known."

Gene and Eugenia got up to go: they didn't want to miss any of the four hours that were allotted for the visit with their son. Before they left, Gene said, "You'll let us know if you find anything, won't you?"

Over the next few weeks, Gilbert continued to track down sources. Many of them, including the Barbees, remained convinced that Willingham was guilty, but several of his friends and relatives had doubts. So did some people in law enforcement. Willingham's former probation officer in Oklahoma, Polly Goodin, recently told me that Willingham had never demonstrated bizarre or sociopathic behavior. "He was probably one of my favorite kids," she said. Even a former judge named Bebe Bridges—who had often stood, as she put it, on the "opposite side" of Willingham in the legal system, and who had sent him to jail for stealing—told me that she could not imagine him killing his children. "He was polite, and he seemed to care," she said. "His convictions had been for dumb-kid stuff. Even the things stolen weren't significant." Several months before the fire, Willingham tracked Goodin down at her office, and proudly showed her photographs of Stacy and the kids. "He wanted Bebe and me to know he'd been doing good," Goodin recalled.

Eventually, Gilbert returned to Corsicana to interview Stacy, who had agreed to meet at the bed-and-breakfast where Gilbert was staying. Stacy was slightly plump, with pale, round cheeks and feathered dark-blond hair; her bangs were held in place by gel, and her face was heavily made up. According to a tape recording of the conversation, Stacy said that nothing unusual had happened in the days before the fire. She and Willingham had not fought, and were preparing for the holiday. Though Vasquez, the arson expert, had recalled finding the space heater off, Stacy was sure that, at least on the day of the incident—a cool winter morning—it had been on. "I remember turning it down," she recalled. "I always thought, Gosh, could Amber have put something in there?" Stacy added that, more than once, she had caught Amber "putting things too close to it."

Willingham had often not treated her well, she recalled, and after his incarceration she had left him for a man who did. But she didn't think that her former husband should be on death row. "I don't think he did it," she said, crying.

Though only the babysitter had appeared as a witness for the defense during the main trial, several family members, including Stacy, testified during the penalty phase, asking the jury to spare Willingham's life. When Stacy was on the stand, Jackson grilled her about the "significance" of Willingham's "very large tattoo of a skull, encircled by some kind of a serpent."

"It's just a tattoo," Stacy responded.

"He just likes skulls and snakes. Is that what you're saying?"

"No. He just had—he got a tattoo on him."

The prosecution cited such evidence in asserting that Willingham fit the profile of a sociopath, and brought forth two medical experts to confirm the theory. Neither had met Willingham. One of them was Tim Gregory, a psychologist with a master's degree in marriage and family issues, who had previously gone goose hunting with Jackson, and had not published any research in the field of sociopathic behavior. His practice was devoted to family counseling.

At one point, Jackson showed Gregory Exhibit No. 60—a photograph of an Iron Maiden poster that had hung in Willingham's house—and asked the psychologist to interpret it. "This one is a picture of a skull, with a fist being punched through the skull," Gregory said; the image displayed "violence" and "death."

Gregory looked at photographs of other music posters owned by Willingham. "There's a hooded skull, with wings and a hatchet," Gregory continued. "And all of these are in fire, depicting—it reminds me of something like Hell. And there's a picture—a Led Zeppelin picture of a falling angel. . . . I see there's an association many times with cultive-type of activities. A focus on death, dying. Many times individuals that have a lot of this type of art have interest in satanic-type activities."

The other medical expert was James P. Grigson, a forensic psychiatrist. He testified so often for the prosecution in capital-punishment cases that he had become known as Dr. Death. (A Texas appellate judge once wrote that when Grigson appeared on the stand the defendant might as well "commence writing out his last will and testament.") Grigson suggested that Willingham was an "extremely severe sociopath," and that "no pill" or treatment could help him. Grigson had previously used nearly the same words in helping to secure a death sentence against Randall Dale Adams, who had been convicted of murdering a police officer, in 1977. After Adams, who had no prior criminal record, spent a dozen years in prison—and once came within seventy-two hours of being executed—new evidence emerged that absolved him, and he was released. In 1995, three years after Willingham's trial, Grigson was expelled from the American Psychiatric Association for violating ethics. The association stated that Grigson had repeatedly arrived at a "psychiatric diagnosis without first having examined the individuals in question, and for indicating, while testifying in court as an expert witness, that he could predict with 100-percent certainty that the individuals would engage in future violent acts."

AFTER SPEAKING TO STACY, Gilbert had one more person she wanted to interview: the jailhouse informant Johnny Webb, who was incarcerated in Iowa Park, Texas. She wrote to Webb,

who said that she could see him, and they met in the prison visiting room. A man in his late twenties, he had pallid skin and a
closely shaved head; his eyes were jumpy, and his entire body
seemed to tremble. A reporter who once met him described him
to me as "nervous as a cat around rocking chairs." Webb had
begun taking drugs when he was nine years old, and had been
convicted of, among other things, car theft, selling marijuana,
forgery, and robbery.

As Gilbert chatted with him, she thought that he seemed
paranoid. During Willingham's trial, Webb disclosed that he had
been given a diagnosis of "post-traumatic stress disorder" after he
was sexually assaulted in prison, in 1988, and that he often suffered from "mental impairment." Under cross-examination,
Webb testified that he had no recollection of a robbery that he
had pleaded guilty to only months earlier.

Webb repeated for her what he had said in court: he had
passed by Willingham's cell, and as they spoke through a food
slot Willingham broke down and told him that he intentionally
set the house on fire. Gilbert was dubious. It was hard to believe
that Willingham, who had otherwise insisted on his innocence,
had suddenly confessed to an inmate he barely knew. The conversation had purportedly taken place by a speaker system that
allowed any of the guards to listen—an unlikely spot for an inmate to reveal a secret. What's more, Webb alleged that Willingham had told him that Stacy had hurt one of the kids, and
that the fire was set to cover up the crime. The autopsies, however, had revealed no bruises or signs of trauma on the children's
bodies.

Jailhouse informants, many of whom are seeking reduced
time or special privileges, are notoriously unreliable. According
to a 2004 study by the Center on Wrongful Convictions, at North-
western University Law School, lying police and jailhouse informants are the leading cause of wrongful convictions in capital
cases in the United States. At the time that Webb came forward

against Willingham, he was facing charges of robbery and forgery. During Willingham's trial, another inmate planned to testify that he had overheard Webb saying to another prisoner that he was hoping to "get time cut," but the testimony was ruled inadmissible, because it was hearsay. Webb, who pleaded guilty to the robbery and forgery charges, received a sentence of fifteen years. Jackson, the prosecutor, told me that he generally considered Webb "an unreliable kind of guy," but added, "I saw no real motive for him to make a statement like this if it wasn't true. We didn't cut him any slack." In 1997, five years after Willingham's trial, Jackson urged the Texas Board of Pardons and Paroles to grant Webb parole. "I asked them to cut him loose early," Jackson told me. The reason, Jackson said, was that Webb had been targeted by the Aryan Brotherhood. The board granted Webb parole, but within months of his release he was caught with cocaine and returned to prison.

In March, 2000, several months after Gilbert's visit, Webb unexpectedly sent Jackson a Motion to Recant Testimony, declaring, "Mr. Willingham is innocent of all charges." But Willingham's lawyer was not informed of this development, and soon afterward Webb, without explanation, recanted his recantation. When I recently asked Webb, who was released from prison in 2007, about the turnabout and why Willingham would have confessed to a virtual stranger, he said that he knew only what "the dude told me." After I pressed him, he said, "It's very possible I misunderstood what he said." Since the trial, Webb has been given an additional diagnosis, bipolar disorder. "Being locked up in that little cell makes you kind of crazy," he said. "My memory is in bits and pieces. I was on a lot of medication at the time. Everyone knew that." He paused, then said, "The statute of limitations has run out on perjury, hasn't it?"

Aside from the scientific evidence of arson, the case against Willingham did not stand up to scrutiny. Jackson, the prosecutor, said of Webb's testimony, "You can take it or leave it." Even the refrigerator's placement by the back door of the house turned out to be innocuous; there were two refrigerators in the cramped kitchen, and one of them was by the back door. Jimmie Hensley, the police detective, and Douglas Fogg, the assistant fire chief, both of whom investigated the fire, told me recently that they had never believed that the fridge was part of the arson plot. "It didn't have nothing to do with the fire," Fogg said.

After months of investigating the case, Gilbert found that her faith in the prosecution was shaken. As she told me, "What if Todd really was innocent?"

III

In the summer of 1660, an Englishman named William Harrison vanished on a walk, near the village of Charingworth, in Gloucestershire. His bloodstained hat was soon discovered on the side of a local road. Police interrogated Harrison's servant, John Perry, and eventually Perry gave a statement that his mother and his brother had killed Harrison for money. Perry, his mother, and his brother were hanged.

Two years later, Harrison reappeared. He insisted, fancifully, that he had been abducted by a band of criminals and sold into slavery. Whatever happened, one thing was indisputable: he had not been murdered by the Perrys.

The fear that an innocent person might be executed has long haunted jurors and lawyers and judges. During America's Colonial period, dozens of crimes were punishable by death, including horse thievery, blasphemy, "man-stealing," and highway robbery. After independence, the number of crimes eligible for the death penalty was gradually reduced, but doubts persisted over whether legal procedures were sufficient to prevent an innocent person from being executed. In 1868, John Stuart Mill made one of the most eloquent defenses of capital punishment, arguing that executing a murderer did not display a wanton dis-regard for life but, rather, proof of its value. "We show, on the contrary, most emphatically our regard for it by the adoption of a rule that he who violates that right in another forfeits it for himself," he said. For Mill, there was one counterargument that carried weight—"that if by an error of justice an innocent person is put to death, the mistake can never be corrected."

The modern legal system, with its lengthy appeals process and clemency boards, was widely assumed to protect the kind of "error of justice" that Mill feared. In 2000, while George W. Bush was governor of Texas, he said, "I know there are some in the country who don't care for the death penalty, but . . . we've adequately answered innocence or guilt." His top policy adviser on issues of criminal justice emphasized that there is "super due process to make sure that no innocent defendants are executed."

In recent years, though, questions have mounted over whether the system is fail-safe. Since 1976, more than a hundred and thirty people on death row have been exonerated. DNA testing, which was developed in the eighties, saved seventeen of them, but the technique can be used only in rare instances. Barry Scheck, a co-founder of the Innocence Project, which has used DNA testing to exonerate prisoners, estimates that about eighty percent of felonies do not involve biological evidence.

In 2000, after thirteen people on death row in Illinois were exonerated, George Ryan, who was then governor of the state, suspended the death penalty. Though he had been a longtime advocate of capital punishment, he declared that he could no longer support a system that has "come so close to the ultimate nightmare—the state's taking of innocent life." Former Supreme Court Justice Sandra Day O'Connor has said that the "execution of a legally and factually innocent person would be a constitutionally intolerable event."

Such a case has become a kind of grisly Holy Grail among opponents of capital punishment. In his 2002 book *The Death*

Penalty, Stuart Banner observes, "The prospect of killing an innocent person seemed to be the one thing that could cause people to rethink their support for capital punishment. Some who were not troubled by statistical arguments against the death penalty—claims about deterrence or racial disparities—were deeply troubled that such an extreme injustice might occur in an individual case." Opponents of the death penalty have pointed to several questionable cases. In 1993, Ruben Cantu was executed in Texas for fatally shooting a man during a robbery. Years later, a second victim, who survived the shooting, told the Houston *Chronicle* that he had been pressured by police to identify Cantu as the gunman, even though he believed Cantu to be innocent. Sam Millsap, the district attorney in the case, who had once supported capital punishment ("I'm no wild-eyed, pointy-headed liberal"), said that he was disturbed by the thought that he had made a mistake.

In 1995, Larry Griffin was put to death in Missouri, for the drive-by shooting of a drug dealer. The case rested largely on the eyewitness testimony of a career criminal named Robert Fitzgerald, who had been an informant for prosecutors before and was in the witness-protection program. Fitzgerald maintained that he happened to be at the scene because his car had broken down. After Griffin's execution, a probe sponsored by the NAACP's Legal Defense and Educational Fund revealed that a man who had been wounded during the incident insisted that Griffin was not the shooter. Moreover, the first police officer at the scene disputed that Fitzgerald had witnessed the crime.

These cases, however, stopped short of offering irrefutable proof that a "legally and factually innocent person" was executed. In 2005, a St. Louis prosecutor, Jennifer Joyce, launched an investigation of the Griffin case, upon being presented with what she called "compelling" evidence of Griffin's potential innocence. After two years of reviewing the evidence, and interviewing a new eyewitness, Joyce said that she and her team were convinced that the "right person was convicted."

Supreme Court Justice Antonin Scalia, in 2006, voted with a majority to uphold the death penalty in a Kansas case. In his opinion, Scalia declared that, in the modern judicial system, there has not been "a single case—not one—in which it is clear that a person was executed for a crime he did not commit. If such an event had occurred in recent years, we would not have to hunt for it; the innocent's name would be shouted from the rooftops."

"MY PROBLEMS ARE SIMPLE," Willingham wrote Gilbert in September, 1999. "Try to keep them from killing me at all costs. End of story."

During his first years on death row, Willingham had pleaded with his lawyer, David Martin, to rescue him. "You can't imagine what it's like to be here, with people I have no business even being around," he wrote.

For a while, Willingham shared a cell with Ricky Lee Green, a serial killer, who castrated and fatally stabbed his victims, including a sixteen-year-old boy. (Green was executed in 1997.) Another of Willingham's cell-mates, who had an IQ below seventy and the emotional development of an eight-year-old, was raped by an inmate. "You remember me telling you I had a new celly?" Willingham wrote in a letter to his parents. "The little retarded boy. . . . There was this guy here on the wing who is a shit sorry coward (who is the same one I got into it with a little over a month ago). Well, he raped [my cellmate] in the 3 row shower week before last." Willingham said that he couldn't believe that someone would "rape a boy who cannot even defend himself. Pretty damn low."

Because Willingham was known as a "baby killer," he was a target of attacks. "Prison is a rough place, and with a case like mine they never give you the benefit of a doubt," he wrote his parents. After he tried to fight one prisoner who threatened him, Willingham told a friend that if he hadn't stood up for himself several inmates would have "beaten me up or raped or"—his thought trailed off.

Over the years, Willingham's letters home became increasingly despairing. "This is a hard place, and it makes a person hard inside," he wrote. "I told myself that was one thing I did not want and that was for this place to make me bitter, but it is hard." He went on, "They have [executed] at least one person every month I have been here. It is senseless and brutal. . . . You see, we are not living in here, we are only existing." In 1996, he wrote, "I just been trying to figure out why after having a wife and 3 beautiful children that I loved my life has to end like this. And sometimes it just seems like it is not worth it all. . . . In the 3½ years I been here I have never felt that my life was as worthless and desolate as it is now." Since the fire, he wrote, he had the sense that his life was slowly being erased. He obsessively looked at photographs of his children and Stacy, which he stored in his cell. "So long ago, so far away," he wrote in a poem. "Was everything truly there?"

Inmates on death row are housed in a prison within a prison, where there are no attempts at rehabilitation, and no educational or training programs. In 1999, after seven prisoners tried to escape from Huntsville, Willingham and four hundred and fifty-nine other inmates on death row were moved to a more secure facility, in Livingston, Texas. Willingham was held in isolation in a sixty-square-foot cell, twenty-three hours a day. He tried to distract himself by drawing—"amateur stuff," as he put it—and writing poems. In a poem about his children, he wrote, "There is nothing more beautiful than you on this earth." When Gilbert once suggested some possible revisions to his poems, he explained that he wrote them simply as expressions, however crude, of his feelings. "So to me to cut them up and try to improve on them just for creative-writing purposes would be to destroy what I was doing to start with," he said.

Despite his efforts to occupy his thoughts, he wrote in his diary that his mind "deteriorates each passing day." He stopped working out and gained weight. He questioned his faith: "No God who cared about his creation would abandon the innocent." He seemed not to care if another inmate attacked him. "A person who is already dead inside does not fear" death, he wrote.

One by one, the people he knew in prison were escorted into the execution chamber. There was Clifton Russell, Jr., who, at the age of eighteen, stabbed and beat a man to death, and who said, in his last statement, "I thank my Father, God in Heaven, for the grace he has granted me—I am ready." There was Jeffery Dean Motley, who kidnapped and fatally shot a woman, and who declared, in his final words, "I love you, Mom. Goodbye." And there was John Fearance, who murdered his neighbor, and who turned to God in his last moments and said, "I hope He will forgive me for what I done."

Willingham had grown close to some of his prison mates, even though he knew that they were guilty of brutal crimes. In March, 2000, Willingham's friend Ponchai Wilkerson—a twenty-eight-year-old who had shot and killed a clerk during a jewelry heist—was executed. Afterward, Willingham wrote in his diary that he felt "an emptiness that has not been touched since my children were taken from me." A year later, another friend who was about to be executed—"one of the few real people I have met here not caught up in the bravado of prison"— asked Willingham to make him a final drawing. "Man, I never thought drawing a simple Rose could be so emotionally hard," Willingham wrote. "The hard part is knowing that this will be the last thing I can do for him."

Another inmate, Ernest Ray Willis, had a case that was freakishly similar to Willingham's. In 1987, Willis had been convicted of setting a fire, in West Texas, that killed two women. Willis told investigators that he had been sleeping on a friend's living-room couch and woke up to a house full of smoke. He said that he tried to rouse one of the women, who was sleeping in another room, but the flames and smoke drove him back, and he ran out the front door before the house exploded with flames. Witnesses maintained that Willis had acted suspiciously; he moved his car out of the yard, and didn't show "any emotion," as one volunteer firefighter put it. Authorities also wondered how Willis could have escaped the house without burning his bare feet. Fire investigators found pour patterns, puddle configurations, and other signs of arson. The authorities could discern no motive for the crime, but concluded that Willis, who had no previous record of violence, was a sociopath—a "demon," as the prosecutor put it. Willis was charged with capital murder and sentenced to death.

Willis had eventually obtained what Willingham called, enviously, a "bad-ass lawyer." James Blank, a noted patent attorney in New York, was assigned Willis's case as part of his firm's pro-bono work. Convinced that Willis was innocent, Blank devoted more than a dozen years to the case, and his firm spent millions, on fire consultants, private investigators, forensic experts, and the like. Willingham, meanwhile, relied on David Martin, his court-appointed lawyer, and one of Martin's colleagues to handle his appeals. Willingham often told his parents, "You don't know what it's like to have lawyers who won't even believe you're inno-cent." Like many inmates on death row, Willingham eventually filed a claim of inadequate legal representation. (When I recently asked Martin about his representation of Willingham, he said, "There were no grounds for reversal, and the verdict was abso-lutely the right one." He said of the case, "Shit, it's incredible that anyone's even thinking about it.")

Willingham tried to study the law himself, reading books such as "Tact in Court, or How Lawyers Win: Containing Sketches of Cases Won by Skill, Wit, Art, Tact, Courage and Eloquence." Still, he confessed to a friend, "The law is so complicated it is hard for me to understand." In 1996, he obtained a new court-appointed lawyer, Walter Reaves, who told me that he was appalled by the quality of Willingham's defense at trial and on appeal. Reaves prepared for him a state writ of habeas corpus, known as a Great Writ. In the byzantine appeals process of death-penalty cases, which frequently takes more than ten years, the writ is the most critical stage: a prisoner can introduce new evidence detailing such things as perjured testimony, unreliable medical experts, and bogus scientific findings. Yet most indigent inmates, like Willingham, who constitute the bulk of those on death row, lack the resources to track down new witnesses or dig up fresh evidence. They must depend on court-appointed lawyers, many of whom are "unqualified, irresponsible, or over-burdened," as a study by the Texas Defender Service, a nonprofit organization, put it. In 2000, a Dallas *Morning News* investigation revealed that roughly a quarter of the inmates condemned to death in Texas were represented by court-appointed attorneys who had, at some point in their careers, been "reprimanded, placed on probation, suspended or banned from practicing law by the State Bar." Although Reaves was more competent, he had few resources to reinvestigate the case, and his writ introduced no new exculpatory evidence: nothing further about Webb, or the reliability of the eyewitness testimony, or the credibility of the medical experts. It focussed primarily on procedural questions, such as whether the trial court erred in its instructions to the jury.

The Texas Court of Criminal Appeals was known for upholding convictions even when overwhelming exculpatory evidence came to light. In 1997, DNA testing proved that sperm collected from a rape victim did not match Roy Criner, who had been sentenced to ninety-nine years for the crime. Two lower courts recommended that the verdict be overturned, but the Court of Criminal Appeals upheld it, arguing that Criner might have worn a condom or might not have ejaculated. Sharon Keller, who is now the presiding judge on the court, stated in a majority opinion, "The new evidence does not establish innocence." In 2000, George W. Bush pardoned Criner. (Keller was recently charged with judicial misconduct, for refusing to keep open past five o'clock a clerk's office in order to allow a last-minute petition from a man who was executed later that night.)

On October 31, 1997, the Court of Criminal Appeals denied Willingham's writ. After Willingham filed another writ of habeas corpus, this time in federal court, he was granted a temporary stay. In a poem, Willingham wrote, "One more chance, one more strike / Another bullet dodged, another date escaped."

Willingham was entering his final stage of appeals. As his anxieties mounted, he increasingly relied upon Gilbert to investigate his case and for emotional support. "She may never know what a change she brought into my life," he wrote in his diary. "For the first time in many years she gave me a purpose, something to look forward to."

As their friendship deepened, he asked her to promise him that she would never disappear without explanation. "I already have that in my life," he told her.

Together, they pored over clues and testimony. Gilbert says that she would send Reaves leads to follow up, but although he was sympathetic, nothing seemed to come of them. In 2002, a federal court of appeals denied Willingham's writ without even a hearing. "Now I start the last leg of my journey," Willingham wrote to Gilbert. "Got to get things in order."

He appealed to the U.S. Supreme Court, but in December, 2003, he was notified that it had declined to hear his case. He soon received a court order announcing that "the Director of the Department of Criminal Justice at Huntsville, Texas, acting by and through the executioner designated by said Director . . . is hereby directed and commanded, at some hour after 6:00 p.m. on the 17th day of February, 2004, at the Department of Criminal Justice in Huntsville, Texas, to carry out this sentence of death by intravenous injection of a substance or substances in a lethal quantity sufficient to cause the death of said Cameron Todd Willingham."

Willingham wrote a letter to his parents. "Are you sitting down?" he asked, before breaking the news. "I love you both so much," he said.

His only remaining recourse was to appeal to the governor of Texas, Rick Perry, a Republican, for clemency. The process, considered the last gatekeeper to the executioner, has been called by the U.S. Supreme Court "the 'fail-safe' in our criminal justice system."

IV

One day in January, 2004, Dr. Gerald Hurst, an acclaimed scientist and fire investigator, received a file describing all the evidence of arson gathered in Willingham's case. Gilbert had come across Hurst's name and, along with one of Willingham's relatives, had contacted him, seeking his help. After their pleas, Hurst had agreed to look at the case pro bono, and Reaves, Willingham's lawyer, had sent him the relevant documents, in the hope that there were grounds for clemency.

Hurst opened the file in the basement of his house in Austin, which served as a laboratory and an office, and was cluttered with microscopes and diagrams of half-finished experiments. Hurst was nearly six and a half feet tall, though his stooped shoulders made him seem considerably shorter, and he had a gaunt face that was partly shrouded by long gray hair. He was wearing his customary outfit: black shoes, black socks, a black T-shirt, and loose-fitting black pants supported by black suspenders. In his mouth was a wad of chewing tobacco.

A child prodigy who was raised by a sharecropper during the Great Depression, Hurst used to prowl junk yards, collecting magnets and copper wires in order to build radios and other contraptions. In the early sixties, he received a Ph.D. in chemistry from Cambridge University, where he started to experiment with fluorine and other explosive chemicals, and once detonated his lab. Later, he worked as the chief scientist on secret weapons programs for several American companies, designing rockets and deadly fire bombs—or what he calls "god-awful things." He helped patent what has been described, with only slight exaggeration, as "the world's most powerful nonnuclear explosive": an Astrolite bomb. He experimented with toxins so lethal that a fraction of a drop would rot human flesh, and in his laboratory he often had to wear a pressurized moon suit; despite such precautions, exposure to chemicals likely caused his liver to fail, and in 1994 he required a transplant. Working on what he calls "the dark side of arson," he retrofitted napalm bombs with Astrolite, and developed ways for covert operatives in Vietnam to create bombs from local materials, such as chicken manure and sugar. He also perfected a method for making an exploding T-shirt by nitrating its fibers.

His conscience eventually began pricking him. "One day, you wonder, What the hell am I doing?" he recalls. He left the defense industry, and went on to invent the Mylar balloon, an improved version of Liquid Paper, and Kinepak, a kind of explosive that reduces the risk of accidental detonation. Because of his extraordinary knowledge of fire and explosives, companies in civil litigation frequently sought his help in determining the cause of a blaze. By the nineties, Hurst had begun devoting significant time to criminal-arson cases, and, as he was exposed to the methods of local and state fire investigators, he was shocked by what he saw.

Many arson investigators, it turned out, had only a high-school education. In most states, in order to be certified, investigators had to take a forty-hour course on fire investigation, and pass a written exam. Often, the bulk of an investigator's training came on the job, learning from "old-timers" in the field, who passed down a body of wisdom about the telltale signs of arson, even though a study in 1977 warned that there was nothing in "the scientific literature to substantiate their validity."

In 1992, the National Fire Protection Association, which promotes fire prevention and safety, published its first scientifically based guidelines to arson investigation. Still, many arson investigators believed that what they did was more an art than a science—a blend of experience and intuition. In 1997, the International Association of Arson Investigators filed a legal brief arguing that arson sleuths should not be bound by a 1993 Supreme Court decision requiring experts who testified at trials to adhere to the scientific method. What arson sleuths did, the brief claimed, was "less scientific." By 2000, after the courts had rejected such claims, arson investigators increasingly recognized the scientific method, but there remained great variance in the field, with many practitioners still relying on the unverified techniques that had been used for generations. "People investigated fire largely with a flat-earth approach," Hurst told me. "It looks like arson— therefore, it's arson." He went on, "My view is you have to have a scientific basis. Otherwise, it's no different than witch-hunting."

In 1998, Hurst investigated the case of a woman from North Carolina named Terri Hinson, who was charged with setting a fire that killed her seventeen-month-old son, and faced the death penalty. Hurst ran a series of experiments re-creating the conditions of the fire, which suggested that it had not been arson, as the investigators had claimed; rather, it had started accidentally, from a faulty electrical wire in the attic. Because of this research, Hinson was freed. John Lentini, a fire expert and the author of a leading scientific textbook on arson, describes Hurst as "brilliant." A Texas prosecutor once told the Chicago *Tribune*, of Hurst, "If he says it was an arson fire, then it was. If he says it wasn't, then it wasn't."

Hurst's patents yielded considerable royalties, and he could afford to work pro bono on an arson case for months, even years. But he received the files on Willingham's case only a few weeks before Willingham was scheduled to be executed. As Hurst looked through the case records, a statement by Manuel Vasquez, the state deputy fire marshal, jumped out at him. Vasquez had testified that, of the roughly twelve hundred to fifteen hundred fires he had investigated, "most all of them" were arson. This was an oddly high estimate; the Texas State Fire Marshals Office typically found arson in only fifty percent of its cases.

Hurst was also struck by Vasquez's claim that the Willingham blaze had "burned fast and hot" because of a liquid accelerant. The notion that a flammable or combustible liquid caused flames to reach higher temperatures had been repeated in court by arson sleuths for decades. Yet the theory was nonsense: experiments have proved that wood and gasoline-fuelled fires burn at essentially the same temperature.

Vasquez and Fogg had cited as proof of arson the fact that the front door's aluminum threshold had melted. "The only thing that can cause that to react is an accelerant," Vasquez said. Hurst was incredulous. A natural-wood fire can reach temperatures as high as two thousand degrees Fahrenheit—far hotter than the melting point for aluminum alloys, which ranges from a thousand to twelve hundred degrees. And, like many other investigators, Vasquez and Fogg mistakenly assumed that wood charring beneath the aluminum threshold was evidence that, as Vasquez put it, "a liquid accelerant flowed underneath and burned." Hurst had conducted myriad experiments showing that such charring was caused simply by the aluminum conducting so much heat. In fact, when liquid accelerant is poured under a threshold a fire will extinguish, because of a lack of oxygen. (Other scientists had reached the same conclusion.) "Liquid accelerants can no more burn under an aluminum threshold than can grease burn in a skillet even with a loose-fitting lid," Hurst declared in his report on the Willingham case.

Hurst then examined Fogg and Vasquez's claim that the "brown stains" on Willingham's front porch were evidence of "liquid accelerant," which had not had time to soak into the concrete. Hurst had previously performed a test in his garage, in which he poured charcoal–lighter fluid on the concrete floor, and lit it. When the fire went out, there were no brown stains, only smudges of soot. Hurst had run the same experiment many times, with different kinds of liquid accelerants, and the result was always the same. Brown stains were common in fires; they were usually composed of rust or gunk from charred debris that had mixed with water from fire hoses.

Another crucial piece of evidence implicating Willingham was the "crazed glass" that Vasquez had attributed to the rapid heating from a fire fuelled with liquid accelerant. Yet, in November of 1991, a team of fire investigators had inspected fifty houses in the hills of Oakland, California, which had been ravaged by brush fires. In a dozen houses, the investigators discovered crazed glass, even though a liquid accelerant had not been used. Most of these houses were on the outskirts of the blaze, where firefighters had shot streams of water; as the investigators later wrote in a published study, they theorized that the fracturing had been induced by rapid cooling, rather than by sudden heating—thermal shock had caused the glass to contract so quickly that it settled disjointedly. The investigators then tested this hypothesis in a laboratory. When they heated glass, nothing happened. But each time they applied water to the heated glass the intricate patterns appeared. Hurst had seen the same phenomenon when he had blowtorched and cooled glass during his research at Cambridge. In his report, Hurst wrote that Vasquez and Fogg's notion of crazed glass was no more than an "old wives' tale."

Hurst then confronted some of the most devastating arson evidence against Willingham: the burn trailer, the pour patterns and puddle configurations, the V-shape and other burn marks indicating that the fire had multiple points of origin, the burning underneath the children's beds. There was also the positive test for mineral spirits by the front door, and Willingham's seemingly implausible story that he had run out of the house without burning his bare feet.

As Hurst read through more of the files, he noticed that Willingham and his neighbors had described the windows in the front of the house suddenly exploding and flames roaring forth. It was then that Hurst thought of the legendary Lime Street Fire, one of the most pivotal in the history of arson investigation.

ON THE EVENING OF OCTOBER 15, 1990, a thirty-five-year-old man named Gerald Wayne Lewis was found standing in front of his house on Lime Street in Jacksonville, Florida, holding his three-year-old son. His two-story wood-frame home was engulfed in flames. By the time the fire had been extinguished, six people were dead, including Lewis's wife. Lewis said that he had rescued his son but was unable to get to the others, who were upstairs.

When fire investigators examined the scene, they found the classic signs of arson: low burns along the walls and floors, pour patterns and puddle configurations, and a burn trailer running from the living room into the hallway. Lewis claimed that the fire had started accidentally, on a couch in the living room—his son had been playing with matches. But a V-shaped pattern by one of the doors suggested that the fire had originated elsewhere. Some witnesses told authorities that Lewis seemed too calm during the fire and had never tried to get help. According to the Los Angeles Times, Lewis had previously been arrested for abusing his wife, who had taken out a restraining order against him. After a chemist said that he had detected the presence of gasoline on Lewis's clothing and shoes, a report by the sheriff's office concluded, "The fire was started as a result of a petroleum product being poured on the front porch, foyer, living room, stairwell and second floor bedroom." Lewis was arrested and charged with six counts of murder. He faced the death penalty.

Subsequent tests, however, revealed that the laboratory identification of gasoline was wrong. Moreover, a local news television camera had captured Lewis in a clearly agitated state at the scene of the fire, and investigators discovered that at one point he had jumped in front of a moving car, asking the driver to call the fire department.

Seeking to bolster their theory of the crime, prosecutors turned to John Lentini, the fire expert, and John DeHaan, another leading investigator and textbook author. Despite some of the weaknesses of the case, Lentini told me that, given the classic burn patterns and puddle configurations in the house, he was sure that Lewis had set the fire: "I was prepared to testify and send this guy to Old Sparky"—the electric chair.

To discover the truth, the investigators, with the backing of the prosecution, decided to conduct an elaborate experiment and re-create the fire scene. Local officials gave the investigators permission to use a condemned house next to Lewis's home, which was about to be torn down. The two houses were virtually identical, and the investigators refurbished the condemned one with the same kind of carpeting, curtains, and furniture that had been in Lewis's home. The scientists also wired the building with heat and gas sensors that could withstand fire. The cost of the experiment came to twenty thousand dollars. Without using liquid accelerant, Lentini and DeHaan set the couch in the living room on fire, expecting that the experiment would demonstrate that Lewis's version of events was implausible.

The investigators watched as the fire quickly consumed the couch, sending upward a plume of smoke that hit the ceiling and spread outward, creating a thick layer of hot gases overhead—an efficient radiator of heat. Within three minutes, this cloud, absorbing more gases from the fire below, was banking down the walls and filling the living room. As the cloud approached the floor, its temperature rose, in some areas, to more than eleven hundred degrees Fahrenheit. Suddenly, the entire room exploded in flames, as the radiant heat ignited every piece of furniture, every curtain, every possible fuel source, even the carpeting. The windows shattered.

The fire had reached what is called "flashover"—the point at which radiant heat causes a fire in a room to become a room on fire. Arson investigators knew about the concept of flashover, but it was widely believed to take much longer to occur, especially without a liquid accelerant. From a single fuel source—a couch—the room had reached flashover in four and a half minutes.

Because all the furniture in the living room had ignited, the blaze went from a fuel-controlled fire to a ventilation-controlled fire—or what scientists call "post-flashover." During post-flashover, the path of the fire depends on new sources of oxygen, from an open door or window. One of the fire investigators, who had been standing by an open door in the living room, escaped moments before the oxygen-starved fire roared out of the room into the hallway—a fireball that caused the corridor to go quickly into flashover as well, propelling the fire out the front door and onto the porch.

After the fire was extinguished, the investigators inspected the hallway and living room. On the floor were irregularly shaped burn patterns that perfectly resembled pour patterns and puddle configurations. It turned out that these classic signs of arson can also appear on their own, after flashover. With the naked eye, it is impossible to distinguish between the pour patterns and puddle configurations caused by an accelerant and those caused naturally by post-flashover. The only reliable way to tell the difference is to take samples from the burn patterns and test them in a laboratory for the presence of flammable or combustible liquids.

During the Lime Street experiment, other things happened

that were supposed to occur only in a fire fuelled by liquid accelerant: charring along the base of the walls and doorways, and burning under furniture. There was also a V-shaped pattern by the living-room doorway, far from where the fire had started on the couch. In a small fire, a V-shaped burn mark may pinpoint where a fire began, but during post-flashover these patterns can occur repeatedly, when various objects ignite.

One of the investigators muttered that they had just helped prove the defense's case. Given the reasonable doubt raised by the experiment, the charges against Lewis were soon dropped. The Lime Street experiment had demolished prevailing notions about fire behavior. Subsequent tests by scientists showed that, during post-flashover, burning under beds and furniture was common, entire doors were consumed, and aluminum thresholds melted.

John Lentini says of the Lime Street Fire, "This was my epiphany. I almost sent a man to die based on theories that were a load of crap."

HURST NEXT EXAMINED a floor plan of Willingham's house that Vasquez had drawn, which delineated all the purported pour patterns and puddle configurations. Because the windows had blown out of the children's room, Hurst knew that the fire had reached flashover. With his finger, Hurst traced along Vasquez's diagram the burn trailer that had gone from the children's room, turned right in the hallway, and headed out the front door. John Jackson, the prosecutor, had told me that the path was so "bizarre" that it had to have been caused by a liquid accelerant. But Hurst concluded that it was a natural product of the dynamics of fire during post-flashover. Willingham had fled out the front door, and the fire simply followed the ventilation path, toward the opening. Similarly, when Willingham had broken the windows in the children's room, flames had shot outward.

Hurst recalled that Vasquez and Fogg had considered it impossible for Willingham to have run down the burning hallway without scorching his bare feet. But if the pour patterns and puddle configurations were a result of a flashover, Hurst reasoned, then they were consonant with Willingham's explanation of events. When Willingham exited his bedroom, the hallway was not yet on fire; the flames were contained within the children's bedroom, where, along the ceiling, he saw the "bright lights." Just as the investigator safely stood by the door in the Lime Street experiment seconds before flashover, Willingham could have stood close to the children's room without being harmed. (Prior to the Lime Street case, fire investigators had generally assumed that carbon monoxide diffuses quickly through a house during a fire. In fact, up until flashover, levels of carbon monoxide can be remarkably low beneath and outside the thermal cloud.) By the time the Corsicana fire achieved flashover, Willingham had already fled outside and was in the front yard.

Vasquez had made a videotape of the fire scene, and Hurst looked at the footage of the burn trailer. Even after repeated viewings, he could not detect three points of origin, as Vasquez had. (Fogg recently told me that he also saw a continuous trailer and disagreed with Vasquez, but added that nobody from the prosecution or the defense ever asked him on the stand about his opinion on the subject.)

After Hurst had reviewed Fogg and Vasquez's list of more than twenty arson indicators, he believed that only one had any potential validity: the positive test for mineral spirits by the threshold of the front door. But why had the fire investigators obtained a positive reading only in that location? According to Fogg and Vasquez's theory of the crime, Willingham had poured accelerant throughout the children's bedroom and down the hallway. Officials had tested extensively in these areas—including where all the pour patterns and puddle configurations were—and turned up nothing. Jackson told me that he "never did understand why they weren't able to recover" positive tests in these parts.

Hurst found it hard to imagine Willingham pouring accelerant on the front porch, where neighbors could have seen him. Scanning the files for clues, Hurst noticed a photograph of the porch taken before the fire, which had been entered into evidence. Sitting on the tiny porch was a charcoal grill. The porch was where the family barbecued. Court testimony from witnesses confirmed that there had been a grill, along with a container of lighter fluid, and that both had burned when the fire roared onto the porch during post-flashover. By the time Vasquez inspected the house, the grill had been removed from the porch, during cleanup. Though he cited the container of lighter fluid in his report, he made no mention of the grill. At the trial, he insisted that he had never been told of the grill's earlier placement. Other authorities were aware of the grill but did not see its relevance. Hurst, however, was convinced that he had solved the mystery: when firefighters had blasted the porch with water, they had likely spread charcoal-lighter fluid from the melted container.

Without having visited the fire scene, Hurst says, it was impossible to pinpoint the cause of the blaze. But, based on the evidence, he had little doubt that it was an accidental fire—one caused most likely by the space heater or faulty electrical wiring. It explained why there had never been a motive for the crime. Hurst concluded that there was no evidence of arson, and that a man who had already lost his three children and spent twelve years in jail was about to be executed based on "junk science." Hurst wrote his report in such a rush that he didn't pause to fix the typos.

V

"I am a realist and I will not live a fantasy," Willingham once told Gilbert about the prospect of proving his innocence. But in

February, 2004, he began to have hope. Hurst's findings had helped to exonerate more than ten people. Hurst even reviewed the scientific evidence against Willingham's friend Ernest Willis, who had been on death row for a strikingly similar arson charge. Hurst says, "It was like I was looking at the same case. Just change the names." In his report on the Willis case, Hurst concluded that not "a single item of physical evidence . . . supports a finding of arson." A second fire expert hired by Ori White, the new district attorney in Willis's district, concurred. After seventeen years on death row, Willis was set free. "I don't turn killers loose," White said at the time. "If Willis was guilty, I'd be retrying him right now. And I'd use Hurst as my witness. He's a brilliant scientist." White noted how close the system had come to murdering an innocent man. "He did not get executed, and I thank God for that," he said.

On February 13th, four days before Willingham was scheduled to be executed, he got a call from Reaves, his attorney. Reaves told him that the fifteen members of the Board of Pardons and Paroles, which reviews an application for clemency and had been sent Hurst's report, had made their decision.

"What is it?" Willingham asked.

"I'm sorry," Reaves said. "They denied your petition."

The vote was unanimous. Reaves could not offer an explanation: the board deliberates in secret, and its members are not bound by any specific criteria. The board members did not even have to review Willingham's materials, and usually don't debate a case in person; rather, they cast their votes by fax—a process that has become known as "death by fax." Between 1976 and 2004, when Willingham filed his petition, the State of Texas had approved only one application for clemency from a prisoner on death row. A Texas appellate judge has called the clemency system "a legal fiction." Reaves said of the board members, "They never asked me to attend a hearing or answer any questions."

The Innocence Project obtained, through the Freedom of

Information Act, all the records from the governor's office and the board pertaining to Hurst's report. "The documents show that they received the report, but neither office has any record of anyone acknowledging it, taking note of its significance, responding to it, or calling any attention to it within the government," Barry Scheck said. "The only reasonable conclusion is that the governor's office and the Board of Pardons and Paroles ignored scientific evidence."

LaFayette Collins, who was a member of the board at the time, told me of the process, "You don't vote guilt or innocence. You don't retry the trial. You just make sure everything is in order and there are no glaring errors." He noted that although the rules allowed for a hearing to consider important new evidence, "in my time there had never been one called." When I asked him why Hurst's report didn't constitute evidence of "glaring errors," he said, "We get all kinds of reports, but we don't have the mechanisms to vet them." Alvin Shaw, another board member at the time, said that the case didn't "ring a bell," adding, angrily, "Why would I want to talk about it?" Hurst calls the board's actions "unconscionable."

Though Reaves told Willingham that there was still a chance that Governor Perry might grant a thirty-day stay, Willingham began to prepare his last will and testament. He had earlier written Stacy a letter apologizing for not being a better husband and thanking her for everything she had given him, especially their three daughters. "I still know Amber's voice, her smile, her cool Dude saying and how she said: I wanna hold you! Still feel the touch of Karmon and Kameron's hands on my face." He said that he hoped that "some day, somehow the truth will be known and my name cleared."

He asked Stacy if his tombstone could be erected next to their children's graves. Stacy, who had for so long expressed belief in Willingham's innocence, had recently taken her first look at the original court records and arson findings. Unaware of Hurst's report, she had determined that Willingham was guilty. She denied him his wish, later telling a reporter, "He took my kids away from me."

Gilbert felt as if she had failed Willingham. Even before his pleas for clemency were denied, she told him that all she could give him was her friendship. He told her that it was enough "to be a part of your life in some small way so that in my passing I can know I was at last able to have felt the heart of another who might remember me when I'm gone." He added, "There is nothing to forgive you for." He told her that he would need her to be present at his execution, to help him cope with "my fears, thoughts, and feelings."

On February 17th, the day he was set to die, Willingham's parents and several relatives gathered in the prison visiting room. Plexiglas still separated Willingham from them. "I wish I could touch and hold both of you," Willingham had written to them earlier. "I always hugged Mom but I never hugged Pop much."

As Willingham looked at the group, he kept asking where Gilbert was. Gilbert had recently been driving home from a store when another car ran a red light and smashed into her. Willingham used to tell her to stay in her kitchen for a day, without leaving, to comprehend what it was like to be confined in prison, but she had always found an excuse not to do it. Now she was paralyzed from the neck down.

While she was in an intensive-care unit, she had tried to get a message to Willingham, but apparently failed. Gilbert's daughter later read her a letter that Willingham had sent her, telling her how much he had grown to love her. He had written a poem: "Do you want to see beauty—like you have never seen? / Then close your eyes, and open your mind, and come along with me."

Gilbert, who spent years in physical rehabilitation, gradually regaining motion in her arms and upper body, says, "All that time, I thought I was saving Willingham, and I realized then that he was saving me, giving me the strength to get through this.

I know I will one day walk again, and I know it is because Willingham showed me the kind of courage it takes to survive."

Willingham had requested a final meal, and at 4 p.m. on the seventeenth he was served it: three barbecued pork ribs, two orders of onion rings, fried okra, three beef enchiladas with cheese, and two slices of lemon cream pie. He received word that Governor Perry had refused to grant him a stay. (A spokesperson for Perry says, "The Governor made his decision based on the facts of the case.") Willingham's mother and father began to cry. "Don't be sad, Momma," Willingham said. "In fifty-five minutes, I'm a free man. I'm going home to see my kids." Earlier, he had confessed to his parents that there was one thing about the day of the fire he had lied about. He said that he had never actually crawled into the children's room. "I just didn't want people to think I was a coward," he said. Hurst told me, "People who have never been in a fire don't understand why those who survive often can't rescue the victims. They have no concept of what a fire is like."

The warden told Willingham that it was time. Willingham, refusing to assist the process, lay down; he was carried into a chamber eight feet wide and ten feet long. The walls were painted green, and in the center of the room, where an electric chair used to be, was a sheeted gurney. Several guards strapped Willingham down with leather belts, snapping buckles across his arms and legs and chest. A medical team then inserted intravenous tubes into his arms. Each official had a separate role in the process, so that no one person felt responsible for taking a life.

Willingham had asked that his parents and family not be present in the gallery during this process, but as he looked out he could see Stacy watching; whatever calm he had obtained was lost, and with his last breaths he cursed her. The warden pushed a remote control, and sodium thiopental, a barbiturate, was pumped into Willingham's body. Then came a second drug, pancuronium bromide, which paralyzes the diaphragm, making it impossible to breathe. Finally, a third drug, potassium chloride, filled his veins until his heart stopped, at 6:20 p.m. On his death certificate, the cause was listed as "Homicide."

After his death, his parents were allowed to touch his face for the first time in more than a decade. Later, at Willingham's request, they cremated his body and secretly spread some of his ashes over his children's graves. He had told his parents, "Please don't ever stop fighting to vindicate me."

In December, 2004, questions about the scientific evidence in the Willingham case began to surface. Maurice Possley and Steve Mills, of the Chicago *Tribune*, had published an investigative series on flaws in forensic science; upon learning of Hurst's report, Possley and Mills asked three fire experts, including John Lentini, to examine the original investigation. The experts concurred with Hurst's report. Nearly two years later, the Innocence Project commissioned Lentini and three other top fire investigators to conduct an independent review of the arson evidence in the Willingham case. The panel concluded that "each and every one" of the indicators of arson had been "scientifically proven to be invalid."

In 2005, Texas established a government commission to investigate allegations of error and misconduct by forensic scientists. The first cases that are being reviewed by the commission are those of Willingham and Willis. In August, 2009, the noted fire scientist Craig Beyler, who was hired by the commission, completed his investigation. In a scathing report, he concluded that investigators in the Willingham case had no scientific basis for claiming that the fire was arson, ignored evidence that contradicted their theory, had no comprehension of flashover and fire dynamics, relied on discredited folklore, and failed to eliminate potential accidental or alternative causes of the fire. He said that Vasquez's approach seemed to deny "rational reasoning" and was more "characteristic of mystics or psychics." What's more,

Beyler determined that the investigation violated, as he put it to me, "not only the standards of today but even of the time period." The commission is reviewing his conclusions, and plans to release its own report. The commission will likely narrowly assess the reliability of the scientific evidence. But some legal scholars believe that its findings could eventually lead to Texas becoming the first state to acknowledge that, since the advent of the modern judicial system, it had carried out the "execution of a legally and factually innocent person."

Just before Willingham received the lethal injection, he was asked if he had any last words. He said, "The only statement I want to make is that I am an innocent man convicted of a crime I did not commit. I have been persecuted for twelve years for something I did not do. From God's dust I came and to dust I will return, so the Earth shall become my throne."

DAVID GRANN *is a staff writer at* The New Yorker *magazine and author of the* New York Times *bestseller* The Lost City of Z: A Tale of Deadly Obsession in the Amazon. *The piece about Cameron Todd Willingham is one of a dozen true stories included in Grann's latest book,* The Devil and Sherlock Holmes: Tales of Murder, Madness, and Obsession, *which was recently published by Knopf Doubleday.*

Coda

Days before the government commission on forensic science was scheduled to hear testimony from Dr. Craig Beyler about his findings, Governor Rick Perry removed the body's long-standing chairman and two of its members. Perry insisted that the three commissioners' terms had expired and the changeover was "business as usual." But the chairman, Sam Bassett, who had previously been reappointed and had asked to remain, told the *Houston Chronicle* that he had heard from Perry's staffers that they were "concerned about the investigations we were conducting." Another of the removed commissioners told the Associated Press that Perry's office had informed her that the Governor was "going in a different direction."

Pamela Colloff

FLESH AND BLOOD

FROM *Texas Monthly*

I

CHARLES DICKERSON WAS the only officer on duty on
March 1, 2008, when the call came into the Rains County sheriff's office just after four-thirty in the morning that there had been
a shooting at the Caffey residence. The Caffeys lived in a modest
cabin set deep in the woods along a one-lane gravel road outside
Alba, a rural community of 492 people halfway between Sulphur
Springs and Tyler. Most folks around Alba and Emory, the nearby
county seat, knew the family; Penny played piano at Miracle Faith
Baptist Church, and her husband, Terry, was a home health aide
and lay preacher. Their daughter, Erin, worked as a carhop at the
Sonic. They also had two sons: Matthew, known as Bubba, who
was in the seventh grade, and Tyler, a fourth-grader. The Caffey
children—who had been home-schooled for three years—were
shy and well mannered, though sixteen-year-old Erin was the least
reserved. A slight, pretty blonde, she was known for her beautiful

singing voice, which she showcased in soaring gospel solos at Miracle Faith on Sundays.

Dickerson headed east along U.S. 69 and turned down the road that led through the woods to the Caffeys' house, following the crooked path as it rambled beneath pine canopies and over dry creeks, past a neighbor's hand-lettered sign that read, "Acknowledge thine iniquity—Jeremiah 3:13." Daybreak was still a few hours off, and the road beyond the glare of his headlights was pitch-black. Dickerson strained to see a mailbox or a landmark that might orient him to his surroundings, but the houses were few and far between. At a bend where the trees thinned out, he spotted a murky orange glow in the distance. As he drove nearer, he could see that a house was on fire. Dickerson realized that he was looking at the Caffey home.

The cabin appeared to have been burning for some time; the structure was engulfed in flames, and the metal roof had begun to buckle under its own weight. Dickerson radioed his dispatcher to mobilize the county's volunteer fire departments and sped down the road to Tommy Gaston's house, where the 911 call had originated.

Gaston, a genial man with a head of white hair, was the Caffeys' closest neighbor, and he looked relieved to see the sheriff's deputy at his door. Just beyond him, sprawled across the living room floor, was Terry Caffey. He had been shot five times: once in the head, twice near his right shoulder, and two more times in the back. His face and upper body were caked with blood. Although it was a cold night, the 41-year-old was wearing a T-shirt, pajama bottoms, no shoes, and a single wet sock. He had stumbled and crawled five hundred yards from his home, where he had been left for dead, to Gaston's—a journey that had taken him nearly an hour, all told. Along the way, he had fallen into a creek, where he had almost drowned, but he had kept moving, staggering toward Gaston's house as the fire behind him grew more intense. There was so much blood that Dickerson could not tell where he had been shot. "They're all gone," Caffey told the sheriff's deputy, his voice breaking. "Charlie Wilkinson shot my family."

THE AMBULANCE WAS about to pull away from Tommy Gaston's house when sheriff's investigator Richard Almon, who had hurried to the scene, climbed inside. "I don't think I'm going to make it," Caffey sputtered, straining to catch his breath. Almon crouched beside the gurney and asked him a few hurried questions. Charlie Wilkinson was his daughter's boyfriend, Caffey told the detective, and he and his wife had recently demanded that Erin stop seeing him. Charlie had broken into the house and shot Caffey and his family as they slept.

Almon clambered out of the ambulance and shared what he had learned with chief deputy Kurt Fischer. In rural communities as small as Alba and Emory, there are no strangers, and Fischer shook his head when he heard Charlie's name. His boys were friends with the clean-cut high school senior and had fished and gone four-wheeling with him many times before; in fact, Fischer told the detective, he had spotted Charlie's car parked outside Matthew Waid's trailer while driving to the crime scene. Waid was a few years older than Charlie, and Charlie and his buddies sometimes drank at his place and stayed the night.

All the lights were out in the rundown blue single-wide when Fischer and sheriff's deputy Ed Emig pulled up outside. A teenager whom Fischer did not recognize groggily came to the door; he was unsure if Charlie had spent the night or not, but he agreed to let the officers in. Fischer walked from room to room, stepping over piles of dirty clothes and empty beer cans as he went, startling Waid and his girlfriend from their sleep. Fischer told them he needed to talk to Charlie Wilkinson.

As Fischer continued down the hall, he saw that a blanket covered the empty door frame of one bedroom. Pulling the blanket back, he shone his flashlight inside. He could see Charlie lying on a mattress, awake, wearing only blue jeans. A semiautomatic handgun lay on the floor beside him.

"Charlie—it's Kurt," Fischer said. "Let me see your hands."

"What's going on?" Charlie said. He hesitated, and Fischer thought he might reach for the gun.

"Let me see your hands," repeated the chief deputy.

He led Charlie outside in handcuffs and sat him on the porch; he read the teenager his Miranda rights and told him that he was being taken in for questioning. The Caffey family had been attacked and killed earlier that morning, Fischer informed him. Charlie hung his head and was quiet.

"Were you involved in this?" Fischer asked.

"No, sir," Charlie said, shaking his head. "I got drunk last night and passed out."

Deputy Emig went inside to get Charlie a shirt and his cowboy boots. As Emig carried them out to the porch, he noticed that they were spattered with blood. The officers put Charlie in the back of the squad car, where he stared out the window in silence as they drove through the woods toward Emory in the predawn gloom.

At daybreak, the fire was still smoldering. Volunteer firefighters had struggled for several hours to put out the flames, but the house had burned down to its foundation. Later that day, when the bodies of the two Caffey boys were pulled from the rubble, one firefighter, overcome with emotion, fell to his knees.

AFTER CHARLIE WAS brought to the county jail, Fischer obtained a search warrant from the justice of the peace and returned to the trailer to collect any evidence that might tie Charlie to the crime scene. In the living room, he found a camouflage-colored purse with a driver's license inside it belonging to Erin Caffey. He began searching the back bedroom where Charlie had been found. There was no overhead light, so he pulled a blanket off one of the windows to illuminate his view. Spent shell casings lay scattered across the carpet, and next to the mattress sat a box of ammunition. Fischer picked up a black-and-white Western shirt, and a used condom slipped onto the floor.

Near the closet, he lifted up a blanket that was piled on the floor and noticed a shock of blond hair. For an instant, he thought he had found a doll. He pushed the hair aside to get a better look and watched, dumbfounded, as two eyes opened.

A girl was sitting with her back to the wall, in a fetal position. Fischer drew his gun and commanded her to show him her hands, but she just stared at him.

"What's your name?" Fischer asked.

"Erin," she stammered. Fischer recognized her from her driver's license photo.

The chief deputy brought her into the living room, where Matthew Waid and his girlfriend sat on the couch. Fischer had already informed the couple that the Caffey family was dead. Waid stared at the girl in disbelief and confirmed that she was Erin Caffey.

"How did you get here?" Fischer asked her.

Erin stood wide-eyed in her pajamas, bewildered, as she surveyed the room. "I don't know," she mumbled. "Where am I?"

II

Erin's pastor, Todd McGahee, once joked that if he had five more of her, he could fill his church on Sundays. Erin was cute and petite, with blue-gray eyes and a flirtatious smile, and she thrived on attention. Boys often came to Miracle Faith just to see her, and several of them credited her with bringing them closer to Jesus. At the Sonic on Emory's main drag, she was the only car-hop who delivered her orders wearing roller skates, and most afternoons, her admirers parked on whichever side of the drive-in she was waiting on. Yet despite her effect on boys, she struck people as hopelessly naive. "She gushed innocence," remembered a coworker (who, like many teenagers interviewed for this story, asked to remain anonymous). "A lot of guys flirted with her, and she would just blush and smile and duck her head down and skate inside and tell me, 'That guy wanted my number!' And I'd say, 'Did you tell him that your mom would be answering the phone?'"

Terry and Penny Caffey were protective—some said overly protective—of their daughter. Her homeschooling had begun when she was thirteen, after the family had moved to Alba from Celeste, a small town about an hour's drive away. Terry and Penny had wanted to be closer to Miracle Faith, where they were then serving as the church's youth ministers. Erin and her brothers had initially enrolled in their new public schools; she started the eighth grade at Rains Junior High, and Bubba and Tyler attended Rains Elementary. Then, that fall, an incident at the junior high had upset Terry and Penny: A girl who had been showing interest in Erin had kissed her in the hallway. The Caffeys abruptly pulled their children out of school a month into the academic year, and Penny began teaching them a Bible-based curriculum at home. She and Terry hoped that the individual instruction might benefit Erin, who had been diagnosed with attention deficit disorder and lagged behind her classmates. It was an isolated existence for an otherwise social girl whose life was largely circumscribed to Miracle Faith and her parents' house, six miles from town.

Faith was the cornerstone of the Caffeys' lives. They attended Bible study on Wednesday nights and church every Sunday and set aside several hours each week to rehearse gospel songs—with Penny playing piano, Bubba on guitar and harmonica, and Erin singing vocals. (Tyler, the youngest, preferred to play outdoors.) Terry and Penny had met at a revival meeting in Garland when she was 21 and he was 24, and their strong Baptist faith had always bound them together. Above their driveway hung a polished cedar plank with the inscription: "The Caffeys—Joshua 24:15." The verse, which Terry had committed to memory, was a reminder that they had chosen a righteous path: "If it seem evil unto you to serve the Lord, choose you this day whom ye will serve . . . as for me and my house, we will serve the Lord." Their children also shared their devotion. Bubba used to witness to whoever would listen, and Erin cried tears of joy when she sang her Sunday church solos—so much so that sometimes she had to stop, mid-verse, to collect herself. "I know there's no such thing as perfect, but in my book, they were," said Tommy Gaston, who was a frequent guest in their home and played in a gospel band with Penny.

When Erin turned sixteen, in July 2007, she got her driver's license and an old Chevy pickup and started working at the Sonic. "She was *so* sheltered," said her co-worker. "It was like she was seeing the world for the first time." One day at a church fellowship meeting, Miracle Faith's new youth director came upon Erin making out with a teenage boy. Several kids had already seen her sitting on a picnic table behind the church, kissing the boy while he eased his hand up her shirt. Erin had invited him over to her house before and considered him to be her boyfriend. But Terry and Penny, who separated the two teenagers that day at Miracle Faith, were deeply embarrassed by her behavior. "You're not going to see that boy no more," Terry told her.

CHARLIE WILKINSON WAS not the most polished guy to take an interest in Erin. He always seemed to be broke, and he drove a beat-up 1991 Ford Explorer that had to be push-started. He was good-looking in an unassuming kind of way, with sandy hair and light-blue eyes, and he nearly always wore Wranglers, black cowboy boots, and an oversized black Western hat. (On

MySpace, he went by the name Hillbilly.) He had met Erin at the Sonic a few weeks before the start of his senior year, having just returned home from boot camp at Fort Sill, Oklahoma, with his Texas National Guard unit. Charlie would later remember the electricity of the moment when Erin had glided up to his car window to deliver his order. "Instant vibe," he said, snapping his fingers.

Charlie lived in the country with his father, his stepmother, a stepbrother, a stepsister, and a half-sister. His dad worked at a paper mill outside Dallas. His mother had moved to Del Rio after his parents divorced, and he saw her only once or twice a year. An avid hunter, he spent much of his time fishing and tracking wild hogs through the brush, and like most of his friends, he was proficient with a firearm. He planned to go on active duty after graduation. He had never been arrested, and at school, he had no serious disciplinary problems—but he was hotheaded, and other students knew it was easy to get a rise out of him. "Some guys would really tease him and pick at him until he would get angry," remembered a classmate. Charlie might strike his desk or storm out of the classroom when he was provoked, but he usually walked away from a fight.

Throughout the fall, Charlie visited the Sonic to see Erin. For Halloween, she dressed up as a fifties carhop, coasting around the Sonic in a homemade pink-and-white poodle skirt with a pink scarf knotted at her neck. Shortly after that he worked up the nerve to ask her out. She was instantly taken with him, and Charlie too seemed to be infatuated. "He was totally in love with her and considered her his soul mate," Dion Kipp Jr., a friend of Charlie's, later told investigators. "Charlie talked about Erin twenty-four-seven." Though the Caffeys would not allow Charlie to take Erin out alone, the two teenagers still managed to spend much of their time together. Charlie dropped by the Sonic every afternoon during Erin's half-hour break, and at night, he was a frequent guest at the Caffeys' house. If Erin and her

brothers built a bonfire in the backyard after supper, as they often did, he lingered by her side. At nine o'clock, the Caffeys
made sure that Charlie was headed for the door—but after he
said goodbye, Erin usually called him and talked to him until
her ten o'clock phone curfew. (On the weekends, they had until
eleven.) Charlie also began attending church at Miracle Faith.
"What I knew of Charlie, he seemed like a nice boy," said Pastor
McGahee. "I don't think anyone worried about him and Erin at
first. We thought it was just puppy love."

In December Erin asked her parents if she could return to
public school. Her brothers had already reenrolled that fall after
Bubba, who was thirteen, told them that he missed his friends,
and the Caffeys—who were eager to free up time for Penny to
earn some extra income—agreed to let Erin go back before
Christmas. At school, where she enrolled as a freshman, she and
Charlie were inseparable; they ate lunch together and walked
down the hall hand in hand, and sometimes they slipped away to
Erin's pickup to fool around. Terry began allowing them to go
out for dinner every now and then, with the assurance that
Charlie would have Erin home no later than nine-thirty. Often
they went to a friend's house where they could be alone, and after
Christmas, they had sex for the first time. One night not long
afterward, Charlie pulled his car over on a country road, knelt on
the pavement, and presented Erin with his grandmother's en-
gagement ring. It was a promise ring, he told her. Though it was
not a formal proposal, he was declaring his intentions.

Penny noticed the ring on Erin's finger a few days later at a
church function and ordered her to give it back. Charlie was playing basketball outside the fellowship hall that afternoon, and Terry
pulled him aside. "This is totally inappropriate," he told the boy,
who shrugged. "You're promising yourself to my daughter? Do
you realize she is sixteen years old?" Terry had already begun
to grow uneasy with how fast the relationship seemed to be
moving. He did not care for Charlie, and he was not happy

about how much time the high school senior was spending with his daughter. He had never gotten over Charlie's nonchalant attitude when they first met; Terry had come home from work, and Charlie—his legs slung over the side of Terry's armchair—had not bothered to stand up or shake his hand. "I don't like that boy," Terry used to tell Penny. "If he can't show me any respect, how does he treat our daughter?"

From then on, the Caffeys limited Erin's time with Charlie to once a week, in their home, under their watch. Furious with her parents, Erin told her aunt that she planned on running away to be with Charlie when she turned seventeen. More and more she and her mother were at odds, and Erin once called Charlie in tears to report that Penny had slapped her in the heat of an argument. Then, in early February, Penny overheard Erin giggling one night past her phone curfew—Erin had sneaked her cell phone into her room to call Charlie. Penny informed her daughter that she was grounded. Erin's car keys and phone were taken away, and for weeks, her parents drove her to and from school. Worst of all, as far as Erin was concerned, Charlie's weekly visits to the house were suspended.

KILLING HER PARENTS, Erin told Charlie, was their best option. She talked about the idea relentlessly. In school, she brought up the subject once or twice a day; during a lunch break in mid-February, a junior overheard her tell Charlie that killing her parents was the only way they could be together. Charlie, who turned eighteen that month, wanted to be with Erin, and he promised to do whatever it took to make her happy. His father used to joke that he had "lost puppy dog syndrome"—he tried to help whoever was down on his luck; Erin was someone he wanted to rescue. Charlie told several friends that he intended to kill her parents. Still, sometimes he seemed ambivalent about their plan. He only wanted to run away with Erin, he told a buddy. As late as two days before the murders, he gloomily admitted to the same friend that he wished he could just get her pregnant so the Caffeys would have no choice but to accept him. But Erin was insistent. She was too young to have a baby, she said, and as long as her parents were alive, she and Charlie would have to be apart. "She had him around her finger, pretty much," said a girl who was a senior at the time. "She could get him to do whatever she wanted. She asked for something, she got it."

At Miracle Faith, people sensed that something was wrong in the Caffey home. Penny was withdrawn for most of February, and she declined to go on a women's church retreat, saying that she needed to spend more time with her family. At church functions, Erin was aloof and distracted. During a Valentine's Day dinner that was hosted by her youth group, she stood idly by, too preoccupied to even fill water glasses. The pastor's wife, Rebecca McGahee, was deeply troubled by her demeanor later that month, when she sang at her grandfather's funeral. Terry's father had died of a heart attack on February 21, and though none of the Caffeys had been close to him, they performed "Amazing Grace" in his honor. Terry and Bubba played harmonica, with Penny on piano. But Erin—whose jubilant singing often brought parishioners to their feet—turned in a listless, halfhearted performance. Her voice faltered, and her cousin, who did not have her natural talent, outshone her. Rebecca sensed that something was spiritually wrong with the girl. "Erin's anointing had lifted," she said. "She couldn't sing a lick."

On February 27, three days before the murders, the Caffeys demanded that Erin break up with Charlie. Earlier that day, Penny had stopped by the local library, at her sister's suggestion, and gone online to look at Charlie's MySpace profile, which had included comments about having sex and getting drunk. When Erin came home that afternoon, her father and mother were waiting for her in the living room. "It's over," Terry told her.

"You're breaking up with him today. I mean, it's over now." To their surprise, she did not protest. She had wanted to break things off with Charlie for a while, she tearfully confessed, but had not been sure how. Before the family left for Bible study, Erin promised that she would end things with Charlie.

III

"You're Erin Caffey?" chief deputy Fischer asked the girl again. She nodded and looked as if she might throw up. In her flower-print pajamas, with her blond hair pulled back into a ponytail, she seemed sweet and guileless. She glanced apprehensively around the trailer. She was disoriented, and Fisher thought that she appeared to be under the influence of some kind of drug.

"Can you tell me what happened?" Fischer asked.

"Fire," she said, her voice trailing off.

Erin was taken by ambulance to the Hopkins County Memorial Hospital, in Sulphur Springs, where she was given a full medical assessment. At the suggestion of Detective Almon, she was interviewed in the hospital's trauma room by Shanna Sanders, the young, personable chief of police for the Rains Independent School District who was on a first-name basis with most of the high school's students. Sheriff's deputy Serena Booth sat in. At the time, Erin was believed to be a victim—a girl who, investigators presumed, had been kidnapped after the murders.

Gently, Sanders asked Erin what she remembered. In a timid, childlike voice that Sanders had to strain to hear, Erin spoke haltingly, offering few details. She seemed confused, repeatedly telling the officers that she was fourteen years old. She had woken up in a house full of smoke, she said. There had been "two guys with swords" dressed in black who had ordered her to get down on the floor. Though she was unsure how she had gotten to the trailer, she said, she did remember trying to call her "friend"

Charlie and being unable to reach him. Then she drank "some stuff" that was offered to her at the trailer, and she could not recall anything afterward. She was teary at the start of the interview, but otherwise she showed little emotion. When Sanders asked if she had anything else to say, Erin whispered, "They're coming after me."

Sanders and Booth would later reflect on the fact that Erin had not smelled like smoke, and Sanders regretted that she had turned away to give Erin some privacy when her maternal grandmother, Virginia Daily, had come to tell her that her father had, miraculously, survived the attack. But that morning, the two officers felt only pity for the soft-spoken girl who had just lost her mother and two brothers. They stayed with her for five hours until she was released from the hospital, then offered to accompany her and her grandparents to the intensive care unit at the East Texas Medical Center in Tyler to see Erin's father. "You're a tough little girl," Sanders told her.

HER STORY WAS already beginning to unravel, though, as Charlie was being questioned at the sheriff's office in Emory. Detective Almon, a plainspoken Navy veteran with a blunt, intense manner, led the interrogation, while Texas Ranger John Vance assisted. At the outset, Charlie muttered, "I'm in a lot of trouble." Almon informed Charlie that he had been identified by a victim who had survived the attack and asked him to tell them exactly what had happened the previous night. If Charlie was startled by the news that he had left behind an eyewitness, he did not give himself away. Slowly, though, he began to parcel out information. Erin had called him the day before, Charlie said. She was, he recounted, "still pretty pissed off about her parents telling us we could not see each other." Once again, she told him that she wanted them dead. Charlie had urged her to just run away, but Erin had said, "No, kill them."

Around one-thirty the next morning, he told Almon, he and a friend had gone to the Caffey home. The friend, whom he initially refused to identify, was his hunting buddy Charles Waid, Matthew's younger brother. The twenty-year-old needed money, and Charlie had promised him $2,000 if he would help him kill the Caffeys—cash that Erin had told Charlie he would find in a lockbox inside the house. They brought along Waid's girlfriend, a bubbly high school senior named Bobbi Johnson, whose silver Dodge Neon they were driving. According to Charlie, Johnson did not know what the boys' plans were but had insisted on coming with them. Charlie told the detective that when they first drove up, the Caffeys' dog had barked so much that they decided to leave, but Erin called him on his cell phone afterward and promised to keep the dog quiet when he returned. And so with Waid behind the wheel of the Neon, they went back to the Caffeys' house.

The threesome picked Erin up at the end of her parents' driveway and rode around for an hour, talking about what to do. Charlie told the detective that he asked Erin several times to consider running away, but she was emphatic that she wanted her parents dead. Finally, they turned back toward the Caffey home and parked down the road. It was agreed that Charlie would kill Erin's parents, and Waid would take care of the two boys so no witnesses would be left behind. "I ain't got no conscience," Charlie said to the investigators about his decision to follow through on Erin's wishes. "I joined the Army to do whatever needed to be done without thinking." As for her parents, he said, "I intended to kill them because I thought I was in love."

According to Charlie, the girls had stayed behind in the car while he and Waid went inside. They entered through the front door, which Erin had left open. Armed with a .22-caliber pistol and two samurai swords, they moved through the house with brutal efficiency. Charlie crept into Terry and Penny's first-floor bedroom and fired at them until his gun jammed. He handed the gun to Waid, who fixed the .22 and fired two more shots. They left the room, and then Charlie came back and cut Penny's throat to make sure she was dead. The sound of gunfire had woken Bubba and Tyler, who called out for their parents and then locked themselves in Erin's room.

Charlie told the detective that when he and Waid were satisfied that Erin's parents were dead, Waid instructed him "to go get the kids" because "little ones talk." Charlie had balked, and Waid, in return, threatened to leave. Charlie went upstairs and told the boys to come out of Erin's room and go to their beds. "They were scared, and I could not stand to look at their faces," he said. Bubba tried to put up a fight by kicking Charlie, and when he did, Waid, who was still downstairs, raised the .22, aimed at the balcony where the brothers stood, and shot Bubba in the face. He fell to the floor and did not move again. Charlie, who had narrated the night's events with stoic detachment, broke down as he recounted how Waid had then come upstairs and stabbed eight-year-old Tyler. "I could not do it," he said, covering his face with his hands. "Why did he have to die?" Yet Charlie said he thought he had also stabbed Tyler at least once.

After the killing spree, Charlie told the detective, he had carried a suitcase of Erin's belongings, which she had previously packed, out to the car. She seemed happy, he remembered. She smiled and said, "I'm glad that's over." He and Waid went back inside and retrieved the lockbox, which Charlie opened using the combination that Erin had given him. The take, along with the contents of Terry's wallet and Penny's purse, amounted to $375 and some change, he said. Then they used their pocket lighters to set fire to furniture and clothes and bedsheets. As they hurried down the gravel road away from the Caffeys' home, the teenagers could see that the house was ablaze.

They drove down back roads for a while to blow off steam.

Later that night, he told the detective, Waid dropped him and Erin off at the trailer, where they had sex. "I hope that God forgives me," Charlie added.

THE INVESTIGATION MOVED FORWARD quickly on Saturday afternoon. Almon learned that Erin's toxicology test—she had been screened for Rohypnol, GHB, and other drugs that can cause memory loss—had come back negative. She also showed no symptoms of smoke inhalation. Chief deputy Fischer picked up Bobbi Johnson outside the restaurant where she washed dishes, and he pulled Charles Waid over driving her car. Johnson, who had recently played a minor role in the Rains High School production of *Oklahoma!*, seemed to be in high spirits. At the sheriff's office that afternoon, she played dumb with the officers until they told her they had Waid and Wilkinson in custody, at which point she admitted what she knew. Waid, who held out the longest, finally confessed under Almon's relentless questioning.

Their detailed accounts of the night were consistent with Charlie's. A former special-ed student with a heavy-lidded gaze, Waid showed no remorse, and he casually recounted how he had killed the two boys. Before the conclusion of the interview, he added a detail to the story that Charlie had left out. As they had driven away from the burning house, he said, Erin had cried out, "Holy shit, that was awesome!"

While the suspects were being questioned in the sheriff's office in Emory, Erin's grandparents were driving her to the hospital in Tyler, escorted by Chief Sanders and Deputy Booth. Just a few minutes into the drive, however, Sanders' cell phone rang. It was Fischer, calling to inform Sanders that Erin had been implicated in the Caffey murders and she needed to be placed under arrest. For a moment, Fischer heard only dead silence on the other end of the line. Sanders passed the phone to Booth. "You want us to do what now?" Booth asked, incredulous.

Sanders pulled her squad car into a parking lot, and the Dailys followed. She informed them that she had been instructed to arrest their granddaughter in connection with the Caffey murders and requested that Erin step out of the car. Virginia Daily became hysterical and grabbed Erin's face. "Did you have any part in this?" she demanded.

"No, Grandma," Erin told her, crying.

As a juvenile, Erin could not be taken directly to the sheriff's office for questioning and so she appeared that afternoon before a justice of the peace. "After everything we had heard, I was picturing a monster, for lack of a better word," said Sergeant Vance. "Here was someone who had dreamed up a scheme to murder her family and manipulated people into carrying out her plan. And then in walks this tiny, meek, blond-headed girl who couldn't fight her way out of a wet paper sack." The judge informed Erin of her rights and asked if she would be willing to speak with investigators. She declined to meet with the Texas Ranger or Detective Almon, electing to make a written statement instead. The brief account, put down in her girlish handwriting, echoed what she had told Chief Sanders: There had been smoke and strangers with swords, and she could not remember much else. She was taken to the juvenile detention center in Greenville, where she was held on charges of capital murder.

Less than 24 hours after the murders, Waid, Johnson, Charlie, and Erin were all in custody.

IV

Terry Caffey was discharged from the hospital several days later and went to stay with his sister in the town of Leonard, about an hour's drive from Alba. For a man who had been shot five times and climbed out the window of a burning house, he could consider himself lucky; he had a broken nose, two fractured cheekbones, and minor nerve damage in his right arm. "I remember the nurse coming in and saying, 'Mr. Caffey, you can go home now,'" Terry told me when I visited him this spring. "All I heard was the word 'home.' I thought, 'I don't have a home. I don't have a family to go home to.' And I remember weeping, just weeping uncontrollably.

"I laid on my sister's couch for a few days, and that's when the despair hit me. I decided that I was going to go back to my property and end my life. I was going to lay down and shoot myself right there on the spot where I lost my family. I wanted to die where they died. And then I decided, no, there's been enough bloodshed. I'm going to take all of the pain pills they gave me—all the depression medication, the Xanax, everything—drink me a bottle of Jim Beam, put a hose in the tailpipe of my daughter's pickup, run it up to the window, and just fall asleep and not wake up again.

"So two or three days I pondered on this. Somebody brought me a Bible and told me to read the book of Job. Well, I'd read the story countless times before, but I read it again and it was almost like I was there with Job. He lost everything, his whole family, all his worldly possessions, but he did not lose his faith, and God blessed him doubly. That turned me around and got me thinking that God might have a plan for me. He didn't bring me through all that for nothing.

"I went back to our property as soon as I was better. There was nothing left but the subfloor and the metal roof. I spent days out there picking through the ashes. I would get on my hands and knees and just dig. I didn't find much—a Hot Wheels car; a broken ceramic cup; a horseshoe-shaped belt buckle that the kids gave me for Christmas. I ended up buying me a used RV, and I moved it back up on my land. Everybody said I was crazy for going back, but it brought me healing. I put my RV right on the spot where my house once stood, and I stayed out there about four months. I was so stubborn, I thought, 'I'll be darned if somebody is going to run me off of our property. When I leave, it will be when I'm ready and when God's ready for me to leave.' Some nights it was pitch-black by the time I got home, and I had to work up the courage to get out of the car. I bought me a nine-millimeter pistol and I slept with it beside me."

Twice a week, Terry made the trip to Greenville to see his daughter. He could not ask Erin any of the questions he longed to know the answers to; her lawyer had warned him that their conversations were being recorded and anything Erin said could be used against her at trial. And so Terry sat opposite the only other surviving member of his family—the girl who investigators were telling him had wanted him and his wife and sons dead—and conversed with her about subjects as mundane as the weather. Terry found the visits agonizing, but he felt compelled to be in the presence of his only living child. His daughter looked fragile and anxious in her orange prison jumpsuit, and at the end of every visit, he made sure to tell her that he loved her. During the many hours in which they made polite conversation, he ventured only once to ask her a question of substance. It was a question that preoccupied him more than his doubts about her innocence. "Were me and your mom good parents?" he asked her as they sat on opposite sides of the Plexiglas divider. Yes, Erin assured him, blinking back tears. She couldn't have asked for a better mom or dad.

GIVEN THE COMPLEXITY that four capital murder cases posed for a small, rural county, the Texas attorney general's office was asked to assist the Rains County district attorney in bringing the four defendants to trial. Assistant attorney general Lisa Tanner, a seasoned prosecutor who has sent four men to death row in her eighteen years as a trial lawyer, was assigned to the case. "This was not the most brutal or cold-blooded case I had ever prosecuted," she told me. "But when you took all the different factors and put them together—how young and seemingly normal the perpetrators were; how ruthless they were; how stupid they were; how cavalier they were; how utterly undeserving this family was—it was, without question, the most disturbing case I'd ever dealt with."

The crime also defied easy explanation. Though Charlie and Waid had been drinking that night, neither was using drugs. Erin's desire to have her parents killed did not appear to be motivated by any mistreatment or trauma; her court-mandated psychological evaluation failed to point to any evidence of abuse in the Caffey home. Yet Tanner had no doubt that Erin had masterminded the crime. "The phone records really did it for me," she said. "When I saw the phone records, I realized that it didn't matter if a single one of the other defendants testified against her. We were still going to be able to convict her of capital murder."

The phone records corroborated a pivotal point in Charlie's account of the murders. "From 11:46 p.m. until 12:48 a.m. that night, Erin called him six times from inside the Caffey house," Tanner said, reading from the case file. "But the kicker was from 1:22 a.m. to 1:58 a.m., when she called him seven more times. That comported completely with what Charlie told us, which was that she kept calling and saying, 'Where are y'all? What's the holdup? Hurry up. Come back, and I'll keep the dog quiet.'"

Tanner sat down with Terry Caffey and showed him the phone records this past June. She needed to explain to him why prosecutors were asking the court to certify Erin as an adult. (If certified, she would face the same punishment at trial as an adult, including life without parole—with one notable exception: Even when certified, a juvenile cannot receive the death penalty.) Tanner was in the difficult position of briefing the victim of a crime who also happened to be the parent of the perpetrator. "It was an awful thing to have to do, to lay out to a man that his daughter wanted him dead and was responsible for the deaths of the rest of his family," Tanner said. "I brought all of the relevant documents and pictures, and we went through everything. I showed him photos of the suitcase that Erin had packed and the burned-out lockbox that was open to the combination that she had given Charlie. I showed him the statement that a friend of hers had given to investigators about how Erin had wanted them to be killed. I told him about her and Charlie having sex afterwards, which was by far the hardest thing to have to tell him. Terry cried a lot and kept asking, 'Why?' He said, 'I don't understand. We didn't see any of this coming.'"

And yet, after Terry had seen every last piece of evidence, he continued to visit Erin and never wavered in his support, standing beside his daughter at each court appearance holding her hand. For the many people who puzzled over his loyalty, there were many others, in the pews of Miracle Faith and elsewhere, who understood it as the scriptural imperative of unconditional love. Terry drew particular sustenance from a passage in Romans, chapter 12: "Bless them which persecute you," a principle that, in the end, informed his wish that his family's killers be spared the death penalty. "My heart tells me there have been enough deaths," Terry wrote in a letter to the Rains County district attorney, Robert Vititow, this past fall. "I want them, in this lifetime, to have a chance for remorse and to come to a place of repentance for what they have done. Killing them will not bring my family back." He asked that Charlie Wilkinson and Charles Waid receive sentences of life in prison without parole. After consulting with the attorney general's office, Vititow honored his wishes and offered them a plea deal. In November they each pleaded guilty to three counts of capital murder.

At their sentencing hearings in January, Terry rose to address each of them in the courtroom. He spoke first to Waid, who remained impassive, and then to Charlie. "In time, God has shown me what it means to forgive," Terry said as Charlie's eyes shone with tears. "Charlie Wilkinson, I want to say to you today, I forgive you. Not so much for your sake, but for my own. I refuse to grow into a bitter old man. If I want to heal and move on, I must find some forgiveness in my heart, and that has been the hardest thing I have ever had to do because you took so much from me."

V

Today Terry lives in a tidy brick house in Wills Point, about thirty miles southwest of Alba, just down the road from the cemetery where Penny and the boys are buried. He became an ordained minister in April, and he gives his testimony most weekends at local churches, using his family's story as an object lesson in forgiveness. To the astonishment of many of his closest friends, he remarried last year. Terry found a good listener in Sonja Webb, a pretty divorcée he met in the course of his work as a home health aide. Webb was raising two sons on her own. She asked him to lunch last June, and they never ran out of things to talk about.

"Terry missed being a husband and a father," Tommy Gaston says. "He needed somebody to lay down beside him at night who he could tell his troubles to." They said their vows in October at Miracle Faith, just a few feet from where Terry's wife's and sons' caskets had rested seven months earlier. Webb's boys—Blake, who is seventeen, and Tanner, who is nine—bear a passing resemblance to Bubba and Tyler. Terry, who shares a warm relationship with his stepsons, says that, like Job, he has been doubly blessed for never faltering in his faith in God.

Once a month, Terry makes the three-hour trip to Gatesville, where Erin is incarcerated. At his urging, she received a lesser sentence than life without parole; he wanted to make sure that she had something to live for, he said. And so Erin accepted a plea deal—two life sentences to be served concurrently, plus an additional 25 years—which ensures that with good behavior she will be eligible for parole when she is 59 years old. Now that she has pled out and the specter of a capital murder trial is gone, their conversations are no longer restricted, and Terry is free to ask his daughter whatever he wants to know. Yet when I visited him, he seemed hesitant. "I've got so many questions, and I don't want to hit her with them all at once," he said. He has, thus far, chosen to accept the story line she has provided him: She was planning on running away that night, but then she changed her mind. The phone calls, she told her father, were to dissuade Charlie from coming at all. It was Charlie who had wanted the family dead, and when he came to the house, she had been powerless to stop him.

"I think she thought Charlie was just blowing smoke," Terry said. "I don't think she actually thought he would go through with it. I *know* my daughter. She cried one time when we were in my truck and I ran over a squirrel; she's tenderhearted. No kid's an angel, but I know what she is capable of, and I know she's not capable of murder."

ERIN TOLD ANOTHER VERSION of her story to Israel Lewis, the mental health counselor who was hired to evaluate her for the defense. When she spoke to Lewis, Erin insisted that Charlie had a volatile temper; he had killed her family after she had broken up with him and then framed her. "I have worked with some good liars, but Erin was one of the best," said Lewis, who has nineteen years' experience counseling juvenile offenders. "She seemed totally sincere and genuine, and I would have put my license on the line to say that she was telling me the truth. She spoke with tears in her eyes—'God will save me. He knows I'm innocent.' I cried every time I left her jail cell."

Only after learning the details of the criminal investigation did Lewis realize that Erin had been manipulating him. He continued to visit her at the county jail, but what disturbed him most, at the end of a year of counseling, was the realization that he could no more explain why she had wanted her family killed than on the day he had first met her. She remained a mystery. "You could not have paid her to say anything negative about her parents," he said. "I still long for the day when I know what was hurting her bad enough to make such a decision."

Erin declined my interview requests, but the three other defendants each agreed to sit down with me and revisit the early morning of March 1, 2008. They all gave similar accounts, with Erin serving as the driving force behind the killings. Johnson, who is serving a forty-year sentence, recalled how Charlie had repeatedly asked Erin to consider running away as the group had driven around before the murders. "Charlie kept saying, 'Are you *sure* you want to do this?'" Johnson recounted. "And she said, 'Why are you asking me this? If you love me, you'll do it.'" (Explaining her own inability to put the brakes on the plan, Johnson said, "I just wanted to go home, but Charlie said it was too late, that I was already involved. He said that if anybody said anything to anyone, that person would be taken care of. I was scared shitless.") Erin had seemed elated after the killings, Johnson explained, and said that she was "free." In fact, Johnson said, Erin had wanted to get out of the car to make sure that everyone was dead. And it was Erin who had insisted that her brothers be killed, according to both Johnson and Waid. The boys picked on her, Erin had said, and she didn't want them to be left in foster care. "They were ridiculous reasons—not even reasons—just an excuse," Waid told me. "When we pulled away from the house, she was happier than a kid on Christmas morning."

One afternoon this spring, I visited Charlie at the Polunsky

Unit, in Livingston, the imposing, maximum-security prison that is best known for housing death row. Now nineteen, he looked impossibly young for someone who will never step beyond the guard towers and concertina wire again. He wore a starched white inmate's uniform, a buzz cut, and a doleful expression. He was frank about the horror of what he had done and made no excuses for himself. "If I was sitting on my jury, I would have stuck the needle in my arm," he told me. At the same time, he said, Erin was given ample opportunity to call off the plan. "It was her idea," he said. "If at any time she would have said, 'Well, we're not going to do it after all,' it never would have happened."

He had no ill words for the people he had so viciously attacked. Of the Caffeys, he painted a nostalgic portrait. "You know them family pictures that they print in movies and stuff?" he said. "The old-timey ones with the white fence? When I was at their house, that was what the family was like. They were perfect." When I visited the subject of his role in Tyler's murder, he grew quiet and studied his hands, his eyes slowly filling with tears. "I don't really like to talk about that," he said.

It was when he spoke about Erin that his voice softened and grew sentimental. "I would have done anything for her," he said. "She was very smart. Very caring. I don't know why she wanted it done, why it had to be like that, but she was a very nice person." Weeks after the killings, when he was being held at the county jail on $1.5 million bond, he had been devastated to learn from his defense attorney that Erin had, in fact, asked a previous boyfriend to kill her parents too. Sergeant Vance had interviewed the boy whom Erin was caught kissing at Miracle Faith, and he had told the Texas Ranger that Erin had spoken to him about her desire to have them killed—several months before she had started dating Charlie.

"It made me question a lot of things," Charlie said, his voice trailing off. "After months of pushing me and convincing me and all this, I got to thinking that maybe all I was was just a tool."

He had not spoken to her since the morning of the crime, and he is barred from communicating with her ever again; he will forever have to wonder if she wanted her parents dead so that she could be with him or simply so that she could be free of her family's control. "I don't know what's wrong with her head," he said. "She needs to have it looked at."

But Charlie was more bewildered by Erin's behavior than bitter. Knowing everything he knew, I asked him, did he still love her? He thought for a moment before answering my question, and I studied his face behind the Plexiglas. "Once you love somebody, you can't quit," Charlie said. "You always will."

PAMELA COLLOFF *has been a staff writer at* Texas Monthly *since 1997. She is a graduate of Brown University and was raised in New York City. In 2001, she was a finalist for a National Magazine Award in public interest. Her work has also appeared in* The New Yorker, *and has been anthologized in the 2008 and 2007 editions of* Best American Crime Reporting *and the 2006 edition of* Best American Sports Writing. *She lives in Austin, Texas.*

Coda

During fifteen years of writing about true crime, no other story has spooked me the way "Flesh and Blood" did. I did not sleep well while I was writing about this case. The innumerable questions it inspired preoccupied me. Was Erin Caffey mentally ill? What had Terry Caffey not told me? Were Charlie Wilkinson and Charles Waid both sociopaths? Was Bobbi Johnson completely blameless? What was I missing?

Because all four defendants chose to plead out before their cases went to trial, few details about the murder were publicly known when I began reporting this story. My very first interview was with Terry Caffey, who could not have been a more likable, generous, or gracious person. Incredibly, he had only kind words for his daughter, whom he saw as a naive teenager manipulated by an obsessed boyfriend. He placed the blame for the crime entirely on the two young men who committed the killings. It was only when I read the case file that I realized the disconnect between Terry's account and the terrible reality of this crime. When my story was published, Terry wrote to express his disappointment in the way that I had characterized his daughter. "I know she had her part in it—I'm not saying she didn't," he wrote in an e-mail. But he was frustrated, he explained, that I had put "the blame all on Erin" and made it look like "Erin twisted their arms and made them do it." He wished I had instead written "a story of hope and forgiveness and moving on."

Had Erin chosen to talk to me, as her three codefendants did, that might have been easier to accomplish. While I was reporting this story, I sent her a long letter asking for the opportunity to sit down and talk with her, but never received a response. To my knowledge, she has still not agreed to talk with any reporter—or investigator, for that matter—to explain her side of the story.

Erin Caffey is currently serving her sentence at a women's prison in Gatesville, Texas, and is not due to be released until 2051, when she will be fifty-nine years old.

Jeffrey Toobin
_____

THE CELEBRITY DEFENSE

FROM *The New Yorker*

ON THE MORNING of March 11, 1977, Detective Philip Vannatter, of the Los Angeles Police Department, arrived at his desk in the West L.A. division to find a report that had been placed there a few hours earlier. The document recounted how patrol officers had gone to the home of Samantha Gailey, a thirteen-year-old girl who lived in the San Fernando Valley, after her mother called police to say that Samantha had been raped by Roman Polanski, the movie director, who was forty-four at the time.

"In those days, I was too busy raising kids and paying bills to go to many movies," Vannatter recalled recently. "But of course I knew who Polanski was, because of Sharon Tate." Seven and a half years earlier, Tate, who was married to Polanski, and four other people were killed at the couple's home, in Benedict Canyon, by members of Charles Manson's "family."

Vannatter read the file and went to interview Gailey and her mother, reported on his findings to prosecutors in the district attorney's office, and then took the girl and the mother to speak to the lawyers themselves. According to Vannatter, "The prosecutor decided that we should go to the hotel where Polanski was staying and execute a search warrant"—to find, among other things, photographs of Gailey that she said Polanski had taken and quaalude pills like the one she said the director had given her. "The head of the D.A.'s office there told me to do the search but not to arrest him," Vannatter recalled. "They said they didn't want to do an arrest, but to do the case more slowly, through a grand-jury investigation. I was very unhappy when I heard about that. I thought we had plenty of evidence to arrest him, and that's what I thought we should do."

So, in the early evening, Vannatter and his partner went to the Beverly Wilshire hotel, in Beverly Hills, where Polanski was staying. "As we were walking through the lobby, I saw Polanski getting out of the elevator," Vannatter said. "I walked up to him and placed him under arrest. I thought, The heck with this. I wasn't going to let those D.A.s tell me how to do my job. Why not arrest the guy? Any other person would have been arrested. So I said I'm going to do what is right.

"After I read him his rights, I asked him to take me upstairs to his room, so I could do the search," Vannatter went on. "I noticed that he had something in his hand, and he was just about to drop it. So I put my hand under his and said, 'Why don't you drop it into my hand instead of on the floor?'" Polanski placed a single quaalude in Vannatter's palm.

In Suite 200, Polanski was jittery but cooperative. "As we say on the farm, he was nervous as a hen on a hot rock. He kept asking me for the quaalude back, so he could take it and calm down," Vannatter said. "By the time we got back to the station house, he told me he had had sex with her." (The question of exactly when Polanski first admitted having sex with Gailey is a matter of dispute.)

But the case did not end there, and, almost thirty-three years later, it's still not over. On March 24, 1977, a Los Angeles

County grand jury indicted Polanski on six felony counts, including rape by use of drugs and furnishing a controlled substance to a minor. On August 8, 1977, pursuant to a plea bargain, Polanski pleaded guilty to the least serious of the charges against him, having unlawful sex with a minor—statutory rape. On the eve of his sentencing hearing, which was scheduled for February 1, 1978, Polanski fled to Europe, and he has not returned.

Earlier this year, on September 26th, he was detained in Switzerland after American authorities made a provisional request for his arrest. Last week, Polanski's lawyers provided the deed to his apartment in Paris, the final piece of security to raise $4.5 million for a bail package that had been approved by the local courts. Under the terms of the arrangement, Polanski was then released to house arrest at his chalet, known as Milky Way, in the Swiss ski resort of Gstaad, having spent sixty-seven days in a Zurich detention center. The large amount of bail, and a requirement for him to wear an electronic monitoring bracelet, might seem extreme for a seventy-six-year-old man; but, considering that Polanski is one of the most famous fugitives from American justice in the world, his release from prison under any terms at all may seem like a generous deal for him.

The question of whether Polanski's celebrity has helped or hurt him hovers over his lengthy legal battle. For Vannatter, the lesson in Polanski's long flight from justice is that celebrities enjoy special privileges in the legal system—a subject on which he possesses a unique vantage point. Seventeen years after arresting Polanski, Vannatter, with his partner Tom Lange, led the investigation of the murder of O. J. Simpson's ex-wife, Nicole Brown Simpson, and her friend Ronald Goldman. (Simpson was acquitted.) "I just think that celebrities get a sweetheart deal, more than the average guy does," Vannatter, who retired from the L.A.P.D. in 1996 and moved, part-time, to a farm he bought in Indiana, said. "I never believed in that."

It is easy to see why Vannatter and many others find such a

moral in Polanski's story. Polanski has enjoyed a comfortable exile in Europe, where until this year he not only avoided prison but continued to make films. For decades, his conviction for a felony sex crime existed mostly as a footnote in a long and eventful life. But the Polanski story suggests an alternative view, too. Over the years, there have also been times when he has been penalized for his celebrity status. Mostly, celebrity warps the criminal process, and not always in a predictable direction. In Polanski's case, the effect of his celebrity was doubly, and inconsistently, pernicious; it obscured both how badly Polanski treated his young victim and how badly the legal system treated him.

POLANSKI'S PERIOD OF HOUSE ARREST will mark a return to an alpine village that has long been a favorite escape for him. Friends of Polanski brought him to Gstaad to help him recover from his grief over the murder of Sharon Tate. On that visit, in the late sixties, Polanski discovered that Gstaad was, he wrote in an autobiography, "the finishing school capital of the world [with] hundreds of fresh-faced, nubile young girls of all nationalities." At the time, "Kathy, Madeleine, Sylvia and others whose names I forget played a fleeting but therapeutic role in my life. They were all between sixteen and nineteen years old. . . . They took to visiting my chalet, not necessarily to make love—though some of them did—but to listen to rock music and sit around the fire and talk." He described sitting in his car outside the schools at night, waiting for his "date" to climb out over the balcony after roll call. At this age, Polanski wrote, the girls "were more beautiful, in a natural, coltish way, than they ever would be again." The autobiography, "Roman, by Polanski," was published in 1984, seven years after his guilty plea, and suggests a lack of contrition about his actions. While exile and tragedy have been persistent themes in Polanski's life, so, too, has a sexual obsession with very young women. He started dating the actress

Nastassja Kinski when he was in his mid-forties and she was in her mid-teens. He has been together with his wife, Emmanuelle Seigner, since he was fifty-one and she was eighteen.

And then, of course, there is the criminal case involving thirteen-year-old Samantha Gailey. In his autobiography, he wrote of the day that Vannatter arrested him, "I was incredulous; I couldn't equate what had happened that day with rape in any form." In an interview two years after the crime, with Martin Amis, Polanski spoke in even blunter terms: "When I was being driven to the police station from the hotel, the car radio was already talking about it. . . . I couldn't *believe.* . . . I thought, you know, I was going to wake up from it. I realize, if I have *killed* somebody, it wouldn't have had so much appeal to the press, you see? But . . . fucking, you see, and the young girls. Judges want to fuck young girls. Juries want to fuck young girls—*everyone* wants to fuck young girls!"

Roman Polanski has led the kind of life that has already called forth multiple biographies. He was born in Paris in 1933, and his survival into adulthood must count as something close to a miracle. His father, a Jewish émigré from Poland whom Polanski described as a "struggling entrepreneur," made the extraordinarily unwise decision to return his family to Kraków in 1936. After Hitler's invasion, the family was confined to the city's ghetto. His mother, four months pregnant, was taken to Auschwitz and gassed; his father was carried off, too, but somehow survived. On March 14, 1943, the Germans completed the liquidation of the ghetto.

"He has a world view which has been informed by terrible events, unspeakable events, that have never soured him as a person. There is no bitterness, no anger, though there is memory," Jeff Berg, his longtime agent, who spoke to Polanski while he was jailed, told me. "Roman is not defeated by anything," Peter Gethers, who edited his autobiography and wrote two screenplays with him, said. "He doesn't regret the things that happen to him, because he understands that things just happen. He is neither in denial nor apologetic about his life. He wouldn't use the word, but it's a very existential approach to life."

Polanski's early life seems to have instilled in him a voraciousness for experience—intellectual, physical, sexual. Amid the deprivations of postwar Poland, the young Polanski became an accomplished actor, skier, bicycle racer, fencer, mimic, and artist. Summer camp changed his life. "I became Troop 22's head of entertainment," he wrote in his autobiography. "Organizing, directing, and starring in all our Boy Scout shows. I had discovered my vocation."

In the early fifties, Polanski joined the threadbare Polish film community in Lodz. He made a handful of experimental shorts. His first full-length feature was "Knife in the Water," a dark, atmospheric drama about a married couple who pick up a young stranger on the way to an excursion on their boat. It earned Polanski an Academy Award nomination in 1963 for Best Foreign Language Film. "I flew into L.A. first class and was met by a huge limousine sporting a Polish flag on the fender," he wrote. (He lost to Federico Fellini, for "8½.")

Polanski landed in Hollywood at a propitious moment. "It was a great time in the movie business," Peter Bart, then the vice-president for production at Paramount and later the editor of *Variety*, said. "It was possible to be a great artist and make pictures that made money, too." Shortly after Polanski's Oscar nomination, Paramount acquired the rights to Ira Levin's book "Rosemary's Baby," a satanic thriller. After Polanski rejected Bart's initial requests that he direct the movie version, Bart asked his boss at Paramount, Robert Evans, to intervene. "Bob called up Roman and said, 'What have you got to lose? If you come to L.A., the worst thing that can happen is that you are going to have the best sex of your life.' Roman said, 'I'll be there.'"

"Rosemary's Baby" became a huge success, and Polanski found himself a member of a celebrated generation of young actors and directors, including Warren Beatty, Jack Nicholson, Martin Scorsese, Francis Ford Coppola, and Brian De Palma. "For the first time, we were making money," Bart said. "Roman started to like this community. He loved the fast life. He became a real star. He got good tables in restaurants. That had not been part of his life. You could see him change, to a degree. The un-thinkable happened to Roman—he was actually happy."

Polanski even found a woman he loved, a young actress named Sharon Tate, and they married on January 20, 1968. When Tate was pregnant with their first child, she and Polanski rented a house on the quiet and remote Cielo Drive.

IT WAS SHORTLY BEFORE DINNER on August 9, 1969, when Polanski, who was in London, received the phone call. His maid had found the bodies: Tate, who was eight and a half months pregnant; Jay Sebring, a Hollywood hair stylist; Wojtek Frykowski, a friend of Polanski's from Poland; and Abigail Folger, Frykow-ski's girlfriend and an heiress to the Folger coffee fortune. (Steven Parent, who had been visiting the estate's caretaker, was shot outside.) Tate had been stabbed sixteen times, Folger twenty-eight, and Frykowski fifty-one (and shot twice). The word "PIG" was written in Tate's blood on the front door.

For months, the crime was unsolved, and it became the subject of a torrent of speculation, with some insinuations directed at Polanski. *Time* noted that "Sharon and Polanski circulated in one of the film world's more offbeat crowds." The innuendo wounded Polanski, who assisted the police, and offered a reward for leads. Finally, on December 1st, the police announced that the case had been solved. Most of the Manson "family" members who had conducted the attacks were already in custody. Manson had no connection to Polanski, or to any of the victims.

"Sharon's death is the only watershed in my life that really matters," Polanski wrote. "Afterward, whenever conscious of enjoying myself, I felt guilty." After months of wandering, and much skiing, and eventually running out of money, Polanski directed a movie version of "Macbeth," which was a critical and commercial debacle. A little later, his friend Robert Evans asked him to direct a script, by Robert Towne, about the murky origins of modern Los Angeles. Polanski was reluctant, but Evans courted him by hosting a Passover Seder, with Kirk Douglas presiding and Sidney Korshak, the mob fixer, arranging the catering. Polanski agreed to direct "Chinatown." That film, which came out in 1974 and features a victim of incest trying to protect her daughter from the same fate, earned Polanski his next Academy Award nomination. (He lost to Coppola, for "The Godfather, Part II.")

In the years after Tate's death, Polanski lived a gilded itinerancy, mostly in Europe. He shot "The Tenant," a thriller in which he also starred, in Paris, and directed "Rigoletto" at the Bavarian State Opera, in Munich. In his autobiography, Polanski recounted an evening in Munich in late 1976 when he and a journalist friend went on a double date. At Polanski's hotel suite, the journalist stayed with his date, whom Polanski knew only as "Nasty," and "I took the other girl, a stunning blonde, to bed. By the time I surfaced the journalist had gone. Nasty was half-asleep in an armchair in the sitting room. Taking her by the hand, I led her back into the bedroom. We never repeated this threesome, though I saw a lot of both girls thereafter." Nasty was Nastassja Kinski, an aspiring German actress. Kinski spoke little English, and Polanski spoke no German. She was, according to Polanski, fifteen years old.

Late in the fall of 1976, French *Vogue* asked Polanski to guest-edit its Christmas edition. He took Kinski to the Seychelles and used photographs taken of her there in the issue. He then secured an assignment from *Vogue Hommes*, also based in Paris, to shoot a feature on adolescent girls, to "show girls as they really were these days—sexy, pert, and thoroughly human," he wrote in his autobiography.

Polanski headed to Los Angeles, where he was preparing to direct an adaptation of "The First Deadly Sin," a novel by Lawrence Sanders, concerning a serial killer. He mentioned the *Vogue* assignment to a friend, Henri Sera, who suggested that the younger sister of a woman he was dating might make a good subject. This tip led Polanski to make an appointment to meet Samantha Gailey and her mother at their home in the suburb of Woodland Hills, on February 13, 1977. During the visit, Susan Gailey, a divorced actress who had played small roles in "Police Woman" and "Starsky and Hutch," did most of the talking. Also at the meeting was Susan Gailey's boyfriend, who was an editor at *Marijuana Monthly*. As Gailey later testified before the grand jury, Polanski showed her the *Vogue* Christmas issue and explained that his current project was to feature "young girls seen through his eyes and possibly an interview." Gailey recalled telling Polanski that her daughter was thirteen, "because I thought maybe she was too old. I thought he might want younger girls."

ALTHOUGH THE LEGAL CASE involving Polanski remains controversial and unresolved, the underlying facts are largely undisputed. Except for a few specific details, what happened between Polanski and Samantha Gailey is pretty clear.

At that first encounter with Samantha, at her home, Polanski claims to have been "disappointed" because she was "a good-looking girl but nothing sensational." Still, Polanski arranged to return a week later to take some photographs of Samantha. He arrived at about 4 P.M. on February 20th; Susan had laid out a selection of clothes that the girl might wear. Polanski said at first that he wanted to shoot in Benedict Canyon, but, concerned with the fading light in the late afternoon, he agreed with Susan's suggestion that he go to some scrubby hills just behind the Gailey home. Susan asked to go along—so that she could take her own pictures—but, she testified, "He said, No, that he would

rather be alone with her because she will respond more naturally."

Polanski selected some clothes and drove Samantha to a hillside near her home. They walked and Polanski started taking
pictures. He took a number of shots of her in different shirts and
then, according to Samantha's grand-jury testimony, "He said,
'Here, take off your top now.'" She did, and they finished the
session at about six-thirty in the evening, after Polanski had shot
about two rolls of film. "She had nice breasts," Polanski wrote.
"I took pictures of her changing and topless." Samantha did not
tell her mother about the topless photos. When they returned
to the house, Susan's boyfriend gave Polanski several issues of
Marijuana Monthly to give to Jack Nicholson, in the hope of
obtaining an interview with him.

Polanski then flew to New York to do research on police procedures for "The First Deadly Sin." When he returned to L.A., he
made an appointment to see Samantha on March 10th. Polanski
again arrived in the late afternoon, greeted her mother, and drove
off with Samantha. They went first to the home of a friend, the
actress Jacqueline Bisset, who lived on Mulholland Drive, in
the Hollywood Hills. They took about fifty pictures, but the
light was fading, and there were several guests on the premises.
So Polanski called Jack Nicholson's house, on the other side of
Mulholland. He reached Helena Kallianiotes, a professional
belly dancer who worked as a caretaker for Nicholson as well as
for Marlon Brando, who owned the compound. She told Polanski to come over.

Kallianiotes let Polanski and Samantha in, then chatted with
them in the kitchen. Samantha said she was thirsty. Polanski
poured glasses of Cristal champagne for the three of them. Kallianiotes left, and Polanski began taking pictures of Samantha
sipping the champagne. "I just kept drinking it for pictures," she
testified. Polanski again asked her to pose topless, which she did.
"We weren't saying much now, and I could sense a certain erotic

tension between us," Polanski wrote. Samantha dialled her mother, at Polanski's request, and he told Susan that they would be later than expected. Susan also spoke to Samantha, who told her that she was fine.

After the phone call, Polanski asked Samantha to pose in Nicholson's outdoor Jacuzzi. Polanski produced a yellow pill container with a quaalude broken into three parts. When he offered Samantha part of the pill, she hesitantly accepted. "I think I must have been pretty drunk or else I wouldn't have," she testified. (Polanski does not mention the pill in his book.)

Samantha removed all her clothes, except for her underwear, before entering the Jacuzzi. "I was ready to get in and he said, 'Take off your underwear.' So I did and then I got in," she testified. Polanski took more photographs of her, then removed his clothes and joined her in the Jacuzzi. When Polanski moved toward her, Samantha said she wanted to get out because her asthma was acting up. (This was not true; she'd never had asthma.) "I had to get out because of the warm air and the cold air or something like that," Samantha testified that she had said. She also said that she wanted to go home. Polanski wrote that "she said she'd stupidly left her medication at home." He encouraged her to join him in Nicholson's swimming pool instead, which she did. After a few moments, she left the pool and went inside to the bathroom.

At this point, Gailey's story and Polanski's diverge somewhat. She told the grand jury that he approached her in the bathroom "and told me to go in the other room and lie down." She went into the room, then asked again to go home. He said he would take her home later. He began kissing her, and then began performing oral sex on her. "I was ready to cry. I was kind of—I was going, 'No. Come on. Stop it.'" In light of the champagne and the quaalude, Samantha said, "I was kind of dizzy, you know, like things were kind of blurry sometimes. . . . I was mostly just on and off saying, 'No, stop.'"

Polanski began having intercourse with her and asked whether she was on the pill (she said no) and when her last period was (she couldn't remember). Polanski said, " 'Oh, I won't come inside of you then,' . . . then he lifted up my legs farther and he went in through my anus," despite her saying that she didn't want him to. Samantha said she did not fight back physically, "because I was afraid of him," though she continued to ask him to stop.

In his book, Polanski described the sexual encounter this way: "We dried ourselves and each other. She said she was feeling better. Then, very gently, I began to kiss and caress her. After this had gone on for some time, I led her over to the couch. There was no doubt about her experience and lack of inhibition. She spread herself and I entered her. She wasn't unresponsive."

While Polanski and Gailey were in the bedroom, Anjelica Huston, Nicholson's girlfriend, arrived at the house. Soon after, Polanski and Gailey made an awkward departure—"I didn't mention making love in the TV room, though that must have been pretty obvious," he wrote. Samantha had hurried out before he did. "I was sitting in the car and I was crying," Gailey testified. According to Polanski, Samantha "talked a lot during the drive home" and mentioned that she was studying "A Midsummer Night's Dream" in school. "I tried not to wince when she started spouting Shakespeare in a strong Valley accent." Before they reached the Gailey home, she testified, he said to her, "Don't tell your mother about this, and don't tell your boyfriend either. . . . This is our secret."

Inside the house, Susan Gailey thought that her daughter was "weird looking." Samantha told her, out of Polanski's earshot, that she had invented a case of asthma, and then hastily retreated to her bedroom. Polanski showed Samantha's mother and her sister, Kim, the photographs from the first session, on the hillside. When they saw Samantha topless, the atmosphere in the room turned tense. According to Susan's testimony, "Kim stepped back. And I kind of stepped back. And the dog peed on the floor and

Kim went for the dog and threw her out. And she doesn't do that. It must have been some kind of energy thing happening." (After the dog's accident, Kim testified, "Roman gave me a big speech on how to take care of dogs.")

Samantha's boyfriend came over later that night, and she told him what had happened. Kim overheard them, and informed Susan. Enraged at the news, Susan Gailey called the police. The police arrived after 11 P.M. and took a statement from Samantha, and then took her to a hospital, where she was examined. By the following evening, Vannatter had placed Polanski under arrest.

ON THE NIGHT OF POLANSKI'S ARREST, his entertainment lawyer helped arrange his release on bail of twenty-five hundred dollars. The lawyer then quickly hired Douglas Dalton to take the criminal case. Dalton's representation of Polanski is now well into its fourth decade.

Once one of the most prominent lawyers in Los Angeles, Dalton has not practiced for years. "I turn eighty this year, and I've been retired for ten years," Dalton told me, as we sat in front of the fireplace in his Tudor-style mansion, near Hancock Park. "But I've kept my law license active for this one case, just because I feel what happened to Roman was so wrong. The system was totally out of control."

Polanski's arrest, on March 11, 1977, set off what was usually described as a media frenzy, even if the press reaction seems almost quaint when judged by the standards of the cable-news and Internet era. Crowds of photographers greeted Polanski at his court appearances, and Johnny Carson made jokes about him ("Close Encounters with the Third Grade"). But, by and large, Dalton was free to build his best defense—and, at least initially, to use Polanski's celebrity to his advantage. "We investigated this case and expected it to go to trial," Dalton told me.

The early signs were not promising for Polanski. Samantha

Gailey's grand-jury testimony, which she gave on March 24, 1977, laid out a damaging case against him. On the issues of drugs and coercion, Vannatter's investigation established important points of corroboration. Undeveloped photos in Polanski's camera showed Gailey in Nicholson's Jacuzzi, and her drinking champagne. A pill bottle found in Polanski's hotel room featured a prescription for quaaludes. Gailey's concoction of the asthma attack, which Polanski acknowledged, suggested that she was trying to escape from him. Anjelica Huston also agreed to testify for the prosecution.

But the Polanski defense had options, particularly at a time when rape cases were treated in different ways than they are now. In her grand-jury testimony, Gailey acknowledged that she was not a virgin (she had had sex twice with her boyfriend, who was seventeen) and that she had once accidentally taken a quaalude. California had a rape shield law, which would have limited what Gailey could be questioned about on the stand, but it wouldn't have protected her entirely from public scrutiny. That process had begun. Dalton told the press, "The facts indicate that before the alleged act in this case, this girl had engaged in sexual activity. . . . We want to know about it, we want to know who was involved, when. We want to know why these other people were not prosecuted. And this is a thing we want to fully develop." Likewise, the character and behavior of Susan Gailey might have come into play in a trial. Susan could have been portrayed as a neglectful parent who, in essence, offered up her daughter in order to ingratiate herself with a famous director. In the climate of the time, it mattered little that attacks on Samantha and her mother might not have been relevant (or true); rape defendants had been acquitted with less.

Samantha's father, who was a lawyer, lived in another state, and he arranged for her to be represented by a Los Angeles attorney named Lawrence Silver. (Silver, who is still her lawyer, did not respond to requests for comment.) He allowed Gailey to give testimony before the grand jury (which is a closed proceeding), but, mindful of the fate that often awaited rape victims, he did not want her to have to appear in a public trial. Dalton artfully leveraged Silver's concern for Gailey into a critical advantage for Polanski.

Throughout the spring and summer of 1977, Dalton and the prosecutors skirmished over access to evidence (Gailey's underwear was cut in half, so that both sides could test it) and other procedural issues. Any notion of a plea bargain stalled when the government insisted that, according to the policy of the district attorney's office, Polanski be allowed to plea only to the most serious count against him—in this case, rape with the use of drugs, which carried a sentence of at least three years. Dalton wanted a misdemeanor plea or, at most, a plea to the least serious count, statutory rape, which would likely incur a shorter sentence. Silver wrote a letter saying that Gailey did not want to testify, and her family did not want her to, either:

> *Long before I had met any other attorney in this case, my clients informed me that their goal in pressing the charges did not include seeking the incarceration of the defendant, but rather, the admission by him of wrong-doing and commencement by him, under the supervision of the court, of a program to ensure complete rehabilitation. . . . Whatever harm has come to her as a victim would be exacerbated in the extreme if this case went to trial.*

A reporter had told him that this "promised to be one of the most sensational Hollywood trials," Silver wrote. "This is not the place for a recovering young girl."

This was perhaps the clearest example of Polanski's celebrity helping him: the attention drove the victim to try to withdraw from the case. And so the D.A.'s office agreed to allow Polanski to plea to felony statutory rape, the least serious count in the indictment, which he did, on August 8, 1977.

At the insistence of the prosecution, Polanski received what's known as an "open plea"—that is, a plea where his sentence was left to the discretion of the judge, Laurence J. Rittenband. At the hearing, Polanski said he knew that the maximum sentence for his crime was "one to fifteen-twenty years in state prison." The prosecutor, Roger Gunson, asked Polanski, "Who do you believe will decide what your sentence will be in this matter?"

"The judge," Polanski said.

"Who do you think will decide whether or not you will get probation?"

"The judge."

Silver read his letter in open court. Midway through, Rittenband interrupted him. "I think some of the reporters are taking notes," he said. "You might read a little slower, so that they will be able to get this."

THE PLEA BARGAIN IS THE MOMENT when the case pivoted from the story of what Polanski did to Samantha Gailey to the story of what the system did to him. Polanski's detractors focus on the first, his supporters on the second, but the two are intertwined, and both were shaped by the influence of Polanski's celebrity.

Polanski's fate was now in the hands of Judge Rittenband, who had, by 1977, established himself as an eccentric figure on the Los Angeles legal scene. A New York–born prodigy, Rittenband went straight from high school to New York University Law School; too young to take the bar exam after earning his law degree, Rittenband filled the time by acquiring an undergraduate education at Harvard. Wounded in the Second World War, he moved to California, started practicing law, and won appointment as a judge in 1961. Rittenband presided in the Santa Monica courthouse and could be a querulous, domineering presence on the bench. He snared many of the high-profile cases that tend to occur in that tony region of Los Angeles County—Elvis and Priscilla Presley's divorce, a child-custody case involving Marlon Brando, a paternity suit against Cary Grant.

Rittenband was a peripheral Hollywood player—a lifelong bachelor who juggled several girlfriends and enjoyed the friendship of movie stars at the Hillcrest Country Club. He also seems to have sought out the news media more than other judges. As Rittenband assumed control of the case, Polanski's celebrity, heretofore an important advantage for him, became more of a mixed blessing.

Since the nineteen-seventies, in California and elsewhere, criminal sentencing has changed dramatically, particularly with regard to the role of the judge. "California used to have a wide-open system, where the law gave the judge a lot of discretion about how long to sentence someone," Robert Weisberg, a professor at Stanford Law School, said. That system, which was known as "indeterminate sentencing," evolved into the current, very different regime, which is known as "determinate sentencing." Judges now have far less latitude, and discretionary parole has been abolished for most crimes in California. Sentences are more severe. Today, an adult defendant who pleaded guilty to statutory rape in California would likely receive about three years in state prison.

In addition, the sentencing process has become more formalized, with the judges being required to present explicit findings concerning how they reached decisions. Three decades ago, especially in Rittenband's courtroom, a case would often be resolved with an off-the-record understanding among the lawyers and the judge. Dalton was hoping for a deal that would lead to probation.

After Polanski's guilty plea, his chances for a light sentence at first seemed good. In the previous year, according to Polanski's defense team, none of the convictions for statutory rape in Los

Angeles County resulted in a sentence to state prison, although many defendants spent time in county jails or lockups. (How many defendants had been allowed to plea down from charges as serious as those against Polanski is another question.) The report in the case by the probation officer, Irwin Gold, read more like the words of a starstruck fan than like those of a law-enforcement officer. After a lengthy summary of Polanski's tragic past, Gold wrote, "Possibly not since Renaissance Italy has there been such a gathering of creative minds in one locale as there has been in Los Angeles County during the past half-century. The motion-picture industry has proved [a] magnet to many of them." As for Polanski's crime, Gold wrote:

> *There was some indication that circumstances were provocative, that there was some permissiveness by the mother, that the victim was not only physically mature, but willing; as one doctor has additionally suggested there was the lack of coercion by the defendant who was, additionally, solicitous regarding the possibility of pregnancy. It is believed that incalculable emotional damage could result from incarcerating the defendant whose own life has been a seemingly unending series of punishments.*

Alvin E. Davis, the psychiatrist Gold cited, seemed equally smitten, writing that incarceration "would impose an unusual degree of stress and hardship because of [Polanski's] highly sensitive personality and devotion to his work." Davis saw the rape as the result of the "loss of normal inhibitions in circumstances of intimacy and collaboration in creative work, and with some coincidental alcohol and drug intoxication." In the report's twisted recitation, Polanski's proffer of alcohol and drugs to a child becomes exculpatory; his claim of a "lack of coercion" is accepted as fact.

But on September 16, 1977, three days before Polanski was to be sentenced, Rittenband called the lawyers in the case to an off-the-record private meeting in his chambers—a meeting that remains a crucial point of controversy in the case. According to Dalton, Rittenband said that he had decided to order Polanski to go to the state prison at Chino for a "diagnostic study" of his mental state, which might take as long as ninety days, under a California law that allowed for evaluation of prisoners before sentencing. Assuming that the report from the psychiatrists at Chino would be favorable, Dalton later wrote in a court filing, the judge told the lawyers that "the diagnostic study at Chino would constitute defendant Polanski's punishment and that there would be no further incarceration." At the meeting, the prosecutor and the probation officer told Judge Rittenband that it was inappropriate to use a diagnostic study as a punishment, but the judge ignored them, and an improvisational sentence was not, in fact, unusual for its time.

Rittenband made another request: he asked for what Dalton, in a 2008 affidavit, called a "charade of arguing our respective positions at the Probation and Sentencing Hearing on September 19." Dalton told me, "Rittenband said, 'You both argue. You argue for a prison sentence, and you argue for probation.' But it was all for show"—he had already made up his mind. (Gunson, the prosecutor, agrees with this version of events.) Three days later, at the public hearing, Gunson and Dalton did as Rittenband instructed. Rittenband also kept to his script and ordered the mental evaluation at Chino.

Dalton expressed no real objection to the diagnostic sentence, because his client appeared to be on a glide path to avoiding real prison time. "All we needed was a good psychiatric report, and Roman would have been free," Dalton said. But the defense lawyer made what turned out to be a miscalculation. At the September 16th meeting in Rittenband's chambers, Dalton asked the judge to stay the order of incarceration until Polanski could complete work on a new directing project. In another example of Polanski's privileged status, Rittenband said that he would publicly authorize a reprieve of only ninety days, but he told Dalton, off the record, that he would have the option of asking for further stays, until the film was finished.

POLANSKI'S PLAN TO DIRECT "The First Deadly Sin" had fallen through after his arrest, but he was quickly hired to direct a remake of the 1937 film "The Hurricane," which was to be produced by Dino de Laurentiis, a major figure in middlebrow seventies cinema. Polanski was happy to get the work, even if it appeared likely to fall below his usual aesthetic standards. (The plot was to include pearl divers getting caught in a giant clam.) "Dino's faith in me showed I had ceased to be a complete Hollywood outcast," Polanski wrote. He wanted Kinski to play the female lead. "Although Dino was bowled over by her looks, he doubted if she could acquire a sufficient command of English before shooting began."

De Laurentiis asked Polanski to go to Europe, to set up a West German distribution deal. While there, Polanski was photographed at an Oktoberfest celebration in Munich, sitting amid a group of attractive young women, and smoking a cigar. The picture went out on the U.P.I. wire, and was printed in the September 29, 1977, edition of the Santa Monica *Evening Outlook*, with a caption stating that Polanski "enjoys the companionship of some young ladies at the Munich, Germany, Oktoberfest." The photograph infuriated Rittenband, who believed that Polanski was abusing the privilege of the stay of his sentence. Rittenband gave an interview to a gossip columnist (even then an unusual thing for a judge to do in a pending case), Marylin Beck, who reported that "Roman Polanski could be on his way to prison this weekend." Polanski's celebrity was turning against him.

Rittenband ordered Dalton to bring Polanski back to Santa Monica for a hearing about why the stay should not be revoked. At the hearing, on October 24th, Dalton called witnesses, in-

cluding de Laurentiis, who established that Polanski had a legitimate business reason for being in Germany. Rittenband was
persuaded to leave the stay in effect, but he declined to extend
the ninety-day limit. Given the uncertainty of Polanski's situation, de Laurentiis fired him. (The film, directed by Jan Troell
and starring Mia Farrow, was released in 1979, to dismal public
response.) Polanski entered the Chino prison shortly before
Christmas and was released, when his evaluation was complete,
forty-two days later, on January 29, 1978. According to a letter
to Rittenband from Chino's associate superintendent, "Staff are
in agreement the granting of probation in this case would be in
the best interest of all concerned."

On January 30th, the day after Polanski was released—and two
days before he was to be officially sentenced—Rittenband summoned the lawyers for another private meeting. Rittenband said
that he was unhappy with the diagnostic report, which he called
a "whitewash." This was, to be sure, an understandable reaction,
given that the Chino report, like the earlier probation report,
was extremely deferential toward Polanski. But Rittenband also
expressed discomfort with the way his rulings had been received by the public. He had changed his mind again, saying
that he had decided to impose an additional prison sentence.
The Judge said he was considering limiting the further punishment to forty-eight days—to complete the original ninety
days—but only if Polanski then agreed to leave the United States
for good. (Polanski did not have a green card; he is a French
and Polish citizen.) At a meeting the next day, with Lawrence
Silver, Gailey's lawyer, also present, Rittenband said, according
to Dalton, that "there was nothing which could be produced by
the defense that would influence him regarding his intended
sentence."

Dalton informed Polanski of the latest dispiriting turn of
events. It wasn't clear what Rittenband was going to do, although
it did seem that there would be more prison time in Polanski's

future—perhaps just forty-eight days, or perhaps more. (It was also not clear how Rittenband planned to enforce his deportation plan. State judges have no authority over immigration matters.) Polanski wrote in his autobiography, "Since it was clear that I had served my forty-two days in Chino for nothing, an obvious question arose: what had I to gain by staying? The answer appeared to be: nothing." In fact, Polanski had the right to appeal any sentence that Rittenband might impose, although prevailing would be a long shot. But Polanski decided that he had trusted the American legal system long enough. That evening, without telling Dalton, he took a British Airways flight to London. By the following morning, when Dalton appeared in front of Rittenband to announce that Polanski had fled, the director had flown on to Paris. At what would have been the sentencing hearing, on February 1st, Rittenband issued a bench warrant for the arrest of Polanski, who was now a fugitive.

FIVE DAYS LATER, on February 6th, Rittenband held a press conference in his chambers to denounce Polanski for fleeing and to reveal that he planned to sentence him in absentia. He confirmed that he had wanted Polanski to leave the country after his release. Dalton responded by filing a motion to have Rittenband recused from the case for bias. (Holding a press conference about a pending case was one of the grounds.) Rittenband agreed to be replaced, though he refused to acknowledge any wrongdoing; if Polanski had returned, his case would have been heard by a different judge. In subsequent years, Rittenband nevertheless vowed to sit on the bench until Polanski came back, but he retired in 1989, and died in 1993, at the age of eighty-eight.

Polanski settled into a spacious apartment on the Avenue Montaigne. By August, 1978, seven months after fleeing the States, he was shooting his next film, "Tess," a movie version of Thomas Hardy's "Tess of the d'Urbervilles," starring Nastassja Kinski, who was still in her teens. (The story features an older man who either seduces or rapes the young Tess.) The film won Polanski his third Academy Award nomination. (He lost to Robert Redford, for "Ordinary People.")

Thus began Polanski's fruitful, if somewhat circumscribed, years of exile. "Roman is a superstar in the streets of Paris," his friend Thom Mount, who produced three of Polanski's movies, said. "He walks into a restaurant, and the headwaiter faints." Polanski's status as a fugitive from American justice has made it difficult, but not impossible, for him to continue to direct major films. "The case was more than just background noise," Jeff Berg, his agent, said. "It determined what he could do and where he could do it and with whom he could work." (Berg is the chief executive of International Creative Management, where I am also a client.) The terms of the Franco-American extradition treaty do not compel either country to extradite its own citizens, but Polanski has had to be careful in his travels; the United Kingdom, for example, has been off-limits. It was seven years between "Tess" and "Pirates," a misbegotten seafaring adventure starring, of all people, Walter Matthau. Two years later, in 1988, Polanski released "Frantic," a thriller set in Paris, with Harrison Ford and Emmanuelle Seigner, who was then his girlfriend. It turned out to be his last production with a major American studio. In 1989, he married Seigner, and over the following decade they had two children.

The legal case against Polanski largely faded from view. Every few years, Dalton made an overture to resolve the case, but the prosecutors always insisted that Polanski return to the United States first. Polanski refused to expose himself to that level of uncertainty. In 1997, Dalton came close to brokering a resolution, which would have required no further prison time for Polanski; according to Dalton, the judge assigned to the matter,

Larry Fidler, had more or less signed off on the plan but insisted that the final hearing be televised. (Fidler, through a spokesman, denied imposing this condition. Gunson supports Dalton's recollection.) In any event, Polanski scuttled the plan.

The last turn in the case began, oddly enough, with perhaps the greatest triumph of Polanski's career. Polanski and his producing partners had pieced together financing to produce an adaptation of a Polish memoir, first published in 1946, called "Death of a City." The story of a musician who survived the Warsaw ghetto while his entire family perished, the movie was called "The Pianist," and it was released in 2002; it proved to be a perfect vehicle for the director, who turned seventy the following year. At last, Polanski's long-sought Oscar seemed within reach.

THE SUCCESS OF "THE PIANIST" raised the question of whether Polanski would return to Los Angeles for the Academy Awards, and the Los Angeles *Times* ran a story about his long exile. "I saw that article, and it piqued my interest," Marina Zenovich, a documentary filmmaker, told me. "Then a little while later I saw Samantha Geimer on Larry King." Over the years, Geimer, née Gailey, had become an increasingly vocal supporter of Polanski's return. In 1993, Polanski reportedly agreed to pay five hundred thousand dollars to Geimer as a settlement in a civil suit. (It apparently took several years, and more legal wrangling, for the money to be paid.) She never backed down from her grand-jury testimony, but as she moved toward her forties, with a family of her own, Geimer urged the district attorney to allow Polanski to return without having to go to prison. On February 23, 2003, Geimer and her lawyer, Lawrence Silver, appeared on "Larry King Live." Silver said, "What happened that day, both to Polanski and to some extent the American judicial system—I really think it was a shameful day." Zenovich recalled, "That didn't make sense to me. So I decided to investigate the case myself." A few weeks later, Polanski won the Oscar for Best Director; he remained overseas for the ceremony.

In a previous documentary, Zenovich had become obsessed with her subject, the French businessman, politician, and actor Bernard Tapie; now she focussed the same fanatical level of attention on the long-dormant Polanski legal drama. Zenovich created an especially damning portrait of Judge Rittenband, complete with interviews with his girlfriends. Most important, Zenovich tracked down a player whose role had been unknown to Polanski's team. David Wells was a deputy district attorney who had worked briefly on the case before Gunson took over, and he told Zenovich that he had spoken secretly with the judge and pushed him to be tougher. Wells said that he had brought Rittenband the photograph of Polanski at Oktoberfest. "What I told him was . . . 'Look! He's giving you the finger. He's flipping you off,'" Wells told Zenovich. "He said, 'What? What? He's not getting away with that.'" (Wells has recently recanted this part of his interview, telling The Daily Beast, "I lied. . . . I thought it made a better story if I said I'd told the judge what to do." He declined to speak with me.) Wells's lobbying of Rittenband raised the spectre of prosecutorial and judicial misconduct and thus possible grounds for a dismissal of the case.

Zenovich's documentary, "Roman Polanski: Wanted and Desired," premiered at the Sundance Film Festival in 2008 and was broadcast on HBO later that year. The force of celebrity had buffeted the case once more. It had helped Polanski by persuading his victim to support a plea deal, and by inspiring a fawning probation report; it hurt him by drawing suspicion to his legitimate travel to Germany and prompting Rittenband's erratic decisions. Celebrity now helped by drawing Zenovich's attention, which, in turn, led to new questions about the case against him. His lawyers decided to make yet another attempt to resolve it.

Dalton recruited Chad Hummel, a partner at the Los Angeles firm of Manatt, Phelps & Phillips, to help with the case. Armed with Zenovich's fresh disclosures, Hummel and Dalton separately met with the prosecutors to whom the Polanski file had been passed. (Gunson had retired in 2002.) Their answer was the same as their predecessors': no deal until Polanski returned. The question for his lawyers now became whether the misconduct by Wells and Rittenband was so egregious that a judge might dismiss the case even in the face of Polanski's refusal to submit to the jurisdiction of American courts.

There was a precedent of sorts. In July, 2002, *Vanity Fair* had run a long article about the restaurant Elaine's, in New York. The piece included an anecdote from Lewis Lapham, then the editor of *Harper's*, who said that Polanski, while in New York on the way to Los Angeles for Sharon Tate's funeral, had made a pass at a woman at Elaine's, telling her, "I will make another Sharon Tate out of you." Polanski denied it, noting that he had not stopped in New York on his way from London, and sued *Vanity Fair*'s parent company, Condé Nast, in British courts. (Condé Nast also owns *The New Yorker*.)

In light of Polanski's checkered personal history, his decision to sue for injury to his reputation was presumptuous, to say the least. This was especially true because Polanski was what's known as a "libel tourist," who was using Britain's libel laws, which favor the plaintiff, to sue an American magazine. Even more audaciously, Polanski declined to go to England, fearing extradition in his statutory-rape case. *Vanity Fair* asked the court to dismiss the lawsuit, but in February, 2005, the Law Lords, Britain's highest court, ruled that Polanski did not have to appear in person in order to pursue the case. (After a trial in which Polanski testified by video link, the jury awarded him about ninety thousand dollars.) The British decision was obviously not binding on an American court, but it suggested that he might be able to win in the United States, too, without showing up.

In December, 2008, the Polanski defense team filed a motion in L.A. County Superior Court, asking that the case be dismissed on the ground that Polanski had been deprived of due process of law. (The lawyers submitted Zenovich's documentary as an exhibit.) On February 17, 2009, Hummel appeared before Judge Peter Espinoza to argue the case. (The transcript noted, "Defendant Polanski not present in court.")

The diagnostic session at Chino, Hummel told Judge Espinoza, "was intended to be his entire sentence. . . . So this notion that somehow there was a fleeing from a sentence is not true." Hummel went on, "In our system, we simply cannot tolerate back-room communications between prosecutors and judges that influence a sentence and that cut out the defendant and his counsel from those communications. . . . That's at the heart of this request." Lawrence Silver joined in Polanski's motion, saying, "The time has come for this case to end, Your Honor."

The D.A.'s office responded with barely concealed rage. "This case is about a 44-year-old defendant who plied a 13-year-old girl with drugs and alcohol, then against her consent, committed acts of oral copulation, sodomy and sexual intercourse upon her," the attorneys wrote in a brief. "Petitioner's flight, whatever his motivations, and his failure to take responsibility for his crimes is at the heart of the extraordinary delays in this case."

Polanski's lawyer clearly made an impression on Judge Espinoza, who said that there had been "substantial . . . misconduct that occurred during the pendency of this case." Ultimately, though, he rejected Polanski's motion, under what is known as the "fugitive disentitlement doctrine." Espinoza ruled that Polanski "is not entitled to request any affirmative relief from this Court, as he remains at large." Polanski's team asked a three-judge Court of Appeal panel to intervene, and on July 30th that court gave them a surprising victory. In a departure from its usual practice, the court directed Espinoza to show cause why he should not hold "an evidentiary hearing, without requiring [Polanski's] physical presence, to determine whether the case should be dismissed in furtherance of justice." The Court of Appeal may have been subtly inviting the trial court to throw out the prosecution. It was perhaps Polanski's biggest court victory in thirty-two years—and, in the upside-down world of his case, the worst thing that could have happened to him.

STEVE COOLEY, who was elected in 2000, is the fifth Los Angeles County district attorney to preside over the Polanski prosecution. Cooley first won the job as the law-and-order alternative to his predecessor, Gil Garcetti, who was widely criticized for his handling of several high-profile cases, most notably the O. J. Simpson trial. Notwithstanding the passion of Cooley's argument, Polanski appeared to be making progress in the courts in the summer of 2009. Cooley had to respond.

Over the years, the district attorney's efforts to bring Polanski back to the United States seem to have been half-hearted. According to a chronology released by the D.A.'s office, prosecutors have made only a handful of significant gestures to international authorities, and there have been long gaps in even this effort. (The chronology lists nothing, for example, during the periods 1982 to 1985, 1989 to 1993, and 1995 to 2004.) The first time a provisional request for Polanski's arrest in Switzerland was actually prepared was on September 22, 2009. E-mails obtained by the Associated Press show that prosecutors in Los Angeles tracked Polanski as he moved between Austria and Switzerland in late September and weighed which country had a better extradition arrangement with the United States. "I don't have experience with any Austrian extraditions so I don't know how 'friendly' they would be to extradition on such a case," Diana Carbajal, a deputy district attorney, wrote in one message. This sudden rush of interest ended with Polanski's arrest on the night of September

26th, as he arrived at the Zurich airport, to attend a ceremony in his honor at that city's film festival.

The timing clearly suggests that the Los Angeles District Attorney's office moved to arrest Polanski because he seemed to have a real possibility of winning in the courts. Cooley has said, "It's about completing justice. Justice is not complete when someone leaves the jurisdiction of the court." Polanski's lawyers thus have to wonder whether, by bringing the motion to dismiss the case, they effectively prompted their client's arrest. Did Polanski's motion, meritorious though it might be, backfire? "There was prosecutorial misconduct and we felt we had to bring it to the court's attention," Dalton told me. "We had to do it."

AFTER POLANSKI'S ARREST, the value of his celebrity went through its most precipitate rise and fall. Polanski's friends, many of them also celebrities, swept in with public, fervent support. The S.A.C.D., the French dramatic writers' guild, sponsored a petition, which said that Polanski had been arrested "in a case of morals." It went on, "Filmmakers in France, in Europe, in the United States and around the world are dismayed by this decision. It seems inadmissible to them that an international cultural event, paying homage to one of the greatest contemporary filmmakers, is used by the police to apprehend him." Signers included Woody Allen, Martin Scorsese, Pedro Almodóvar, and eventually several hundred others from around the world. Bernard-Henri Lévy organized another petition, drawing support from Steven Soderbergh, Neil Jordan, Sam Mendes, Diane von Furstenberg, and Mike Nichols as well as Salman Rushdie and Milan Kundera. This one said, "We ask the Swiss courts to free him immediately and not to turn this ingenious filmmaker into a martyr of a politico-legal imbroglio that is unworthy of two democracies like Switzerland and the United States. Good sense, as well as honor, require it." Nicolas Sarkozy, the French President, called Polanski's arrest "not a good administration of justice." The producer Harvey Weinstein wrote about Polanski's "so-called crime."

With equal rapidity, an anti-Polanski backlash swept in. The petitions made no reference to the facts of the case, no acknowledgment of the seriousness of his crime, and no recognition that sex with a child—the rape of a child—was worthy of condemnation. Columnists across the political spectrum, from feminists on the left to conservatives on the right, found common cause in revulsion at both Polanski and his famous friends. Katha Pollitt wrote in *The Nation*, "It's enraging that literary superstars who go on and on about human dignity, and human rights, and even women's rights (at least when the women are Muslim) either don't see what Polanski did as rape, or don't care, because he is, after all, Polanski—an artist like themselves." The *Wall Street Journal*'s drama critic wrote, "Anyone who lives in a tightly sealed echo chamber of self-congratulation, surrounded by yes-men who are dedicated to doing what he wants, is bound to lose touch with reality." Polanski's public supporters, from Sarkozy to Weinstein, decided to discuss the matter no further. In the court of public opinion, the backlash won. The legalities were left to the Swiss courts.

As in the United States, the advantage in the legal battle in Switzerland shifted, over time, to Polanski. He was initially denied bail—understandably, as there was a "risk of flight"—and incarcerated in a small prison, built around a stone-paved courtyard. He could see the tops of a few trees and a bit of the sky from the barred window of his cell, and was allowed an hour of exercise per day. On October 2nd, Dalton, Hummel, and Reid Weingarten, a Washington lawyer, met with Justice Department officials to ask them not to make a formal extradition request. The lawyers did not succeed, but the official demand for extradition did not go to the Swiss until three weeks later. Polanski's

lawyers put together a package of guarantees that included elec-
tronic monitoring and most of his personal financial assets, and
that persuaded an appellate court to release him to his chalet.
His legal challenges to the extradition order have only just begun, and probably will not be resolved until next spring.

Still, it appears likely that at some point Polanski will be returned to California, and there he will face a legal situation of
daunting complexity. So much time has passed that it is difficult
to know for sure how a court today would apply the rules in effect in 1977. Some sort of settlement—an agreement on a short
prison term, perhaps—remains a theoretical possibility, but according to one member of Polanski's camp, "We have basically
given up on making any sort of deal with Cooley. He won't talk
to us." On December 10th, the Court of Appeal will hear arguments on the question of whether an evidentiary hearing can be
held in Polanski's absence. If the court grants such a hearing,
Polanski will be able to call prosecutors to the witness stand,
including perhaps Cooley himself. The prospect of a hearing
about government misconduct may bring the district attorney's
office to the bargaining table at last.

If Polanski were to lose his case in the Court of Appeal, the
advantage would shift to Cooley. A trial may be complicated, or
perhaps even impossible, because the original file in the case
went missing, and had to be re-created years later. It appears that
Polanski will face some time in a California state prison upon
his return: the extradition request stipulates, "The maximum
time that Mr. Polanski could be sentenced to prison . . . is two
years." Meanwhile, the director, who is wealthy but not nearly
as rich as such near-contemporaries as Steven Spielberg and
George Lucas, has had lawyers in Paris, Zurich, Washington,
Los Angeles, and Dallas, where Dalton's son works on the case.

Polanski will await the next turn in his own story in the elegant confines of Milky Way, which has a spectacular view of the
Alps. Shortly before his arrest, Polanski had nearly finished

editing his latest film, "The Ghost," a political thriller starring
Ewan McGregor, Pierce Brosnan, and Kim Cattrall. The story
concerns a former prime minister of Great Britain, whose troubled tenure leads him to settle in the United States to write his
memoirs. According to the trailer, the protagonist's flight into
exile came about because of "one decision I made . . . which
wasn't in the interests of the U.S.A." It is Polanski's first film
since "Chinatown" to be set primarily in the United States, but,
given his legal difficulties, he had to use locations in Germany as
substitutes for the New England setting. Through intermediar-
ies, Polanski worked on the post-production process from his
prison cell, and he will complete the project from the more con-
genial surroundings of his vacation home. Given the vertiginous
shifts in fortune that he has endured throughout his life, Polanski is well suited to live with the current uncertainties, and the
movie will be released, on schedule, early next year.

JEFFREY TOOBIN, *a staff writer at* The New Yorker *and senior ana-
lyst at CNN, is the author of five books, most recently* The Nine: Inside
the Secret World of the Supreme Court.

Coda

The legal skirmishing in Polanski's case continued inconclu-
sively into early 2010. The Swiss authorities refused to relieve
him from house arrest, finding that Polanski remained a risk of
flight. Back in California, the Polanski legal team kept coming
close, but still failed to reach a resolution of the case as long as
the defendant refused to return. In separate hearings in the Court
of Appeal and then back again in front of Judge Espinoza, the
judges expressed misgivings about the way Polanski had been

treated, but still refused to resolve the case with him still out of the country. The stalemate endured.

The Ghost Writer premiered, to a customary Polanski reaction. The film drew respectful reviews, but little business, in the United States; it drew raves in Europe. At the Berlin film festival, Polanski won the award for best screenplay, though he was not in a position to appear in person. "Even if I could, I wouldn't," Polanski said, "because the last time I went to a festival to get a prize I ended up in jail."

Nadya Labi

THE SNATCHBACK

FROM *The Atlantic*

ON A HUMID THURSDAY AFTERNOON in February, I am
riding in a rented van in Central America with a man who ab-
ducts children for a living. The van's windows are tinted, and
Gustavo Zamora Jr. is speeding east on a two-lane highway
toward Siquirres, a town buried in the lush abundance of eastern Costa Rica. Gus is planning to snatch Andres, a 9-year-old
American boy who has been claimed by too many parents. Sitting behind me is one of them: Todd Hopson, a 48-year-old
lawyer from Ocala, Florida, who considers himself the boy's
father, by rights of love and U.S. law. Ahead of me in the front
passenger seat is Gus's 22-year-old son and partner, Gustavo
Zamora III.

"That's too far for a switch," the elder Zamora, 53, is saying,
pointing to a hotel 10 miles outside of Siquirres. His plan is to
use two vehicles for what he calls the "recovery," or "snatchback."
Once he gets Andres, he intends to drive a white Toyota SUV to
a switch point, where he will abandon the SUV and put Andres
in the van. That way, any witnesses to the snatchback will report

seeing the SUV headed west in the direction of the capital, San José—while in fact Gus and Andres will be in the van headed southeast toward Panama. But this hotel won't work. "We definitely can't come all the way back down this way," Gus says: "I want to make time."

Even by the standards of this American age of divorce, when byzantine custody arrangements are commonplace, Andres's situation is complex. His biological mother, Helen Zapata, who is from Costa Rica but now lives in America, was married to Todd Hopson for just under three years. Now they are divorced—but they continue to share custody of Andres and, until recently, lived together in Florida. Todd never formally adopted Andres, but he and Helen got an official document in Florida in June of 2008 acknowledging Todd's legal paternity. They also asked a Florida court to declare Andres "born of their marriage," a request that was granted the following September and applied retroactively to 2004, the year they divorced.

"I got to thinking—what if something happens to me, and Andres has Helen's last name? Andres wouldn't be entitled to any rights or benefits," Todd told me. "I'm a lawyer and should have been thinking about those things earlier, but I didn't."

At the end of June 2008, Helen flew to Costa Rica to spend time there and, with Todd's support, to enroll in a drug clinic to kick a cocaine habit. Every year, Helen and Andres traveled to Costa Rica to visit not only Helen's relatives, but also those of Jason Alvarado, who is Andres's biological father. So that June, as usual, Andres went along, though he didn't want to go—he didn't want to miss Little League season in Ocala, for one thing. Before Helen left the U.S., she called Jason in Costa Rica, asking if he would look after Andres for a few days and saying that she planned to go job-hunting in Costa Rica so that she could move there permanently. "I lied to him" to hide the drug problem, Helen concedes. When Jason learned Helen's true whereabouts he called Todd in Florida, thanking him for everything he'd done for Andres and telling him, Todd says, that he planned to raise the boy himself.

Todd felt blindsided. He had thought Andres would be visiting with Helen's mother and told me he had "no idea that Jason had any interest" in having custody of Andres. As Todd saw it, Jason had never previously tried to gain custody or in any way contributed to Andres's care. "If you're going to be the father," Todd says, "you don't let someone else pay the freight."

Todd consulted with the U.S. Embassy in Costa Rica, which advised him to proceed with his plan to pick up Andres in early August. But when Todd flew to Costa Rica, Jason would not let him talk to the boy. Todd was livid. He had hoped to reason with Jason, but he realized that the man had no intention of backing down. So Todd got an injunction from a San José court ordering Jason to surrender Andres, and he and Helen accompanied the Costa Rican police when they went to Jason's office to deliver it. Jason still refused to relinquish Andres, and Todd says the police told him that they didn't have the right under Costa Rican law to enter Jason's home and take the boy. Todd returned to Florida while Helen stayed in Costa Rica. Later in August, Jason challenged Helen's maternal fitness in light of her drug habit and won temporary custody of Andres from a different Costa Rican court.

The Hague Convention on the Civil Aspects of International Child Abduction was drafted in 1980 to resolve custodial claims between what are known as the "taking parent" and the "left-behind parent." To date, 81 nations, including the United States, in 1988, have agreed to the treaty. The State Department, which enforces the treaty in the U.S., currently has more than 2,000 active cases involving nearly 3,000 children abducted from the U.S. or wrongfully retained abroad. In 2008, it opened 1,082 new files, an increase of more than 25 percent over 2007. (The increase reflects a rise in transnational marriages, and consequently transnational divorces, as well as growing awareness of the Hague Convention.)

Todd considered filing a Hague application with the State Department, but he was skeptical that it would amount to anything because he distrusted what he dismissed as the corrupt legal system in Costa Rica. The application, he feared, could take months to process. He wavered between feelings of fury and utter helplessness. "It breaks my heart," he said to me. "I don't have any control." Determined to regain some, he surfed the Internet for security agencies in Costa Rica, thinking, "I'll hire some bodyguards and just take Andres." A man Todd spoke to at one agency said he didn't do child recoveries but could recommend someone who did: Gus Zamora. "That's all he does," the man said.

Gus, a former U.S. soldier, has dyed brown hair and a tidy moustache. He wears Oakley sunglasses and a gold necklace with a pendant shaped like a diver. A martial-arts tattoo adorns the back of his left hand. In Gus's mind, he's never stopped being a soldier. In Tampa, his home, he drives a royal-blue BMW with the license plate ABN RGR, referring, respectively, to his time as a member of the 101st Airborne Division and as an Army ranger. When on assignment, like on this scouting mission through eastern Costa Rica, he talks about conducting "recon" and moving his "assets." His dark eyes flit from side to side, taking stock of his surroundings, and he rarely stops talking, dispensing instructions, expletives, and commentary about his travels to 64 countries and counting.

As Gus continues to drive east, evaluating prospective switch points, we pass pineapple fields before turning left off Highway 32 toward Siquirres. In a minute or so, we are at the town square, a stretch of grass dominated by soccer goalposts. Gus points to a bench where he says a bus picks up Andres for school each day.

Musing aloud, Gus runs through potential scenarios. Where's the best spot to grab Andres? At the bus stop, on his way to school? A possibility, but Jason or Jason's father sometimes waits with the boy there. At the school itself? Maybe, depending on how far it is from Highway 32. During one of Helen's supervised visits with Andres at the home of Jason's parents?

Across the street from the square is a yellow house with a black iron gate. Todd identifies it as the home of Andres's paternal grandparents, where Helen has her custodial visits. Gus likes what he sees; Helen could walk through the gate with Andres to the waiting SUV. "They could come and get in," Gus says. "This is a straight shot. The highway's right up here," allowing a quick getaway.

"It's a very short route," Todd agrees.

"I like that a lot better. She can walk out the door," Gus says. "She walks down the street, gets in the van. Boom, gone . . ."

HELEN AND JASON GREW UP in Siquirres. They met as teenagers and started dating seriously when she was 17 and he was 19. Jason moved to San José to attend dental school; Helen finished high school and followed him there. After two years, they began to grow apart. Jason told me he broke up with Helen because she cheated on him. Shortly thereafter, Helen told Jason she was pregnant. According to Helen, Jason wanted her to have an abortion. Jason denies this, adding that he promised to take responsibility for the child if he proved to be the father.

A few weeks later, Helen met Todd Hopson, 18 years her senior. The divorced father of an adult daughter, he was vacationing by himself at a golf resort on the outskirts of San José. Though neither spoke the other's language, he and Helen ended up spending the rest of his vacation together, touring the Costa Rican capital.

When Todd returned to the U.S., he talked to Helen by phone and exchanged letters with her; a friend of Helen's acted as interpreter. Todd invited Helen to Florida. When she told him she was pregnant, he said he had already suspected that, and reiterated his invitation. Bringing along the friend as a trans-lator, Helen flew to Florida and moved in with Todd. (The trans-lator left after a couple of weeks, and Helen now speaks English.)

Two months later, Helen's appendix burst, and she was hospitalized in Ocala. The next day, September 6, 1999, she gave birth to a boy. Todd held the infant before Helen did, mar-veling at his shock of black hair. When Andres left the hospital, a week before his mother did, Todd cared for him. Todd also paid the hospital bills, which came to $25,000, and financially supported Andres from then on.

Shortly after giving birth, Helen called Jason to tell him he had a son. Jason wanted to make sure that the boy was his, so he asked Helen to send him blood samples, which she did. Jason sent the samples to a laboratory in Costa Rica, and when the test confirmed that he was the father, he wanted to acknowledge his son legally.

When Andres was a year old, Jason flew to Ocala to get a copy of the birth certificate, which named no father. Even though she hadn't intended to cooperate, Helen helped Jason obtain it, and invited him home, where he visited with her, Andres, and Todd. Jason then registered his paternity with the Costa Rican consul-ate in Miami, but he didn't pursue custody, because, he told me, he was willing to allow Andres to live with his mother. In 2001, Helen married Todd.

Meanwhile, Todd bonded with Andres. As a toddler, Andres would cry and chase the car when Todd went to work. When Andres grew older, Todd helped him with his homework and shuttled him to and from school. When Andres developed a fas-cination with baseball, Todd nurtured it, taking him to batting cages, hiring a private coach, and cheering him on at games. In 2008, they attended spring training for the Yankees, where Andres was thrilled to be within 15 feet of his favorite player, Alex Rodriguez.

Meanwhile, Helen chafed at the quietness of Ocala, escaping

to Orlando for days at a time. She liked to throw on tight jeans and high heels and revel in the attention she attracted. Soon, she was seeking out more dangerous highs.

"I've been 100 percent the father and, over the last year, maybe 80 percent the mother," Todd told me.

"Andres trusts Todd more than he trusts me," Helen says.

IN JULY OF 2008, Todd says, Andres called him from Costa Rica in tears. Andres said he wanted to go home and asked, "Daddy, would you come and get me?" Todd counseled him to be patient, promising that he would come to bring him home soon.

Todd Hopson does not come across as the sort of person who would hire a kidnapper. His idea of excitement is watching *Seinfeld* reruns. He is quick with a one-liner if conversation flags. He clears his throat repeatedly, a nervous tic that may be related to his fondness for cigars. During most of our time in Costa Rica, he wore the same outfit—a khaki shirt with lots of pockets, jeans, and bright-white sneakers. But while Hopson may seem like a softie, his resolve is strong: he would rather break the laws of Costa Rica than his word to Andres.

In late August, even before Todd filed a Hague application, he contacted Gus Zamora, who was feeling the pinch of the recession. It had been nine months since his last recovery. "If somebody asked me to find his dog or cat on a roof, I'd do it," he joked. Gus offered to do the job for $25,000, including expenses—about a third of his usual rate. Still, Todd had to borrow money against his house to pay the fee. Gus planned to take two trips to do the recovery, and Todd agreed to pay him $10,000 before the first and $15,000 before the second.

In September, Gus flew from Tampa to Costa Rica to rendezvous with Helen and do reconnaissance in Siquirres. From the start, Helen resisted doing a recovery; she didn't want to break any laws and possibly jeopardize her ability to return to Costa Rica. Todd felt he needed her cooperation, however, because she had access to Andres—and Andres's passport had her last name on it. (A child traveling with adults without the same last name might raise suspicion.) At Todd's insistence, Helen agreed to meet with Gus.

One day, while doing surveillance with Helen, Gus saw an opportunity to grab Andres. But Helen called him off, deciding instead to rely on the local lawyer she'd hired to regain custody. By February, however, Helen was fed up. She had just returned from a visit with Andres, and she was furious that she could not take him anywhere—not even an ice-cream shop— on her own.

"After I go through all the pain and drama of childbirth, they come and take my son away," she told me. "Hell, no. I decided, 'Gus, come here. I'm not waiting for the law, for Jason, for nothing.'"

THE ASSIGNMENT SEEMED STRAIGHTFORWARD. Helen had access to Andres through her visitation privileges. Todd had assured Gus that Andres wanted to leave Costa Rica. Under these circumstances, how hard could it be to snatch Andres from Jason or from his paternal grandparents, who often cared for him while Jason, the town dentist, was at work? But Gus had learned from the previous recoveries he had conducted—54 of them, by his count—to proceed with caution.

The price of a mistake, after all, could be imprisonment. Agents like Gus risk arrest for kidnapping or related charges if they're caught. When Gus first started doing child recoveries, in the late '80s, he worked for a man named Don Feeney, who pioneered the practice through his company, Corporate Training Unlimited, in Fayetteville, North Carolina. In 1993, Feeney was arrested on kidnapping charges for trying to recover two American girls from their mother in Iceland. He served one year in an Icelandic jail.

The risks remain high. In 2006, two agents were arrested in Lebanon for taking two girls from their father. The mother, who had hired the agents, spent seven weeks hiding in Lebanon with the girls because she, too, faced kidnapping charges. Gus says he himself has never served jail time—but a warrant for his arrest, for kidnapping, was issued in Mexico in 1997. (The charges were subsequently dropped.) To reduce the likelihood of his being charged with kidnapping, Gus says, he insists that the parent who hires him be present during a recovery.

A successful snatchback is only the beginning of the journey. Sometimes, the child doesn't want to go. Early this year, Gus says, an American father agreed to pay him $70,000 to recover his 10-year-old daughter from Japan, assuring him that the girl would acquiesce. Gus went to the Philippines to prepare an escape route by boat. He then flew to Tokyo and, accompanied by the father, hustled the girl into a van as she left home. "That little girl screamed bloody murder," Gus told me. "She was beating at the windows. Contrary to everything we'd been told, she definitely did not want to go." After a day of unsuccessfully trying to calm the girl down, he released her. (He says he received half of his fee up front; he wasn't paid the remainder.) Gus says he would never snatch an unwilling child—though he also describes recoveries in which a resistant child grew more willing over time.

Even if a child wants to go, exiting a country can be challenging, because the forsaken parent will usually report the snatchback to the local authorities. In 2000, George Uhl, a neurologist from Maryland, hired Gus to find and recover his 2-year-old son. The boy was traced to western Hungary, where his mother had left him with her parents. After Gus helped Uhl take the boy, French police intercepted Uhl at Charles de Gaulle airport on his way home. Uhl was released that same day, but his son was returned to the boy's mother. Gus blames Uhl for failing to follow instructions. He says he told Uhl to pay cash for a direct flight to the United States; Uhl's mistake was choosing to connect through Paris. At the time, however, there were no direct flights to the U.S. from Venice, where Uhl was dropped off.

In 2007, a woman hired Gus on behalf of her daughter to retrieve her two granddaughters, then 5 and 4, who had allegedly been abused by their father, the daughter's ex-husband, in Ankara, Turkey. The father had won custody in the Turkish courts and kept the girls' passports, making it hard for Gus to get the girls out of Europe. Traveling with the grandmother and mother, he got the girls to a neighboring country, but the mother could not get papers from the U.S. Embassy for both girls to travel to the States. The mother and the girls have since gone into hiding. (Names and identifying details have been withheld here because the grandmother and mother's lawyers say the girls are at risk of more abuse if they are located.) The grandmother blames Gus. "I gave him $86,000, and he left us stranded," she told me. But Gus says he had set up an exit route for the family through a third European country, adding that the grandmother stiffed him for $25,000.

GUS DEMANDS OBEDIENCE from his clients, and tends to view questioning from them as an affront. Some of his gripes are justified; his clients can be unreliable partners. "The client can be your worst enemy," he says. "Every now and then you get a perfect client, but unfortunately in this business, you're dealing with people who are damaged. They're on their own special shelf." Custody battles as intractable as the ones that call for Gus's services rarely involve uncomplicated actors.

Helen raised Gus's hackles from the start. He didn't trust her, but he felt he had to work with her because it was she, not Todd, who had access to Andres. While she visited with Andres on the front porch, Helen explained, the grandfather usually went to karate class. That left only the grandmother, who spent a lot of time talking on the phone. It seemed to be a situation from which Andres could be easily extricated.

So as dusk falls on a Friday in February, a day after our initial reconnaissance, I am sitting in the SUV, parked around the corner from the yellow house, while Helen visits with Andres on the porch, waiting for an opportunity to take him and make a break for it. Gus has told her not to try anything unless she has a few minutes when she is completely unobserved. But she is having trouble. In the seat behind me, Gus's son is reading aloud text messages from Helen. "She still looking," Helen texts, referring to Andres's grandmother. "She don't move."

A police car passes by. "We've been standing in this spot too long," Gus says. It's a normal patrol, he adds, but if the car returns, he's inclined to leave. Then Helen texts: "We can't do it today." Gus puts the SUV in gear and drives past the yellow house and a royal-blue Toyota Camry—Jason's car—parked in front of it.

The following Monday, I am waiting with Gus and Todd in the parking lot of the motel Gus has chosen as the switch point. Inside, the motel has rooms with mirrored ceilings and rainbow-colored wallpaper; the outside is a garish purple. But Gus has been attracted by subtler selling points: it's only a three-minute drive from the yellow house, and its parking lot is set back from Highway 32, concealed by palm trees. The SUV and the van are parked there, side by side.

Gus is sitting on the back ledge of the van, wearing black cargo pants and a silky gray shirt. Todd is standing nearby, running his hands through his hair, which is slick with sweat. Every few minutes, he takes his cell phone out of his shirt pocket and looks down at it, pushing his glasses up on his nose. When the phone rings at last, Todd jumps. Helen has arrived for her visit, and she has put Andres on the line.

"Hey, Papi, how are you doing?" Todd says, using his nickname for Andres. "You ready to come home soon? What'd you do if you see me? You come running to me, huh?"

Rain starts pouring down, so we take refuge in the van. Gus says the weather reminds him of his days as a ranger in the late 1970s, when one of his instructors, a Vietnam vet, ordered the men to strip off their ponchos in torrential rain. "Men," Gus says, recalling the sergeant's instructions, "the best time to catch the enemy with his pants down is when he's under a poncho, in a defensive situation, with a cup of coffee, feeling sorry for himself. That's when you should be moving against his position."

From the porch of the yellow house, Helen texts that the grandfather hasn't gone to karate. As it becomes clear that, once again, Helen is being too closely observed to initiate the snatchback, Todd grows visibly frustrated and wonders aloud whether one solution might be to slow down "the old man" long enough to keep him from impeding the snatchback. "What if you hire a couple of lowlifes . . . ?"

"It would take me time to fucking do that," Gus says. For all his tough talk, he doesn't seem eager to break down doors.

"Okay, okay," Todd says. "I was just thinking. I don't mean hurt him, but just to, to delay him, to stall him."

Gus doesn't respond. He later tells me that he hasn't been paid enough for that kind of job.

BREAKUPS KNOW NO BORDERS. Lovers from different countries connect, conceive, and in some cases, combust. Their children must weather the aftermath; in the worst cases, they are abducted by a parent and made to live underground. The Hague Permanent Bureau, which collects information about the Convention on the Civil Aspects of International Child Abduction and advises countries about its implementation, does not keep comprehensive global statistics on this phenomenon. But in

1994, the U.S. State Department's Office of Children's Issues, which handles family abduction cases, had four staff members; today, it has 57.

The convention was designed to mediate cross-border tugs-of-war. Any country that has agreed to the treaty promises to respect the custodial decisions of the other contracting countries. The convention's goal is to secure the "prompt return" of a child who has been "wrongfully removed to or retained in" another contracting country. The convention specifically defines *prompt*: a judge or administrator in the country where the child is being held is supposed to render a decision within six weeks. The judge is not authorized to make a decision about custody; his job is to determine whether the child should be returned to his "habitual residence" so that the courts in that place can exercise their jurisdiction.

According to the Permanent Bureau's latest statistics, based on surveys of member nations in 2003, in 68 percent of cases, the parent who initially flees abroad with a child is the mother. After a marital separation, mothers are more likely to have primary custody, and many "taking mothers" cite domestic violence as their reason for running off with their kids. Indeed, the most popular defense against a "prompt return" of a child is Article 13B of the convention—that the child would suffer a "grave risk." Another common defense is Article 12, which, after a year has elapsed since the abduction or wrongful retention, allows a judge to take into account whether the child has "settled into its new environment."

"You'll see this when you look at compliance reports," says Martha Pacheco, Abduction Unit chief at the Office of Children's Issues. "The child will not be returned quickly, for whatever reason. A year goes by, two years go by, and then the argument is made by the taking parent that the child has settled in the country and it will be traumatic for the child to go back. It's not fair—it's a catch-22."

The left-behind parent faces tough odds. Many countries, especially in Asia and the Middle East, have not signed the convention. Those countries have a tendency to favor the rights of their nationals, even if they're the taking parents. Japan has one of the worst records among non-Hague countries. The State Department is handling 73 outstanding cases involving 104 children who have been abducted to or retained in Japan by parents.

The predicament of Walter Benda is typical. In 1995, he was living with his wife of 13 years in her home country of Japan. According to Benda, he wanted to return to the U.S. and she did not. One day, she disappeared with their two daughters. "Please forgive me for leaving you this way," she wrote in a note she left. The Japanese police, Benda says, would not investigate what they viewed as a family matter; it took him three and a half years to find the girls. He never won visitation rights. "It took a couple of years before the courts even interviewed my children," he recalls. "By that time, they'd been brainwashed and didn't want to see their father."

Sometimes even countries that have agreed to the Hague Convention are no better. For instance, the State Department has more than 500 open cases involving 800 children abducted to or retained in Mexico. The convention has no enforcement mechanism; it's up to the judicial system of a member nation to make its court's decision stick. According to the Hague's own statistics from a 2003 study, only 51 percent of all applications end with the child's return to the left-behind parent. When the abducting parent does not consent to give up the child, judges take an average of 143 days to order a return—a far cry from the six weeks mandated by the convention. (Costa Rica, which agreed to the convention in 1998, did not respond to the Hague survey, so it is not included in these statistics.)

In addition to pursuing the matter as a civil issue through the convention, a left-behind parent can press authorities to bring criminal charges against the taking parent. This can result in an

Interpol "red notice" calling for police to arrest the taking parent, with a view toward extradition. That's likely what happened last April, when a Russian mother was arrested in Hungary after abducting her daughter in France from her ex-husband, who was badly beaten during the abduction. The mother was extradited to France to face charges of kidnapping and complicity in the assault; she was later freed.

Gus Zamora, for his part, is generally dismissive of what he calls "the Vague Convention." But he's seen it work. In 2004, Hal Berger's then-wife abducted their son from California to South Africa. A year later, he filed a Hague application, spending hundreds of thousands of dollars in legal fees and eight months in South Africa during the litigation; finally, South Africa's Supreme Court ordered the boy's return to the U.S. Berger, his estranged wife, and their son flew back together on the same plane. But 10 months later, she took off with the son again, using fake passports to return to South Africa. Berger went back to the South African courts—but this time he hired Gus, in case the courts ruled against him, or his estranged wife fled a third time. After spending hundreds of thousands more, a night in jail, and more than a month in Africa, Berger won his case in the South African courts in December 2007 and flew home with his son.

More often than not, Gus gets involved when his clients have lost patience with the courts. When parents come to him in desperation, he asks them three questions: Do they have custodial rights? Do they have an idea where their kids are? And can they afford his fee?

One morning in November of 2005, an engineer (who asked that his name and other identifying details not be used here because of pending legal issues) left his home in the Midwest for work, carrying the lunch his wife had packed for him. A few hours later, he picked up a voice mail from her saying that she had taken their 2-year-old daughter shopping and wouldn't be reachable for a while. Only that evening did he learn that she'd fled to India. The engineer flew to Mumbai, hoping to reconcile. But the marriage seemed irretrievable. On his lawyer's recommendation, he filed for divorce and custody after he returned to the U.S. in January. Ten months later, the engineer called Gus, who advised him to let the custody issue play out in the courts first. Shortly thereafter, the engineer won a default custody judgment in a court in his home state when his ex-wife didn't show up to contest it. At the end of 2006, he flew to Mumbai and met Gus. He returned home with his daughter days later. A kidnapping case is still pending against the engineer in Mumbai.

"DON'T DRIVE FAST, especially on the wet roads," Gus counsels Helen, who is standing under the awning of the purple motel, watching the rain pour down. It's 6 a.m. on Tuesday. The parrots are chirping, and the palm trees bend under the weight of the water. "Take your time and get here," Gus adds. "It's only a couple of minutes."

Gus is prepping Helen to snatch Andres at the bus stop. If a stranger like Gus tried to grab the boy, witnesses might intervene, and the police would react immediately. But a mother calling out to her son and inviting him to step into her car might not trigger an alarm. Ordinarily, Gus would ride along in the car with Helen, but he doesn't trust her. He also has doubts about whether Andres will go with his mother. He has more faith in Todd's relationship with the boy, so he has decided that Todd should be in the SUV with Helen. Gus and his son will wait in the getaway van at the purple motel, preparing for a run to the Panama border.

Wearing a striped scarf to cover her distinctive auburn curls, Helen drives into Siquirres. Rain lashes the windshield. Schoolkids carrying backpacks walk into the curve of their umbrellas. Hunching low in the middle of the backseat to avoid detection,

Todd warns Helen not to drive off the edge of the road, which drops precipitously into a deep gutter.

Helen pulls over alongside a Baptist church. We can see the town square and the bus stop where Andres gets picked up for school, a block away. Cars swoosh by on the slippery road. The windshield wipers swing back and forth. The weather is a problem. The bus stop has no shelter, so whoever drops off Andres is likely to wait with him in the car, to keep the boy dry until the bus arrives.

Todd and Helen are running out of chances. Helen is supposed to have another visitation at the yellow house later today. Todd, Gus, and Gustavo are scheduled to fly back to the United States tomorrow. A solo practitioner, Todd has cleared his court schedule only until the end of the week. And he can't afford to hire Gus for a third trip.

At 7:00, a white bus stops on the town square. No one boards it. There are no schoolkids at the bus stop. "I don't see any activity," Todd says, sighing.

Time passes. The only sounds are the relentless pounding of the rain, the *swish* of the wipers, and Helen's occasional sniffs.

Suddenly, Helen sits bolt upright. "That's Jason. You see?" A blue Camry heads toward us and turns left onto the street perpendicular to ours. She warns Todd to duck down.

"So where's Andres?" Helen says, perplexed. Why didn't Jason pull over at the bus stop? Why did he turn onto the side street instead? Could Andres's bus stop be located on that side street—not by the square, as she had thought? She asks Todd whether she should check out the side street. He encourages her to go.

"I don't know if we should," she says, even as she turns the ignition, inching forward and looking from side to side. She turns right, following the route the blue car took.

"Oh, here," Helen gasps, looking at two boys in identical uniforms—dark-blue polo shirts and khaki pants—standing along the side of the road. She puts down the passenger-side window, shouting: "Come, Andres! *Ven,* Andres!"

The shorter and slimmer of the two boys, who has close-cropped hair and a light scar on his brow, stares at her. His brown eyes widen, and he steps forward slightly. Then he looks at the other boy, looks back at Helen, and shakes his head.

"He says no," Helen says, putting up the window.

"Did Chino see me?" Todd asks, referring to Andres's companion, who is his uncle. Helen says yes. Todd tells Helen to get out of the car and get Andres.

"He doesn't want me to," she says.

"Go out and get him, Helen," Todd says, his voice rising in frustration. "Just go out and get him." Helen drives on. Todd moves aggressively into the space between the front seats, directing Helen to do a U-turn and return to Andres. She obeys, warning Todd that Andres's bus is coming.

"I don't care, because we're made. Let's go," Todd shouts. "I'm going to get him. Just go!" Helen sniffs, and Todd orders her to stop the SUV. He leaps out and goes to Andres, who is wearing an olive-green backpack.

"Let's go," he says, touching Andres's shoulder. "Come on, buddy!"

Helen adds her encouragement from the driver's seat. "Come, Andres!"

Andres hesitates, glances at Chino, and then walks quickly to the open door of the SUV. Todd throws himself into the SUV behind Andres and slams the door. "Go!" he shouts.

Helen hits the accelerator.

"Hi, buddy," Todd says to Andres, hugging him. "How are you, sweetie?"

"Hi," Andres mutters. He's clearly unnerved.

"Don't worry, Papi," Todd assures him. "It's going to be okay."

In the rearview mirror, Helen can see Chino running toward the yellow house. Todd tells her to focus on the road. "Nice and easy," he says. But Helen careens around the corner, narrowly missing an old man on a bicycle as she swerves to avoid an oncoming bus. As she drives, she keeps asking Andres why he refused to come to her. "He's scared," Todd says.

Helen turns onto Highway 32, smack into a long line of traffic. Todd kisses Andres. "Who's following us?" Andres asks. Helen keeps glancing behind us, worried that Jason will be there. As the SUV creeps forward in the traffic, she pounds the heel of her right hand on the steering wheel, shouting at the cars. "They need to move!"

"It's okay, it's okay, buddy," Todd keeps saying to Andres, who sits rigidly, staring out of eyes that seem to have lost their ability to blink. "That car just happened to be behind us. I don't think they were following us."

The palm trees in front of the purple motel come into view, and Helen turns sharply to the right before veering left and screeching to a halt. Gus and his son are waiting in the van, eyebrows raised.

Helen, Todd, Andres, and I jump out of the SUV. Gustavo hustles us into the van.

"Let's go," Gus shouts from the driver's seat.

Helen remembers that she's left the keys in the SUV.

"Leave 'em," Gus barks. "Everybody duck down—you especially," looking at Helen. "Your big head has got to duck down. Don't worry about anything. Just stay down until we get a safe distance away."

Gus roars out of the parking lot and turns left onto the highway, heading east. A blue Camry speeds past us in the opposite direction.

AT GUS ZAMORA'S HOME IN TAMPA are two huge black safes containing dozens of machine guns, pistols, and rifles— enough artillery, he explains, to outfit a SWAT team of 10 men.

(Gus also trains bodyguards.) Inside his office, the shelves are crammed with textbooks like *The Shooter's Bible* and *Gun Parts*. The closet is jammed with model airplanes and shooting trophies. On the walls are pictures and statues of bald eagles; a clock with a camouflage pattern on its face and bullets arrayed around its circumference; certificates attesting to esoteric skills, including one from the "Methods of Entry School" for a course in "surreptitious entry techniques"; newspaper clippings with photos of beaming families; and a handwritten letter from a third-grader in Texas. "Dear Gus," the girl writes, "I remember you, and I hope I can see you sometime."

Born in Gary, Indiana, in 1955, Gus joined the Army in 1977, and served in the 1st Ranger Battalion, an elite infantry unit; a rapid-deployment force based in Vicenza, Italy; and the 101st Airborne Division. He met his wife, Vicki, in the service and left the Army in 1984 to prepare, he says, for the birth of their first child. He received an honorable discharge and started working for a series of private security companies. After a stint with a company based in Brownsville, Texas, Gus landed in northern Costa Rica, working on a report about the Contras in Nicaragua for the U.S. Council for World Freedom. Gus stayed in the area, providing protection for John Hull, an American rancher who helped the CIA deliver aid and weapons to the Contras. (A Senate subcommittee later collected evidence that Hull had been engaged in drug trafficking; he was also indicted for murder in Costa Rica. "What's a little murder when you're overthrowing a government?" Gus says. "That's part of the process.") Gus then made his way to Don Feeney's company, Corporate Training Unlimited, in the late '80s. Feeney's first recovery case, involving the rescue of a 7-year-old girl who'd been taken to Jordan by her father in 1988, had touched off an international incident; the State Department ended up expressing regret to Jordan. Gus, who speaks Spanish fluently, covered Latin American operations for Feeney.

After spending time in that Icelandic jail in 1993, Feeney cooled on the child-recovery business. But Gus was hooked. "I remember calling Gus and saying, 'I've got a case. There's almost no money in it, but I believe the child is in real danger,'" Feeney recalled when I spoke to him recently. "Thirty minutes later, he was at the front door of the office, saying, 'When do we leave?'"

Gus thrives on the feeling that he's doing good while having fun. He embraces the travel with the gusto of a tourist, collecting information about a well-placed bar, a cozy Italian restaurant, the best hotel Jacuzzi. When he has to plan an escape route over water, he'll often go scuba diving for a few days while he makes contacts. Despite his specialized military skills, his real expertise seems to be the ability to network—and to talk his way out of a predicament. He's more fixer than commando.

Gus is paid to take on risk. But his critics say that he also exposes others to danger. When I asked Feeney whether anyone was harmed during his or Gus's recoveries, he responded, "No. I'm not going to tell you that nobody ever got smacked around a bit. But by the time we were gone on the plane, they got up and dusted themselves off." The people guarding the child are not the only ones in jeopardy. If an operation goes wrong, a reclaiming parent risks not only jeopardizing any legal case, but also arrest or physical injury. Even worse, a child may be harmed. (Critics of Gus's line of work often cite this risk, but I haven't heard of a case where a child was actually physically hurt.)

Even if a recovery proceeds safely, a child may be traumatized. "One of the most psychologically devastating aspects of family abduction is the sudden, unexpected rupture," Liss Haviv, the executive director of Take Root, an organization composed of formerly abducted children, explained to me recently. "Being recovered may produce the same result. Whether your situation ultimately improves or not, you learn once again that any- and everything can change in the blink of an eye. How do you trust after that?"

Gus insists that no one has been physically harmed during his recoveries. But military-style operations may result in casualties; that's what may have happened in 2000, when Gus and George Uhl picked up Uhl's 2-year-old son in western Hungary. Uhl's ex-wife, Katharina Gotzler, had left the child there with her parents. Gus and Uhl went to the grandparents' home to retrieve the boy. What came next is contested.

Gus says he waited in the getaway car while Uhl, an American associate, and two Hungarian "assets" went inside to snatch the boy. (When I spoke recently to Gus's assistant on the job, she did not corroborate that Gus was in the car during the recovery, saying she could not recall the specific events.)

Gotzler was in Munich at the time. When she didn't hear from her father that night, she called the neighbors and asked them to check on him, according to her attorney, Donald Cramer. The neighbors found the boy gone, and the grandfather dead.

A German court found that Uhl "had the son abducted with the assistance of armed kidnappers. In the course of this abduction, the grandfather came to his death." Cramer added, "Zamora's belongings were checked at the hotel—he had Tasers, weapons of all sorts, and ropes."

According to Gus, one of the Hungarian men had told him the grandfather smoked a cigarette during the recovery, worrying that he'd be blamed for not protecting the boy. "We had somebody check the phone records from that apartment," Gus says. "The grandfather called his daughter in Germany. She called him back several times, and when she arrived, he was already on the couch dead. We believe that she literally tore him apart on the phone and stressed him out so much that he had a heart attack and died." Gus says the autopsy reported that the cause of death was natural and that the estimated time of death was four hours after the abduction. Prosecutors in Hungary did not press charges.

Uhl has not seen his son since he was stopped at the Paris airport on his way home. (He declined to be interviewed for this article.)

THE DAY AFTER THE SNATCHBACK in Siquirres, *Diario Extra*, a popular tabloid in Costa Rica, reports that while Andres was waiting for the bus, a white Toyota SUV stopped, and two women and a man "violently grabbed" him. The newspaper lists Helen, an aunt, and a U.S. national named "Hotson" as suspects. The article includes a photo of Andres and instructs anyone who spots him to call the police. Jason's wife is quoted: "We are confident, given that only a few hours have gone by, that they would not be able to take him out of the country."

But while the police search for Andres in a white Toyota SUV, we are speeding toward Panama in a beige Dodge Caravan. Andres and Helen lie against each other in the backseat, and Todd is prone against the side door. Gus is at the wheel.

"Andres looks good," Todd says. "That was some shock and awe."

After nearly an hour, Gus has fought his way through traffic to the turnoff to Limón. Except for some overhanging palm trees and piles of trash, the road is clear. At Gus's say so, we sit up. Helen pulls off Andres's dark-blue shirt so he can exchange it for a white T-shirt that says CORNERSTONE MIDDLE SCHOOL.

"You want to go home, right?" Todd says.

Andres nods.

"You remember, I promised," Todd says. "Did you think Daddy wasn't going to come for you?"

Andres shakes his head.

Todd tells Andres that he's left his room exactly the same and that a package has arrived all the way from Japan for him—a customized baseball glove.

"Your hair looks great, buddy," Todd says, kissing him and

observing that he's grown a little Mohawk. Gus's son informs Todd that the correct term is *faux-hawk*.

Andres takes care with his appearance; he is a handsome boy who looks like a miniature version of his favorite Yankee, A-Rod. He tells Todd that he's started using a hair gel called Gorilla Snot. Later, he asks if he'll be able to buy the gel in Florida. Throughout the journey, Andres says little, but he seems most concerned about having "forgotten" things—like the hair gel, his clothing, his iPod charger, his Nintendo DS, and, most important, two of his baseball gloves. He had taken them with him to Costa Rica, even though he didn't play much baseball in Siquirres.

As "What's Love Got to Do With It?" plays on the radio in the background and the ocean crests by the side of the road, Todd tells Andres, "I was so angry when I came down and they wouldn't let me have you."

Andres says nothing. But he smiles a few minutes later when Todd cracks a joke about the snatchback, saying: "I was going to tell you, 'Come with me if you want to live.'"

Gus drives past dilapidated shacks with corrugated-iron roofs, huddles of thin brown cows, and fields of banana plants, their bunches of fruit cradled in bright-blue plastic bags. After an hour, we arrive at Sixaola, a town that shares a narrow river with Panama and lies in the shadow of a border crossing. Trucks idle on a graffiti-covered concrete overpass that runs through the town. Gus's plan is to get Todd and his family to Panama without passing through an official border stop. Presenting them to immigration officials in Costa Rica at this point is too risky.

Gus frets about finding his contact, a Nicaraguan who owns a motorboat in Sixaola. Luckily, "the Nica," as Gus calls him, is at his home—a rickety contraption consisting of sheets of iron on a wooden base. The Nicaraguan goes off to fetch the boat. While we wait, Gus reverses the van, rocking it back and forth on the edge of an embankment, which is littered with rotting banana peels and tin cans. Finally, he manages to squeeze the van next to a pigpen in the backyard of the man's home.

Andres gets out of the van. He plays with a purple band on his wrist and fingers his faux-hawk until a blue boat pulls up to the embankment. He steps into the rocking boat. The engine sputters to life. Minutes later, the captain hops onto Panamanian soil and ties the boat to a banana plant. Todd, Andres, and Helen walk across a stretch of swamp and step into a black pickup with tinted windows that Gus has arranged to have waiting for them.

IT'S TIME FOR THE LITTLE LEAGUE play-offs between the Red Sox and the Bulls at the Ocala Rotary Sportsplex. Andres— HOPSON displayed on the back of his dark-blue shirt—stands on the first-base line next to his teammates, listening to "The Star-Spangled Banner" with his hat over his heart. The music stops, and Andres's coach shouts, "All right, gentlemen, let's go out there and throw some balls!" Soon, Andres is up at bat. He goes down in the count, two strikes against him. He stares through his mirrored sunglasses at the pitcher, a scrawny boy with a mean right arm, and swings at the next ball. The bat connects and he races to first, sliding in safe.

It's as if Andres never left Ocala. He wakes up every day at 7:10 a.m., takes a shower, and has a bowl of Lucky Charms. Then Todd drives him to the Cornerstone School, a private school with banners along its halls promoting MUTUAL RESPECT and APPRECIATION—NO PUT DOWNS. Miss Candice, his third-grade teacher, says she has observed no ill effects from his absence. He does his assignments on time, and he is the Four Square star of the playground. Todd's relationship with Helen broke down, however, not long after their return, and he asked her to move out.

Todd considered taking Andres to a psychologist, but he decided against it because the boy seemed fine. In response to my direct questions, Andres says that the Alvarados treated him well but that he doesn't miss anything about Costa Rica. He didn't play baseball in Siquirres. It's "funner" in Ocala, where he plays baseball three times a week. He says he knew his dad would come for him. Andres doesn't like to talk about Costa Rica. If anyone asks where he was, he told Todd upon his return, "I'm going to say it's a long story."

But as Jason Alvarado sees it, the story is simple. Helen Zapata and Todd Hopson kidnapped Andres. Andres, he says, had been adjusting well to Siquirres; he had even been president of his class. Jason says he doesn't want to appear ungrateful to Hopson for raising Andres. Still, he believes Andres's care should be a matter between him and the boy's mother. "Now that his mother seems not to be able to take care of him, I don't see why he has to stay" in the U.S., Jason says. "They have always known I'm the father. I have always been there for him emotionally and economically." Todd, for his part, says that Jason never spent "one centavo" on Andres's care; Jason counters that he sent money to Helen.

In theory, the U.S. State Department agrees with Jason's view. "We cannot condone the violation of the law of another sovereign territory," a State Department spokesperson says of private recovery attempts. Yet when Todd informed the State Department that he had, with Gus Zamora's help, recovered Andres, the woman helping with his Hague application responded by e-mail, "We all breathed a collective sigh of relief on hearing that Andres and Helen are back home in Florida with you." She went on to explain that Costa Rica had "a steep learning curve" about the convention, and said of Hopson's application, "We frankly do not know how it might have worked in your case."

Jason is giving them another chance to find out: in late May, he filed his own Hague application, requesting his son's prompt return.

NADYA LABI *is a freelance writer. A former staff writer at* Time *magazine and senior editor at* Legal Affairs, *she contributes to* The Atlantic, Wired, *and other magazines.*

Coda

Around the time the article ran, Interpol issued a red notice requesting the arrest of Todd Hopson and Helen Zapata for kidnapping Andres. Todd's not worried, however. He's certain that Jason Alvarado's Hague application will go nowhere. "Florida doesn't recognize dual fathership. You can only have one father," he says. "And I'm the legal father in Florida."

Todd and Helen continue to live apart. In March 2010, Helen was arrested for possession of crack cocaine; Todd paid her jail bond. Helen says it was all a "misunderstanding."

Despite his turbulent year, Andres appears to be thriving. According to Todd, he received an A-plus in two of his courses. He was also one of twenty-three kids in Ocala selected to try out for the Little League World Series. In February, Gus and his son visited Todd and Andres, and a local TV station interviewed them. But Andres won't talk about Siquirres. As Todd puts it, "He's turned the page."

Jason Alvarado has not. He is pursuing his Hague application, and plans to give a deposition in Ocala in April 2010.

Peter Savodnik

THE CHESSBOARD
KILLER

FROM GQ

THE MANIAC TRUNDLES THROUGH a silent forest. He is a
stout man, thick, with a heavy gait. He's with a woman, name
unknown, and they are enveloped by birch trees rising fifty,
sixty feet into a white-gray sky. They are talking about something important. What is love? Is love for real, or is it a ruse, a
make-believe ambrosia? She doesn't know he's had this conversation before. The Maniac is practiced. He has a very low
voice, sturdy hands, thick wrists. When he talks he has an almost
preternatural concentration. He wants to be understood. He
never lies. This is important; in court, he will tell everyone: I
always say exactly what I think.

She admits to him: She didn't know he was so serious. The
Maniac, after all, is a clerk at a grocery store. He had approached
her maybe a half-hour ago, started chatting, making jokes, ram-
bling, opining, discoursing on . . . intimacy. She doesn't know
he has a whole theory of intimacy. "The closer a person is to you,
and the better you know them, the more pleasurable it is to kill
them," he would later say. Then he'd offered her a cigarette.

She'd cupped the cigarette while he lit the match, then laughed at something he said. He suggested they take a walk in the park. She didn't even know him, had no reason to trust him, but she wanted another cigarette. She said yes.

They walk over branches, wrappers, cigarette butts, past bottles, a stuffed animal, a used condom, a disposable razor. Somewhere far away they can hear trails of moving laughter, other people walking, carousing, but here, in this particular swath of wood, there is only the trees and shadows. They can no longer see the road. He says something—later he will try to remember, unsuccessfully, exactly what it was he said—and then he laughs. Suddenly, he thinks he sees something flash across her face, which is plain and unmemorable, like a terrible gestalt, like many disparate pieces of information coalescing into an anticipation of . . . what? She knows, of course, about the disappearances. Everyone does. By this point—late spring 2006—nearly fifty people have vanished into the woods. She knows about the park, the Maniac, the faceless animal no one knows or has seen or is even sure is a man or a single human being. They talk about him on television every night, constantly. He is part of the daily chatter coursing through the ancient apartment blocs that ring the park.

But the grocery clerk?

The grocery clerk. Suddenly she seems certain that the man with the low voice, the man talking to her about the anatomy of love, the sanctity of the human bond, is the Maniac. She stops walking. Suddenly she is very, very tired. She throws her arms around a tree trunk and falls to the ground sobbing, squeezing her eyes shut tight. The Maniac is startled. How could she have known?

Now there are pieces of bark pressed against her cheek, a scratch on her neck. She begins talking to herself. She is incoherent. He can't remember what he said to her. What did he say? Later, in court, the Maniac will recount the penultimate moment with a great and fastidious love. As she clings to the tree, he can't help it—it's awful to say, he knows—but he starts to laugh again, and when she says, "Are you going to kill me?" he has no choice but to reply: "Yes."

IN THE MONTHS following his July 2006 arrest, Alexander Yurievich Pichushkin, now 34, achieved the only goal he ever set for himself, a goal he shared with so many mass murderers before him: Around the world, he was hailed as a monster. He was feared and hated. His name became a symbol of death, and he was catapulted into the international pantheon of serial killers. All the big news organizations—CNN, the *New York Times*, the BBC—aired or published long stories about the most dangerous man in Russia. Criminologists, psychologists and serial-killer aficionados worldwide weighed in online with theories and speculations. Pichushkin had transcended Pichushkin. He was now the Maniac.

The fascination surrounding the Maniac reflected the enormity of his crimes, which seemed somehow deeply Russian—oversized. Ted Bundy was convicted of 30 homicides; Jeffrey Dahmer, 15; Ken Bianchi, the Hillside Strangler, 10; the Canadian pig farmer Willie Pickton, 26. Jack the Ripper was believed to have been guilty of between 11 and 15 murders; David Berkowitz, the Son of Sam, got away with six. The Maniac was convicted of 48. He claimed he'd actually killed 63 people, and there have been reports he may have killed more. A definitive tally is unlikely. No matter the precise figure, Pichushkin inhabits an exclusive club. Only a few serial killers have been more prolific, including Andrei Chikatilo, also Russian, with 53 victims, in 1994, and Yang Xinhai, who was convicted of taking 67 lives in central China from 1999 to 2003. In the annals of serial killers, Alexander Pichushkin is one of the greatest monsters who has ever lived and killed.

The press—first the Russians, then foreign reporters—called

him the Bitsevsky Park Maniac and then the Chessboard Killer because the police supposedly found a chessboard in his apartment—incorrect—and because Pichushkin is Russian, and Russians are supposed to like chess. It's true the police found a piece of paper with a chessboard drawn on it and the names of Pichushkin's victims and the dates of their murders scrawled into the squares. But "Chessboard Killer" is misleading. It suggests Pichushkin would have stopped killing when he reached 64, the number of squares on a chessboard, as if his mission was to fill up a chessboard of death, as if he thought of murder as a game. No one close to the victims or the investigation believes this. During the trial, Pichushkin told the court that "for me, life without killing is like life without food for you." He killed because that is what he did. He had no "signatures" like, say, Robert Lee Yates (who shot all his victims in the head with a .25-caliber handgun) or Jerry Brudos (who amputated various body parts). He never sent the cops or journalists any coded, Zodiac-like messages. He drank heavily, the way many Russian men without prospects drink cheap vodka and sometimes beer and smoke endlessly and expect to die in their late fifties, and he worked at the grocery store. He had no friends or girlfriends, no perversions other than bloodlust.

"He's a regular guy," says Andrei Suprunenko, an investigator at the Prosecutor General's Department of Homicide and Armed Robbery. "He's strong. He exercises. He used to lift weights. He doesn't even have any tattoos." Suprunenko, a trim and balding man with a blonde moustache and large, pale eyes, spent months questioning the Maniac after his arrest. He probably knows him better than anyone, including Pichushkin's own family. He insists the Maniac is a very boring person, a very ordinary person, maybe the most ordinary person in the whole world.

BITSEVSKY PARK IS A LONG, rolling forest filled with birch trees, streams, clearings, crossings, the occasional path or bench or green garbage bin. There is an equestrian complex and a psychiatric facility. In the winter, it's popular with cross-country skiers. The woods extend from Balaklavski Prospekt, on the north end, to the MKAD, the multilane beltway that encircles Moscow, several miles south. It encompasses just over 5,500 acres. (New York's Central Park occupies 843.) Surrounding the park are tens of thousands of people living in anonymous apartment blocs, which are massive and speckled with satellite dishes and clotheslines. Many people here call this part of Moscow— rusting, concrete, a half-hour by metro from the center of the city—the *zhora mira*, or "asshole of the world."

Natasha Pichushkina, the Maniac's mother, moved into a two-bedroom *khrushchovka* at 2 Khersonskaya, entrance No. 2, on the fifth floor, a six-minute walk from the north end of Bitsevsky Park, when she was eleven years old. That was 1963. The five-story *khrushchovki* were the Soviet Union's first public housing projects and named after then-premier Nikita Khrushchev, and even though they were cramped, dark, dank, charmless and overflowing with tenants, they were the first single-family homes most of these families had ever lived in. They were an improvement. Natasha Pichushkina grew up on Khersonskaya Street. She had a family of her own there and knew everyone on the block. So did her son, Alexander Pichushkin, the Maniac, and until the night he was arrested, he lived most of his life at 2 Khersonskaya, where he slept on a couch in the first bedroom, which doubled as a living room. Natasha slept, alone, on a queen-sized bed ten feet from her son. Her husband, Pichushkin's father, moved out before his son had turned one. (The couple apparently maintained contact and, in fact, had a second child, but they never lived under the same roof again.) In the second bedroom were Pichushkin's younger sister, Katya; her husband, also named Alexander; and their son, 6-year-old Sergei, or Seriozh. Everyone except the Maniac is still there.

Pichushkin rarely left the neighborhood. Ten of his victims

lived in the same four-building complex where he lived—four from 2 Khersonskaya; two from 4 Khersonskaya, next door; three from 6; and one from 8. Unlike the later, massive, public-housing projects, the buildings here are low-lying, compact, with single-lane roads coming in and out and narrow strips of park in between. It takes two minutes to walk from 2 Khersonskaya to 8 Khersonskaya. Everyone knows everyone else: the babushkas, the girls who work at the newspaper kiosk, the kids kicking soccer balls in the courtyard, the old men smoking cigarettes.

In the beginning, in 2001, 2002, people just disappeared—pensioners, bums, local fixtures—and no one really noticed. Or, in some cases, family members would wait the requisite three days and then file a missing-person report with the militia, but the militia rarely did anything. No one on Khersonskaya or at the kiosks and vegetable stands on Kakhovka or any of the cops who were supposed to patrol the apartment blocs and metro stations north of the park made any connections. And then, inevitably, the families started talking to each other. There were fears, speculations. Nobody knew anything; therefore, everybody did. The babushkas on the apartment stoops would wonder aloud about the disappearing Lyoshas, Nikolais, Viktors. *Lyosh gedeye?* (Where's Lyosha?) *Nashyol rabotu v Khimkeye.* (He found a job in Khimky.) *Daladno. Vozmozhno on umer.* (Bullshit. He probably died.) *On piyaniy.* (He's a drunk.) One theory held that the Chechens were to blame. Chechen construction crews sometimes kidnap able-bodied men and force them into slave labor. No one knows how often this happens; it happens. So, for a while, people blamed the Chechens or maybe the Azeris—anyone *chorniy*, or "black," which meant anyone not Slavic. But then, in November 2002, an invalid named Alexei Pushkov vanished. Then they didn't think it was the Chechens anymore.

Then, in early or mid-2003, the people on Khersonskaya began to think that it was someone they knew. There were too many connections between those who had gone missing. By then, the count had reached fifteen or twenty. No one had come back; no one expected they would. That's because the people on Khersonskaya, like so many Russians squeezed into crumbling housing complexes, understood something that Westerners cannot really understand: In this place, only certain people matter, and they were not those people. All the authorities cared about was order—snow-plowed streets, a metro that ran on time, quiet, *stabilnost*. If you impose order on the serfs—and make sure they have a slab of meat, a shot of vodka and a woman to sleep with at night in a small, dry, warm cave—you can go to bed assured they won't revolt. Russians know this and wallow in it, and on Khersonskaya Street and the streets and apartment blocs around Bitsevsky Park, they knew they were alone and no one cared what happened so long as they stayed put. The disappearances were signs of their smallness. With each disappearance, they became smaller, more fearful. The rumors metastasized. They thought it might be a woman. Or a pack of killers, with knives. Or a psychiatric patient who had escaped from the nearby institution. Or the mafia. These were the things they said when they drank and smoked on their apartment stoops, or ran into each other in the stairwells of the old *khrushchovki* or the grocery store, and wondered where the men were disappearing to.

Then came November 2005. That was the month Nikolai Zakharchenko, 63, turned up dead in the woods. He was the first body. He was the first one who hadn't just gone missing, but was found, tagged, determined beyond any reasonable doubt to have been murdered. For the first time since the disappearances started four years earlier, the people on Khersonskaya and up and down the wide, gray boulevards, began to see the ghastly threads like connective tissue that seemed to connect all the faces that had disappeared or been forgotten, and they imagined that something terrible had happened. That was when the outline of a horrifying possibility emerged and a new terror began rippling through the apartment blocs, the icy boulevards and metro stations on the orange and gray lines that hug the park, which was now a haunted ground, snowy and forbidden. That was when "Bitsevsky Park Maniac," or "Bitsa Maniac," entered the local lexicon and then the national discourse and then, eventually, the global airwaves, the chat rooms brimming with anonymous posters waxing cryptic about the invisible monster prowling the wilds of southern Moscow.

IT IS DECEMBER 2007. It is snowing and perfectly black outside. The neon billboards and the Ladas—boxy, Soviet, four-door—on the *prospekt*, the boulevard, are far away. Natasha Pichushkina is sitting on her son's bed in the family's apartment at 2 Khersonskaya, and she is crying. She is a small woman, about five-four, with dyed reddish-purplish hair, a weak voice, and a wanness, a sickliness, that has been ironed into her face. An odor—sweat, cooking oil—pervades the whole apartment, which is cluttered with DVDs, old furniture and an ancient refrigerator bearing two faded photographs of her son at 8 or 9. It's dark except for the bluish glow coming from the television. On the other side of a narrow doorway, her grandson Seriozh is playing a video game that involves hunting down barnyard animals. Natasha is saying that Alexander—Sasha, the Maniac—used to be close with his nephew, but Seriozh hasn't seen him in almost a year-and-a-half and he's beginning to forget him. Seriozh was four, she says, the last time he saw his uncle. "He used to ask, 'Where's Sasha?'" she says. "But now he doesn't. He doesn't know where he is. He doesn't know who he is."

She takes out Sasha's collection of pins, which look like the kind of pins any little boy growing up in the Soviet Union might collect. There are pins commemorating the 1980 Olympics in Moscow, pins with Leo Tolstoy's silhouette, Lenin pins, a pin from

Minsk, a pin from the Russian Far East—92 pins in all. She is trying to describe her son. She has photographs of him when he was a little boy, but those are too precious to give away. "You should take them," she says of the pins. "What can I do with these things?"

What else did Sasha like to do? She says he had a cat named Mursik and a fish tank. She says he liked frogs. Echoing Suprunenko, the detective, she stresses how "ordinary" he was. She says he liked Soviet movies, and he loved the television adaptation of Alexander Dumas' *Countess of Monsoreau.* (During the trial, Pichushkin said he sometimes had to hurry up and finish off a murder before he could rush home, undress, shower—in some cases, scrubbing the blood out of his hair or from under his fingernails—and watch the latest installment of *Countess,* usually with his mother.) She's says he's very brave and has a "strong personality" and always does what he wants. Corroborating her son, she says he never lies. Then she tells a story about a lie he once told. One night, Sasha announced he was going for a walk in the park. There were men disappearing almost every week back then, and she and her daughter, Katya, pleaded with him not to go, but Sasha said he wasn't going to let the Maniac stop him.

Does she know why her son became the Maniac? Was it his father abandoning the family? Did something happen when he was little? This is the question that keeps surfacing and resurfacing. It's an impossible question, and the only question that really matters now, and every time it comes up, Natasha Pichushkina cries and shakes her head and stares through a window at the darkened courtyard below. "I know now that I raised my son very poorly," she says. "I can't say what I did wrong. I just tried to raise him like a normal mother." She glances at the photographs of Sasha, which have been taped to the refrigerator. In both pictures he stares straight at the camera, unsmiling. She shakes her head, covers her face. After a long time, she looks up and turns her gaze to the television set. Finally she says, "I think I didn't know my son very well."

Now she sees her son every two weeks, when she visits him at the prison in the center of the city, about a forty-five-minute metro ride from Khersonskaya Street. This is a temporary routine. Soon, Pichushkin will be transported to a permanent facility far from Moscow. She says she brings him Zolotaya Yava Classic cigarettes, cheese and *salo*, or salted lard. She says that visits are for one hour, and that they never talk about what he did or why he is there. Sometimes, she says, she runs out of things to say. "If I don't think too much about everything that's happening, I can go on," Natasha Pichushkina says. "But what happened is never going away. It will never be the same." He loved her, she says, and still loves her, but the enormity of his crimes makes it hard to restore any sense of normalcy. When Natasha Pichushkina takes her grandson to the playground most mornings, she almost always sees someone related to someone her son murdered.

NATASHA FYEDOSOVA LIVES with her mother and daughter in an apartment, at 8 Khersonskaya, that is identical to Natasha Pichushkina's, at 2 Khersonskaya. The kitchen, which is no more than 25 square feet, has a table, a gas-lit stove and two chairs. Natasha, 26, is smoking Vogue cigarettes and wears a T-shirt that says JUICY. She has been talking about her father, Pichushkin, Khersonskaya Street, the cops, the investigation. She serves instant coffee. Luydmilla Fyedosova, her mother, comes in and out. She is watching something on television with her granddaughter, Natasha's daughter, 8-year-old Nastia.

Until Zakharchenko, the first body they found, the Maniac had a routine. He would single out his victim, then hover, circle, watch. He was religious about this. "Pichushkin would wait for hours until his victims were all alone, and then he would approach them," says Fyedosova, whose father, Boris Fyedosov, was victim No. 36. (Fyedosova, who attended all 46 days of the Maniac's trial, has become something of a Pichushkin authority.) He would usually begin with small talk, something Russians tend to avoid, or questions about a mutual acquaintance or a family member. (During the trial, victims' relatives were permitted to ask the Maniac questions. Natasha Fyedosova asked Pichushkin what he talked about with her father before he killed him. The Maniac replied that they talked about her.) Fyedosova, who has a pale, round face and dirty blonde hair, is nearly expressionless as she talks. She recites the many things she has learned about the Maniac with an almost robotic straightforwardness that is disarming and sad. "There was total shock when we heard it was Sasha Pichushkin," Fyedosova says. "He was always very calm, always by himself." She says she was upset by the Maniac's choice of victims. "I thought it was strange that he only wanted to kill people he knew," she says. "If he had killed people he didn't know, in another neighborhood, it wouldn't have been as bad, but he killed people he knew." Indeed, the Maniac befriended people—he acquired them—so he could kill them. Among his favorite books, says his mother, was an aging Russian translation of Dale Carnegie's *How to Win Friends and Influence People*.

Victim No. 32, an unidentified middle-aged man who disappeared in the late spring or early summer of 2003, was typical of the Maniac's victims, Fyedosova says. Pichushkin had been watching him for at least an hour. He had been smoking and drinking on a bench, legs crossed, next to a bus stop around the corner from Pichushkin's apartment. He was an obvious target, but it was warm outside, and there were too many people, perched on their apartment stoop or peering out of an open window or simply strolling down the street, for Pichushkin to approach. Finally, everyone but his target disappeared, heading inside to their apartments or ducking into the grocery store, and for a few minutes No. 32 was all alone, sitting, smoking, scanning the Ladas heading past the grocery store and kiosks toward the wall of birch trees: the park. Pichushkin, filled with an enormous excitement, came up to the man and began talking.

A few minutes later, they were strolling down the two-lane road toward Bitsevsky Park. It was early evening, and the trees loomed over the power lines on Balaklavski Prospekt, and a red-blue sky stretched across the forest. No. 32 must have been in a sour mood, or perhaps he was just hung over. The Maniac, during the trial, described him as distracted, irritable. As they neared the park, Pichushkin tried to placate him. Perhaps he was worried No. 32 would do something that might disrupt his own death. The excitement had been building inside him for so many hours, the anticipation of this final release was so great, that it would have been painful—unjust—if the inebriated, foul-smelling, melancholy crank had somehow escaped. Pichushkin studied No. 32's profile as they crossed the *prospekt*. Now they were finally entering the last, abbreviated chapter of this little man's life, and a bottomless rage filled up the Maniac. He was absorbed by a terrible, almost unimaginable fear that his soon-to-be victim would somehow do something to save himself—and deprive the Maniac of what belonged to him—and he wanted to tear off the little man's head right there, but he had to wait, just a few minutes longer, until they were inside the protective cloak of trees. As they were about to enter the woods, Pichushkin recalled, he asked the man if he had any wish. " 'My wish is to stop drinking,' " the man said, according to Pichushkin. And Pichushkin replied: " 'I promise you, today will be the day you stop drinking.' "

He always took them to one of two wells that burrowed deep into the ground to a feeder pipe that was part of the city's sprawling sewer system. He knew exactly how to get there and how long it would take, how many words would need to be spoken before he could attack. As he trudged through the woods, toward the well, No. 32 apparently did not ask too many questions about where they were going or why. He walked or, more likely, stumbled. He was still a little drunk. Sometimes, when they would arrive at the well, Pichushkin would offer his prey another drink and then propose a toast to his dead dog. Pichushkin did not say what he talked about with No. 32 before he killed him. (Being one of the Maniac's anonymous victims, he was unrepresented at the trial by any family members who could have pressed the Maniac about the details surrounding his death.) And then, suddenly, he took out a hammer or wrench used for removing nails—he is believed to have worn a jacket on each of his hunting expeditions—and struck No. 32 once or twice in the head, hard, but not hard enough to kill him. He wanted his victims to see the person who was taking their lives. Sometimes he would force shards of a broken vodka bottle into their skulls before pushing them down the well. If they weren't dead before they plunged thirty feet into the ground, the fall killed them. The Maniac did not say what condition No. 32 was in before he pushed him down the well. Later, some of the bodies turned up at a waste-water treatment center about five miles away, having meandered in a northeasterly direction through the underground tunnels, but no one ever connected the bodies to the disappearances near Bitsevsky Park. Many bodies never turned up. At least 13 corpses, including, presumably, that of victim No. 32, became clogged in one of the feeder pipes. Sewage authorities, who said the corpses posed no threat to public drinking water, said they have not removed the bodies because that would require shutting down the city's waste-water system for several hours, if not longer.

HE PREFERRED MEN. Only two, or maybe three, of his victims were women. Unlike Andrei Chikatilo, the sexually dysfunctional sexual predator, or Bundy, who preferred college co-eds, or Bianchi, who raped his victims before strangling them, Pichushkin didn't want sex. Sex was beneath him. He sought something more pure: an untainted death. What he loved was the leeching away of life, the quiet terror surrounded by trees, shadows, birds. This is not to say that killing was not sexual for Pichushkin. The way the Maniac talked about killing—he would tell the court that one's first murder is like "first love"— made it sound like killing was a biological imperative. He has said he sometimes ejaculated when he killed. "For the serial killer, the process of preparing to kill and killing is an erotic experience," says Alexander Bukhanovsky, a psychiatrist and serial-killer expert famous in criminal-justice circles for helping authorities find Chikatilo in the early 1990s. But sex—sexual intercourse with other people—is not erotic for serial killers, Bukhanovsky says. What is erotic is killing and all the associations, the mental links and scents and symbols of taking someone else's life. For Pichushkin, the biting wind in winter, in the early evening, the birch trees, the blood of old men, a fresh snow, splattered, kaleidoscopic, the crunch of ice and branches, the reverberations of a distant laughter . . . these were the sources of his sexual energies and the vessel that brought these stirrings to their natural and gruesome apex.

Natasha Fyedosova, who has known Pichushkin's sister, Katya, 26, since they were little, says Pichushkin never had any interest in girls, never talked about sex or made jokes or looked at women the way boys or men often look. Could Pichushkin have been gay? She shakes her head dismissively. When the subject of Pichushkin's sexual orientation comes up with his mother, Natasha Pichushkina, she interjects, "My son was actually going to marry someone." Whom did he plan to marry? She shrugs. She says she never met her. Suprunenko, the detective, also rules out the possibility that Pichushkin is homosexual. He says Pichushkin didn't have any sexual longing for men; he just didn't care about women. Bukhanovsky agrees. So does Pavel

Kachalov, a psychoanalyst at Moscow's Serbsky Institute, where Pichushkin was evaluated after being arrested and ultimately found competent to stand trial. No one, it seems, considers it even remotely possible that Pichushkin was gay. And maybe they're right.

But there's something else: In Russia, which remains violently homophobic, it may be that people have a hard time believing a gay man is capable of the kind of power or force of will that defined the Maniac. The Maniac is a maniac, and he's evil, and everyone says so, but he is also very much a man in the way that Russians think of men. He is, in fact, a frighteningly ordinary man: rough, crude, prone to heavy drinking, a smoker, without any future or sense of his place in the world. He works because he needs money, but not a lot. He unloads canned vegetables, moves boxes, talks to almost no one. He has no trajectory or forward momentum. He is not exactly disdainful of those with goals; he is unaware there are any goals to strive for.

So he kills. He follows his passions, like adolescent currents. He does this when he feels like it, which is often. The first time he was 18. That was July 27, 1992. The victim was Mikhail Odichuk. They'd been classmates, and Pichushkin had invited Odichuk on an outing. He was very open. He told Odichuk he wanted to kill someone; they could do it together; he said it would be a joint introduction into the art of life-taking. Odichuk had tagged along, half in jest, not sure what to expect. When Pichushkin realized that Odichuk wasn't serious about killing anyone, he killed Odichuk instead.

Then he waited nine years. He'd been questioned by the police about Odichuk's death, and the police let him go because Pichushkin was utterly unremarkable, Pichushkin was like them, Pichushkin was like everyone, and only someone who was unlike everyone else, who was remarkable, singular, could kill. But nine years is a long time to wait, especially for someone who says killing is as important to him as eating is to other people.

There is another consideration: Pichushkin understood very well that when he started killing, not dabbling or experimenting à la Odichuk, but really killing, and killing wantonly, he wouldn't stop and that this would be the last thing he did and that even though it might last a long time—there would be pauses, codas, like a sonata—he was embracing his fate and this fate would be monumental and irreversible. He must have been enthralled by this idea. But perhaps he was afraid of it, too. He may even have tried to quash it. There is a story (unverified) that has circulated through the apartments on Khersonskaya that in late 2001 or 2002, after he had resumed killing but before most of his victims had died, Pichushkin wandered into one of the police stations near the park and declared for all to hear that he killed people, not once or sometimes but on a regular basis, as if this were his chosen métier. "Because that is what I do," Pichushkin is said to have said. As the story goes, the cops laughed in Pichushkin's face and called him a drunk and told him to go home, which he did.

In any event, his nine-year respite ended May 17, 2001, when he killed Yevgeny Pronin, victim No. 2. Over the course of the next eight weeks, he would kill nine more people. This killing spree within a killing spree culminated on July 21, when victim No. 11, Victor Volkov, disappeared. That fall and winter the killing continued, but it was less feverish; six or seven people were snuffed out during this stretch. Then, on February 23, 2002, Pichushkin tried and failed to kill Maria Viricheva. Viricheva, who was pregnant at the time, fell down the well Pichushkin pushed her into, and then somehow got herself to a hospital. At the hospital, she was reported by Russian newspapers to have told the *militsioneri*, the police, about the attack in the park. The cops asked for Viricheva's registration papers. (Millions of Russian citizens in Moscow live there illegally; jobs outside the capital are scarce.) Viricheva said she didn't have any papers, and the cops told her that if she stayed quiet about her attack they'd stay quiet about her "illegal habitation." Viricheva, now in prison for an unrelated incident, opted to stay in Moscow.

The Maniac killed three more people in the two weeks following Viricheva. Then, a month later, he encountered Mikhail Lobov, age 13. It's unlikely he knew Lobov, who didn't come from one of the apartment houses on Khersonskaya, and it's unclear where exactly they met—probably on Kakhovka Prospekt, near the metro station, where the kids with leather jackets and multiple piercings drink vodka from large plastic containers and hang out next to the moveable flower stands and the dumpling kiosks. But once the pair entered the forest, Pichushkin did not stray from his script. A fifteen-, maybe twenty-minute slog through the snowy woods. Cigarettes. A few swigs of whatever they were drinking. Some faux-camaraderie—"*Tiy menya uvazhaesh, i ya tebya uvazhaiyu, tak davai vipe'em!*" or "You respect me, and I respect you, so let's drink!" And then the surprise blow to the head, followed by a shove down the well.

Then Pichushkin turned and exited the park—but didn't notice that Lobov's jacket had caught on one of the metal fittings inside the well. Lobov managed to crawl out of the well and, once outside the park, found a cop. "This guy tried to kill me," he told the cop, but the cop told Lobov to go home. A week later, Lobov was back at the Kakhovskaya metro station when he happened to see Pichushkin, who would tell everyone in court that it didn't matter what Lobov said about him or what happened in the park or anything to anyone because nobody would believe a punk who hung out at metro stations with beggars and other punks, which is true everywhere and especially in Russia. But Lobov began screaming and clawing at his hair, and he grabbed one of the *militsioneri* standing outside the station and started pointing and shouting and telling the cops they had to do something. But they did nothing. Once again, they told him to scram. All this came out in the Russian press years later, after Pichushkin had killed at least another 25 people—about one a month, on average, from 2001 to 2006, before he was finally arrested.

THE MOST IMPORTANT FACT about Nikolai Zakharchenko—the first body—is not that he was the first body. It's that he was victim No. 41. That means at least 40 people vanished—were murdered—before the police, and then the detectives at the Interior Ministry and the Prosecutor General's Office, realized there was a serial killer in Moscow.

"Before perestroika, the system was better," says Alexander Bukhanovsky, the psychiatrist and serial-killer expert. "There was a process. It was more methodical. Now the police don't know very much." Yuri Antonyan, a Moscow lawyer who teaches at the Institute for Humanities Education and co-authored a leading text on serial killers, says: "It may take about 30 or 40 murders until serial killers are found in our country. In Great Britain, it takes only seven or eight." In the United States, he says, it usually takes about the same time as it does in Britain; sometimes, it can be a bit longer. The bottom line, Bukhanovsky says, is that the Maniac's desire to kill vastly exceeded the system's capacity to stop him—or even recognize that he existed.

The system, of course, is not really a system. That's because Russia has never had a genuine rule of law. The only people who have ever mattered are the people who own the law, the power, or *vlast*, which is to say the Kremlin and its many clients. Until not so long ago, the southern precincts of Moscow, the asshole of the world, with their Martian-like apartment complexes and indistinguishable avenues peppered with gray facades and fast-food joints and a new, neon gaudiness, were a series of medieval villages teeming with peasants. Before the revolution, the peasants lived on postage-stamp subsistence farms that were muddy, crowded and reminiscent of a Bruegel canvas. Maybe they had a pig, some chickens, a goat. Then, after the 1917 revolution, the peasants were herded into *kommunalki*, or communal-housing projects, and they were forcefully urbanized and told that they were now members of the newly concocted proletariat even though they didn't know what that meant. And then, about fifty years ago, they were given one- or two-bedroom *khrushchovki*, and they were happy inside their tiny hives with their dim lights and ceilings stretching seven feet high because they had never had anything that was theirs, and now they had somewhere to drink at night, and eat their slab of meat and procreate somewhere other than a common room they shared with their mothers and fathers and their children. Nina Asanova, a forensic psychiatrist who has spent years working in Russia's criminal-justice system, calls these people "dead souls."

That forty or fifty or a hundred or several thousand dead souls might disappear into a snowy wood probably bothered no one in the power. "These are people," Asanova says, "without money surrounded by alcoholism and a kind of primitive, brutal sex. As for the bums, they're not protected at all. The police aren't going to worry about them. It was a very rational decision the Maniac made, killing these people." Had he hewed to his own script—tossing his victims into sewage pipes—it's unlikely the Maniac would have ever been caught. Of course, once the higher-ups at the Prosecutor General's Office learned what was going on—once bodies began appearing in Bitsevsky Park, and a crippling fear enveloped the city, and the people crammed into their rusting dens on Khersonskaya Street and then their neighbors and then everyone else, all the urban peasants, began screaming for something to be done—it was only eight months before Pichushkin was arrested, which Suprunenko (correctly) notes is "excellent as far as tracking down serial killers is concerned."

THE DISCOVERY OF ZAKHARCHENKO'S CORPSE not only marked a turning point for the authorities or the people on

Khersonskaya Street. It also pointed to something important going on inside the Maniac. In Pichushkin's mind, Zakharchenko's
killing was a boundary of sorts, a dotted line that delimited the
Maniac who wanted to kill from the Maniac who wanted to be
known.

All along, or at least since he began killing in earnest in 2001,
Pichushkin had been consumed by an irreconcilable conflict:
He wanted to kill and he wanted everyone to know he was the
killer. He felt an intense, almost overwhelming need to murder,
and he deeply craved the respect and adulation of others. During
the trial, Pichushkin treated the assembled to a story. One night,
he was watching television with his mother and sister at home,
and there was a report about the serial killer terrorizing Bitsevsky Park. His sister suddenly exclaimed: "It's so fascinating.
This mad man, he's so fascinating. Who is he?" And Pichushkin
had to fight very hard—he was practically bursting—not to tell
her she was sitting next to him.

But after Zakharchenko, the conflict inside the Maniac began
to seethe and overflow. Now he killed aggressively, openly, leaving bodies in the snow, the mud, sprawled across a grassy plain,
tucked between the trees. The worst, says Natasha Fyedosova,
was the corpse they found by the side of one of the streams that
runs through the park. He had been killed at least two days earlier, and it was snowing, and some wild dogs had found him first.
"There was a doctor walking his dog," she says, "and he saw one of
these wild dogs, and the dog had a bone in his mouth, and the
doctor, because he's a doctor, knew the bone was human." The
"permanent tension," in Bukhanovsky's words, pitting Pichushkin against Pichushkin was nearing its climax, and everyone on
Khersonskaya could feel it. An awful quiet, a waiting, descended
on the *prospekt* and the apartment-caves and the courtyards and
the grocery store and the kiosks. People talked about hearing
shouts and cries echoing through the forest. There were sight-
ings, imaginings. Children no longer ventured into the woods.

The woods, the park, was now a blackened netherland, a symbol of something that was happening around them, something that was happening to them. The babushkas, the "voices of the old wisdom," as Natasha Fyedosova says, talked about Satan paying a visit one winter's night to Moscow.

After they found him, there were people, journalists, television commentators, who compared Pichushkin to Dostoevsky's Rodion Raskalnikov, who killed because he needed the money but really because he believed he had a right to kill. This feels a bit too neat. Dostoevsky, after all, was railing against a Russia that had lost its faith. Pichushkin comes from a Russia that never had any faith to begin with. Raskalnikov found redemption after he reclaimed his God; Pichushkin had no God to reclaim. Post-Soviet Russia is a country that has been reengineered so many times that the old ideologies, traditions and religiosities are little more than old, mildewy, sapped of any application or relevance. Unlike Dostoevsky's pre-Bolshevik, nineteenth-century Russia, in which those who believed battled those who did not, there is no battle in Pichushkin's Russia. That battle ended several decades ago, and now there are very few people, irrespective of who they are or how much power they exercise, who believe in anything—God, truth, beauty, love—except for a raw and primal violence. The Maniac is their cause and effect.

PICHUSHKIN MUST HAVE KNOWN the end was near. He must have sensed that the civil war inside him was erupting and that soon he would do something stupid and they would find him. Corpses were appearing regularly, and now that the Prosecutor General's Office was involved and everyone knew there was a maniac out there, there were police scouring the park twenty-four hours a day—uniformed officers, plainclothes cops, cops on horseback—and they were narrowing their search, talking to everyone, compiling sketches of possible suspects.

But in the very end, it was the Maniac's decision. All the victims' family members, the prosecutors, most everyone with any connection to the case, say Suprunenko and his team did a superb job. But in the very end, it was Pichushkin who hand-delivered Pichushkin to the police.

He had gone on a walk with Marina Moskavalyeva, a co-worker at the grocery store. She had told him that she'd left a note for her son saying she was with Sasha Pichushkin. He kept saying to himself, once they were in the park, that he shouldn't kill her because they'd know it was him. But he wanted to. So Moskavalyeva had to die.

A few hours later, when Moskavalyeva hadn't come home and her son was watching television and saw that they'd found another body in the park and that it was a woman, he called his father, and then they called the police. "We had the note," Suprunenko says, "and we had video footage of Pichushkin and this woman getting on the metro at Novye Cheryomushki and getting off at Konkovo"—on the orange-line, which is to the immediate west of the park—"so we naturally suspected Pichushkin."

It's worth pointing out that the Maniac, who had made a point of never lying, lied about killing Marina Moskavalyeva. There had been other lies, of course, ten million tiny deceptions meant to lure his victims into the park, but these had been sec-ondary prevarications about the details or circumstances sur-rounding the upcoming death, not death itself. No one had ever asked Pichushkin point blank if he had ever killed anyone. But then Moskavalyeva's son, before picking up the phone to call his father, who would then call the police, rang Pichushkin. Pichushkin, after all, was supposed to be taking a stroll with his mother. But when he reached Pichushkin, Pichushkin said he hadn't seen Moskavalyeva. He lied knowing everyone would know he was lying.

Two nights later, on July 16, 2006, close to midnight,

everyone—Natasha Pichushkina, Katya, little Seriozh and, of course, the Maniac—was about to go to sleep at 2 Khersonskaya when suddenly· someone was knocking at the door. This was strange; usually you had to hit the buzzer to be let into the building. Outside, they could hear voices, a radio dispatcher. They looked out the window and there were cars on the one-lane road; there were lights and noise, people circling around. Natasha Pichushkina says she opened the door very slowly, and when she did, a column of men in uniforms pushed through the narrow corridor crammed with jackets and sandals and old boxes, through the musty doorway into the little bedroom where Alexander Pichushkin was about to tuck in for the night. In under a minute, Natasha Pichushkina says, the tiny, two-bedroom *khrushchovka* was flooded with heavily armed riot police: boots, automatic rifles, handcuffs. "They were kind to me," she says. "They said they just wanted to talk to him about some burglaries that had happened, but I thought there were a lot of police for a burglar, and I asked Sasha, 'Did you rob someone?' and he said, 'No.'" Natasha Pichushkina added that her son did not resist when the police took him away. He didn't say anything at all.

After Pichushkin was escorted out of the building, they gave her some documents stating exactly what he was being accused of, and she had a hard time saying anything or moving or sitting down or thinking. She couldn't focus. They stayed all night—the cops, detectives, forensics experts—turning her apartment upside down looking for things that might send her son to prison forever.

"WE WERE IN SHOCK when we realized how many people he'd killed," says Andrei Suprunenko, sitting behind his desk at department headquarters, wearing a black turtleneck and charcoal jacket, smoking promiscuously. His office is a disaster. It reeks of smoke and a permanent grime and there are garbage bags filled to capacity, a painting of a topless woman, a desk over-flowing with loose-leaf papers, notepads, magazines. The investigator has a strange, protean quality: first angry, then pensive, then facetious. Asked why Pichushkin preferred the woods, he says, "Have you ever tried killing someone on the street in broad daylight?"

"In the beginning," he says, "we only had 13 bodies. And then Pichushkin began to tell us that he'd killed more than 60 people." Pichushkin told him about the well, the sewage main—his entire M.O.—and Suprunenko began to understand the fates of all those people who had disappeared. "He wanted to talk," Suprunenko says. "All maniacs want to talk."

He remembers Pichushkin talking about killing people. They would sit there, in one of the holding cells, Suprenenko on one side, Pichushkin on the other, under a fluorescent light, smoking. Pichushkin would wander when he spoke, meandering in and out of his exploits, his life-takings. Suprenenko says he always stared at Pichushkin when Pichushkin was talking to him. "It made him feel important," he says. "I told him I admired him, and he liked that, and then he opened up. It was very important for Pichushkin that people think he was a hero, so I made him feel like a hero."

What emerged from months of questioning, months of plying Pichushkin with sandwiches and cigarettes and pretending that he was a brilliant, cunning evil genius—an artist, really—was not the supernatural Maniac everyone had imagined but a face-less quantity, someone no one could latch onto or read or organize into a tidy, psychological portrait. He was like peering into a glass darkly and trying to find some edifice or substrate, something real and easily explainable, something three-dimensional, with a clearly delineated character and personality, with tastes and preferences and ideas about things and people, God, art, beauty, the human quest for meaning—and finding nothing. It was this nothingness, this maddening air or space or darkness that fueled the shock and confusion—on Khersonskaya Street, where every-one knew Pichushkin, and across Russia and everywhere else. Dave Reichert, who was the lead detective and, later, sheriff on the Green River Killer investigation outside Seattle in the 1980s and 1990s, says the public's fascination with serial killers boils down to this inability on a fundamental, human level to under-stand them. "Nobody can figure them out," says Reichert, now a Republican congressman from Washington state. "How can we as normal human beings begin to comprehend that kind of be-havior. We never can answer that question."

ON OCTOBER 24, 2007, following his trial, Alexander Pichushkin was found guilty of murdering 48 people. Through-out the trial, he insisted that he'd actually killed 63 people—one victim shy of a complete chessboard but 10 people more than Andrei Chikatilo managed—but authorities could only muster evidence to prosecute Pichushkin for 48.

On October 29, Pichushkin was sentenced to life in prison. One week later, his attorney filed an appeal. Not long ago, he almost certainly would have been shot in the back of the head, the way executions happened in the Soviet Union, but Russia imposed a moratorium on the death penalty in 1996. The Bit-sevsky Maniac has prompted many politicians and talk-show hosts to call for bringing it back.

VALENTINE'S DAY, 2008. The Maniac is in a cell on a closed-caption television screen, laughing. Actually, there are five tele-vision screens—four medium-sized televisions, to the left and right, and one large plasma television hanging behind everyone. The Maniac envelopes his audience. We are in the recently renovated Supreme Court of Russia, on Povarskaya Street in the center of Moscow, and almost everyone is here: Natasha

Fyedosova, Pichushkin's lawyer, Pavel Ivannikov, the three judges, the prosecutor in his royal-blue, military-style uniform, the babushkas and younger men and the girls, in glasses, jeans, whispering into their cell phones, who lost somebody, who are scared to look too closely at the television screens filled with the face of the Maniac, who looks bored, amused, angry. He stares. He has long digits. He never looks directly at the video camera in his cell. He is talking to someone we can't see. With his black, button-down shirt and black T-shirt, and his hair, close-cropped, tussled, he looks almost fashionable. Then he stops laughing—he laughs infrequently and only for a second or two—and resumes staring. Beneath the stare is a grin, ironic, fleeting; the grin appears and disappears; it morphs into a frown, which morphs into a look of incredulity, which morphs into a stare. Now he is talking. The volume is turned low, and it's hard to make out what they're saying. Natasha Pichushkina is not here. Nor is Andrei Suprunenko. The television cameras and reporters circle round the families. There are one-thousand photographs being taken simultaneously—of the babushkas, eyes red, the courtroom, fluorescent-lit, with mauve wallpaper, a Russian tricolor behind the judges, the Maniac. The Maniac poses unwittingly in his television cage. "The Maniac in real time," says one of the cameramen.

Now one of the babushkas is saying, "Where is the body? Where is my body?" She is talking about her husband, who disappeared one night down a snowy path into the woods. The babushkas from Khersonskaya Street look scared in this place, which is steel, glass and marble. The judges ask Pichushkin if wants to say anything. Pichushkin utters three words during the whole proceeding: *Nyet, nyet, nyetuy.* "No, no, there's nothing." Pavel Ivannikov loosens his tie and says that even though his client has been convicted of some very heinous crimes, the judges should have mercy and reduce the sentence to 25 years. He says what he has to say.

The judges disappear into their chambers. Forty minutes later they reemerge and declare that the sentence stands. Pichushkin will never go free. Soon he will be moved from the jail in Moscow to a maximum-security prison in the north or maybe the Ural Mountains. They do not say where he will be sent to; this is the way they do things; only his mother will know, and she will not be able to see him often; it will be at least a one-night train ride away.

Now everyone is leaving the courtroom, and Pichushkin is putting his hands behind his back so someone we cannot see can handcuff him. He is disappearing. No one here will ever see him again. He is almost gone.

PETER SAVODNIK *has written for* The Atlantic, Harper's Magazine, GQ, Condé Nast Traveler, W, Time, The Washington Post, *the* Los Angeles Times, *and a slew of other venues. He was previously based in Moscow and now lives in New York. His first book, on Lee Harvey Oswald's two-and-a-half years in the Soviet Union, is slated to be published by Basic Books in 2011.*

Coda

Alexander Pichushkin sits in a prison somewhere far from Moscow—to the east, in a vast forest. Condemned to solitary confinement, he lives a life of total privation: he has no one to talk to, and no one to kill. Russian prisons are notoriously grim—tuberculosis, HIV, violence, and hunger are rampant—and it would not be surprising if he dies before too long.

Meanwhile, Pichushkin's mother, Natasha, is condemned to her own species of solitude. She still lives in the tiny, two-room apartment on Khersonskaya Street—where else would she go?—and everyone is still there: her grandson, Seriozh, and her daughter, Katya, and her daughter's husband, Sasha. But there is a great and immovable death in this apartment, which is already so small and cramped one can barely breathe. Her son will always be a part of this place, even though he is no longer her son exactly; he is now a monster, and no one can forget that ever. In case she tries to, there will always be her neighbors, many of whom lost sons and fathers to Pichushkin, all of whom know who she is. She is no longer Natasha Pichushkina. She is now and will always be the mother of the Bitsevsky Park Maniac.

I think about the apartment on Khersonskaya Street sometimes, and Natasha and Seriozh, who can barely remember his uncle by now. After our first meeting, Natasha gave me the pins her son used to collect when he was a little boy. For a while, I kept the pins in my apartment, in Moscow, and then, before I left Moscow, I shipped the pins back to New York, and now they're tucked away in a cardboard box in the back of my closet. Natasha gave me the pins, I imagine, because they remind her of someone she once loved very much. I keep them because they come from somewhere with a strange and terrible significance, and because I have no idea what to do with them.

THE GREAT BUFFALO CAPER

FROM *5280*

INSIDE A RUN-DOWN HOUSE reeking of weed, two dudes in their thirties and a lady who could've passed for older or younger anxiously scurried about, each throwing together an overnight bag. One of the men was fat and freckled with receding red hair, the other was thin and bony with a receding blond mullet; both of them were covered in tattoos. The lady was visibly pregnant. Finally packed, but clearly unprepared for much of anything, the three spilled from the house into a late-summer afternoon, piled into a clunker of a minivan, and wheeled off. Before leaving their hometown of Dayton, Ohio, they made a pit stop to score an ounce of pot and some cocaine, and then hit the highway, heading as far north as any of them likely had ever been. It was Monday, August 21, 2000, and the gang was bound for St. Johnsbury, Vermont—more specifically, bound for the Fairbanks Museum & Planetarium.

The freckled fat guy was James Boggs, but everyone called him "Boomer," short for "Boomer the Beast," which was ornately inked on his forearm. The house and minivan, a 1985 Chevy

Astro, were his. Only a few months earlier Boomer had finished a 10-and-a-half-year prison stretch for drug trafficking, and when he'd gotten out, as he recently told me, "My momma gave me two grand to get me a house and get me on my feet," and Boomer had applied his momma's scratch to purchasing the crib and modest ride. The skinny guy was Roger Dale Kinney. At the time, at least, he was Boomer's best bud, his "dawg," as Boomer puts it. They'd met on the inside. Kinney had been pinched on an aggravated assault. Doing time, they'd found they had the same interests: tattoos and drugs; and likewise, that they hated the same things: "colored" folk and prison. They'd become so tight that when Kinney got out, Boggs not only let his dawg move in with him, he also welcomed the dawgette, Kinney's lady, "Tish," who was due to give birth in four months.

After they got out of the joint, Boomer and Kinney had managed to land legitimate work, installing cable for the local Time Warner operation. The gig was something they did more to shut up their parole officers than to make money. As far as Boggs and Kinney were concerned, the only real paydays were the tax-free lump sums that came from illegal action. And in those endeavors the ex-cons had made a pact to "hit a lick" as partners. Boomer had been the one who'd met with the contact that hired him for this museum gig, but it was a given that Kinney would be in. Make no mistake, though, Boomer wasn't crazy about Kinney's lady tagging along, what with her being a pregnant chick and all. But Kinney had pointed out that Tish could be the getaway driver. Boomer said "fine," provided "she understands she don't get a cut."

Keeping with Boomer's plan, the gang drove straight through the night. Making only necessary food and fuel stops, they cracked wise about their incipient job. "We're on a buffalo hunt," Boomer said, laughing himself red-faced and adding, in his best TV Tonto voice, "We come to kill the great white buffalo." The joke got funnier as they got more and more stoned. Boomer and Kinney did the smoke-and-coke on the road trip, and as the minivan rolled into St. Johnsbury about 1 p.m. on Tuesday, August 22, some 20 hours after they'd left Ohio, they were sufficiently out of their minds. Yet they were not so far gone that they couldn't see that St. Johnsbury was just about the sleepiest scene in the universe. "I've never seen nothing like this except for on the TV," an awestruck Boomer said, gazing out of the minivan at the quaint storefronts and citizenry. "It's like Mayberry," he said. Boomer didn't even see any cops: "Where's Barney Fife?"

At last they came upon the Fairbanks Museum. Founded in 1889, the brownstone Victorian building sat atop a hill overlooking the town. Seeing it, Boomer got to thinking that this place might be too quiet for the likes of them to get inside, get to the buffalo, and get out without drawing attention. They parked nearby and Boomer got out alone, reached past his sagging beer belly into the pocket of his drooping pants, pulled out the admission fee, and went inside to case the joint. The Fairbanks was all wooden and musty, a two-floored, gorgeous, churchlike curiosity shop packed with display cases of oddities and artifacts, everything from textiles to taxidermy. Boomer saw the surveillance cameras, which his contact for the job had assured him would not be working. Boomer didn't see a single security guard. Near as he could figure, there weren't but maybe 10 people in the whole place. The floorboards creaked under Boomer's boots as he looked for his mark.

And then there it was: the skeleton of a massive bison. The bright white bones rendered a creature some 10 feet long and six feet tall, identified as the "Sacred Buffalo." Even Boomer could see it was a magnificent spectacle. It was positioned with head held high, as if the beast were alive and upon hearing Boomer's approach had raised its skull and snorted. Boomer moved right up close to the buffalo, eased himself alongside a couple of people who were looking at the thing the way he figured smart people who go to museums look at art. He saw the hundreds of tiny carvings in the bones. It was just like in the picture in that *Sacred Buffalo* book the contact had shown Boomer. All over every inch of the bones, even the tiniest ones, were etched scenes of tiny Indians doing Indian things.

Doing his best to be inconspicuous, Boomer surveyed the exhibit space. The best exit option was way in the back. *That's a pretty substantial run*, he thought. And what, he wondered, was outside that door? As the contact had described to Boomer, the Sacred Buffalo was in something akin to an open foyer on the first floor. Above, on either side of the display, were the second-floor balconies, also filled with pieces and open to the public. It wouldn't be a problem getting up there, and Boomer could see there were plenty of chairs. But the chairs appeared to be heavy, and the balcony was a good 20 or so yards removed from the Sacred Buffalo. It wasn't going to be an easy feat to accurately hurl a chair down on the thing. A dude would have to be pretty lucky to hit the Sacred Buffalo, let alone hit it so good that the chair would smash up the son of a bitch.

RUNNING HIS ART MART in the heart of Boulder, Rick Rippberger had seen all kinds of people walk into his store. Buyers, sellers, artists, browsers, they waltzed in buttoned-down or looking like hippie holdovers, some appearing not all that different than the street performers outside on Pearl Street. But Rippberger had never seen anybody like the man who strode into his place on that day in early 1994. The guy was about six-and-a-half feet tall, 250 pounds, muscular, with some of the broadest shoulders Rippberger had ever seen. The man's tan, weathered face was the face of an Indian, or at least Rippberger's idea of an Indian: high cheekbones, prominent nose, narrow, piercing eyes, a long ponytail. In between his cowboy boots and white cowboy hat he wore all denim, except for an oval-shaped belt buckle that might have weighed two pounds.

The man moseyed about the store's inventory—lots of sculptures and paintings of cowboys and Indians, horses, and more than a few buffalo—and then approached Rippberger. In the voice of an Indian, or at least in the slow cadence and understated tone Rippberger associated with Indians, the man introduced himself as the South Dakota–based artist James Durham. "Big Jim" is what folks called him. Art Mart was selling some buffalo-hide robes Durham had made, and he had come to discuss the pricing, wanted to make sure he was being fairly compensated. With that business handled, Big Jim said he had another piece that might interest Rippberger. Durham clarified: It was not a finished piece; rather, it was still just a "vision." Durham believed if he were able to complete the work, it would be spiritual and good and might well change the world. Only thing was, to realize the vision he needed financing. Intrigued by Big Jim, Rippberger invited him out for a meal to hear more.

Durham talked a bit about himself, said he was mixed-blood Indian and pureblood Vietnam veteran and biker. He spoke of his visions: One day, not so long ago, he and some Vietnam-veteran brothers he'd met in 1988 at the Vietnam Veterans Memorial in Washington, D.C., came together in a lodge back East to join in a sweat, that ancient American Indian ritual of purification, and to pray to the Creator for other veterans. Some of the vets brought their families; Durham's wife, son, and daughter came along. Reluctantly, Durham allowed his seven-year-old son, Nick, to join the vets in the lodge.

Midway through the sweat, as Big Jim told Rippberger and would later put in writing, his son passed out. When Nick awoke, he told his father he'd had a vision of his dad in a big green field, wearing buckskin clothes, hair below his belt, with bushy eyebrows. In the boy's dream, Durham had his *chanunpa*—a ceremonial pipe—in his left hand. He was standing on a prairie looking at millions of buffalo. The herd approached Durham and split, creating a path for one big bull buffalo that

walked right up to Durham and spoke to him. It was another
language, but Durham and this buffalo chatted for a while. As
Big Jim wrapped up the story of his son's dream: "Finally, [the
buffalo] started to walk away, but then he stopped. He turned
his head back and looked at [me]. He said something to [me] and
[I] nodded. Then he walked backed into the herd and just disappeared into the millions of them."

Rippberger would be the first to admit he's no expert on
American Indian culture. He grew up in Boulder and did well
financially as the owner-operator of a service station and Potter's
Restaurant. In time, Rippberger sold off the businesses and invested in real estate and other ventures, including the Art Mart,
which he co-owned and operated with his wife. Still, Rippberger knew enough about the Trail of Tears and the White
Man's role in it to feel sympathy, even a smidge of culpability. In
American Indian art, he saw mysticism and nobility and suffering. And so, in Boulder, a town of artsy, politically correct pro-
gressives, Big Jim couldn't have found a more receptive audience
than Rippberger, who was enthralled as Durham spoke of a second vision.

Not long after the sweat, Big Jim fell asleep and dreamed he
saw a buffalo skeleton standing in the middle of a big room with
a high ceiling and a wood floor. He noticed pictures carved onto
all of the bones. Then the buffalo skeleton turned and spoke.
"*Pilamayapelo,*" it said, meaning, "Thank you." When Big Jim
awoke, he told Rippberger, he picked up a sketchbook and drew
the scenes he had seen on the bones. They were the seven sacred
rites of the Lakota people, and a rendering of the Wounded Knee
Massacre and the Battle of the Little Bighorn. Suddenly, as Durham put it to Rippberger, the visions made sense: The Creator
wanted him to scrimshaw, or carve, all of the pictures he had
dreamed onto the skeleton of a buffalo, and to share the buffalo's
teachings, the Lakota tribe's religion, with the world.

Durham showed Rippberger the divinely inspired sketches

he'd done, and estimated it would cost about $30,000 to get the project going, with a few thousand dollars here and there afterward. Big Jim was confident that the finished piece would be a sought-after museum exhibit, and that the money from such a tour would repay Rippberger his initial investment and likely turn a profit. Rippberger was sold. It sounded like a chance to be a part of something "humanitarian" and maybe make some money. He liked the idea so much that he had an idea of his own. Rippberger wanted Big Jim to meet a friend, Peder Lund. The guy had an office in Boulder, across the street from Rippberger's old service station. Lund had money and knew a thing or two about promotion, as he was the owner of a unique publishing house, Paladin Press, which published books like *Hit Man: A Technical Manual for Independent Contractors* and *How to Become a Professional Con Artist.*

ONE MORNING LAST FALL, Peder Lund walked into the conference room of his Paladin headquarters and plopped a cardboard box on the table in front me. Stuck on the side of the box was a computer-generated shipping label that read: HOW TO MAKE $100,000 A YEAR AS A PRIVATE DETECTIVE. It was obviously a box that had once contained copies of that particular title his company had published, but was no longer used for that purpose; as Lund himself had written on it in black marker, the box now contained "Buffalo B.S." "It's all yours," he said, turning to leave, as if the box were a rotting cadaver. "Have at it. I'll be back in a while to see if you have any questions." A quick scan of the box's contents revealed a Buffalo LLC agreement; two art appraisal reports—one from 1997, another from 2000; a thick deposition transcript of James G. Durham in "Sacred Buffalo Inc. vs. Paladin Enterprises Inc."; and a handful of newspaper clippings with headlines like "Police try to flesh out attack on buffalo skeleton."

Rippberger first came to know Lund at the pump. Before Rippberger bought that gas station, he worked there. As a skinny kid with glasses, he would be manning the station and the handsome, curly haired Lund would drive up in whatever his latest sports car was. Lund and the kid would chat. Rippberger thought Lund had a pretty sweet life. "Some of the time when he'd come in on a Saturday morning," as Rippberger said to me recently, "it was hard to tell if he was starting his day or ending his Friday night." They'd pick up their conversation when they bumped into each other around town and became rather friendly. Rippberger's admiration for the dashing Lund grew as he learned that Mr. Nightlife had been a Green Beret in Vietnam, and had parlayed those interests into Paladin Press, a successful imprint specializing in books about weapons, defense, covert operations, and unusual (and sometimes illegal) professions.

Just as Rippberger had predicted, when he and Durham met with Lund, Lund indeed thought the scrimshawed buffalo sounded like a grand idea. Of course, as Rippberger had also figured, if not counted on, Lund had some ideas of his own for what was quickly becoming the Sacred Buffalo project. Paladin has published hundreds of titles, covering everything from jewelry to jihads. Regardless of the subject, virtually all of the books have had two things in common: a tantalizing subject and a pretty incredible story line. That's not to say the books were always well written. Being the shrewd former commando he was, it seemed Lund tried to find book material that was interesting on its face, at least to his audience, along with a paint-by-numbers plot, precisely so he wouldn't have to worry much about the writer lousing up Paladin's investment.

And so Lund liked the Sacred Buffalo project. There was this Durham character and his story, evidently intertwined with the legends of the American Indian, and—*and!*—soon there'd be the buffalo skeleton piece to behold. The three men agreed to Lund's plan of embedding a Boulder-based writer and a photographer with Durham to record the story of the project. The book, which would be entitled *Sacred Buffalo: The Lakota Way for a New Beginning*, would wrap up as the Sacred Buffalo masterpiece was completed, and would be sold concurrent with the buffalo's tour. Of course there would be a tour: museums, universities, wherever. The book would provide a revenue stream all on its own. At the very least, Paladin would sell some copies and generate buzz about Durham and the piece, which might enhance the lure and value of the Sacred Buffalo. After all, the people want to see something that's aesthetically striking, but they also want a story to go along with it.

Rippberger, Lund, and Big Jim formed the Buffalo LLC. Per the terms of the agreement, each had a 33 ⅓ percent share in any profits to be made from the buffalo. Meanwhile, the three struck a gentleman's operating agreement: Paladin would cover the cost of the book; Rippberger and Lund would fund Durham's construction of the Sacred Buffalo; and Durham would create the mystical work of art. And, as the artist and American Indian character he was, Big Jim would tour with the buffalo, sharing his visions with the public. All that was left was to get the scrimshawed buffalo built and get the magical, rolling bones show on the road.

"IN MY DREAM about the Sacred Buffalo," so goes the first sentence of the introduction to the Sacred Buffalo book coauthored by Durham, "I simply walked away at the end without saying a word." And it appears that after many years of talking to all kinds of lawyers and investigators about his buffalo, Big Jim indeed aims to walk away from it and say no more. Last fall, I reached Durham by phone. He suggested that if we were going to talk that we do it in person at his home in South Dakota, but my subsequent calls and e-mails to him in the hopes of scheduling the visit went unreturned. There is, however, the record Big Jim left behind in that 187-page book, chockablock with photographs, fabled history, visions, and dreams.

Once in business with his Boulder-based partners and patrons, Durham returned home to South Dakota and in the summer of 1994 set about his work. First things first: He needed a bison skeleton. Big Jim wrote in the book about his quest to find a worthy buffalo. Evidently, he lay in the middle of a herd of charging bison; he went into a cave and prayed over a rock that reminded him of a "human embryo," only to discover the rock "had been in the stomach of a dinosaur"; he had a staring contest with a buffalo he would have killed with his knife if his wife hadn't been with him. Finally, though, he simply bought a bull buffalo from a rancher. The buffalo was killed in an undisclosed manner. A buddy of his named Les Lutz skinned it, and Durham shipped the bones off to the Ohio State University veterinary school, known for assembling skeletons for museums. The faculty and students were so impressed by the story of Big Jim's visions that they agreed to spend some 780 hours on the process of preparing the bones free of charge.

It should be noted that scrimshawing is not a Native American tradition. It is a nautical art that began with whalers in the early 19th century. Initially, it was not considered art as much as it was a hobby. With time to kill at night, the men aboard ship would whittle designs on the ample supply of whalebones and teeth scattered about their vessels. In time, the handiwork became more sophisticated and a desired folk art. In *Moby-Dick*, Herman Melville refers to "lively sketches of whales and whaling-scenes, graven by the fishermen themselves on sperm whale-teeth. . . ." Big Jim had it in his mind to be the first to apply the tradition to bison bones and represent it as Native American.

A bull buffalo skeleton is comprised of some 180 bones. Even with orbital sanders and X-acto knives, realizing Big Jim's vision, which amounted to etching more than a thousand scenes on the bones, would be an undertaking. He needed a place to work; he needed help. Durham wrote that he searched high and low, traveling to Wyoming and Colorado, hoping for a studio like the one he'd seen in his dream. He ended up renting a dilapidated schoolhouse in the town of Whitewood, South Dakota. As far as Big Jim finding the chosen ones who would assist him in bringing the sacred piece to life, the Creator worked in mysterious ways. Down in Florida, where Big Jim had attended biker week in Daytona Beach, he recruited Harry Lindsay, a fellow Vietnam veteran. Lindsay claimed the boots on his feet were the same ones he wore in Nam, and because he fancied BMW motorcycles his pals called him "Beemer." It was also in Florida that the Great Spirit led Durham to Teri Krukowski, a striking middle-age biker babe and self-described "dancer," who in her spare time had taken up engraving the sort of items a biker babe–dancer would engrave: knives, guns, and motorcycles. Beemer joked that they ought to have T-shirts made with the slogan, "Among the Wretched Ones."

Big Jim, Teri, and Beemer not only worked together in the schoolhouse, engaged in the painstaking and meticulous work of sanding, engraving, and coloring the bones on makeshift desks of plywood on sawhorses; they also lived there together. Durham likened the close quarters to what he and Beemer had experienced in the military. Similarly, there was no mistaking the chain of command: Big Jim was the general, or rather the general-chaplin-shaman-cult-leader-in-chief. He made sure that every day they burned purifying sage and shared the *chanunpa* pipe. He encouraged them to stay spiritually focused and to refrain from cussing. He led house meetings. Smoking Marlboros and drinking shots of espresso, he preached and inspired. Durham had sketched out precisely what scenes he wanted on each bone, and when Teri was carving the "*wiyakas*" on the bison's ribs Durham asked if she knew what they were. She did not. Big Jim explained: "They're all about spirit. Each of them represents a person, 163 people. As I look at each one, I think about a different person I've known. The *wiyakas* each have individuality; they're fat or thin, crooked, each is unique. Like people are."

STANDING ON THE OPEN SOUTH DAKOTA plains, surrounded by hundreds of Indians and tepees, Rick Rippberger watched Big Jim dance around a towering cottonwood tree. The summer sky was clear and the sun was strong. Yet Durham and other Indian men danced around the cottonwood for hours in the blistering heat, chanting what sounded like ancient prayers in ancient repetitive rhythms. Rippberger watched as Durham pierced hooks through his chest flesh; the hooks were attached to long ropes that dangled from the top of the cottonwood. After more time spent dancing and chanting, Big Jim gradually leaned back with hooks in his chest pulling taut the ropes. Farther and farther he leaned back, arms outstretched, the ropes pulling tighter, blood trickling from the pierced holes in his chest, until the massive man's back was nearly parallel with the ground. The hooks snapped loose, flesh ripped, Big Jim stumbled backward, and the hooks were jerked all the way to the very top of the tree and stuck there.

It was the summer of 1994, and with the Sacred Buffalo project under way, Durham had invited Rippberger out to the Pine Ridge Reservation to witness a Sun Dance, a sacred, communal ritual of Great Plains Indians. In the language of the Lakota, the dominant tribe on the Pine Ridge Reservation, the Sun Dance is "*wiwanyag wachipi*," meaning, "dance looking at the sun." Orchestrated by tribes annually in the summer, the Sun Dance is a days-long series of rituals that draws thousands of Indians, who camp, pray, dance, sacrifice, and celebrate together. The buffalo looms large over the Sun Dance as an important symbol, as the great *tatanka* had long been a source of tools, weapons, food, clothing, and therefore inspiration for the American Indians of the Plains. At the literal and ceremonial center of the Sun Dance is a large wooden pole or tree, which serves as something of an altar. Indian men and women dance around it until exhausted, as a form of sacrifice to the Creator, whom they hope will grant them visions and enlightenment. Some men tether themselves to the center pole, as Durham had done, to show a willingness to suffer for the Creator. For similar reasons, some men hook a buffalo skull to their chest and drag it with them as they chant prayers.

Rippberger considered it an honor to have been invited. So that he could come bearing gifts, on the way from Boulder he had purchased dozens of colorful blankets and some 400 pounds of buffalo meat, hauled out in a freezer. He was overwhelmed by the sight of the Sun Dance camp on the massive, open fields. On the prehistoric-looking plains, he spotted hundreds of tepees, tents, campers, and people camped with only sleeping bags and cardboard. At the perimeter of the camp, Rippberger had been stopped by Indians who wanted to know why the White Man was here. As the jittery art dealer tried to explain, Beemer appeared and informed the Indians the guy was with Jim Durham. The Indian men stepped aside. Beemer, who was on foot, directed Rippberger to drive behind him and to positively not veer off course or else pale face might quickly find himself in hostile territory.

Rippberger noticed there was a hierarchy to the camp: Those with the sleeping bags on the outer reaches were the poorest and least influential Indians. The trailers and tents got bigger as he approached the center; these were the Indians of means and power. And this is where Beemer set up Rippberger, among the chiefs and their families, close to the Sun Dance pole, the towering cottonwood. Rippberger noted that Durham indeed must have ranked high on the totem, and then watched Big Jim do his awesome Sun Dance.

Durham writes plenty about himself in *Sacred Buffalo*, but doesn't offer much autobiographical information. He describes himself as a mixed-blood American Indian, but beyond that it's unclear what his heritage is. He wrote that one of his grandfathers was named George Poor Thunder and the other was called Fools Crow. He reveals that he has known "Dr. Bob," meaning that he was a recovering alcoholic, and that he was not a classically trained artist. "[I] got kicked out of art class in seventh grade because I wouldn't draw fruit." He married a woman named Beth, who was in the Navy, and had two children, Nick, and a girl, Crystal. What autobiographical shreds Durham shares in *Sacred Buffalo* are wrapped in visions and profound religious experiences, like the Sun Dance.

After his dance that day in the summer of 1994, Big Jim told Rippberger it was of great significance that his hooks flew to the top of the tree and stuck. It meant the Creator had accepted the Sacred Buffalo, that it was blessed. Shortly thereafter, however, Rippberger and Lund came to think the thing was cursed. Four months became six months, then eight months, and Big Jim and his crew still had not finished the Sacred Buffalo, and they kept asking the Boulder White Men for more and more money. It's unclear how much Big Jim paid Beemer and Teri. Ostensibly the Boulder bankroll was to cover the salaries, food, and rent. But when it was close to a year in, and Rippberger and Lund had invested approximately $30,000 apiece, their financial benevolence began to waver. There were heated telephone exchanges over cash flow. One especially tense moment occurred when the bank called to inform Durham that a Buffalo LLC check supposed to cover the rent for the studio hadn't arrived. Big Jim threw down the phone, and, almost directly quoting from the movie *Top Gun*, said to Beemer, "His mouth is writing checks his ass can't cover."

IN THE SUMMER OF 1995, more than a year since the project had begun, Durham at last gazed upon the completed masterpiece. It was just as he had seen in one of his many visions: He sat on a chair in a room of wooden floors with a high ceiling, alone with his buffalo (alone, that is, except for his *Sacred Buffalo* book coauthor and a photographer). And Big Jim spoke. Moved by the mighty bison he had created, Durham proclaimed, "Power like this hasn't been seen in a long time. It'll flat-out walk tomorrow. It'll walk around the world."

The Sacred Buffalo's inaugural tour wasn't quite the globetrot Durham and the LLC imagined. Lund had hired his ex-wife, Marsha Lund, to handle the tour and marketing. Marsha had met Lund one night in a Boulder bar, and they ended up married for 10 years. She collected silver and turquoise Native American–inspired jewelry, and considered herself an expert. She wrote a book on the subject for Paladin, which, Lund and his ex determined, gave her some frame of reference to spearhead the Sacred Buffalo run. Initially Marsha felt encouraged by the interest in the buffalo. She thought she had the prestigious Field Museum in Chicago on tap. But, as she recently told me, "Jim insisted on getting on the phone with them, and the next thing I know the lady there calls me back and says she's changed her mind." The tour that did come together began in the winter of 1995 with a one-month exhibit at CAM-PLEX Heritage Center Art Gallery in Gillette, Wyoming, with at least six stops thereafter at similarly modest venues, including a five-day stint at the South Dakota State Penitentiary.

With the Sacred Buffalo roaming such sites, the tensions among the LLC partners intensified. Boxes of *Sacred Buffalo* books went out, as Lund and Rippberger recall, but the total sales revenue for them did not come back. And although Rippberger and Lund believed they were sending checks to cover Durham's expenses to travel with the piece and appear at the venues, Big Jim would call them from the road and say he needed more. The Boulder financiers grew more frustrated, especially because, Rippberger and Lund say, they were covering expenses they hadn't counted on. One day, Lund says, he got a call from Big Jim, who said he needed some money because he was behind in child-support payments; if Durham didn't pay he was going to lose his driver's license and possibly be arrested. "At that point," Lund says, "we were well into the project, and if Durham couldn't travel it would have been over. So I paid him a few thousand dollars for a buffalo-hide robe he'd made. Every time you talked to him, he needed money."

Meanwhile, Durham was growing exasperated himself, although with a different view of the LLC. Big Jim saw his Boulder partners as perpetuating the history of the White Man welching on deals made to Indians. Big Jim was of the opinion that his investors were shirking their end of the deal. As Durham would later say in the media and to attorneys, he'd call the guys in Boulder and tell them he was having to crash on couches and even sleep on the floor of a bar because Lund and Rippberger weren't sending the checks they'd promised. Rippberger, for one, was tired of it all. "I know I was at a point where I didn't care what happened to that buffalo," he says. "I didn't care if I ever saw it again. I just wanted to be done with Jim Durham."

Lund clearly still cared. In May of 1997, just before the final two stops on the buffalo's road trip—the University of Central Florida and the Fairbanks Museum in Vermont—he had the Sacred Buffalo appraised. He hired Bernard Ewell, at the time a Colorado Springs–based art appraiser, to provide the information the Buffalo LLC might need to make decisions about rental fees at museums, a possible sale price, and insurance. Ewell is a self-described Salvador Dalí expert, and he refers to himself as "the Dalí Detective." Regardless of the assignment, however, he promises, "I'll always be up-front and unflinching in my evaluations of the players and their actions."

In his Sacred Buffalo appraisal report, Ewell noted that the task of determining a value was difficult because there were no comparables for a buffalo skeleton scrimshawed with Native

American religion and history. A senior member of the American Society of Appraisers, Ewell stated that his methodology "is not based on a formula of calculation. It is simply the value which was given to me spiritually while I meditated before the Sacred Buffalo on March 12." So inspired, Ewell put the fair market value of the piece at $770,000. However, provided with touring and revenue information as articulated by Lund, Ewell upped that assessment considerably. Lund informed Ewell that the LLC had been paid $15,000 and $20,000 in rental fees by at least two of the venues that had rented it. Based on those numbers, the Dalí Detective theorized that at "5 venues a year @ $25,000," multiplied by 10 years, the piece might be worth an additional $1.25 million.

WHEN JAMES "BOOMER THE BEAST" Boggs finished casing the Fairbanks and returned to the minivan, pregnant Tish was bellied up to wheel. Boomer directed her to cruise around back, behind the museum, as close as she could get to that back door he'd seen from inside. Tish couldn't get that close. Between the van and the door were a good-size parking lot and then a hillside of trees. Boomer announced plain and simple he wasn't going to do it. More like he couldn't do it. Never mind the challenges inside, Boomer said, "What's gonna happen is, I'm going to have to run 250 yards. There's no way I can do it and not get caught and [not] have a heart attack." This didn't sit well with Kinney. "Well, I didn't fuckin' come all this way for nothing," he told Boomer. "I'll do it." Just like that, Kinney shouldered open the van door and the blond mullet was out of sight.

It was about 2 p.m. on that Tuesday, August 22, 2000, when Tish put the van in park. She and Boomer waited. Boomer anxiously pumped his leg. Truth of the matter is, Boomer's an easily rattled guy. On at least one occasion, he described himself as "getting more nervous than a cat shitting razor blades." Imagine how he'd have felt if he'd known the St. Johnsbury police department was only two tiny blocks from the museum. A few long minutes later, the museum back door swung open, and damned if that stickman Kinney didn't come bounding out, running and stumbling through the trees, down the hill, and through the cars in the lot. He breathlessly yanked open the minivan door and jumped in. Tish and Boomer sat there, uncertain of what had happened or didn't happen. They watched as Kinney slammed shut the door and immediately turned to puke out the open window, only the window wasn't open. Dawg ended up vomiting all over the interior of Boomer's Astro. Which, considering the circumstances, Boomer let slide.

Tish and Boomer sat there all catatonic-like until Kinney looked up with one of those well-what-in-the-hell-are-you-waiting-for expressions, and between pants and gags, shouted, "Go! Go! Go!!!!!" Tish punched the gas and then slowed to a meander, driving out through the center of St. Johnsbury like she and the boys were on their way to the local Ben & Jerry's for some Chunky Monkey. No one said anything for about an hour, until they realized that they weren't being followed. Boomer then made the call to the contact, told him it was done. The voice on the other end of the phone, said, "Are you kidding me? Man, you're fucking crazy. That's great." The gang drove straight through the night back to Ohio, now joking, "We killed the great white buffalo," high on adrenaline and the promise of big money.

Thus far, the contact had fronted Boggs only $500 for "traveling expenses"—most of that had gone to the dope and coke—and now they were expecting the agreed-upon payday of $25,000, which Boomer would split with Kinney. All the way home, Kinney kept nagging Boomer, "I want my cut right now." And Boomer kept telling Kinney, "Look, dawg, I'm going to take care of you. We're gonna get paid." When the gang got home, as Boomer puts it, he went to meet with the contact to get paid and was more than a little disappointed: "He gave me four pounds of pot and $1,000. And I was like, 'What the fuck is this? Where's the rest of my money?' And he was like, 'Look Boomer, I just don't have liquid cash that I can give you right now.' He knew I'm a killer, that if you fuck with me you better bring your lunch, and so he's like, 'If you work with me—I mean this is a gift—just work with me and I'll give you the twenty-five. But we gotta wait until insurance money comes through.'"

ARMED WITH THE DALÍ DETECTIVE'S APPRAISAL, Lund obtained an insurance policy for the Sacred Buffalo, covering the piece for up to $1.25 million. In addition, each venue that hosted the Sacred Buffalo provided its own insurance coverage for the piece while it was on display in their care. And because the hit on Durham's creation occurred under the watch of the Fairbanks, it was that museum's policy alone that would be on the hook for the damage. The Fairbanks' insurance on the Buffalo was handled by a company called Acadia Insurance, which, in the weeks following the August 2000 hit, promptly put a claims adjuster on the case. The Acadia investigator was a seasoned professional with more than 15 years' experience, and was primarily responsible for handling cases in the million-dollar range. Although the investigator has since left Acadia for a new insurance firm, he remembers the case well. He remembers it so well that when we recently spoke about the Sacred Buffalo he asked that his name not be used because, he said, "I have a wife and kids, and you're talking about some serious bad guys involved here."

So this "Mr. Acadia" was on the case, finding that the only information the police department could provide at the time, according to Police Chief Richard Leighton, was that a skinny guy covered in tattoos was seen running out of the museum. After all, the Fairbanks ain't exactly the Louvre. And it turned out the intelligence Boomer had received from his evidently well-informed contact about the nonfunctional security cameras was dead-on. In the local press, Big Jim said his best guess as to who was responsible was zealous Christians who rejected American Indian spirituality. Durham didn't have any more answers for the insurance investigator, but Mr. Acadia did receive a copy of Ewell's appraisal report. In his talks with Mr. Acadia, Durham said that there was no point in discussing whether it was possible to repair the Sacred Buffalo because "its spirit had been broken."

Mr. Acadia was suspicious of the values the Dalí Detective had placed on the piece while he had "meditated before the Sacred Buffalo." Likewise, he didn't buy the Christian theory, or, for that matter that the random act of vandalism was random. Mr. Acadia hired his own expert to give an appraisal of the broken buffalo, and meanwhile contracted a private investigator to see what he could find. The PI was Ken Springer of New York–based Corporate Resolutions Inc., which specializes in high-value insurance fraud matters. Based on Corporate Resolutions' legwork, according to Mr. Acadia and Springer, they believed the Sacred Buffalo caper was a scam, and that if any of the Buffalo LLC players was involved in busting up the bison and hoping to collect on an insurance-policy payout, it was most likely Durham. In addition to the alleged back child-support payment situation Lund had described, Springer determined that Big Jim was in financial straits, the details of which the PI would not disclose to me. Nevertheless, Springer told Mr. Acadia, he didn't have proof of a connection.

On November 12, 2000, the expert Acadia hired to examine the damaged bison skeleton and estimate what it would cost to repair the buffalo submitted her findings. Lisa Kronthal was no Dalí Detective, but she was a conservator at the American Museum of Natural History. She examined the buffalo on October 27, two months after the crime, near Columbus, Ohio, where

Beemer and Durham had retreated with the damaged piece. She determined that the buffalo had suffered "significant damage," and that even if repaired it would "never be as strong as it was originally." Kronthal wrote, "It was found after speaking in depth with the artist that although he believes the buffalo has lost all spiritual value, he recognizes that it retains significant historical value. Mr. Durham feels the buffalo should be brought back to an exhibitable state." In the detailed report, which reads like a medical autopsy and breaks down the bone-by-bone cost for repairs, Kronthal came up with a cost of roughly $210,000.

Provided with Kronthal's findings, Mr. Acadia entered into a months-long series of settlement negotiations with the Buffalo LLC and with Durham personally, and, finally, sent the LLC a settlement check for $456,000. "As much as society likes to believe insurance companies like to get out of making payment," Mr. Acadia says, "it's actually a lot easier to make payments than it is to get out of them. That's a fact. Unless you've got [concrete evidence of fraud] or you're a really bad insurance company, you're going to pay the claim and move on. That's how it works. [Our investigator] was like, we know [Durham] did it, but we don't have enough to give you to sink your teeth into. As soon as things started to develop that way, it was obvious that we felt that way. We let [Durham's lawyer] know. Communications with Durham didn't exist after the check was sent. The check was another issue."

Indeed, the check was another issue. From that $456,000 settlement, Lund and Rippberger each took $193,000; they sent Durham the remaining $70,000 and told him he could keep the once Sacred and now broken Buffalo.

Fairborn, Ohio, detective Andy Kindred couldn't believe what he'd just heard. It was March 2001, and a fat, freckled dude just busted with three pounds of pot was giving him some whack-a-doodle story about smashing up some buffalo bones in Vermont six months ago. "I was like, you've got to be shitting me,"

Kindred told me recently. "So I picked up the phone and called the St. Johnsbury P.D., and got Chief Richard Leighton on the phone, and he goes, 'No, that happened. You got the guy? I'll be damned.'"

Boomer had found himself across the table from Detective Kindred that day because, thanks to an informant's tip, the Fairborn police had raided Boomer's home, where he was now living with his girlfriend, Angie. Behind the house, police found a plastic bag in a tree with three pounds of marijuana. "It's not hers," Boomer had blurted. "She don't know nothing about it. It's mine." Possession of three pounds legally implied intent to distribute, and considering Boomer's record, such a conviction would be enough to put him inside for a long time. And faced with the possibility of going away (again) for a long stint, Boomer figured he could strike a deal by providing Sacred Buffalo information.

See, Kinney was no longer Boomer's dawg. First off, Kinney had insulted Boomer's new girlfriend. "Angie had been with a colored man before me," Boomer explained to me. "She had a mixed baby. And Roger was like a big-time racist. I mean, I don't like colored kids either, but that baby didn't have nothing to do with it. So me and him fell out about that." What's more, the contact for the buffalo job never did pay up. And so Boomer decided to tell Detective Kindred everything he knew about the buffalo and more in exchange for a lighter sentence. Boomer revealed the contact for the Sacred Buffalo hit: He swore up and down that it was a dude named Johnny Decker.

In a tape-recorded statement to Kindred, Boomer described himself and Kinney as "the Apple Dumpling Gang," and stated that when this Decker hired him for the job, "he told me that the artist [was his] brother. He told me a couple of times that he'd been to South Dakota. He never told me why." Kindred asked Boomer if he'd ever heard the artist's name. Boomer said, "He showed me a picture of him that was in a book. I don't know if he said his name or not. . . . All I know is [he said] the artist was his brother and that's the one that made the buffalo. . . . Evidently the buffalo was on its last leg. It wasn't a major attraction anymore. It went through the circuit and was about to be retired. There wasn't going to be any money made on it. And supposedly this artist had a deal . . . some type of insurance deal that if anything would ever happen to the buffalo, all proceeds would go to some Indian kids on a reservation. Now this is the story he told me."

Within a matter of weeks, Ohio police officers raided Kinney's house. They found a bunch of gas grills that had been stolen and found the dawg hiding in a bedroom closet. Kinney confirmed Boomer's version of events to law enforcement, to Acadia, and also to the court, as both men pleaded no contest to felony burglary for their roles in the Sacred Buffalo hit. Kinney served 12 months, with his four- to eight-year sentence suspended in exchange for his cooperation with the investigation. And because Boomer had agreed to provide information about the buffalo, along with other, unrelated criminal investigations, he did only 120 days in prison, with his sentence of four to eight years suspended. (According to Detective Kindred, information he received during the buffalo case helped solve a missing-person case.) When Boomer got out of the Vermont prison, with some assistance from Kindred, Boomer worked on getting straight. He and Angie had a baby of their own. But Boomer gave in to his drug addiction and got arrested trying to rob a gas station with a knife. When we spoke last fall, Boomer was on the front end of a three-year sentence in Ohio at the Warren Correctional Institution.

Although Boomer agreed to testify against Johnny Decker in any future criminal proceedings related to the Sacred Buffalo caper, there weren't any future criminal proceedings. According to Mr. Acadia, lawyers once involved in the case, law enforcement in Ohio, and Boomer, it just so happened that this Decker fellow was in business with the FBI. The way Boomer puts it,

Decker was a "federal informant." The way the now-retired Detective Andy Kindred puts it, Decker "did a lot of work for the FBI" knocking around Ohio and Indiana and associating with motorcycle gangs as a tipster, and the Feds determined that wherever Decker was or wasn't, and regardless of whatever role he did or did not play in the Sacred Buffalo job, he was too valuable to get caught up in it. In other words, whoever planned the Sacred Buffalo caper and hired Decker to be the middleman was either dumb lucky or a master of the scam.

APPARENTLY UNCONCERNED ABOUT Boomer and Kinney, in 2002 Big Jim filed suit against Lund and Rippberger, arguing that he should have received a third of the insurance settlement. He claimed that, according to the LLC agreement, any profit from the Sacred Buffalo was to be equally divided three ways. Lund and Rippberger countered successfully by claiming their agreement established that all profits would be split three ways, provided the two financiers first recouped their investment plus a 100 percent return on their investment, which was equal to the $193,000 each took out of the Acadia payment. In memos to a Buffalo LLC lawyer on the matter, Lund instructed the attorney to fight Big Jim's suit because it was "ridiculous." On principle, as Lund put it, he told his attorney not to settle. The case dragged on into March 2004, when Lund's attorney deposed Durham. Well into the hours-long deposition, Durham took it upon himself to solicit a settlement.

"I want two cows, 40 blankets," he said. In the flow of the transcript, the opposing counsel is clearly stunned and attempting to collect his thoughts when he says, "Let me write this down." Durham's own lawyer then asks his client, "Are you serious about this?" To which Durham replies: "You're damn right I'm serious. . . . Two cows, breeding cows. That means breeding stock, male, female. Two cows, 40 Pendleton blankets. Good

ones. . . . Two chain saws for Sun Dance to cut our arbor down
so we can dance, and half the money they took over what they
had coming. Forty blankets, 65,000 bucks, two chain saws, and
two cows. Any thief would take that. I ain't paying your attorney's fees. I will go to hell first. . . . I'll walk away. You can
make fun of us forever." Lund and Rippberger's attorney rejected the offer, and shortly thereafter the case withered away.

Rick Rippberger no longer has anything to do with the Art
Mart in Boulder. He's divorced from his wife and thereby
divorced from the business. After he got his piece of the Acadia
payment, he deferred to Lund on the business of the lawsuit
Durham had filed against them; nor did Rippberger closely follow the news of Boomer and Kinney. Until we spoke in a Denver coffee shop last fall, he says, he'd never even heard the name
Johnny Decker. "I didn't even know who he was," Rippberger
said. He had on aviator-style glasses with lenses tinted a rose
color, which seemed uniquely suited for his worldview. Visibly
frustrated, he took off the glasses. "You know what this did for
me? I mean, I'm that type of guy that trusts everybody, all right?
And with this whole thing, and as far as Native Americans, I
have the worst taste of Native Americans in my mouth."

In the *Buffalo* book, Durham wrote "There's another old saying. 'It's not for sale.' I wish that were true of religion. People
without any real spiritual knowledge try to run a sweat lodge—
or a vision quest—for a fee. They learn to sing a couple of songs
and to go through the motions and then they offer to run sweats
for people who will pay the price. The people who pay have no
idea how much preparation and prayer goes into running a real
sweat lodge ceremony, or that the adviser for a vision quest must
be spiritually responsible for them. At best, the people who pay
to go to a sweat lodge just waste their time and money; at worst,
they can be hurt bad. Unlike religion, true spirituality isn't for
sale." But as far as Durham was concerned, the Sacred Buffalo
was for sale.

Big Jim restored the Sacred Buffalo, or, hell, who knows, maybe he had the Sacred Buffalo restored. In any case, the buffalo was put into exhibitable form. And in January 2002, while Boggs and Kinney were coming as clean as they could to authorities, and Rippberger and Lund were fending off Durham's suit, Big Jim sold the Sacred Buffalo. An acquisitions director for an international museum chain, Edward Meyer, bought the piece. When I spoke with Meyer on the phone this fall, he wouldn't disclose how much he'd paid for it, but he said it was the third most expensive purchase he'd ever made in the 30 years he's been in the business. He would say that the priciest piece he's ever bought, which was a matter of public record, was a makeup case once owned by Marilyn Monroe, which Meyer purchased for $265,000.

Before we hung up, Meyer mentioned that the buffalo wasn't the only thing he bought from Durham. He also purchased a human skeleton nailed to a crucifix. What makes the human skeleton piece even more interesting, and controversial, and therefore attractive to Meyer, is that on the bones, every inch of the bones, Durham had scrimshawed scenes from the Bible. "To this day," Meyer says, "I would say it's the most controversial piece in our collection. And we have some 25,000 items. His work is spectacular. The crucifix is beautifully woodworked, and the scrimshaw is incredible. He has told the New Testament and Acts of the Apostles, but from an Indian viewpoint based on his religious upbringing, I guess, in missionary schools. Visually, it is disturbing. People don't see skeletons hanging on crosses. It's a one-of-a-kind." Meyer says the human skeleton exhibit is on display at his venue in London, England, and that as of just last year the Sacred Buffalo could be seen at his museum in San Antonio, Texas. Oh, of course, the name of the international exhibition and museum operation Meyer oversees: It is Ripley's Believe It or Not!

As the executive editor of Denver's city magazine, 5280, MAXIMIL-
LIAN POTTER *writes or edits many of that monthly's narrative and investigative features. His bylined work has earned honors including two
National Magazine Award nominations for Public Interest and Reporting; the American Bar Association's top prize for legal reporting, the
Silver Gavel; and a prestigious Michael Kelly Award selection, recogniz-
ing "the fearless pursuit and expression of truth." Since he has been
executive editor,* 5280 *has earned four National Magazine Award nominations. Potter, thirty-eight, lives in Denver with his (patient) wife and
two sons. He has been a staff writer at* Premiere, Philadelphia, *and*
GQ *magazines. This is the second time Potter's work has been anthologized in* The Best American Crime Reporting.

Coda

"Evergreen" is one of those journalistic terms used to describe a
topic believed to have enduring relevance. The circumstances
that became "The Great Buffalo Caper" presented as such. Which
is why when a former magazine editor and good pal, Christo-
pher Connelly, tipped me to the mystery some six years ago, I
figured I had time to get to it. Sure, enough, the characters and
crime at the heart of the darkly comedic saga were still very
much *animated.* As my editor for this story, Geoff Van Dyke,
put it, the whole thing was like something straight out of a Coen
Brothers film. And so it remains: Nearly a year after the story
was published in *5280,* a man contacted me wanting to know if
the "Caper" was, in fact, true. I assured him it was and inquired
as to why. The man explained that "Big Jim" was the organizer
behind a cross-country motorcycle race. He explained that
Big Jim was billing the thing as the "Hoka Hey," a *Cannonball
Run*–style contest that would begin in Key West, Florida, and
end some 7,000 miles later in Homer, Alaska. There, the winner,

according to the race's promotional materials, will receive a "HALF MILLION DOLLARS in ALASKAN GOLD." (The caps, it should be noted, are *not* mine.) The gentleman on the phone said he'd read the rules of entry; it appeared the $1,000 registration fee was nonrefundable; and, the man said, he doubted the legitimacy of the race. Making clear I had no knowledge of the intriguing competition I could only offer my opinion that the man's suspicions seemed well founded to me. For what it's worth, the Hoka Hey was originally scheduled for August 2009, but it was "delayed" and rescheduled for Summer 2010, if you want in.

Ernest B. Furgurson

THE MAN WHO SHOT
THE MAN WHO
SHOT LINCOLN

FROM *The American Scholar*

For there are some eunuchs, which were so born from their mother's womb; and there are some eunuchs, which were made eunuchs of men; and there be eunuchs, which have made themselves eunuchs for the kingdom of heaven's sake. He that is able to receive it, let him receive it.

—MATTHEW 19:12

ONE MORNING IN SEPTEMBER, 1878, a tired traveler, five feet four inches tall, with a wispy beard, arrived at the office of the daily *Pittsburgh Leader*. His vest and coat were a faded purple, and his previously black pants were gray with age and wear. As he stepped inside, he lifted a once fashionable silk hat to disclose brown hair parted down the middle like a woman's. Despite the mileage that showed in his face and clothes, he was well-kept, and spoke with clarity. He handed the editor a note from an agent at the Pittsburgh rail depot, which said: "This will introduce to you Mr. Boston Corbett, of Camden, N.J., the avenger of Abraham Lincoln. Mr. Corbett is rather bashful, but at my solicitation he concluded to call on the *Leader* editor as an old soldier."

The newspaperman realized that this was no joke. He remembered the photographs of this man, spread across the North after he shot the assassin John Wilkes Booth thirteen years earlier, in April 1865. He invited him to sit and talk. Corbett told him that he was homeless, almost penniless, and headed to Kansas to stake a claim. The railroad agent had suggested that he come to the newspaper to tell his story, on the chance that someone would help him on his way.

Asked what had happened since he entered history by shooting Booth that early morning in Virginia, Corbett said that despite his fame, he had nothing. The photographer Mathew Brady had taken his portrait, and published it by the thousands, but all the hero got in return was a few copies. He had worked at his trade of hat finisher in New York, then lived in Camden while employed in Philadelphia. He showed the editor his credentials as a guard at the great Philadelphia Centennial Exposition of 1876. Now his luck had run out. He lost his job in Philadelphia and could not find work, so decided to head for wide-open Kansas, determined to get there if he had to walk. So far he had paid $4.21 for rail fare, but come on foot much of the way to Pittsburgh. That morning he had sought out the local manager of the Pennsylvania Railroad, without success. He was going back that afternoon.

The editor of the *Leader* did not say how long they talked, or record how much Corbett told him about his earlier life. But Corbett was always willing to tell how he got his name:

Born in London in 1832, he came to America with his family when he was seven. They settled in Troy, New York, where he learned the hat trade, soon becoming a journeyman and taking his skills to other cities around the East. The beaver hats then so much in style were made of animal furs matted and repeatedly washed in a solution containing mercury nitrate, a process called carroting because it turned the fur a distinct shade of orange. Hat finishers like Corbett labored in close quarters, inhaling vapors laden with mercury. A year after he married, his young wife died with their stillborn daughter. He was despondent, and began wandering, working by day and drinking by night. Adrift in Boston, he underwent a born-again experience inspired by a Salvation Army evangelist. He felt a calling. It shook his life so profoundly that he decided to change his name to honor the place where he first saw the light, as Christ had changed the names of Saul and Simon when he called them. Since then his first name had been not Thomas, but Boston.

There was much more to his story: In Boston, he let his hair grow long in imitation of Jesus, became a street-corner preacher, and harangued his fellow workers for cursing and wenching. But the streets were still full of sin, and he was young, only twenty-six, and lonesome. One night in July, two women mocked him and beckoned him down from his soapbox. He was tempted. Fearful that he could not resist such strumpets, he went to his room, took a pair of scissors and carefully castrated himself. Then he proceeded to a prayer meeting, had dinner and took a walk before seeking emergency aid at Massachusetts General Hospital.

In his own mind, he had done as the Bible said: he had made himself a eunuch for the kingdom of heaven's sake. He said years later that he felt divinely instructed; he wanted to "preach the gospel without being tormented by animal passions." The grisly experience may have removed him from sexual temptation, but the rest of his life proves that it did not remove his manhood.

After weeks recovering, he moved to New York and became a loud and constant presence at the Fulton Street Meeting, a lunchtime prayer gathering in lower Manhattan, organized by the Young Men's Christian Association. He was too fervent for his co-worshipers, who called him a fanatic. When he testified or led prayers, he added an emphatic "er" to his words, saying

"Lord-er hear-er our prayer-er. . . ." In his loud, shrill voice, he shouted "Amen" and "Glory to God!" to approve anything he liked. Those around him tried to shush him, but failed.

Corbett was living in this emotional fever when war came in 1861, and he enlisted in the Twelfth New York Volunteers two days before the regiment sailed for Washington. He was eager to get at the Rebels: "I will say to them, 'God have mercy on your souls'—then pop them off." Morning and night, he prayed in the corner of his tent, despite the jeers of rough fellow soldiers. His resistance to military authority, to any authority below that of Christ, got him into the guard-house, and sometimes had him marching back and forth with a knapsack full of bricks. Even then he kept his Bible in hand, ranting at his comrades for their sins.

He was not afraid of the highest brass; in parade formation in Washington's Franklin Square, when colonel and future general Daniel Butterfield cursed the regiment for misbehavior, Corbett stepped forth and defied him to his face. He was punished, but not repressed. He announced that he would quit the army when his first hitch was up, no matter what. When the hour came, he was on picket duty, but laid down his weapon and marched off. A court martial fined him two months pay, yet he kept reenlisting. The Twelfth New York was among the 12,500 Union troops captured, then paroled by Stonewall Jackson's Confederates at Harper's Ferry just before the battle of Antietam in September 1862. The following year, Corbett switched to Company L of the Sixteenth New York Cavalry, a regiment that spent much of its time chasing John Mosby's Confederate raiders on the outskirts of Washington.

By mid-1864, U.S. Grant had marched the great Federal army from its winter camps along the Rapidan River to the suburbs of Richmond, a hundred miles south of the Union capital. But behind the lines, Mosby's partisan horsemen still harassed Federal outposts and communications, striking and then disappearing into the northern Virginia countryside, tying down many times their own numbers and keeping Washington on edge.

That June, Mosby's riders surprised Corbett and a detachment of Company L who were looking for them near Centreville. Official records say the Union troopers were loafing about after a meal and unprepared when the Rebels struck; Corbett's version was, "I faced and fought against a whole column of them, all alone, none but God being with me, to help me, my being in a large field and they being in the road. . . ." *Harper's Weekly* would make him a hero, reporting that the Yankee cavalrymen "were hemmed in . . . and nearly all compelled to surrender except Corbett, who stood out manfully, and fired his revolver and twelve shots from his breech-loading rifle before surrendering, which he did after firing his last round of ammunition. Mosby, in admiration of the bravery displayed by Corbett, ordered his men not to shoot him, and received his surrender with other expressions of admiration."

But when Corbett was out of Mosby's hands, he got what turned into a death sentence to thousands of other captives—he was sent first to Lynchburg, then to the pine woods of Georgia, into the hellhole of Andersonville prison. Soldiers of both sides suffered in prison camps North and South, but Andersonville was the worst of the horrible lot. Although it existed for barely a year, about 45,000 captured Union troops were sent there, and of these nearly 13,000 died of disease, malnutrition and exposure to the elements. Corbett endured, preaching, praying and comforting his fellow inmates. "Bless the Lord," he said later, "a score of souls were converted, right on the spot where I lay for three months without any shelter."

After the war, he would testify for the prosecution in the longrunning trial of Captain Henry Wirz, commandant of the camp, the only Confederate soldier executed for war crimes. He told of seeing prisoners dragging ball and chain in the sun;

he said the place "was in a horrible condition of filth"; the swamp around the stream that flowed through the stockade "was so offensive and the stench so great that he wondered that every man there did not die; the maggots were a foot deep"; prisoners dug roots and dried them to eat; men who carried the dead out to be buried were allowed to bring back firewood, only to hear taunts of "That's right; sell off a dead man for wood!" from fellow sufferers. When Corbett himself was sent out to gather firewood, he managed to slip away, but within hours was tracked down by hounds and brought back.

Then, after he had been held for five months, General Grant allowed the resumption of prisoner exchanges. Because Corbett was suffering with scurvy, diarrhea and fever, he was among the emaciated but lucky hundreds sent back north, a skeleton on crutches. Of thirteen other Yankees captured with him, only one survived.

Corbett stayed in an Annapolis hospital three weeks, until he was strong enough to take thirty days leave. He had reason to be deeply vengeful as he rejoined his regiment at Vienna, Virginia, ten miles west of Washington. Writing to a woman who had tended soldiers returning from Andersonville, he said the thousands of their comrades lying under Georgia soil were "monuments of the cruelty and wickedness of this Rebellion—the head of all the rebellions of earth for blackness and horror. Those only can feel the extent of it who have seen their comrades, as I have, lying in the broiling sun, without shelter, with swollen feet and parched skin, in filth and dirt, suffering as I believe no people ever suffered before in the world."

On April 15, the morning after John Wilkes Booth shot Lincoln at Ford's Theater, the Sixteenth New York deployed into a cordon thrown about Washington in hopes of snaring the attacker before he could escape to the South. The troopers did not realize the president had died until they approached the capital and saw flags at half mast. The regiment split into detachments that rode out to follow every rumor of Booth's where-abouts. Between these sorties, Corbett was asked to lead prayer one night at Washington's Wesley Chapel. "O Lord," he intoned, "lay not innocent blood to our charge; but bring the guilty speedily to punishment." The regiment had the honor of riding in the president's funeral procession on April 19, a solemn parade along Pennsylvania Avenue between thousands of mourning citizens and buildings draped in black.

For another five days, Corbett and his detachment continued their vigil until a bugle sounded "Boots and Saddles" and brought them running to their stable. They mounted up, and with Lieutenant Edward Doherty leading, they clattered to the office of Lafayette C. Baker, chief of War Department detectives, across from Willard's Hotel at Fourteenth and Pennsylvania. Doherty went in, emerged with two other detectives, and rushed with twenty-six cavalrymen to the Sixth Street wharf to board the steamer *John S. Ide*. They set out down the Potomac toward Fredericksburg in pursuit of the assassin.

Booth and David Herold, one of his accomplices, had escaped into southern Maryland, where they hid at Dr. Samuel Mudd's house, then in swamps and barns until they borrowed a rowboat and slipped across the wide Potomac into Virginia. Following a tip, Doherty's troopers came ashore at Belle Plain on Aquia Creek at about 10 o'clock that Monday evening and spread across country, rapping farmers out of bed for questioning. The next day they tracked Booth to the Rappahannock River, and shuttled across on a rude scow that carried eight men and horses at a time. That night they traced him to the Garrett farm, just west of Port Royal. After a detective threatened the reluctant Garrett with hanging, the farmer's son pointed to the barn where the fugitives were hiding. That is where Corbett picked up the story three weeks later, when he testified before the military court trying the remaining conspirators.

He told how the soldiers surrounded the barn, and Lieutenant

Doherty and the detectives carried on a long back-and-forth conversation with Booth, trying to persuade him to give up. "He positively declared he would not surrender, saying, 'Well, my brave boys, you can prepare a stretcher for me. . . . make quick work of it; shoot me through the heart.'" But Booth said his accomplice wanted to come out, so Herold emerged and was quickly searched and tied up. Immediately after that, detective Everton J. Conger set fire to hay in the barn.

Corbett said, "The position in which I stood left me in front of a large crack—you might put your hand through it, and I knew that Booth could distinguish me and others through these cracks in the barn, and could pick us off if he chose to do so." He could have shot Booth easily, but "as long as he was there, making no demonstration to hurt any one, I did not shoot him, but kept my eye on him steadily." Then he saw Booth "taking aim with the carbine, but at whom I could not say. My mind was upon him attentively to see that he did no harm, and when I became impressed that it was time that I shot him, I took steady aim on my arm, and shot him through a large crack in the barn."

When Booth's body arrived at the Washington Navy Yard, Corbett was immediately proclaimed a hero by the public. He sat for photographer Brady, in several poses alone and in one standing with Doherty. The newly promoted captain towers over him, but Corbett stands at ease with forage cap tilted over his eyes, his pistol holster huge on one hip, his other hand grasping his saber, his boots tall and polished—the strange little sergeant whose cavalry brothers found him "cheerful and heroic under circumstances of intense suffering and great provocation."

But Secretary of War Edwin M. Stanton, detective chief Baker and others were not interested in Corbett as hero; they were furious that he had shot Booth before he could be captured. They wanted the assassin alive, to question him and to conduct a show trial, trying to prove that the conspiracy involved Confederate President Jefferson Davis, who had not yet been caught. Some charged that Corbett had acted against orders, others that he fired without orders. He insisted that he pulled the trigger only when he saw the assassin raise his carbine.

On the scene, Corbett had explained simply that "Providence directed my hand." Days later, he wrote a letter, published by the *New York Times*, refuting "many false reports in the papers charging me with violation of order, &c. . . ." Lieutenant Doherty had cleared him of blame, he said, and commended him to General Grant for his action. Corbett wrote that "when I saw where the ball had struck him—in the neck, near the ear—it seemed to me that God had directed it, for apparently it was just where he had shot the President."

Corbett was offered one of Booth's pistols as a keepsake, but declined it. When someone offered him $100 for the pistol with which he had shot Booth, he also declined, saying it belonged to the government. But if the government wished to reward him, he said, it might let him keep his little horse. It was not worth much, but he had become attached to it after riding it through so much history.

The Committee on Claims conducted more than a year of hearings before deciding to award Lafayette Baker and the detective, ex-colonel Conger, $17,500 each from the $75,000 reward posted by the Federal government. That generated so much public protest that the committee's report was disapproved. But after it was revised, the biggest single share still went to Conger, while the enlisted cavalrymen who chased Booth down, including the sergeant who shot him, got precisely $1,653.85 each.

That did not sustain Corbett long; by some accounts, he was robbed of his share soon after he got it. He returned to New York, back at the downtown prayer meetings where he had spoken before the war. He preached temperance to shipyard workers, and ventured onto the lecture circuit. But that career fizzled because his advertised lectures invariably turned out to be raging sermons instead. In 1869 he found work as a hatter in

Philadelphia and became pastor of a Methodist mission across the Delaware River in Camden. Stacked in one corner of his kitchen there, he kept half a dozen rough benches for use by the worshipers who came to hear his nightly sermons. When a reporter asked him about John Wilkes Booth, he said, "I felt I was doing my duty to my God and my country. To this day I feel justified in my course. Were the ghosts of twenty assassins to arise against me, they could not disturb a calm Christian spirit."

Corbett was Christian, but not calm. Losing his job was not the only reason he left Philadelphia and headed west. He was not pursued by the ghosts of twenty assassins, but he had received threatening letters; he suspected that he was targeted by Confederate sympathizers bent on revenge. He stayed briefly with an ex-comrade in Company L, who wrote that Corbett had "been driven from pillar to post," that "he preaches with a pistol in his pocket," that "after he says his prayers he lies down at night with a loaded revolver under his pillow," that "he moans pitifully" in his sleep. "It almost seems my house was haunted while he was there."

Although Corbett was "a good man, a pure and devout Christian of spotless life," his friend went on, "I declare I was glad when he was gone, he was so unhappy, so uneasy, so strange. He is no lunatic. He is no fool. He is a good man in every way. But wherever he goes he says Nemesis pursues him, and the trouble spirits of revenge will not let him rest. He is in constant fear of assassins."

Corbett made it to Cloud County, Kansas, and homesteaded 80 acres on seemingly worthless land eighteen miles southeast of Concordia. He was convinced that admirers of Booth had created a secret order sworn to avenge him. He built himself a sod and stone dugout, with holes in the walls so he could fire out at interlopers. He lived as a recluse, wandering the countryside on his cherished little black horse Billy. A friend said he always had a "watchful, wary countenance . . . he always seemed to be on the lookout for something."

Often when he saw someone approaching, he dismounted, drew his pistol and lay waiting in the grass until he saw who it was. He was a deadly marksman—one Kansan alleged that he had seen him bring down a barn swallow with his pistol. Neighbors said he fired warning shots if they happened to ride across the borders of his claim. Such behavior brought him before a hearing in Concordia, where he whipped out his gun and shouted "Lie, lie, lie!" But because it was Corbett, the authorities sent him back to his shanty with just a warning. He was active with the local Salvation Army, and a friendly judge tried to help him by arranging lectures, but as before he drove audiences away with his "shouting, ranting, street preacher religion—'Repent and ye shall be saved!'" A Presbyterian minister invited him to talk about his war experiences, and Corbett took the occasion seriously, even buying a new coat and shirt. But what he delivered was another shouted "disconnected exhortation."

Other war veterans sympathized with Corbett; an old cavalryman and legislator arranged a job for him as a doorkeeper in the Kansas House of Representatives at Topeka. This worked out for a few months, but each day his piety was offended by the doings of the prairie politicians around him. Eventually, on February 15, 1887, he could stand it no more. Just after the morning prayer, he drew his pistol and threatened the speaker of the House, abruptly adjourning the legislature. He kept the floor, waving his weapon and threatening legislators, reporters and staff. There are many versions of exactly what provoked him; one says he was disrespected by the House staff, another that he exploded when he heard pages mocking the opening prayer. As he raged, lawmakers hid under desks and spectators scattered; he held the floor until police crept up behind him, grabbed his pistol and took him away.

After long testimony, a probation judge in Topeka declared

Corbett "hopelessly insane" and committed him to the state asylum. A reporter recalled his shooting of Booth, and said sadly that the "bloody deed, which so effectually blighted his life. . . . has finally followed him into a straight-jacket."

Sadly, but not finally: Occasionally Corbett threw fits of anger at the asylum, but at other times he was a model patient. He was allowed to join other inmates in outdoor exercises until on May 26, 1888, a friend of the superintendent's son came visiting, and tied his "smart Indian pony" near the gate. The old cavalryman saw his chance. Dawdling behind his group, pretending to admire the spring blossoms, he leaped into the saddle and galloped away. The patients he left behind shouted excitedly, but this was not unusual at the asylum, so at first attendants did not realize what had happened. They spotted him when he was half a mile down the road, "whipping that pony at every jump" with the rawhide quirt the boy had left hanging on the saddle. "To all appearance the only reason that pony was running was because he couldn't fly," said a witness. "At a turn in the road, Corbett looked back and swung his straw hat around his head, and thus waved farewell to the hospital and his late companions." A few days later, a letter came saying the horse could be reclaimed at Neodesha, Kansas, 75 miles south. Corbett had spent two nights there with an old soldier who had suffered with him at Andersonville. He borrowed train fare, covering it with a draft on the $15 he had left in a Concordia bank. Then he departed, saying he was headed for Mexico.

What happened to him after that is not known, but widely rumored. Every few months some newspaper out west reported that he had appeared in a neighboring county, or was working in the gold fields of Nevada, or had died in a Minnesota forest fire. In 1900, a Topeka patent medicine magnate said a certain John Corbett had been peddling his products up and down Texas and Oklahoma for several years, always being careful not to step over the Kansas line. He was convinced that this Corbett was really Boston. But among other discrepancies, this Corbett stood six feet and weighed 188 pounds; after extensive interviews and depositions, he was convicted of perjury in trying to collect Boston's abandoned property and $1,300 in accumulated government pension. In 1913, after chasing rumors for a quarter century, state officials concluded that "it is safe to say that no one in Kansas knows the whereabouts of Boston Corbett." In 1958, Boy Scouts erected a stone monument on Corbett's homestake, decorated with a plaque and a pair of big pistols.

The phrase "mad as a hatter" was already familiar more than 150 years ago; it appeared in Edinburgh's *Blackwood Magazine* in 1829, and Thackeray used it in *Pendennis* in 1850, when Corbett was learning the hat trade at which he worked for two decades or more. Through the years, doctors began to recognize the poisonous side effects of the mercury used in many medical treatments and in industrial procedures such as hatmaking. Among the victims' symptoms they listed irritability, nervousness, fits of anger, anxiety, insomnia, low self control, exaggerated response to stimulation, fearfulness and violent behavior. The worst damage came from mercury made airborne into tiny droplets and breathed into the lungs—exactly what had happened to Boston Corbett.

On December 1, 1941, the U.S. Public Health Service banned the mercury process in hatmaking.

ERNEST B. "PAT" FURGURSON *was a Washington and foreign correspondent and syndicated columnist for the* Baltimore Sun *before turning his full attention to American history. In the past two decades, he has done four books about the Civil War—*Chancellorsville 1863: The Souls of the Brave; Ashes of Glory: Richmond at War; Not War But Murder: Cold Harbor 1864; *and* Freedom Rising: Washington in the Civil War, *all published by Alfred A. Knopf. His work has also appeared in* National Geographic, Smithsonian, Reader's Digest, American Scholar, *and other magazines.*

Coda

This piece on Boston Corbett isn't based on the kind of traveling, buttonholing reporting that I loved during my first life, as a newspaperman. It's the result of digging into all kinds of musty paperwork, from the shorthand record of the Lincoln assassins' trial to pension applications at the National Archives to the Seventeenth Annual Report of the Kansas Historical Society. But many of the juiciest quotes and descriptions are indeed from old newspapers—the *Pittsburgh Leader* and *Titusville Morning Herald*, the *Waterloo Iowa State Reporter* and *Cincinnati Enquirer*, the *Butte Daily Miner* and the *Portland Journal*, not to mention the usual suspects, like the *New York Times*, the *Washington Post* and *Harper's Weekly*. In those hand-set, pre-Mergenthaler days, provincial papers had their own personalities. For me today, coming across a lively piece by some anonymous prairie reporter of the 1800s is almost—but not quite—as much fun as was that first gin & tonic atop the Caravelle after a hot day in the Delta.

David Kushner

THE BOY WHO HEARD
TOO MUCH

FROM *Rolling Stone*

IT BEGAN, AS IT ALWAYS DID, with a phone call to 911.
"Now listen here," the caller demanded, his voice frantic. "I've
got two people here held hostage, all right? Now, you know
what happens to people that are held hostage? It's not like on the
movies or nothing, you understand that?"

"OK," the 911 operator said.

"One of them here's name is Danielle, and her father," the
caller continued. "And the reason why I'm doing this is because
her father raped my sister."

The caller, who identified himself as John Defanno, said that
he had the 18-year-old Danielle and her dad tied up in their
home in Security, a suburb of Colorado Springs. He'd beaten the
father with his gun. "He's bleeding profusely," Defanno warned.
"I am armed, I do have a pistol. If any cops come in this house
with any guns, I will fucking shoot them. I better get some help
here, because I'm going fucking psycho right now."

The 911 operator tried to keep him on the line, but Defanno
cut the call short. "I'm not talking anymore," he snapped. "You

have the address. If I don't have help here now, in the next five minutes, I swear to fucking God, I will shoot these people." Then the line went dead.

Officers raced to the house, ready for an armed standoff with a homicidal suspect. But when they arrived, they found no gunman, no hostages, no blood. Danielle and her father were safe and sound at home—alone. They had never heard of John Defanno, for good reason: He didn't exist.

"John Defanno" was actually a 15-year-old boy named Matthew Weigman—a fat, lonely blind kid who lived with his mom in a working-class neighborhood of East Boston. In person, Weigman was a shy and awkward teenager with a shaved head who spent his days holed up in his room, often talking for up to 20 hours a day on free telephone chat lines. On the phone, he became "Lil' Hacker," the most skilled member of a small band of telephone pranksters known as "phreaks." To punish Danielle, who had pissed him off on a chat line, Weigman had phoned 911 and posed as a psycho, rigging his caller ID to make it look like the emergency call was coming from inside Danielle's home. It's a trick known as "swatting"—mobilizing SWAT teams to exact revenge on your enemies—and phreakers like Weigman have used it to trigger some 200 false raids in dozens of cities nationwide.

"When I was a kid, a prank was calling in a pizza to a neighbor's house," says Kevin Kolbye, an FBI assistant special agent in charge who has investigated the phreaks. "Today it's this."

Like a comic-book villain transformed by a tragic accident, Weigman discovered at an early age that his acute hearing gave him superpowers on the telephone. He could impersonate any voice, memorize phone numbers by the sound of the buttons and decipher the inner workings of a phone system by the frequencies and clicks on a call, which he refers to as "songs." The knowledge enabled him to hack into cellphones, order phone lines disconnected and even tap home phones. "Man, it felt pretty powerful for a little kid," he says. "Anyone said something bad about me, and I'd press a button, and I'd get them."

But in the end, those close to Weigman feared that his gift would prove to be his downfall. "Matt never intended on becoming the person he became," says Jeff Daniels, a former phreaker who befriended Weigman on a chat line. "When you're a blind little tubby bald kid in a broke-ass family, and you have that one ability to make yourself feel good, what do you expect to happen?"

MATTHEW WEIGMAN WAS BORN BLIND, but that was hardly the only strike against him. His family was a mess. His father, an alcoholic who did drugs, would drag the terrified Matt across the floor by his hair and call him a "blind bastard." His dad left the family when Weigman was five, leaving Matt and his older brother and sister to scrape by on his disability pension and what their mother earned as a nurse's aide. For Weigman, every day was a struggle. "There were times I hated being blind," he recalls. At school, as he caned his way through the halls, other kids teased him about how his eyes rolled out of control. "Kids can be cruel, because they don't understand what they're doing," he says. "They can't even begin to fathom what they're causing, and that stuff eats at your mind."

At age four, Matt surprised his mother by making out flashing bulbs on the Christmas tree. After that, he could perceive faint lights—and he exploited the ability for all it was worth. He cooked for himself by feeling his way around the kitchen—eggs here, frying pan there, toaster over there—and refused to stop, even after he burned himself. He shocked his brother by climbing on a bicycle and tearing down the road, using the blurry shadows for guidance. He taught himself to skateboard, too. To build his confidence, his mom's new husband let the eight-year-old Matt drive his car around the empty parking lot at Suffolk

Downs, a nearby racetrack. "It made me feel a lot better," Weigman recalls. "I thought, 'I'm doing something that people who see can do.'"

And he could do one thing even better than sighted people: hear. Weigman became obsessed with voices, music and sounds of all sorts. He could perfectly mimic characters he heard on the Cartoon Network, and he played his favorite songs on a small keyboard by ear. He would also dial random numbers on the phone, just to hear who picked up—and what kind of response he could elicit from them. He fondly recalls the first time he called 911, at age five, and duped them into sending a cop to his door.

"You need the police?" the officer asked.

"No," Weigman replied. "I'm just curious. I wanted to see what the operator would do."

The cop reprimanded the boy sharply. "I wouldn't do that no more," he said.

But Weigman was hooked. In real life, he was gaining weight and dodging bullies, struggling to find a place to fit in. By age 10, however, he had found the perfect escape: a telephone party line. The service—a precursor to Internet chat rooms—allows multiple callers to talk with each other over the phone. Despite the rise of online video streaming, there are still scores of telephone party lines scattered across the country, an odd and forgotten throwback to a pre-digital world. Compared to texting or video chat, the phone lines have a unique appeal: They offer callers a cloak of anonymity coupled with the visceral immediacy of live human voices. Some call to socialize, others for phone sex.

Hoping to give Weigman a social network beyond the confines of his tiny bedroom, a friend had slipped him the number of a free party line known as Studio 55. The second Weigman called, a new world opened up to him. He heard voices. Some were talking to each other. Others piped in only occasionally, listening in as they watched TV or played video games. Weigman found he could decipher each and every ambient sound, no matter how soft or garbled. Many of the callers were social misfits and outcasts: ex-cons and bawdy chicks and unemployed guys with nothing better to do all day than talk shit to a bunch of complete strangers. People without a life. And that's when it hit Weigman: *No one here could see each other. They were all just disembodied voices.* "We're all blind right now," he announced to the group.

Weigman wasn't a freak anymore. But he was about to become a phreak.

TELEPHONE PHREAKING ISN'T NEW: The practice, which dates back half a century, was the forerunner of computer hacking. In 1957, a blind eight-year-old named Joe Engressia accidentally discovered that he could whistle at the precise frequency—2,600 hertz—used to control phone networks. A pioneering phreak named John Draper later realized that the free whistles given out in Cap'n Crunch cereal boxes also replicated the exact same tone. Kids with a mischievous streak and too much free time were soon competing to see who could achieve the most elaborate phone hack. A tech-savvy student named Steve Wozniak, who would soon invent something called Apple with his friend Steve Jobs, once used a series of high-pitched whistles to make a free international call to the Vatican to prank the pope.

As he listened in on the party lines, Weigman began pressing random numbers on his phone, just to see what would happen. Once he held down the star button and was surprised to hear a computerized voice say, "Moderator on." He had no idea what it meant. But when he hit the pound key, the voice suddenly began ticking off the private phone number of every person in the chat room. Weigman had discovered a secret tool through which a party-line administrator could monitor the system. Now, whenever someone on the line trash-talked him, he could quietly access their number and harass them by calling them at home.

By 14, Weigman was conning his way through AT&T and Verizon, tricking them into divulging insider information—like supervisor identification numbers and passwords—that gave him full run of the system. If he heard a supervisor's voice once, he could imitate it with eerie precision when calling one of the man's underlings. If he heard someone dialing a number, he could memorize the digits purely by tone. A favorite ploy was to get the name of a telephone technician visiting his house, then impersonate the man on the phone to extract codes and other data from unsuspecting co-workers. Once he called a phone company posing as a girl, saying he needed to verify the identity of a technician who was at "her" door. Convinced, the operator coughed up the technician's company ID number, direct phone line and supervisor—key information that Weigman could later put to nefarious use, like cutting off a rival's phone line.

There seemed to be no limit to what he could do: shut off your phone service, dig up your unlisted cellphone number, even listen in on your home phone—something only a handful of veteran phreaks can pull off. Celebrities were a favorite target. Weigman claims to have hacked and called the cellphones of Lindsay Lohan ("She was drunk, and my friend tried to have phone sex with her") and Eminem ("He told me to fuck off"). Last year, during the presidential campaign, Weigman heard a YouTube video of Mitt Romney's son Matt dialing his dad. Weigman listened closely to the touch tones, deciphered the candidate's cellphone number—and then made a call of his own. "Mitt Romney!" he said. "What's going on, dude? Running for president?" Weigman says Romney told him to shove the phone up his ass, and hung up.

In addition to relying on his heightened sense of hearing, Weigman picked up valuable tips on phone hacking from other phreaks on the party lines. One of the most valuable tricks he learned was "spoofing"—using home-brewed or commercial services, such as SpoofCard, to display any number he chose on the caller-ID screen of the person he phoned. Intended for commercial use—allowing, say, a doctor to mask his home phone number while calling a patient—SpoofCard is perfectly legal and available online for as little as $10. Some services let callers alter their voices—male to female—as well as their numbers.

Weigman performed his first "swat" at age 14, when he faked an emergency call from a convenience store down the street from his home. "Listen," he told the 911 operator, "there's a robbery here! I need you to show up right now!" Then he hung up and called his brother, who was standing watch outside the store. "Oh, God, dude!" his brother told him. "There's police everywhere!"

"Really?" Weigman replied in awe. Over the phone, he heard sirens wail in the darkness.

WEIGMAN BEGAN SPENDING SEVERAL HOURS a day talking shit on assorted party lines. When someone on the line would challenge him or piss him off, he would respond by faking a 911 call and sending an armed SWAT team to their door. "I probably did it 50 or 60 times," he says.

He spent most of his time on party lines like Jackie Donut and Boston Loach, which teemed with lowlifes, phreakers and raunchy girls whom Weigman calls "hacker groupies." Men on the party lines competed to see who could score the most. "A lot of guys on there were looking for free phone sex," says Angela Roberson, a tongue-pierced blonde from Chicago who got to know Weigman on Boston Loach. The 34-year-old Roberson, who stumbled on the line one night when she was bored and drunk, found its rough-and-tumble community oddly appealing. "You can sit and talk smack to whoever you want to," she says. "You get to live in a whole different world." Weigman might be overweight and blind and stuck in his room, but the party line provided him with plenty of opportunities the real world didn't offer. When asked how much phone sex he had, he says, "Oh, Jesus, man—too much."

Weigman soon realized that one caller on the party line got his way with the hacker groupies more than anyone else. Stuart Rosoff, a middle-aged party-liner from Cleveland, had started out as a teenager making obscene phone calls and ended up serving three years in prison. Overweight and unemployed, with a hairy chest and thick mustache, Rosoff cruised the party lines for girls, introducing himself as Michael Knight, after David Hasselhoff's character on *Knight Rider*. He was also a member of a gang of phreaks nicknamed the Wrecking Crew.

When Rosoff didn't get what he wanted on the party line, he turned ugly. "Stuart was a malicious phreaker," says Jeff Daniels, the former phreak who hung out on the party line. "He was limited in knowledge, but good at things he knew how to do." One time, showing off to Weigman, Rosoff singled out a woman who had refused him phone sex and called the police in her hometown, scrambling the caller ID to conceal his identity. The woman, he told the cops, was abusing her kids—causing the 911 operator to dispatch police officers to her door. Having proven his power, Rosoff called the woman back and demanded phone sex again. If she didn't want to do it, he added generously, he would gladly accept it from her daughter.

"Stuart was like a mentor to Matt," says Roberson. "They would joke around and threaten to shut each other's phones off just because they were bored." It wasn't long, however, before Weigman surpassed Rosoff as a phreaker. He began to harass the older man, disconnecting his phone and digging up his personal data to use for leverage and revenge. Phreakers call this "the information game," and Weigman was the undisputed master. Rosoff was soon reduced to groveling on the chat lines, begging Weigman to leave him alone.

Roberson felt threatened by Weigman and by Rosoff, who kept pestering her for phone sex. Once, after a confrontation with Weigman, she picked up her phone only to hear the high-pitched squeal of a fax machine in place of the dial tone. It had been rigged to last all night. Despite Weigman's denials, Roberson claims he also hacked into her voicemail. To protect herself from attacks, she became close to another member of Rosoff's gang, eventually moving in with him and taking part in one of the Wrecking Crew's pranks.

Roberson was surprised when she learned that Weigman was just a teenager. "I would have never thought that he was a 16-year-old," Roberson says. "He was smart, and he was feared." When Weigman called up a party line, he would brashly announce his presence in the chat room with a little smack talk: "How you doing, you motherfuckers?" He might be an overweight blind kid, but on the party lines, he could be whoever he wanted. "That's why he did what he did," says Roberson. "He was insecure, but he could be powerful here."

As Weigman's reputation as a phreaker surpassed even Rosoff's, his hobby became an obsession. In a single month, he would place as many as 40,000 calls—ranging from a few seconds in length to several hours. He dropped out of 10th grade, spending all day on the phone. His mother was proud that he had found something he was good at and glad he had finally made some friends, if only on the phone. "She left it alone because it was my social outlet," Weigman says. Matt was also using his newfound skills to bill purchases to bogus credit cards, snagging everything from free phone service to Dunkin' Donuts gift cards. ("I love Dunkin' Donuts!" he says.)

Weigman became a master of what phreakers call "social engineering"—learning phone-industry jargon and using it to manipulate telecommunications workers. One day, Weigman picked up the phone and dialed AT&T. Two rings, then a voice: "Thanks for calling, this is Byron. How can I help you?"

"How you doing, Byron?" Weigman asked, adopting the tone of an older man, one at ease with his own authority.

"Good," Byron said. "And you?"

"I'm doing all right. My name is William Jones. I'm calling you with AT&T asset protection. I'm actually working on a customer-fraud issue. We need to write out a D order." In a few short sentences, Weigman had appropriated the name, voice and lingo of a real AT&T agent, ordering a rival's phone to be disconnected.

"What's the telephone number?" Byron asked. Weigman rattled off the name and number on his rival's account. Then, to authorize access, he gave Byron the AT&T security-ID code belonging to Jones.

For a moment, the phone filled with the sound of rattling computer keys being struck by expert fingers.

"Looks like it's paid in full," Byron said, puzzled.

"Yeah," Weigman said, "we're looking at a fraud account, sir. We're just going to have to take that out of there."

As Byron filed a disconnection order, Weigman made idle chitchat in his "Jones" persona, speculating on the twisted minds of phone phreaks. "Deep down, I know that they know someday they're going to get caught up, you know?" he told Byron. "They just really don't think about it. It's crazy."

The words applied to Weigman himself. By now, he had "stoolies" on the party lines eager to do his bidding. As his power on the phones grew, he began to change. Unable to take the teasing and the pity he got for being blind, he grew sneering and mean, lowering his voice, adopting a manly bluster. Using the phone to lash out at others, he directed all the rage he felt at the world against his fellow phreaks. To prove his prowess, he targeted Daniels, a 37-year-old from Alabama who had been arrested for phone hacking as a teenager. "He was calling my landlord and telling him I was a child molester and that I killed people," Daniels claims.

Still, there was something sympathetic about the kid. "To me, he was still a boy," Daniels says. Having been to jail himself, he didn't want Weigman to make the same mistakes he had. So he got Weigman's attention the only way he could: by beating him at his own game. When Weigman refused to stop the phone attacks, Daniels tracked down the teenager's detailed personal information, including his Social Security number. That earned him Weigman's respect, and the two became friends. They would talk for hours on the phone at night, Weigman's put-on baritone suddenly replaced by a more childish tone. "He was not the big shot he made himself out to be," Daniels realized.

Weigman opened up about his miserable and impoverished life, crying as he told Daniels how much he longed to see the world with his own eyes. His weight fluctuated from boyishly pudgy to extremely obese, and he was spending more and more time locked in his room upstairs, listening to Nirvana and Muddy Waters. One time, a teacher took his class to a blues club in Boston, and the music seemed to capture what he was feeling: the poverty, the despair, the sense of being trapped. "He lived in a jail at home," says Daniels. "He lived in a box."

Daniels urged him to drop the macho bullshit on the party lines and stop drawing attention to himself. Weigman agreed to keep his mouth shut and even christened his new self-image with a more stoic nickname. From now, on he would no longer be Lil' Hacker. He called himself "Silence."

ON A JUNE NIGHT IN 2006, James Proulx was watching television at 1 a.m. when a SWAT team suddenly surrounded his home in Alvarado, Texas. A stocky, gray-haired trucker who had recently undergone open-heart surgery, Proulx went to the door, where he was confronted by two armed policemen—their guns pointed directly at him. The officers threw Proulx to the ground, snapped handcuffs on him and put him in the back of a squad car.

They had reason to be suspicious. A call to 911 had come in from Proulx's house; a man identifying himself as Proulx said he was tripping on drugs and holding hostages. He demanded $50,000 so he could flee to Mexico. He also claimed to have killed his wife. If any cops got in his way, he warned, he'd kill them, too.

As the police soon discovered, however, Proulx was just another swatting victim. It turned out that Proulx's 28-year-old daughter, Stephanie, spent time on Jackie Donut. When she clashed with Weigman and others, they decided to strike back. "If a female wouldn't give Matt phone sex," she recalls, "he would call them a fucking bitch and send a SWAT team to their house." Weigman considered Proulx a "crazy chick who would threaten hackers," and he was very direct with her. "You're annoying," he told her. "I might come after you." Four months after Stephanie's father was swatted, police showed up at her home in Fort Worth, Texas, drawn by a fake call to 911.

One afternoon, not long after Proulx was swatted, Weigman came home to find his mother talking to what sounded like a middle-aged male. The man introduced himself as Special Agent Allyn Lynd of the FBI's cyber squad in Dallas, which investigates hacking and other computer crimes. A West Point grad, Lynd had spent 10 years combating phreaks and hackers. Now, with Proulx's cooperation, he was aiming to take down Stuart Rosoff and the Wrecking Crew—and he wanted Weigman's help.

Lynd explained that Rosoff, Roberson and other party-liners were being investigated in a swatting conspiracy. Because Weigman was a minor, however, he would not be charged—as long as he cooperated with the authorities. Realizing that this was a chance to turn his life around, Weigman confessed his role in the phone assaults.

Weigman's auditory skills had always been central to his exploits, the means by which he manipulated the phone system. Now he gave Lynd a first-hand display of his powers. At one point during the visit, Lynd's cellphone rang. "I can't talk to you right now," the agent told the caller. "I'm out doing something." When he hung up, Weigman turned to him from across the room. "Oh," the kid asked, "is that Billy Smith from Verizon?"

Lynd was stunned. William Smith was a fraud investigator with Verizon who had been working with him on the swatting case. Weigman not only knew all about the man and his role in the investigation, but he had identified Smith simply by hearing his Southern-accented voice on the cellphone—a sound which would have been inaudible to anyone else in the room. Weigman then shocked Lynd again, rattling off the names of a host of investigators working for other phone companies. Matt, it turned out, had spent weeks identifying phone-company employees, gaining their trust and obtaining confidential information about the FBI investigation against him. Even the phone account in his house, he revealed to Lynd, had been opened under the name of a telephone-company investigator. Lynd had rarely seen anything like it—even from cyber gangs who tried to hack into systems at the White House and the FBI. "Weigman flabbergasted me," he later testified.

But Weigman's decision to straighten out didn't last long. "Within days of agreeing to cooperate, he was back on the party line, committing his crimes again," Lynd said. Weigman didn't like being cut off from the only community he had. "I was a hardheaded little kid, and I wanted to do what I wanted to do," he recalls. "I didn't think this could be serious." He was also obsessed. "He's not a criminal—he's an addict," says his friend Daniels. "He's addicted to Silence, to Lil' Hacker, to being the person who is big and bad and bold. He's addicted to being the person who can get every girl to do what he asks over the phone."

Daniels, who owns a party line called the Legend System

After Dark, tried to channel Weigman's energy in a more positive direction by giving him a position as a moderator, making
him responsible for managing the phone chats and reining in
jerks like Rosoff. As Weigman ran the calls, he began softening
up. He even had a girlfriend in her 30s, Chastity, whom he had
met on a party line. He seemed calmer since he met her, more
the kid he really was. When they had relationship troubles, he
confided in Daniels rather than swatting her.

Before long, though, Weigman returned to his old ways.
Daniels began hearing from party-liners who said they were being harassed by the kid. "Knowledge is power," Daniels told
Weigman, "but you're using it for the wrong reasons. They're
going to put you in jail, and you being blind isn't going to save
you." But Weigman wouldn't listen. "He saw himself as this
underage blind kid in a poor family," Daniels recalls. "So how
were they going to put him in prison with big guys who might
want to whup his ass?" Unable to reform his friend, Daniels had
to let Weigman go.

When the FBI finally busted the Wrecking Crew, Weigman's
reputation grew. Recordings and details of his fake 911 calls,
including the swatting in Colorado, leaked and spread online.
The attention only made Weigman grow more paranoid and
vengeful. He stepped up his campaign of intimidation, warning
his victims that any cooperation with investigators would warrant new attacks. He told one woman he'd make her life a "living hell" and put her husband out of business. He threatened a
woman in Virginia with a swatting attack—and ended up calling in a bomb threat to a nursing home where her mother worked
in retaliation for her talking to the FBI. He phoned a mother in
Florida and said that if she gave his name to investigators, he'd
kill her baby by flushing it down the toilet.

In 2007, Rosoff and other party-liners pleaded guilty to swatting. "I'm kind of like a nobody in real life," he told the judge.
"I was actually somebody on the phone, somebody important."

In a plea agreement that limited his prison sentence to five years, Rosoff ratted out his rival, saying that Weigman had participated in "targeting, executing and obtaining information to facilitate swatting calls."

But Weigman was still a minor, and the FBI didn't want to go after him. In a sense, he was being offered a break. As long as he cleaned up his act, he wouldn't be prosecuted. All he had to do was walk away before April 20th, 2008—the day he would turn 18. After that, any crime he committed would get him tried as an adult.

LATE ONE NIGHT THAT APRIL, the telephone rang at the New Hampshire home of William Smith, the Verizon fraud investigator who was working with the FBI. When Smith picked up, however, there was no one on the other end of the line. In the nights that followed, it happened again and again. At first, Smith didn't make much of it. Then one night, his wife looked at the caller ID and noticed something strange: It was Smith's work number, even though he was there at home. "Something's not right," she told him.

Smith changed his home number, but it made no difference. The phone would ring again at all hours—this time with Smith's own cellphone as the point of origin. Weigman, he soon learned, was using his skills and his network of stoolies to ferret out Smith's private phone numbers and harass him. And he knew Weigman's history well enough to know exactly where the calls were leading: a swatting attack. "He was fully aware that he might be subject to violence by proxy if Weigman chose to make a false emergency call," Lynd testified.

In the midst of the harassment, Smith called a travel agent and booked a flight for his wife to visit their son in Georgia. Then he called his son to inform him of the travel plans. Minutes later, the phone rang. This time, the caller ID showed his son's phone.

But when Smith picked up, it wasn't his son after all. It was Weigman. Matt was using his phone-company connections to track every call that Smith made and received—and the veteran fraud investigator for Verizon could do nothing to stop him.

Then, one Sunday in May of last year—on a weekend after his wife had flown to Georgia—Smith was working in his yard when a car pulled up. Out stepped three young men, including one with strange, broken eyes. "I'm Matt," the boy told Smith.

Weigman had driven up from Boston with his brother and a fellow party-liner. Standing in the yard, he could make out Smith's dark, shadowy figure against a blotch of white light, and he heard the investigator's familiar Southern accent—the one he had so easily identified on agent Lynd's cellphone. Weigman told Smith he wasn't there to threaten or hurt him—he just wanted to persuade him to call off the investigation. After years of intimidating others, Weigman was now the one who felt intimidated. He wanted it all to stop.

But Smith wasn't having any of it. He went inside and called the police, who quickly showed up. Weigman didn't run. He told the cops he had done things that were "not so nice." When the officers asked what he meant, he said, "swatting." But after a lifetime of being teased and abused, Weigman was unable to see himself as anything but a victim. He was just a young blind kid, and here he was getting bullied again. Smith, he told the officers, had a "vendetta" against him.

Less than two weeks after he showed up at Smith's house, the police knocked on Weigman's door outside Boston and arrested him. Weigman soon found himself being interrogated by an FBI agent. He listened in darkness as the agent dialed a number on his phone. Thirty minutes later, he spouted back the number by heart—and even knew what it was. "That's the main number of the FBI office here in Boston," Weigman told the astonished agent.

But now that Weigman was 18, his powers couldn't save him

anymore. Last January, he pleaded guilty to two felony counts of conspiracy to commit fraud and intimidate a federal witness. In June, he was sentenced to 11 years in prison.

These days, sitting in a small holding cell in a Dallas prison, Weigman bears no resemblance to the hulking psycho he portrayed on the party lines. Dressed in an orange jumpsuit, he's slim and soft-spoken, his head shifting as he talks. "I'm not a monster or a terrorist," he says. "I'm just a guy who likes computers and telephones. I used my ability to do certain things in the wrong way. That's it." As Weigman recounts his story, he slips effortlessly into the voices of the people he met along the way. Every ambient noise—a guard's chatter, a bag unzipping, a computer disc whirring—draws a tic of his attention.

"Let me tell you something, man," he says, his voice a bit like that of a young Elvis. "If I would have been just a little more mature, if I could just rationalize better, I think I would have been all set. If, when I was young, I had a full-time male father figure in my life. . . ." He stammers a bit, then recovers. "Not having my dad didn't really bother me," he says, "but inside, it kind of messed me up a bit."

Above all, though, Weigman is still a teenager. While he expresses remorse over his swatting attacks, he takes giddy pleasure in recounting his other exploits—whether punking celebrities or playing the phone companies like an Xbox. "The phone system and infrastructure is just weak," he says. "I had access to the entire AT&T and Verizon networks at times. I could have shut down an entire area." Then he segues into an earnest pitch for a future job. "I'd love to work for a phone company, just doing what I do legally," he says. "It's not about power. I know the phone and telecommunication systems and can be a crucial part of any company."

In the meantime, he's free to brush up on his skills. Though he's restricted from calling party lines, he has phone access in prison. For a self-described telephone addict, it seems almost cruel, like imprisoning a crackhead with a pipe and a rock. Could he use the prison phone the same way he used his home phone? Could he hack his way, from his prison cell, beyond the guard towers and the razor wire, into the world outside?

Weigman bobs his head and kneads his hands. "I'm sure I could," he says.

DAVID KUSHNER *is a contributing editor of* Rolling Stone *and* Wired, *and the digital culture commentator for National Public Radio's* Weekend Edition Sunday. *His books include* Masters of Doom: How Two Guys Created an Empire and Transformed Pop Culture *(2003);* Jonny Magic and the Card Shark Kids: How a Gang of Geeks Beat the Odds and Stormed Las Vegas *(2005); and* Levittown: Two Families, One Tycoon, and the Fight for Civil Rights in America's Legendary Suburb *(2009). He is an adjunct professor of journalism at New York University. His work has also appeared in publications including* The New York Times Magazine, New York, Details, *and* Discover.

Coda

Writing about a recent crime requires, among other things, persistence and patience. Until the case is over, it can be tough—if not impossible—to get key people to talk. Defendants and attorneys often don't want to risk a heavier sentence on a magazine story. This is what happened with Matt Weigman. His sentencing kept getting delayed, and so did my shot at an interview. Badgering Weigman's attorney, Carlo D'Angelo, became a full-time job. I spent months doing what journalists call a "write around"—reporting around Weigman, talking with whomever I could, poring over court files and transcripts, immersing myself in the phone phreak underworld, but still—no Matt. We could have run the article without Weigman's participation, of course, but we were willing to wait.

Eight months after getting my assignment, Weigman got sentenced, and I made one more call to his attorney. OK, D'Angelo told me, Matt's ready to talk. I flew down to Dallas to meet Weigman. After so much anticipation, I had no idea what to expect. Maybe he wouldn't want to go into much detail. Maybe he'd have some immovable chip on his shoulder. Maybe he could care less about sharing his story with a magazine. But as I sat down across from this kid in an orange jumpsuit, the first thing he did was apologize for the delay. Then he said, "I used to read *Rolling Stone* in Braille!" He's still in jail now.

Skip Hollandsworth

Bringing Down the Dogmen

FROM *Texas Monthly*

THE "SHOW" WAS SCHEDULED to take place on Friday night in a field behind a rundown gas plant about forty miles west of Houston. Chris, a young dogman from the coastal town of Matagorda, was driving up to take on Rob Rogers—or, as he was known in the dogfighting world, White Boy Rob. Chris was a cocky, fast-talking black guy, maybe 25 years old. He had a beauty of a pit bull named BJ, a newcomer to the game but one that had already developed a reputation as a "leg dog." At his last show, BJ had locked his teeth onto his opponent's front left leg, ripped out a chunk of cartilage, and then immediately torn into the right leg, nearly snapping a bone. "Nobody can beat BJ," said Chris. "White Boy Rob ain't going to do nothing to my BJ."

Rogers was one of the best dogmen in Texas, renowned for his ability to work fighting pit bulls—"bull dogs," he called them. He kept thirty dogs at a property in Baytown and at his two-bedroom trailer in Channelview, a blue-collar suburb of Houston, where he lived with his wife and three children. As a fight approached, he would select one dog and put him "on the keep." He would run him for an hour through a cemetery with a thirty-pound chain attached to his collar. He'd make him swim for another hour in an above-ground pool in his backyard, then put him on a treadmill to run some more. Rogers would give the dog vitamins and amino acids and inject him with anti-inflammatory drugs. He'd give the dog very little water in order to lessen bleeding during a fight and make the skin tighter and harder to bite. To keep the animal relaxed, he'd let it stay inside the trailer and sleep at the foot of his bed. "You treat your bull dog with respect and you'll be amazed at what he does for you," Rogers liked to say. "You can tell him where to hit another dog, and he'll hit it."

For this particular show, Rogers had chosen Dozer, a 36-pound male with a coat the color of fried chicken. Dozer was young, just nineteen months old. Usually Rogers didn't bring out one of his dogs until it had reached at least the age of two. But Dozer had what dogfighting aficionados describe as a "hard mouth": He was a vicious biter. Like almost all of Rogers's dogs, Dozer was also known for his "gameness": Once he was ordered to fight, he refused to quit. When Rogers showed up in his old gray Ford van and pulled Dozer from his large crate, a couple of men who had been invited to the show let out low whistles. Dozer looked around, proud as a Thoroughbred, his muscles rippling under his short hair.

One by one, Dozer and BJ were weighed in, each suspended from a scale with a thin cord running under his front legs and around his chest. A member of Chris's team washed Dozer with water, baking soda, warm milk, and vinegar to make sure his coat was not treated with some foreign substance that would inhibit BJ from biting. According to the rules, Rogers had the right to wash BJ, but he was so confident in Dozer that he shrugged his shoulders and told the referee to get the show going.

A wooden box—twelve feet by twelve feet, the walls two feet high—had been constructed in the middle of the field, with a couple of portable industrial lights set up around it. Inside the box, a carpet had been laid down over the grass. The invitation-only crowd of about thirty men stood just outside the box, most of them making bets. Chris and Rogers had each put up $750 for the fight, winner take all. The two men stepped into the box, cradling their dogs in their arms, and quickly turned toward their separate corners so that the dogs could not see each other. "Face your dogs," said the referee.

The dogs were set down on the carpet and turned toward the center of the box. When they finally got a glimpse of each other, it was as if a switch had been flipped. Their heads slunk below their shoulders, and their paws strained against the carpet. The referee shouted, "Release your dogs," and they came flying toward the center of the box with a vengeance, two projectiles colliding in midair.

Dozer immediately buried his teeth in BJ's chest, and just as immediately spit him out. Rogers cursed. BJ obviously had some sort of solution on him—a flea dip, maybe—that was bothering Dozer. Rogers watched as BJ took advantage of the opportunity, driving himself underneath Dozer's jaws and tearing at his front leg.

Rogers snapped his fingers, pointed to BJ's face—the one place where he figured there would be no flea dip—and shouted, "Get it! Get after it!" Dozer responded, his teeth gnashing at BJ's muzzle. BJ pawed backward, blood spurting from his mouth. Blood and urine drenched the carpet. Dozer was so wounded in his front leg that he had trouble standing. But as spectators around the box bellowed, he held onto BJ's chest, his teeth like clamps.

Chris called for a break, and the two dogs were briefly separated. Rogers's and Chris's assistants gave them quick sponge baths and blew on them to cool them off. "Release your dogs!" the referee again called out, but BJ was having no more of it. He refused to walk over the scratch line that had been drawn on the carpet. The referee slowly counted from one to ten. BJ stayed where he was, and Dozer was declared the victor.

Rogers loaded Dozer up in his crate and drove away from the gas plant. It had been a good night. His reputation in the dog-fighting world remained untarnished. He knew that within hours other dogmen would be on the phone swapping tales about his victory, talking up Dozer as White Boy Rob's next great bull dog. He turned onto the highway and headed contentedly back to Channelview, never noticing the black pickup parked behind the trees or the two undercover officers sitting inside watching him.

A FEW MONTHS EARLIER, in the summer of 2007, Stephen Davis and Gary Manning, two officers assigned to the Department of Public Safety's criminal intelligence division in Houston, had been sitting behind their desks when a lieutenant walked in and said that a player in the Houston-area dogfighting game was ready to talk. The two men sighed. They were veteran agents, beefy guys with the kind of oversized biceps and surly expressions you'd expect from bouncers at cheap strip joints. They'd worked undercover for years, usually going by their first names (for this article, their first names have been changed). They had posed as drug dealers, motorcycle gang members, white supremacists, and gun runners. "We didn't want to mess with dogfighting," recalls Manning, who spent six years in the Marines before joining the DPS, in 1994. "We just figured it was piddly shit, something for the local animal-control officers."

Then they started Googling. They learned that the Humane Society of the United States estimates that as many as 40,000 people around the country are involved in dogfighting. On dogfighting Web sites they read message boards filled with comments about everything from the best way to train fighting dogs to tips for treating them when they are injured. They got hold of underground dogfighting magazines and studied ads from pit bull kennels promoting litters of puppies that were the offspring of retired champion dogs.

When they met with the informant, he told them that there were dogmen all over southeast Texas, some raising fighting pit bulls out in the country just as their fathers and grandfathers once had. Other dogmen, the informant said, kept their dogs in their backyards, behind their homes, at the edges of cities. A new generation of inner-city black dogmen had also emerged, holding their shows in abandoned buildings or in the back parking lots of apartment complexes. Brash young gangbangers or wannabe gangsters were even getting into the game, the informant added, sometimes spontaneously staging their shows on street corners, in full view of anyone passing by.

The informant kept going, telling Manning and Davis about unscrupulous dogmen putting cocaine on their dogs' gums, shooting them up with steroids, and then abandoning or unabashedly killing their "curs" (the worst-performing dogs). He brought up the 2006 murder of 27-year-old Thomas Weigner, a prosperous young pit bull breeder and handler, well-known in dogfighting circles around the country, who kept more than 250 fighting pit bulls on a twenty-acre spread in Liberty County, northeast of Houston. At least two gunmen had broken into his home, tied up his family, and then shot him, letting him bleed to death. The Liberty County Sheriff's Department named a rival dogman, 34-year-old William David Townsend, of Montgomery County, as its lead suspect, speculating that he wanted either Weigner's money (Weigner had reportedly won $50,000 in a recent show) or Weigner's best dogs for his own kennel. Townsend was arrested on an unrelated drug charge, then released on bond, at which point he reportedly fled to Mexico, taking some of his best dogs (and maybe some of Weigner's).

Nevertheless, the informant told Manning and Davis, Townsend was still in the game, sometimes slipping back into Texas with one of his dogs for a show.

"Nothing is slowing these guys down, absolutely nothing," the informant said. "They make Michael Vick look like a pussy."

Manning and Davis drove out to have a look at some of the dogmen's homes, including White Boy Rob Rogers's trailer, in Channelview. But the cops quickly realized that their investigation faced one major problem: They had almost no chance of getting close to a dogfight, at least not one involving the better players. Dogmen were like members of a secret society; their shows were invitation-only. And those spectators who got invited were not informed of the show's location until an hour or so before it was to begin—sometimes less. They almost always drove to the shows in cars or trucks with the license plates removed to avoid being identified. Usually, someone would do a "heat run" on the way to a show, doubling back on the route he had just taken to see if any cops were following in an unmarked vehicle.

The cops thought they had caught a break when the informant told them about the Friday-night show between Rogers and Chris. They set up down the street from Rogers's trailer, watched him load a dog into his van, and discreetly followed him. But when he turned down a dirt road and headed behind the gas plant, they came to a stop. Lookouts, no doubt, had been stationed around the field, and Manning and Davis had no idea when the show was actually going to begin. Considering that the only way to make a felony case on a dogfighter is to catch him in the act of dogfighting, they figured they were out of luck.

But they couldn't get the dogmen out of their minds. "There's got to be a way to bring them down," Manning kept saying to his partner. A few days later, they walked into their lieutenant's office and told him that they wanted to do something that had never before been tried in the history of American law enforcement. They wanted to become dogmen themselves.

FOR CENTURIES, dogfighting was perfectly legal. In Rome's Colosseum, gladiator dogs were pitted against one another or against other animals, including wild elephants. One of the more popular forms of entertainment in twelfth-century England was "baiting," in which fighting dogs would be released into a ring with chained bulls and bears. In the colonial United States dogfights were common, and they continued well into the nineteenth century, with formal rules and sanctioned referees. As recently as 1881, the Ohio and Mississippi Railroad advertised special fares to a dogfight in Louisville, Kentucky.

Eventually, because of protests by such groups as the American Society for the Prevention of Cruelty to Animals, states began passing legislation that banned dogfights. By the thirties, dogfighting had been driven almost completely underground. Nevertheless, it remained a culturally ingrained phenomenon that simply refused to go away—a fact that became all too clear when Michael Vick, the quarterback of the Atlanta Falcons, was indicted by a grand jury in July 2007 for operating a dogfighting ring on his Virginia farm and later sentenced to two years in prison. The vast majority of Americans were stunned. Why, they wanted to know, would a young multimillionaire celebrity risk everything to engage in what they regarded as a barbaric practice?

Pit bulls are fast, agile animals with bulging chests, bricklike snouts, jaws that have ten times the crushing power of other dogs', and incredibly strong back legs that allow them to shoot forward like blitzing linebackers. If properly socialized, they can be among the most people-friendly, face-licking pets on the planet: Think of Petey in *The Little Rascals*. But when raised by a dogman, they can be terrifying, capable of brawling for hours at a time, ripping the flesh off their opponents, even disemboweling them if they get the chance.

Dogmen view their fighting pit bulls as nothing less than spectacularly trained athletes. On dogfighting Web sites, dogmen constantly swap stories about famous pit bulls. ("The best pound for pound match dog I have ever seen was 'CH. HOLLY,'" one dogman recently blogged. "She was the K-9 equivalent of Sugar Ray Robinson.") They know the bloodlines of the pit bulls the way horse racing fans know the lineage of Triple Crown contenders. "Let me tell you," Rogers said when I met him recently, "they are beautiful animals. It's amazing to watch two of them face off in the box, studying one another, making a move, then changing strategies and making another move. These dogs think. They're smart. And they get a real joy out of fighting. They're born and bred to fight. I'm telling you, keeping one of these dogs from fighting is just as cruel as keeping a retriever inside the house and not letting him fetch."

Rogers, who is 38, is hardly an unpleasant man. Stocky, with closely cropped dark hair and crooked teeth, he usually dresses in a sleeveless T-shirt, blue jean shorts, and sandals or rubber flip-flops. He has a regular day job, selling salvaged cars to junkyards. His wife is a friendly, outgoing woman, and he proudly describes his three children as "honor roll students." The family attends a small Baptist church in Channelview, just down the road from their trailer, and on birthdays and other special occasions they like to go to Casa Olé, an inexpensive Mexican restaurant. One of Rogers's neighbors describes him as "a nice enough guy who always waves when he sees you driving by."

Raised by a single mother in a blue-collar neighborhood in Houston, Rogers told me that he was "just your average redneck kid who loved to hunt and fish." He loved dogs, he said—"all kinds of dogs, big and little, rottweilers and dachshunds." Except for a few fistfights, he rarely got in trouble as a boy. (His only criminal conviction to date is a misdemeanor charge for an illegal inspection sticker.)

When he was in his early twenties and living in Channelview, he saw his first show. What struck him immediately was not the violence of the dogfighting but the bond between the men and their dogs. "They worked with their dogs like they were teammates," he told me. "And they never let their dogs get too hurt. I learned all that stuff about fighting your dog to the death was just a big lie. If their dogs were losing, they'd pick them up, take them home, get them healed, and let them live to fight another day."

Rogers began reading about the training techniques of such legendary Texas dogmen as Maurice Carver, of San Antonio, the "Silver Fox," who, according to one story on a dogfighting Web site, always arrived for his shows "in his cowboy boots, Stetson hat and usually dressed to kill." Rogers bought some pit bulls and built their loyalty by occasionally giving them a pork bone from Kroger or a stuffed animal to rip apart. ("I bought up every stuffed teddy bear I could find at the Channelview garage sales," he said.) He had the dogs swim with him and his children in the family's plastic pool and in a nearby river. He bought a treadmill for him and his wife but soon started to use it to work a dog while he and the family ate dinner or watched television. Eventually he had a few of his dogs do some "rolls"—brief fights with other dogs, five to ten minutes in length. Then he started doing shows for money. One evening, he took his best dog, Little Punk, to a remote piece of property near Austin to challenge a well-known veteran dogman and his animal, Hogdog. According to the rules, dogmen can't touch their dogs during a fight, but they can get right up beside them and exhort them to fight harder. In the middle of the action, Rogers stepped forward, snapped his fingers, pointed to Hogdog's back legs, and said, "Right there." Little Punk promptly attacked. Rogers then snapped his fingers and pointed at Hogdog's head; Little Punk responded by pulling Hogdog's head straight back, nearly ripping it off his neck. The spectators were amazed at the newcomer's skill. Rogers was like some sort of pit bull whisperer. Hogdog's owner pulled his dog from the fight after 42 minutes, and suddenly Rogers was famous.

In 2002 he began fighting a solid black pit bull named Dipstick. Dipstick was a defensive specialist. He'd wait until his opponent made the first move, then he'd deftly step to the right or left, lock his jaws onto the side of his opponent's face or ears, and start clamping down. Within a couple years—Rogers always gave his dogs plenty of rest between fights—Dipstick became a "grand champion" (a pit bull that has won five matches in a row, an unusual feat in dogfighting).

Dogfighting fame seldom translates to wealth. Rogers rarely won more than $1,000 at a fight (though occasionally the purses went as high as $10,000), and he'd plow much of that money back into food and veterinary supplies for the dogs. Every now and then, he'd agree to train the pit bulls of other dogmen, usually charging between $500 and $1,500. "I didn't mind helping out other guys who were devoted to the sport," he told me. In early 2008 he got a call about two white guys who had opened a new "spot"—a place to hold dogfights—in a small, secluded warehouse on the east side of Houston, just off Interstate 10. They were calling their spot the Dog House, and they wanted to meet the great White Boy Rob and perhaps do a few rolls with him, maybe even pick up some pointers.

"Yeah, I'll talk to them," Rogers said.

MANNING AND DAVIS'S PLAN was to lure Rogers and other dogmen to the warehouse to put on shows, which they would videotape with cameras hidden in the walls or within their clothing. But the informant told them that if they ever hoped to win the dogmen's trust, they were going to have to get in their own box and fight their own dogs.

One afternoon in early 2008, Manning and Davis drove to the informant's house to get their first taste of dogfighting. The informant led them into his garage, where he had set up a box. He brought out a female named Crunch and showed Manning, who was going to be the dogman, how to hold the dog before a fight, how to release it, and how to coach it when the fight began.

The informant then went back outside and returned a minute or two later with another female, named Mercedes. He stood in one corner of the garage with Mercedes and had Manning stand in another corner with Crunch. "Release," said the informant, and just like that, without the slightest provocation, the two dogs came charging, their ears pinned back, their teeth ripping into each other's skin.

Manning and Davis had seen their share of homicide victims and had been in a few bloody fights themselves, but they had never witnessed anything like this. They left as quickly as they could and drove to the nearest bar, dog blood still on their boots. "What the fuck have we gotten ourselves into?" asked Manning.

Four days later, the informant called to say that Rogers had agreed to take a look at the Dog House. When he arrived with a couple of his associates, Manning and Davis were wearing motorcycle boots, blue jeans, and sleeveless T-shirts. They said they were members of a local motorcycle gang that stole ATMs for a living (they'd had a couple of busted ATMs put against the back wall). They offered their visitors something to drink, but Rogers simply stared at the newcomers and their dogs (which the informant had brought to the warehouse earlier). "Let's do a roll," he said.

A nervous Manning, already dripping with sweat, carried Crunch into the box. Rogers brought out a dog from his van, but he told one of his buddies to act as the dog's handler. Rogers wanted only to observe. Manning and Davis looked at each other. If Rogers wasn't on tape, they couldn't pop him for a felony dogfighting charge. "Let's go," said Rogers. "What the hell are we waiting for?"

The dogs were released. Predictably, Rogers's superior dog demolished Crunch, first attacking her front legs, then going for her neck. A desperate Manning, getting down on his hands and knees, kept yelling at Crunch to keep fighting. "Good, Mama!" he shouted, as the informant had taught him. "Kill that other bitch! You can do it!"

Rogers quickly ordered the roll to be stopped. "You don't even have any idea what the hell you're doing, do you?" he asked Manning. He then added, "You're going to kill your dog, right? Your bitch is nothing but a cur."

Manning knew that some dogmen immediately kill a dog that's lost a fight, usually by shooting or electrocuting it. Was that what Rogers expected him to do to prove himself as a real dogman? He stared at Crunch, who was limping and gasping for breath, her tongue jutting from the side of her mouth. "No, man, I'm not killing her," Manning finally said. "She's new to the game. I just wanted to see if she would scratch out."

Rogers nodded. "I'd do the same thing," he said. Apparently Manning had passed the test.

THE NEWS BEGAN TO SPREAD: Two new dogmen had built a spot inside a warehouse, and they were more than happy to let other dogmen hold their shows there for a $20 admission fee. They were also barbecuing wings and ribs on a grill out in the parking lot. Gradually, Manning and Davis built their reputations, mostly with minor dogfighters. In time, Rogers returned to the Dog House too, getting in the box to do some rolls and a couple of shows, dominating everyone who dared to take him on. The cops were smart; they knew that having White Boy

Rob in attendance enhanced their legitimacy. To make sure he kept coming back, they lent him money and agreed to fund part of the purses for his shows. They also bought a couple dogs from him and paid for the dogs' conditioning. It wasn't long before Rogers was treating Manning and Davis as his apprentices.

In the world of dogfighting, Rogers was actually regarded as one of the more honorable dogmen. He didn't shoot up his dogs with steroids. He didn't hang "bait animals" (cats or small dogs) from a pole in a cage and have his pit bulls lunge after them in order to build their aggression. Nor was he a partier. When Manning and Davis once offered to buy him drinks at Hi-10 Cabaret, a topless club, he refused, saying he didn't want to disrespect his wife.

Despite Rogers's training, Manning and Davis's dogs got pummeled in their initial shows. "You dumbass white boys," their black opponents would gleefully yell, driving away at the end of the night, their stomachs full of barbecue and beer. The officers would bandage up their dogs and take them back to their homes in suburban Houston. Their children and neighbors would stare wide-eyed at the battered pit bulls sitting in their garages or chained to metal stakes in their backyards. Late one evening, one of Manning's neighbors, who knew about his undercover work, saw him pull into the driveway and carry out an exhausted pit bull. "Don't ask," Manning said.

In April, only a couple months after opening the Dog House, they received an invitation to bring one of their dogs to a show with a top black dogfighter who lived an hour or so outside Houston. It was a huge break: Manning and Davis figured that if they could win over the crowd at that show, they might, in turn, be able to lure them to the Dog House for more fights— and in the end, make more arrests.

The show was held in a field surrounded by thick woods. Manning and Davis were the only white men in attendance. More than fifty black men, some likely armed with pistols and knives, crowded around the cops and their dog, Brutus, whom they had bought from another Houston dogman a few days earlier. The purse was set at $5,000—each side putting up $2,500. Manning and Davis knew nothing about Brutus, and they were worried the dog would quickly fold, which would enrage the spectators, who had come expecting to see a real fight. Instead, Brutus raced to the middle of the box, grabbed onto his opponent's head, and threw him backward. The fight lasted an amazing two hours and twenty minutes. Toward the end, Brutus was fading, with lacerations all over his body. Manning stepped forward, picked Brutus up in his arms, and forfeited the fight, handing his opponent $2,500. The spectators started applauding, some of them saying it was one of the best shows they had ever seen. "You got a real bull dog in that Brutus," one of them said, slapping Manning and Davis on the back. Though Brutus died a few days later, the two officers realized that they had been accepted as real dogmen.

Soon after, dogmen from around southeast Texas were calling Manning's and Davis's cell phones, wanting to come to the Dog House for a show. A group of dogmen from Louisiana, another hotbed of dogfighting, drove to Houston to check out the Dog House. One dogman brought his girlfriend to watch a show. "What the hell is next?" asked Davis. "A kid's night?"

The dogmen Davis and Manning encountered had all kinds of day jobs: manager of a Jack in the Box, sales representative for an oil-field services company, mail room clerk for a community college, professional baseball player turned high school English teacher. But the person they really wanted to meet was Houston's top black dogfighter, a 42-year-old man known as Fat Don. The rumor was that Fat Don, whose real name was Donald Wayne Woods, had 150 dogs spread out among various properties. At least two of those dogs were grand champions that had won shows with $100,000-plus purses. Fat Don arrived at every show in a Mercedes SUV. He also owned several classic cars and a couple dragsters, which he raced at local tracks. He had supposedly arranged for a pet company to send trucks out to his home, situated behind locked gates in northeast Houston, to deliver giant bags of dog food.

In the fall of 2008, Fat Don finally agreed to meet Manning and Davis at a Denny's. He was short and squat and wore overalls. He had a four-man entourage with him, one of whom stood watch outside the restaurant. For a while, they talked about his grand champions Fat Boy and Cash. Manning and Davis mentioned that they were now "kennel partners" with White Boy Rob. They told Fat Don that they wanted to match one of their dogs against one of his.

Fat Don's eyebrows raised. He had been out of the game for a while and liked the idea of making his comeback against White Boy Rob and his new partners. He agreed to do a show six weeks later.

Rogers put Gemini, a black-and-white pit bull, on the keep. Fat Don went with an all-black dog named Fred. But when they met at the Dog House, Rogers said Gemini was not rested—he had accidentally slipped off his chain in Rogers's yard a few days earlier and gotten into a vicious fight with another dog—and that the show should be forfeited. Manning and Davis were insistent that the show go on: They needed videotape of Fat Don in the box.

The bout was totally anticlimactic. Fred got on top of Gemini, slammed his head to the carpet, and never let up. Gemini seemed disoriented, as if he had suffered a concussion. After a mere twelve minutes, a humiliated Rogers called a halt and had Gemini picked up. "Another day," he said to Fat Don. Manning and Davis handed over their side of the purse—$10,000.

Though Manning and Davis were exhilarated to have nabbed another kingpin, they did have one problem: The top DPS commanders in Austin had been reviewing the dogfighting budget, and they were not happy that so much of their money was flowing into the hands of the dogmen. A couple commanders thought the whole operation was trivial compared with the major crimes that needed to be investigated. A couple others were concerned that animal rights organizations would erupt upon learning that DPS officers had actually been dogfighting themselves. Belinda Smith, the animal cruelty prosecutor for the Harris County district attorney's office, and Stephen St. Martin, another of the DA's top prosecutors, went to Austin to reassure the DPS commanders that Manning and Davis's investigation was perfectly legal. They mentioned that the Dog House had become so well-known that dogmen from around the state and even as far away as Tennessee and Maryland were wanting to arrange shows there.

What's more, Manning and Davis told their commanders that they were convinced they were getting close to William David Townsend, the lead suspect in the 2006 Thomas Weigner murder case. One day Rogers had called and told them that two Mexican brothers had transported Townsend's dog Bisexual over the border. They'd driven her to Rogers's yard to spend the night before a fight the next night in East Texas against a dog from a Louisiana pit bull kennel. Bisexual, so named for a vicious tendency to strike at her opponents' genitals, was one of the most feared pit bulls in Texas dogfighting. If she won her fight against the Louisiana dog, as she was easily expected to do, she'd be a grand champion.

Manning and Davis persuaded Rogers to let them watch the show. Also coming along in another vehicle were two black bodyguards from Houston who had presumably been hired by Townsend to make sure nothing happened to Bisexual. The caravan headed toward the town of Jasper. But when they reached the show's location, the dogman handling the Louisiana dog said the kennel owners, perhaps realizing their dog would be no match for Bisexual, wanted to back out of the fight.

According to Manning, one of the Mexicans then called

Townsend in Mexico. He put the call on speakerphone, and Manning was able to eavesdrop on the entire conversation. He heard the Mexican ask if he should shoot the gringo dogman from the Louisiana kennel. Townsend told him to instead arrange a deal with the kennel owners to obtain the dog that was supposed to fight—or else suffer the consequences. A deal was indeed struck, and the Mexicans disappeared back into Mexico with Bisexual and the Louisiana dog.

"They'll be back to get Bisexual that grand championship," Rogers told Manning and Davis. "I promise they'll be back."

In fact, the Mexican brothers were rumored to be coming back with Bisexual for a show on December 6, and Manning and Davis proposed that on that night teams of DPS and local police officers sweep into three spots, including their own, where several shows would be taking place. Maybe they'd get lucky and nab Bisexual, the Mexican brothers, and Townsend too. At the least, the officers declared, the roundup could bring down close to two hundred dogmen and spectators.

But the DPS commanders ordered the officers to close their investigation and arrest those they already had on videotape. At dawn on a Friday morning in November, more than one hundred peace officers stormed some of the dogmen's homes and various properties where Manning and Davis knew that large numbers of fighting dogs were being kept.

Over the next several days, more suspects were arrested. When it was all over, 85 men, including White Boy Rob and Fat Don, were indicted for either dogfighting (a state felony with a maximum punishment of two years in jail) or being spectators at a dogfight (a class A misdemeanor with a maximum punishment of one year in jail). Animal control officers also confiscated 185 fighting dogs. When Rogers's dogs and their puppies were carried off, his wife and children burst into tears. The dogs were the family pets. Every night, they would curl up on the couch and lie on their backs to be rubbed on their stomachs. "It's not fair," one of the children cried out.

Because dogmen have been known to break into animal shelters to steal confiscated pit bulls, Harris County stationed constables around the facility where the dogs had been taken. But there was no way, Belinda Smith told reporters, to rehabilitate dogs that had been bred to be so wildly aggressive toward other dogs. It was also important, she noted, to keep those dogs, especially the champion dogs belonging to Fat Don and Rogers, from passing on their fighting bloodlines. So the decision was made to euthanize all of them, including the pit bulls that Manning and Davis had used. Before they were put down, the officers showed up to say goodbye. "I'm not much of an emotional guy, and I knew it was the right thing to put those dogs down," said Manning. "But when I was saying, 'Good girl,' to one of my dogs, petting her on the head, she started wagging her tail. It was not easy to walk away from that."

The bust was trumpeted in the news as one of the biggest in the nation, and predictably, most citizens were outraged. Someone commented on the *Houston Chronicle* Web site that dogmen should be tied down, covered with pork chop grease, and mauled by "20 hungry pit bulls." As it turned out, the animal rights organizations were not angry at all that Manning and Davis had fought dogs: They were thrilled that someone had finally gone after the dogmen.

But the writers on the dogfighting Web sites were furious that the informant, one of their own, had become a snitch. (Manning and Davis refuse to comment on whether the informant had struck a deal regarding any previous charges in return for his cooperation.) One described the cops as "scumbags" who'd entrapped the dogmen. On the *Chronicle* Web site, someone who said he wasn't a dogman wrote, "It's laughable that so-called mistreatment of animals gets more attention than many of the horrendous things that happen to humans every day."

Nevertheless, the criminal cases were open-and-shut. By June of this year, almost all the defendants had worked out deals, including Fat Don, who, according to Smith, quietly agreed to a two-year felony sentence. To just about everyone's surprise, however, one of the few dogmen who initially refused to cop a plea was White Boy Rob.

When I talked to Rogers, in early June, he and his family had left their Channelview trailer after receiving death threats and moved into a nearby apartment. Instead of working with dogs, Rogers was spending his evenings taming feral cats, getting them to drink milk out of a saucer he kept right outside the front door. "Maybe I'll get them tame enough that the kids can adopt them," he said.

I asked Rogers what he thought of Manning and Davis, who had just been named officers of the year by a Houston law enforcement organization. His voice almost softened—almost. "It never occurred to me, not once, that those boys were cops. I thought they wanted to be real dogmen, so I taught them how to fight the right way—with dignity and honor, not letting their dogs get chewed up. And I know, deep down, they started loving it as much as I did. I could tell they had the blood for it. But now they get to go free and get all kinds of publicity while I go off to prison."

He paused. "It don't matter. Locking me up ain't nothing compared to what they've already done to my dogs. They even took away our two boxers and killed them. Do you think that's right? Do you think any of those dogs really wanted to be rescued so they could have a needle stuck in their ass? Come on, now, you tell me who the monster is. All of you people who call yourselves civilized go to boxing matches. You watch wrestling, and you watch those Ultimate Fighting Championships on television. What's really the difference here?"

After viewing the DPS videotapes of Rogers standing in the box at the Dog House, exhorting his dogs to keep fighting, Rogers's attorney, Rick Detoto, a respected young Houston criminal defense attorney, knew it would be an uphill battle to get an acquittal. "But I agree with my client. Morally, a juror should have a problem with cops deliberately subjecting all these dogs to abuse in order to arrest someone else," Detoto said. "Would those cops stick a child in a house where a suspected child abuser lives in order to catch him? I don't think so. And I have to say, when you see the undercover officers in those videotapes, they look like they're having a really good time."

Manning and Davis insist they were just playacting and that they were never seduced by Rogers or the other dogmen. But they do admit that their experience taught them about the dogmen's fierce devotion to what they do. "We definitely forced dogfighting around here to go more underground," Manning said. "We've noticed the talk on the dogfighting Web sites has gotten a lot more coded. But we'll never get dogfighting to go away. There will always be a show every weekend night."

Though Rogers believed he could have taken the stand and convinced a jury that dogfighting was a legitimate sport and not a crime, he finally decided in late June to accept an offer from the district attorney's office: He agreed to plead guilty and will serve a one-year felony sentence in county jail, which means he could be out in six months—not bad compared with the two-year sentence he could have received. Smith said she decided to offer him the deal because he had no prior criminal record, which would have allowed a jury to give him probation. But, she added, if he is caught dogfighting again, he can be sent away to prison for two to ten years.

When I asked Rogers if he would ever go back to dogfighting, he said, "I don't know, to be honest with you. But I will tell you that every night, I dream about my dogs making their moves, feinting to the left and then attacking to the right. My dogs were great dogs. They were beautiful, strong dogs. Oh, man, they were beautiful."

SKIP HOLLANDSWORTH, *an executive editor of* Texas Monthly, *writes two or three crime stories a year for the magazine. Since publishing the story about dogfighting in August 2009, he has written about a powerful federal judge in Galveston who for years sexually abused women in his own courthouse, and he also has chronicled the story of a sweet, shy young mother in suburban Houston who suddenly stabbed her husband 193 times and buried him in their backyard.*

Coda

The massive Texas bust ultimately resulted in prison time for sixty Texas dogfighters and spectators (including two women). Since then, the federal government has carried out another dogfighting bust that rounded up thirty top dogfighters in five states, including Texas. But Belinda Smith of the Harris County district attorney's office insists that dogfighting in Texas hasn't been dealt a fatal blow. "It's just gone deeper underground," she says. Determined to bring down the next group of big-time dogfighters who have taken over from Fat Don and White Boy Rob, she has been meeting with various local police departments, hoping to set up more undercover operations. "But, of course, we know when we get them, there's going to be someone ready to step right up to take their place," Smith admits. "It remains the great mystery: Why do men love dogfighting the way they do? Why is it so important to them?"

Ron Chernow

MADOFF AND HIS MODELS

FROM *The New Yorker*

IN FINANCIAL HISTORY, Ponzi schemes—the fraudulent enterprise of paying off old investors with money collected from new ones—are the most peculiar of crimes. Before they are detected, they seem exquisitely pleasing to perpetrators and victims alike. The fraud appears to be a bountiful gift that the confidence trickster, a generous soul and a financial wizard to boot, has bestowed upon a grateful world. Investors frequently revere the schemer, endowing him with magical properties. The schemer, in turn, may come to believe that his scheme isn't altogether shady and that he will someday generate the sensational returns advertised. For the duration of a Ponzi scheme, it may seem like a victimless crime. Not surprisingly, when the impostor is exposed, the victims experience profound hurt and disillusionment, having trusted implicitly in the schemer against a chorus of naysayers.

Charles Ponzi was probably the most colorful and outlandish practitioner of the scheme that bears his name. An Italian immigrant and postman's son who arrived in Boston in 1903, he had charm, imagination, and chutzpah of epic proportions. At first, he worked as a grocery clerk and dishwasher, but he soon got a job with a bank in Montreal that paid exorbitant interest rates and stole money from depositors—invaluable training for his future exploits. After being arrested for forging a signature on a check, Ponzi was clapped into a Quebec jail for twenty months and told his unsuspecting mother that he had landed a job as a "special assistant" to the warden. Returning to the United States, he served a two-year stint in an Atlanta prison for smuggling Italian immigrants into the country.

Ponzi's mind was a small factory for cranking out get-rich-quick schemes. Back in Boston in 1919, Ponzi had the epiphany that secured his place in the annals of financial larceny. An avid stamp collector, he received a letter from Spain that contained a voucher called an International Reply Coupon, which the recipient could redeem for a return-postage stamp at a fixed price in sixty-three countries. Many European currencies had slumped after the war, and Ponzi reasoned that he could buy such coupons, say, in debased Italian lire, redeem them in America, then sell the stamps at a sizable profit. It was an elementary form of currency arbitrage—exploiting discrepancies in the prices of the coupons in different currencies. In December of 1919, Ponzi launched a firm called the Securities Exchange Company—it preceded by more than a decade the creation of the Securities and Exchange Commission in Washington, D.C., established to police swindlers like Ponzi—and wooed investors by promising a fifty-percent return on their money in forty-five days.

Financial fraud is the crime of choice for arrivistes, insecure dreamers with a yearning eye for high society. Desperate to feel rich and important, they tend to be excellent mimics of respectability. The diminutive Ponzi fit the bill perfectly. A dandy in a straw boater with spats and a showy gold-tipped cane, he strutted about Boston, greeting reporters with ready quips and quotable lines, and his press coverage was, at first, highly laudatory.

Like many confidence men, Ponzi preyed first on his own kind, and the Boston Italian community embraced him with delirious joy. As insurance against future trouble, Ponzi also recruited Boston policemen and reporters as investors. In February, 1920, he collected a meagre five thousand dollars; five months later, he was raking in a million dollars weekly. Ponzi's business drew in thousands of investors, bewitched by his supposed prowess. With considerable skill, he portrayed himself as a populist champion who would enable small investors to earn their rightful places in the world. He claimed to accept money from investors as a form of altruism, and they rewarded him with fanatic loyalty.

Ponzi's investment strategy wasn't illegal, and the postal coupons could, in theory, have yielded a profit. In practice, however, the scheme was preposterous and unworkable. Nobody could buy and transport stamps in sufficient quantities to earn the returns that Ponzi promised. In *Ponzi's Scheme* (2005), Mitchell Zuckoff, a journalism professor at Boston University, regards his subject as a chronic dreamer with a cockeyed scheme that went awry. Ponzi was indeed a strange amalgam of petty visionary and big-time crook. Soon after he announced his scheme, postal authorities in Italy, France, and Romania suspended the sale of postal coupons, destroying any chance that Ponzi could implement his plan or reward investors with outsize returns. When anyone pressed him about his investment methods, he hinted that he couldn't reveal his lucrative strategies.

As he paid off old clients with money from new ones, the press scented criminal mischief afoot. The New York postmaster, Thomas G. Patten, pointed out that too few coupons existed to sustain a scheme of such magnitude. When reporters dredged up Ponzi's criminal past in Montreal, complete with mug shots, his fate was sealed. Eight months after he founded the Securities Exchange Company, federal agents padlocked the offices. It turned out that Ponzi had never actually got around to buying many postal coupons and that it was all a colossal hoax. Sentenced to five years in a federal prison in Plymouth, Massachusetts, Ponzi had fancy stationery printed up that said "Charles Ponzi, Plymouth, Mass." He was deported to Italy in 1934, and later made his way to South America, where he died in the charity ward of a Rio de Janeiro hospital in 1949.

Ponzi was convinced that he was a wizard who had stumbled upon a form of financial alchemy that had eluded others. Incapable of moral clarity, he could never quite admit to himself that he was a charlatan and that his scheme was an impossible fiasco. He fooled others because he fooled himself. Right up until the end, he found refuge in fantasies that he might take over a chain of banks or shipping lines that would enable him to pay off his legions of worshipful investors. He never suffered serious remorse or second thoughts.

PONZI'S SCHEME HAS ENJOYED a rich afterlife, often in far more adept hands. As one ponders the scandal of Bernard L. Madoff, who has pleaded guilty to fraud in a scheme thought to have cost nearly sixty-five billion dollars in investor money, one is tempted to say that Ponzi lacked ambition. Madoff imitated Ponzi in a few particulars, such as victimizing his own community (in his case, Jewish) and inventing fictitious returns, but his improvements on the traditional Ponzi scheme are breathtaking.

Where Ponzi pandered to uneducated investors and promised gargantuan returns, Madoff trimmed annual returns to a modest but wondrously reliable eight to twelve percent. Madoff's seductive appeal lay not so much in his purported profits as in his consistency. Although that consistency was far more suspect than his returns, given the volatility of financial markets, the reasonable-sounding profits gave his operation an air of respectability. Wealthy investors could flatter themselves that, far from being greedy, they were sacrificing yield for security. Madoff's method enabled him to swindle rich people who prided themselves on their financial conservatism and sophistication, so that he could appeal to avarice of a quiet, upper-crust sort.

Forever dependent on a growing supply of fresh victims, Ponzi schemers can't be fussy about their clients and are typically in an unseemly hurry to snare them. Here, Madoff made his most audacious innovation. Instead of openly courting investors, he pretended to fend them off. Back in the nineteen-twenties, sophisticated investors joined together in pools that manipulated individual stocks, and such funds acquired a certain cachet. Something similar happened in recent years with hedge funds, which retained snob appeal even when returns flagged. Madoff made it seem impossibly difficult to invest with him. As a rule, his fund was closed to new investors, requiring special introductions to the club. "I know Bernie, I can get you in" was the open sesame whispered throughout the world of Jewish society, where "Uncle Bernie" was affectionately touted as "the Jewish bond." The aura of exclusivity was bogus, of course: he ended up with almost five thousand client accounts.

Even when he deigned to accept people's money, Madoff emphasized his extreme reluctance. "Bernie would tell me, 'Let them start small, and if they're happy the first year or two, they can put in more,'" one investor told the *Wall Street Journal*. Madoff pretended that his investment-advisory business was merely a lucrative sideline for select friends, while his real business lay in a market-making operation that matched buyers and sellers. Thus Madoff posed as a man beleaguered by his own generosity, who took on new clients as a favor to friends. It was a bravura performance.

As word spread that Madoff made heaps of money for investors, he acquired a social glow at the country clubs where he recruited his victims, burnished by his mansion in the Hamptons, his villa on the French Riviera, and yachts moored in various places. Dressed in charcoal-gray bespoke suits from Savile Row and fond of expensive watches, he took on the protective coloration of his environment—a specialty of Ponzi schemers—and both admired and resented the moneyed crowd that he emulated. Only his facial twitches and the ghost of an old stammer gave the lie to his calm, avuncular image. His low-profile approach appealed to a class of investors who would have cringed at Ponzi's crass hucksterism.

Although he came from modest origins in the outer boroughs of New York—he earned the seed money for Bernard L. Madoff Investment Securities from working as a lifeguard at Rockaway Beach and installing sprinkler systems—Madoff clothed himself in establishment credentials. He was a trustee of Hofstra University, a nonexecutive chairman of the Nasdaq stock exchange, and a member of a government advisory panel on securities regulation. Like Ponzi, he posed as a paladin of small investors, and he ingratiated himself with government regulators. Every large Ponzi scheme needs an active network of agents—carnival barkers who pull people into the big tent—and Madoff strategically deployed people in places such as Greenwich, Connecticut, and Palm Beach, Florida. His mystique led prominent personalities—including Steven Spielberg, Mortimer Zuckerman, Senator Frank Lautenberg, Elie Wiesel, Sandy Koufax, and Kevin Bacon—to invest with Madoff directly or through charities they established.

Madoff's spectacular downfall has sparked a cottage industry of journalists trying to fathom his psychopathology. The enigmatic smirk he has shown to the news media, giving the impression of a man savoring a little joke on the world, has only heightened curiosity. In late January, the *Times* business section ran a piece that typed Madoff as a psychopath and quoted forensic psychologists who likened him to Ted Bundy, the serial killer: "They say that whereas Mr. Bundy murdered people, Mr. Madoff murdered wallets, bank accounts and people's sense of financial trust and security." These analysts assumed that Madoff intended from the outset to create a gigantic fraud and destroy thousands of people. Did he?

Although Madoff's scheme dates back to at least the early nineteen-nineties, we understand little about the genesis of his criminal operation. Still, a new biography of another grand-scale Ponzi schemer, to be published next month, allows for some educated guesses. *The Match King*, by Frank Partnoy, a law professor at the University of San Diego, is an engrossing study of Ivar Kreuger, a Swedish financier of the nineteen-twenties and the operator of a global safety-match business so enormous that he was dubbed the Match King. Although his empire started only a few years after Ponzi's scheme imploded, Partnoy calculates that Kreuger's machinations lasted ten times longer and involved sums fifty times larger. He lifted the prosaic Ponzi fraud to a new level of sophistication and engaged in corporate finagling on a dizzying scale.

KREUGER DIDN'T MERELY FABRICATE RETURNS. He was a genuine businessman, backed by factories, mines, and other tangible assets. Like other industrialists, Kreuger planned to amass a huge fortune by manufacturing something ubiquitous and banal, much as John D. Rockefeller had done with kerosene. Kreuger wanted to monopolize the sale of the tiny boxes of safety matches that people used to light stoves or tobacco; cigarette smoking had become faddish among women as well as men in the nineteen-twenties, stoking demand for the product. By the 1929 crash, Kreuger's Swedish Match Company, a subsidiary of his holding company, Kreuger & Toll, had cornered the market on two-thirds of the forty billion matchboxes sold worldwide each year. Kreuger & Toll also earned a reputation as a proficient builder that completed construction projects reliably and on time. John Maynard Keynes extolled Kreuger as "perhaps the greatest constructive business intelligence of his age."

As a young man, Kreuger had rebelled against the monotony of his father's job as a factory manager in a small family match business on the Baltic Sea. The young man hatched grandiose plans as he studied engineering. Like Madoff, Kreuger was somewhat colorless and unassuming. He wore tastefully tailored suits, spoke five languages fluently, and projected an air of stability. He seldom laughed, was ascetic in his eating habits, and, aside from occasional flings with young women, was obsessed by business. A consummate actor who followed a scripted life, he always prepared a face to meet the faces that he met. Partnoy opens his story with Kreuger taking a transatlantic liner in the early nineteen-twenties and staging vignettes to impress other passengers. He undertook detailed preparations for meetings, then made sure specific questions were asked so that he could rattle off the string of facts he had memorized. He punctuated his speeches with meaningful pauses and long stares at the audience. Secretive and aloof, Kreuger, like Madoff, built his mystique by playing hard to get and retreating into a tight little zone of privacy.

Kreuger scarcely merits attention as a personality, although he had charm enough to court another great Swedish enigma, Greta Garbo. As a financial manipulator, however, Kreuger deserves study. In 1922, Swedish Match offered a dividend equal to twelve percent of its share price, which Kreuger & Toll topped with a dividend worth twenty-five percent. Kreuger believed that he could produce such lofty returns on a regular basis. Both his fame and his subsequent undoing came about because he was held hostage to those unrealistically high guarantees.

The alluring dividends dulled the critical faculties of investors, who didn't pry too closely into his affairs. With Europe devastated after the First World War, the only place where Kreuger could raise the vast capital to bankroll his empire was Wall Street. "You haggle about giving me money," Kreuger chided a Swedish banker. "But when I get off the boat in New York I find men on the pier begging me to take money off their hands." In 1923, Kreuger set up a new firm called International Match to act as a conduit for that money. American investors gave Kreuger a rapturous reception: by the time the Great Depression struck, his stocks and bonds ranked as the most widely held securities on Wall Street.

The American connection was all-important to Kreuger because of a daring plan he had concocted to take over the world match industry. He would approach governments with an irresistible deal: he'd lend them money at single digit interest rates if, in exchange, they granted him domestic monopolies on matchbox production. Kreuger always hoped that his interest payments to Wall Street would be equalled by the interest on the money he was lending abroad, giving him the matchbox monopolies for free. But things never quite worked out that way, and he finally had to borrow at much higher interest rates on Wall Street than he received from foreign governments. By late 1927, Kreuger had parlayed his scheme into match monopolies in nearly a dozen countries. The whole operation was premised on an uninterrupted flow of capital from Wall Street, which hinged, in turn, on dangling those hefty returns before investors.

As he doled out stupendous dividends, Kreuger developed a loyal following among American investors, who profited handsomely from his securities. Before the New Deal, there were few disclosure requirements for securities. In the nineteen-twenties, fewer than a third of the firms listed on the New York Stock Exchange even bothered to publish quarterly reports. So it's not surprising that satisfied investors swallowed Kreuger's brief, cryptic statements. With the federal government gripped by a laissez-faire ideology, the states tried to compensate with so-called "blue sky" laws, which regulated the sale of securities to discourage fraud, but they were inadequate to the cunning of a transnational swindler such as Kreuger.

Like Ponzi, Kreuger didn't set out to create a fraudulent enterprise. Nor was he booking only phantom profits. Rather, he aroused exaggerated expectations that he couldn't live up to. Annual returns in the match industry fluctuated wildly, denying Kreuger the steady high earnings he needed. So he turned to the venerable robbing-Peter-to-pay-Paul racket. To pay his dividends, he took out secret loans, imagining that they were temporary, only to have the deception take on a permanent life of its own. Financial engineering had, instead of acting as the servant of his business, evolved into its very essence.

Ivar Kreuger's empire previews the multinational corporations of the nineteen-sixties which regarded themselves as sovereign states and aimed to soar above the regulatory snares of any single country. Like Harold Geneen, of ITT, and other conglomerate chieftains of that era, Kreuger thought that all businesses could be reduced to ledgers studied in the antiseptic atmosphere of a corporate suite. By the late nineteen-twenties, his Swedish Match division alone employed twenty-six thousand people in ninety match plants scattered across the globe. Tellingly, Partnoy's biography doesn't contain a single scene of Kreuger inspecting a factory, chatting with a floor manager or worker, or strolling through one of the forests from which his matchsticks were chopped. Nor, as far as we know, did his bankers or accountants evince the least bit of curiosity about seeing these places. Kreuger's haunts were banks, boardrooms, and government ministries. He was always shopping for tax havens and pliant governments, such as the Duchy of Liechtenstein—"droll little countries with droll little laws," he called them. By striking deals with politicians, he was able to negotiate monopolies that he could never have attained in the marketplace. And countries desperate for Kreuger's loans enabled him to charge their citizens artificially high prices for matches.

Kreuger was a virtuoso at financial shell games, shuffling assets from one subsidiary to another to produce the desired results. He converted corporate balance sheets from transparent tools to instruments of deceit. His maze of companies was so baffling that secret subsidiaries spawned other secret subsidiaries in a never-ending chain of concealment. Anticipating the murky world of Enron and AIG, Kreuger pioneered off-balance-sheet entities, shunting debt to invisible firms and dummy companies. At times, it seemed as if Ivar Kreuger alone understood the corporate behemoth he had created, and he showed how easily legitimate companies, with a little creative accounting, can turn into outlaw enterprises.

Those who wonder how Madoff duped his auditors will find an instructive case study in Partnoy's account of Kreuger's relationship with A. D. Berning, a junior auditor with Ernst & Ernst, the accounting firm that earned lucrative fees from representing Kreuger's business interests. The young functionary prided himself on handling the mogul's account, and was pathetically eager to please him. Berning wasn't disposed to question shocking discrepancies that surfaced in the ledgers, especially after the Kreuger account led to his making partner. The Match King softened him up with perks and presents, inviting him along on fancy trips that stroked the auditor's ego. Berning gradually became complicit in the fraud without ever quite realizing that he had strayed across the line. Later, he achieved heroic stature by his part in exposing the fraud that he had helped to perpetuate. Kreuger's American bankers, the Boston Brahmin house of Lee, Higginson & Company, were no less credulous toward their foremost underwriting client. Every time the firm got too nosy, Kreuger boosted the fees he paid it. Like Madoff, Kreuger presented himself as a public benefactor, but Kreuger did so on a global scale, since he was ostensibly helping to rescue the French and German economies and advising President Herbert Hoover.

As Kreuger slipped deeper into debt and deceit, his personality became impenetrable. In his tightly guarded world, his motto was "Silence, silence, and more silence." For days on end, he sequestered himself in his Stockholm headquarters and warded off unwanted visitors. Outside his boardroom he posted red and green lights to signal to his secretary whether visitors could enter. In his office, he had a dummy phone that rang whenever he stepped on a secret button under his desk; he would then cite urgent business to chase away guests who had overstayed their welcome. At times, he pretended to field calls from Mussolini or Stalin. At one point, he even hired Swedish actors to attend a reception and pose as ambassadors from various countries.

The inner sanctum that Kreuger created and the way he dodged spontaneous encounters presage aspects of how Madoff did business. Madoff operated his investment-advisory business on the seventeenth floor of the Lipstick Building, in midtown Manhattan, in offices that have been described as "icily cold modern." Even though he supposedly managed billions of dollars, he concentrated the operation in a small space, run by a handful of longtime associates and family members, who thus far haven't been charged with any wrongdoing. For a time, his wife, Ruth, supervised the firm's bank accounts. Madoff fostered a subtle climate of fear among investors. He grew testy when quizzed about his methods and forbade investors from discussing their conversations with him. When one client dared to do just that in an e-mail to other clients, Madoff threatened to banish the man from his fund. A tacit understanding arose that Madoff wouldn't discuss financial matters in social settings, preventing confrontations with inquisitive investors or encounters that might surprise him into unwanted revelations. Most of all, Madoff protected himself by being plain elusive. "You couldn't meet Madoff," one banker told the *Wall Street Journal*. "He was like a pop star."

IN THE CLASSIC ACCOUNT *The Great Crash*, John Kenneth Galbraith notes that booms always mask many cases of embezzlement, which come to light during the bust. "Within a few days" of the 1929 crash, Galbraith writes, "something close to universal trust turned into something akin to universal suspicion." Such a climate was bound to undermine Ivar Kreuger, who appeared on the cover of *Time* the week of the crash, perhaps confirming the old journalistic adage that any phenomenon appearing on the cover of *Time* has already peaked. Kreuger's entire career had been predicated on access to American money markets. When they shut down, he couldn't survive long. In 1931, to lay to rest any doubts about his solvency, Kreuger actually boosted the International Match dividend from three dollars and twenty cents to four dollars per share, a promise that only worsened his predicament.

Kreuger had previously skirted the rules but, technically speaking, didn't engage in outright fraud. Only after the crash did he stoop to old-fashioned criminal behavior. He forged a series of Italian treasury bills, misspelling the name of an Italian finance official. However adroit in financial larceny, he was an amateur in more rudimentary forms of crime. Kreuger let it be known that he hoped to revive his sinking fortune by cutting a deal with Mussolini's government, and hinted at other secret deals in the works. Meanwhile, he shifted assets frantically from one account to another to hide an over-all shortage of funds, a shortage on the order of a hundred million dollars.

As rumors spread about his troubles, Kreuger became increasingly reclusive, avoiding meetings with bankers and auditors. He drank and smoked heavily and barricaded himself in a room in Stockholm that he had labelled the Silence Room. By early 1932, the gates of the New York credit markets had slammed shut for Ivar Kreuger. As he foresaw ruin, he grew manic, greeting his bankers on one occasion in yellow silk pajamas and a purple silk dressing gown. As the self-control of this skillful actor crumbled, he started to babble in sudden outbursts and heard imaginary phones ringing and people knocking at the door.

In March, 1932, at the age of fifty-two, Ivar Kreuger left his

Paris apartment and bought a 9-mm. Browning pistol. As a dozen bankers awaited an important meeting with him, he retired to his bedroom, lay in bed, and shot himself in the heart. His suicide note began, "I have made such a mess of things that I believe this to be the most satisfactory solution for everybody concerned." Two weeks later, accountants at Price Waterhouse declared his companies insolvent. He left behind widespread destruction. The venerable house of Lee, Higginson went bankrupt, and one partner had the decency to admit, "I suddenly knew we had all been idiots." Unlike the Madoff scandal, Kreuger's downfall didn't leave investors completely bereft. Swedish Match retained a major portion of the world match market, and Kreuger also left behind substantial gold, timber, iron-ore, and real-estate interests. The trustees of International Match recovered a third of lost investor value after thirteen years—about the same amount that Ponzi's investors eventually recovered.

Frank Partnoy, as a fair-minded biographer, renders a mixed verdict on Ivar Kreuger. "He was not merely the greatest financial fraudster of the century," he writes. "He was a builder, as well as a destroyer." Certainly, Kreuger, like all great Ponzi schemers, had a willing army of dupes and confederates behind him; as is often the case, the victims were so gullible that they seem like eager accomplices to, as well as casualties of, the fraud. And, no less than Ponzi, Kreuger had also deceived himself.

Few financiers become embroiled in Ponzi schemes voluntarily, for the simple reason that such schemes are mathematically certain to fail. At some point, the incoming money cannot keep pace with the outgoing claims, and the fraud must unravel. And so the saga of Ivar Kreuger presents a credible explanation of how giant Ponzi enterprises come about: not as sudden inspirations of criminal masterminds but as the gradual culmination of small moral compromises made by financiers who aren't quite as ingenious as they think. As Charles Baudelaire once said, we descend into hell by tiny steps. Indeed, in pleading guilty last

Thursday, Madoff explained that he had initially thought his fraud would be short-lived. He may well have fancied himself a brilliant money manager. Perhaps, early on, he even had a few good, legitimate years. When his lucky streak suddenly ended, he might have thought that he would temporarily make whole the losses of old investors by giving them money from new ones. And then he was off and running.

An honors graduate of Yale and Cambridge, RON CHERNOW *is one of the most distinguished commentators on business, politics, and finance in America today.* The St. Louis Post-Dispatch *has hailed him as "one of the pre-eminent biographers of his generation," and* Fortune *magazine has dubbed him "America's best business biographer." His first book,* The House of Morgan, *won the National Book Award as the best nonfiction book of 1990. The Modern Library Board voted it one of the hundred best nonfiction books published in the twentieth century. His second book,* The Warburgs, *won the prestigious George S. Eccles Prize for the best business book of 1993 and was cited by the American Library Association as one of the year's ten best works. In reviewing his 1997 collection of essays,* The Death of the Banker, The New York Times *called Mr. Chernow "as elegant an architect of monumental histories as we've seen in decades." His 1998 biography of John D. Rockefeller, entitled* Titan, *was nominated for a National Book Critics Circle Award and remained on the* New York Times *bestseller list for sixteen weeks. Both the* Times *and* Time *magazine voted it one of the ten best books of the year, while* The Times *of London praised it as "one of the great American biographies."*

Mr. Chernow's biography of Alexander Hamilton was published by The Penguin Press *in April 2004. The* New York Times *praised it as "moving and masterly . . . by far the best biography ever written about the man." Excerpted by* Business Week *and chosen as the main selection of both* The Book-of-the-Month Club *and the* History Book Club, *the book spent three months on the* New York Times *bestseller* list and was the first recipient of the George Washington Book Prize for the year's best book about the founding era. A frequent contributor to The New York Times, Mr. Chernow is a familiar figure on national radio and television shows and has appeared in numerous documentaries. He lives in Brooklyn, New York, and recently served as president of PEN American Center, the country's preeminent organization of authors. The Penguin Press has just published his biography of George Washington.

Charles Bowden

The Sicario

FROM *Harper's Magazine*

I AM READY FOR THE STORY of all the dead men who last saw his face.

As I drank coffee and tried to frame questions in my mind, a crime reporter in Juárez was cut down beside his eight-year-old daughter as they sat in his car letting it warm up. This morning as I drove down here, a Toyota passed me with a bumper sticker that read, with a heart symbol, I LOVE LOVE. This morning I tried to remember how I got to this rendezvous.

I was in a distant city and a man told me of the killer and how he had hidden him. He said at first he feared him, but he was so useful. He would clean everything and cook all the time and get on his hands and knees and polish his shoes. I took him on as a favor, he explained.

I said, "I want him. I want to put him on paper."

And so I came.

The man I wait for insists, "You don't know me. No one can forgive me for what I did."

He has pride in his hard work. The good killers make a very

tight pattern through the driver's door. They do not spray rounds everywhere in the vehicle, no, they make a tight pattern right through the door and into the driver's chest. The reporter who died received just such a pattern, ten rounds from a 9mm and not a single bullet came near his eight-year-old daughter.

I wait.

I admire craftsmanship.

The first call comes at 9:00 and says to expect the next call at 10:05. So I drive fifty miles and wait. The call at 10:05 says to wait until 11:30. The call at 11:30 does not come, and so I wait and wait. Next door is a game store frequented by men seeking power over a virtual world. Inside the coffee shop, it is all calculated calm and everything is clean.

I am in the safe country. I will not name the city, but it is far from Juárez and it is down by the river. At noon, the next call comes.

We meet in a parking lot, our cars conjoined like cops with driver next to driver. I hand over some photographs. He quickly glances at them and then tells me to go to a pizza parlor. There he says we must find a quiet place because he talks very loudly. I rent a motel room with him. None of this can be arranged ahead of time because that would allow me to set him up.

He glances at the photographs, images never printed in newspapers. He stabs his finger at a guy standing over a half-exposed body in a grave and says, "This picture can get you killed."

I show him the photograph of the woman. She is lovely in her white clothes and perfect makeup. Blood trickles from her mouth, and the early-morning light caresses her face. The photograph has a history in my life. Once I placed it in a magazine and the editor there had to field a call from a terrified man, her brother, who asked, "Are you trying to get me killed, to get my family killed?" I remember the editor calling me up and asking me what I thought the guy meant. I answered, "Exactly what he said."

Now the man looks at her and tells me she was the girlfriend of the head of the *sicarios* in Juárez, and the guys in charge of the cartel thought she talked too much. Not that she'd ever given up a load or anything, it was simply the fact that she talked too much. So they told her boyfriend to kill her and he did. Or he would die.

This is ancient ground. The term *sicario* goes back to Roman Palestine, where a Jewish sect, the Sicarii, used concealed daggers (*sicae*) in their murders of Romans and their supporters.

He leans forward. "Amado and Vicente"—the two brothers who have successively headed the Juárez cartel—"could kill you if they even thought you were talking," he says.

These photographs can get you killed. Words can get you killed. And all this will happen and you will die and the sentence will never have a subject, simply an object falling dead to the ground.

I feel myself falling down into some kind of well, some dark place that hums beneath the workaday city, and in this place there is a harder reality and absolute facts. I have been living, I think, in a kind of fantasy world of laws and theories and logical events. Now I am in a country where people are murdered on a whim and a beautiful woman is found in the dirt with blood trickling from her mouth and then she is wrapped with explanations that have no actual connection to what happened.

I have spent years getting to this moment. The killers, well, I have been around them before. Once I partied with two hundred armed killers in a Mexican hotel for five days. But they were not interested in talking about their murders. He is.

WE WILL NEVER SEE HIM COMING. He is of average height, he dresses like a workman with sturdy boots and a knit cap. If he stood next to you in a checkout line, you would be unable to describe him five minutes later. Nothing about him draws attention. Nothing.

He has very thick fingers and large hands. His face is expressionless. His voice is loud but flat.

He lives beneath notice. That is part of how he kills.

He says, "Juárez is a cemetery. I have dug the graves for 250 bodies."

I nod because I know what he means. The dead, the 250 corpses, are details, people he disappeared and put in holes in death houses. The city is studded with these secret tombs. Just today the authorities discovered a skeleton. From the rotted clothing, the experts peg the bones to be those of a twenty-five-year-old man. He is one of a legion of dead hidden in Juárez.

That is why I am here. I have spent twenty years now waiting for this moment and trying to avoid being buried in some hole. At that party long ago with the two hundred gunmen, a Mexican federal cop wanted to kill me. He was stopped by the host, and so I continued on with my tattered life. But I have come to this room so that I can bring out my dead, the thousands who have been cut down on my watch. I have published two books on the slaughter of the city, reporting there from 1995, when murder in Juárez ran at two to three hundred a year, until 2008, when 1,607 people were killed. And that is only the official tally—no one really keeps track of those who are taken and never heard from again. I am a prisoner of all this killing.

We sit with a translator at a round wooden table, drapes closed.

He says, "Everything I say stays in this room."

I nod and continue making notes.

That is how it begins: nothing is to leave the room, even though I am making notes and he knows I will publish what he says because I tell him that. We are entering a place neither of us knows. I can never repeat what he tells me even though I tell him I will repeat it. Nothing must leave the room even though he watches me write his words down in a black notebook. I do not even know his name, nor can I verify the particulars of what he tells me. But this killer has come to me with a pedigree, established through the hands that delivered him to me: a man who once used him, a former cartel member and leading state policeman who now has produced him as a favor.

He tells me to feel the tricep on his right arm. It hangs down like a tire. Now, he says, feel my left arm. There is nothing there.

He stands, puts a chokehold on me. He can snap my neck like a twig.

Then he sits down again.

I ask him how much he would charge to kill me.

He gives me a cool appraisal and says, "At the most, $5,000, probably less. You are powerless and you have no connections to power. No one would come after me if I killed you."

We are ready to begin.

I ASK HIM how he became a killer.

He smiles and says, "My arm grew."

He takes a sheet of paper, draws five vertical lines, and writes in the spaces in black ink: CHILDHOOD, POLICE, NARCO, GOD. The four phases of his life. Then he scratches out what he has written until there is nothing but solid ink on the page.

He cannot leave tracks. He cannot quite give up the habits of a lifetime.

I reach for the paper but he snatches it back. And laughs. I think at both of us.

"When I believed in the Lord," he says, "I ran from the dead."

"I had a normal childhood," he insists. He will not tolerate the easy explanation that he is the product of abuse.

"We were very poor, very needy," he continues. "We came to the border from the south to survive. My people went into the *maquilas*. I went to a university. I didn't have a father who treated me badly. My father worked, a working man. He started at the *maquila* at 6:00 P.M. and worked until 6:00 A.M., six days a week.

The rest of the time he was sleeping. My mother had to be both father and mother. She cleaned houses in El Paso three days a week. There were twelve children to feed."

He pauses here to see if I understand. He will not be a victim, not of poverty, not of parents. He became a killer because it was a way to live, not because of trauma. His eyes are clear and intelligent. And cold.

"Once," he says, "my father took me and three of my brothers to the circus. We brought our own chilis and cookies so we did not have to spend money. That was the happiest day of my life. And the only time I went somewhere with my father."

But now we turn to the time he worked for the devil.

He is in high school when the state police recruit him and his friends. They get $50 to drive cars across the bridge to El Paso, where they park them and walk away. They never know what is in the cars, nor do they ever ask. After the delivery, they are taken to a motel where cocaine and women are always available.

He drops out of the university because he has no money. And then the police dip into his set of friends who have been moving drugs for them to El Paso. And send them to the police academy. In his own case, because he is only seventeen, the mayor of Juárez has to intervene to get him into the academy.

"We were paid about a hundred and fifty pesos a month as cadets," he says, "but we got a bonus of $1,000 a month that came from El Paso. Every day, liquor and drugs came to the academy for parties. Each weekend, we bribed the guards and went to El Paso. I was sent to the FBI school in the United States and taught how to detect drugs, guns, and stolen vehicles. The training was very good."

After graduation, no one in the various departments really wanted him because he was too young, but U.S. law enforcement insisted he be given a command position. And so he was.

"I commanded eight people," he continues. "Two were honest and good. The other six were into drugs and kidnapping."

Two units of the State Police in Juárez specialized in kidnapping, and his was one such unit. The official assignment of both units was to stop kidnapping. In reality, one unit would kidnap the person and then hand the victim over to the other unit to be killed, a procedure less time-consuming than guarding the victim until the ransom was paid. Sometimes they would feign discovering the body a few days after the abduction.

That was the orderly Juárez he once knew. Then in July 1997, Amado Carrillo Fuentes, the head of the Juárez cartel, died. This was an "earthquake." Order broke down. The payments to the State Police from an account in the United States ended. And each unit had to fend for itself.

"I have no real idea how and when I became a *sicario*," he says. "At first, I picked up people and handed them over to killers. And then my arm began to grow because I strangled people. I could earn $20,000 a killing."

Before Carrillo's death, cocaine was not easy for him to get in Juárez because "if you cut open a kilo, you died." So he and his crew would cross the bridge to El Paso and score. He is by now running a crew of kidnappers and killers, he is working for a cartel that stores tons of cocaine in Juárez warehouses, and he must enter the United States to get his drugs.

That changed after Carrillo's death. Soon he was deep into cocaine, amphetamines, and liquor and would stay up for a week. He also acquired his skill set: strangulation, killing with a knife, killing with a gun, car-to-car barrages, torture, kidnapping, and simply disappearing people and burying them in holes.

He mentions the case of Victor Manuel Oropeza, a doctor who wrote a column for the newspaper. He linked the police and the drug world. He was knifed to death in his office in 1991.

"The people who killed him taught me. *Sicarios* are not born, they are made."

He became a new man in a new world.

IN THE EYES OF THE U.S. GOVERNMENT, the Mexican drug industry is very organized, its cartels structured like corporations, perhaps with periodic meetings. But on the ground with the *sicario*, there is no structure. He kills all over Mexico, he works with various groups, but he never knows how things are linked, he never meets the people in charge, and he never asks any questions. And so he visits the various outposts of this underground empire, but does so without any map and with no directory of the management. He is in a cell and can betray only the handful of people in his cell. He will never even be certain which cartel organization pays him.

He tells me of a leader—a deputy of Vicente Carrillo Fuentes, the current head of the Juárez cartel—"a man full of hate, a man who even hates his own family. He would cut up a baby in front of the father in order to make the father talk."

He says the man is a beast. He is drifting now, going back in time to a place he has left, the killing ground where he would slaughter and then drop five grand in a single evening. He remembers when outsiders would try to move into Juárez and commandeer the plaza, the crossing. For a while, the organization killed them and hung them upside down. Then, for a spell, they offered Colombian neckties, the throat cut, tongue dangling through the slit. There was a spate of necklacing, the burned body found with a charred stub where the head had been, the metal cords of the tire simply blackened hoops embracing the corpse.

He has lived like a god and been the destroyer of worlds. The room is still, so very still, the television a blank eye, the walls sedated with beige, the exhaust fan purring. His arms at rest on the wood table, everything solid and calm.

But his face is fear. Not fear of me but of something neither of us can define, a death machine with no apparent driver. There is no headquarters for him to avoid, no boss to keep an eye peeled for. He has been green-lighted, and now anyone who knows of the contract can kill him on sight and collect the money. The name of his killer is legion.

He can hide, but that only buys a little time, and he is allowed only one serious mistake and then he is dead. His hunters can be patient. He is like a winning lottery ticket, and one day they will collect. The death machine careens through the streets, guns at the ready, always rolling, no real route, randomly prowling and looking for fresh blood. The day comes and goes, and ten die. Or more. No one can really keep count any longer, and besides, some of the bodies simply vanish and cannot be tallied.

He stares at me.

He says, "I want to talk about God."

I say, "We'll get to that."

He is the killer and he does not know who is in charge. Just as he usually did not know the reason for the murders he committed. He will die.

Someone will kill him. No one will really notice.

NO PLACE IS SAFE, he knows that fact. A family in the States owed some money on a deal, so a fourteen-year-old son and his friend were snatched and taken back over. The man killed them with a broken bottle, then drank a glass of their blood. He knows things like that. Because of what he has done. He knows that crossing the bridge is easy because he has crossed it so many times. He knows all the searches and all the security claims at the border are a joke because he has moved with his weapons back and forth. He knows that everything has been penetrated, that nothing can be trusted, not even the solid feel of the wooden table.

The rough edge of burning wood fires at those shacks of the poor, the acrid smell of burned powder flowing from a spent brass cartridge, an old copper kettle with oil boiling and fresh pork swirling into the crispness of *carnitas*, the caravan of cars passing in the night, windows tinted, and then the entire procession turns and comes by again and you look but do not stare because if they pause, however briefly, they will take you with them to the death that waits, the holes being dug each morning in the brown dirt of the Campo Santo, the graves a guess and a promise gaping up like hungry mouths for the kills of the morning and afternoon and evening, and four people sit outside their house at night and the cars come by, the bullets bark, two die soon after the barrage, and the other two are scooped up by family who drive them from hospital to hospital through the dark houses because no healers will take them in. The killers have a way of following their prey into the emergency rooms in order to finish the work.

His arms are on the wooden table as Juárez wafts across our faces, and we do not speak of this fact.

I cannot explain the draw of the city that gives death but makes everyone feel life. Nor can he. So we do not speak but simply note this fact with our silence. We are both trying to return to some person we imagine we once were, the person before the killings, before the torture, before the fear. He wants to live without the power of life and death, and wonders if he can endure being without the money. I want to obliterate memory, to be in a world where I do not know of *sicarios* and think of dinner and not of fresh corpses decorating the *calles*. We have followed different paths and wound up in the same plaza, and now we sit and talk and wonder how we will ever get home.

I crossed the river about twenty years ago—I can't be exact about the date because I am still not sure what crossing really means except that you never come back. I just know I crossed and now I stumble on some distant shore. It is like killing. I ask him, "Tell me about your first killing," and he says he can't remember, and I know that he is not telling the truth and I know that he is not lying. Sometimes you cannot reach it. You open that drawer, and your hand is paralyzed and you cannot reach it. It is right in front of you but still you cannot reach it, and so you say you don't remember.

He has a green pen, a notebook. He has printouts from the Internet, mainly things about me. He has spent ten hours researching me, he says. Like so many pilgrims, he is in the market for a witness who can understand his life. He has decided I will suffice. He is at ease now. Before, his body was hunched over, shoulders looming, those trained and talented hands. He wore a skullcap that hid his hair and he seldom smiled.

Now he is a different person, a man who laughs, his body almost fluid, his eyes no longer dead black coals but beaming and dancing as he speaks.

"We are not monsters," he explains. "We have education, we have feelings. I would leave torturing someone, go home and have dinner with my family, and then return. You shut off parts of your mind. It is a kind of work, you follow orders."

For some time, his past life has been dead to him, something he shut off. But now it is back. He thinks God has sent me to convey his lessons to others. Like all of us, he wants his life to have meaning, and I am to write it down and send it out into the world. Of course, he must be careful. When he left the life two years ago, the organization put a $250,000 contract on his life. He does not know what the contract currently is, but it is unlikely to be lower. At the moment, God is protecting him and his family, he knows this, but still he must be careful.

"I don't do bad things anymore," he says, "but I can't stop being careful. It is a habit I have. That's how I ensure security for myself. They killed me twice, you know."

And he lifts his shirt to show me two groupings of bullet holes in his belly from separate times when he took rounds from an AK-47.

"I was in a coma for a while," he continues. "I weighed 290 pounds when I went into the hospital, a narco hospital, and I shrank to 120 pounds."

It was all a mistake. The organization believed he had leaked information on the killing of a newspaper columnist, but it turned out the actual informant had been the guy paid to tap phones. So he was killed and "they apologized to me and paid for a month's vacation in Mazatlán with women, drugs, and liquor. I was about twenty-four then."

He sips his coffee. He is ready to begin.

HE NOTES THAT when I asked him earlier about his first killing, he said he couldn't really remember because he used so much cocaine and drank so much alcohol back then. That was a lie. He remembers quite well.

"The first person I killed, well, we were state policemen doing a patrol," he says. "They called my partner on his cell phone and told him the person we were looking for was in a mall. So we went and got him and put him in the car."

Two guys get in the car, identify the target, and leave. They are people paying for the murder.

He and his partner use the police code for a homicide: when the number 39 is spoken, it means to kill the person.

The guy they have picked up has lost ten kilos of cocaine, drugs that belong to the other two men.

His partner drives, and he gets in back with the victim.

The target says that he gave the drugs to someone else. At that moment his partner says, "Thirty-nine," and so he instantly kills him.

"It was like automatic," he explains.

They drive around for hours with the body and they drink. Finally, they go to an industrial park, pry off a manhole, and throw the body in the sewer. For his work, he gets an ounce of coke, a bottle of whiskey, and $1,000.

"They told me I had passed the test. I was eighteen."

He checks into a hotel and does cocaine and drinks for four days.

"The state police didn't care if you were drunk. If you really wanted to be left alone, you gave the dispatcher a hundred pesos and then they would not call you at all."

After this baptism, he moves into kidnapping and enters a new world. Soon he is traveling all over Mexico. He is working for the police, but whenever an assignment comes up he simply gets leave.

A few of the kidnappings he participates in are merely snatches for ransom. But hundreds of others have a different goal.

"They would say, 'Take this guy. He lost 200 kilos of marijuana and didn't pay.' I would pick him up in my police car, I would drop him off at a safe house. A few hours later, I would get a call that said there is a dead body to get rid of.

"This was at the start of my career, after I passed my test. For about three years I traveled all over Mexico. Once I even went to Quintana Roo. I always had an official police car. Sometimes we used planes, but usually we drove. We got through military checkpoints by showing an official document that said we were transporting a prisoner. The document would have a fake case number."

He becomes a tour guide to an alternate Mexico, a place where citizens are transported from safe house to safe house without any records left for courts and agencies. When he arrives someplace, the person has already been kidnapped. He simply picks him up for shipment.

Controlling them was easy because they were terrified.

"When they saw that it was an official car and when I said, 'Don't worry, everything will be fine. You'll be back with your family. If you don't cooperate, we'll drug you and put you in the trunk and I can't guarantee then that you'll see the end of the journey.'"

The drive is fueled by coke. He and his partner always dress well for such work—they get five or six new suits from the organization every few months. They are seldom home but seem to live in various safe houses and are supplied with food and drugs. But no women. This is all business.

THEY HARDLY EVER DO police work; they are working full-time for narcos. This is his real home for almost twenty years, a second Mexico that does not exist officially and that coexists seamlessly with the government. In his many transports of human beings to bondage, torture, and death, he is never interfered with by the authorities. He is part of the government, the state policeman with eight men under his command. But his key employer is the organization, which he assumes is the Juárez cartel, but he never asks since questions can be fatal. They give him a salary, a house, a car. And standing.

He estimates that 85 percent of the police worked for the organization. But, even on a clear day, he could barely glimpse the cartel that employed him. He is in a cell, and above him is a boss, and above that boss is a region of power he never visits or knows. He also estimates that out of every hundred human beings he transports maybe two make it back to their former lives. The rest die. Slowly, very slowly.

In each safe house, there would be anywhere from five to fifteen kidnap victims. They wore blindfolds all the time, and if their blindfolds slipped they were killed. At times, they would be put in a chair facing a television, their eyes would be briefly uncovered, and they would watch videos of their children going to school, their wives shopping, the family at church. They would see the world they had left behind, and they would know this world would vanish, be destroyed, if they did not come through with the money. The neighbors never complained about the safe houses. They would see all the police cars parked in front and remain silent.

They might owe a million, but when the work was finished they would pay everything, their entire fortunes, and maybe, just maybe, the wife would be left with a house and a car. People would be held for up to two years. They were beaten after they were fed, and so they learned to associate food with pain. Once in a great while, the order would come down to release a prisoner. They would be taken to a park blindfolded, told to count to fifty before they opened their eyes. Even at this moment of freedom, they would weep because they no longer believed it possible for them to be released and still expected to be murdered.

"Sometimes," he says, "prisoners who had been held for months would be allowed to remove the blindfolds so they could clean the safe house. After a while, they began to think they were part of the organization, and they identified with the guards who beat them. They would even make up songs about their experiences as prisoners, and they would tell us of all the fine things they would make sure we got when they were released. Sometimes after beating them badly, we would send their families videos of them and they would be pleading, saying, 'Give them everything.' And then the order would come down and they would be killed."

Payment to the organization would always be made in a different city from where the prisoner was held. Everything in the organization was compartmentalized. Often he would stay in a safe house for weeks and never speak to a prisoner or know who they were. It did not matter. They were products and he was a worker following orders. No matter how much the family paid, the prisoner almost always died. When the family had been sucked dry of money, the prisoner had no value. And besides, he could betray the organization. So death was logical and inevitable.

He pauses in his account. He wants it understood that he is now similar to the prisoners he tortured and killed. He is outside the organization, he is a threat to the organization, and "everyone who is no longer of use to the boss dies."

He is now the floating man remembering when he was firmly anchored in his world.

"I want it understood," he says, "that I had feelings when I was in the torture houses and people would be lying in their vomit and blood. I was not permitted to help them."

He is calm as he says this. He alternates between asserting his humanity and explaining how he maintained a professional demeanor while he kidnapped, tortured, and killed people. He says he is feared now because he believes in God. Then he says he could make a good grouping on the target with his AK-47 at 800 yards. He would practice at military bases and police academies. He could get in using his police badge.

The work, he insists, is not for amateurs. Take torture—you must know just how far to go. Even if you intend to kill the person in the end, you must proceed carefully in order to get the necessary information.

"They are so afraid," he explains, "they are usually cooperative. Sometimes when they realize what is going to happen to them, they become aggressive. Then you take their shoes away, soak their clothes, and put a hot wire to each foot for fifteen seconds. Then they understand that you are in charge and that you are going to get the information. You can't beat them too much because then they become insensitive to pain. I have seen people beaten so badly that you could pull out their fingernails with pliers and they wouldn't feel it.

"You handcuff them behind their backs, sit them in a chair

facing a hundred-watt bulb, and you ask them questions about their jobs, number and age of children, all things you have researched and know the answer to. Every time they lie, you give them a jolt from an electric cattle prod. Once they realize they can't lie, you start asking them the real questions—how many loads have they moved to the U.S., who do they work for, and if they are not paying your boss, well, why?

"They will try by this point to answer everything. Then we beat them and let them rest. We show them those videos of their family. At this point, they will give up anything we ask for and even more. Now you have the advantage, and you use this new information to hit warehouses and steal loads, to round up other people they work with, and then you video their families and begin the process again. You know the families will not likely go to the police because they know the guy is in a bad business. But if they do tell the police, we instantly know because we work with the police. We're part of the anti-kidnapping unit. Sometimes the people kidnapped are killed instantly because, after we take their jewelry and cars, they are worthless. Such goods are divided up within the unit, among five to eight people. The hardest thing is when you kill them because then you must dig a hole to bury them. There are two mistakes most people make. They don't pay whoever controls the plaza, the city. Or they dreamed of being bigger than the boss."

But none of this really matters because he never asks why people are kidnapped, nor who they really are. They are simply product and he is simply a worker. Their screams are simply the background noise to the task at hand. Just as calming them or transporting them is simply part of the job.

THERE IS A SECOND CATEGORY OF KIDNAPPING, one he finds almost embarrassing. Someone's wife is having an affair with her personal trainer, so you pick up the trainer and kill him. Or a guy has a hot woman and some other guy wants her, so you kill the boyfriend to get the woman for him.

"I received my orders," he says, "and I had to kill them. The bosses didn't know what the limits were. If they want a woman, they get her. If they want a car, they get it. They have no limits."

He resents people who like to kill. They are not professional. Real *sicarios* kill for money. But there are people who kill for fun.

"People will say, 'I haven't killed anyone for a week.' So they'll go out and kill someone. This kind of person does not belong in organized crime. They're crazy. If you discover such a person in your unit, you kill him. The people you really want to recruit are police or ex-police—trained killers."

All this is a sore point for him. The slaughter now going on in Juárez offends him because too many of the killings are done by amateurs, by kids imitating *sicarios*. He is appalled by the number of bullets used in a single execution. It shows a lack of training and skill. In a real hit, the burst goes right where the lock is on the door because such rounds will penetrate the driver's torso with a killing shot. Twice he was stymied by armored vehicles, but the solution is a burst of full-jacketed rounds in a tight pattern—this will gouge through the armor. A hit should take no more than a minute. Even his hardest jobs against armored cars took under three minutes.

A real *sicario,* he notes, does not kill women or children. Unless the women are informants for the DEA or the FBI.

Here, he must show me. A proper execution requires planning. First, the Eyes study the target for days, usually at least a week. His schedule at home is noted, when he gets up, when he leaves for work, when he comes home, everything about his routines in his domestic life is recorded by the Eyes. Then the Mind takes over. He studies the man's habits in the city itself: his day at work, where he lunches, where he drinks, how often he visits his mistress and where she lives and what her habits are. Between the Eyes and the Mind a portrait is possible. Now there is a meeting of the crew, which is six to eight people. There will be two police cars with officers and two other cars with *sicarios*. A street will be selected for the hit, one that can easily be blocked off. Timing will be carefully worked out, and the hit will take place within a half dozen blocks of a safe house—an easy matter since there are so many in the city.

He picks up a pen and starts drawing. The lead car will be police. Then will come a car full of *sicarios*. Then the car driven by the target. This is followed by another car of *sicarios*. And then, bringing up the rear, another police car.

During the execution, the Eyes will watch and the Mind will man the radios.

When the target enters the block selected for the murder, the lead police car will pivot and block the street, the first *sicario* will slow, the second car of *sicarios* behind the target will pull up beside him and shoot him, the final police car will block the end of the street.

All this should take less than thirty seconds. One man will get out and give a coup de grâce to the bullet-riddled victim. Then all will disperse.

The car with the killers will go to the safe house and leave their vehicle in a garage. It will be taken to a garage owned by the organization, repainted, and then sold on one of the organization's lots. The killers themselves will pick up a clean car at the safe house, and often they return to the scene of the murder to see that everything has gone well.

He sketches this with exactness, each rectangle neatly drawn to delineate a car, and the target's car is filled in and blooms on the page with green ink. Arrows indicate how each vehicle will move. It is like an equation on a chalkboard.

HE LEANS BACK FROM HIS TOIL and on his face is almost the look of a job well done. This is how a real *sicario* performs his work. In the ideal hit, no target is left alive. Should any in the group be injured, they go to one of the organization's hospitals— "If you can buy a governor, you can buy a hospital."

"I never knew the names of the people I was involved with," he continues. "There was a person who directed our group and he knew everything. But if your job is to execute people, that is all you do. You don't know the reasons or names. I would be in a safe house with the kidnapped for a month and never speak to them. Then, if I was told to kill them, I would. We would take them to the place where they would be killed, take off their clothes. We would kill them exactly the way we were ordered— a bullet to the neck, acid on the bodies. There would be cases where you would be killing someone, strangling them, and they would stop breathing, and you would get a call—'Don't kill them'—and so you would have to know how to resuscitate them or we would be killed because the boss never makes a mistake."

Everything is contained and sealed. For a while they used crazy kids to steal cars for the work, but the kids, about forty of them, got too arrogant, talking and selling drugs in the nightclubs. This violated an agreement with the governor of Chihuahua to keep the city quiet. So one night around ten years ago, fifty police, and one hundred and fifty guys from the organization who were to ensure the job was done, rounded up all the kids on Avenida Juárez. They were not tortured. They were killed with a single head shot and buried in one hole.

"No." He smiles at me. "I will not tell you where that hole is."

He has trouble remembering some things.

"I would get up in the morning and do a line," he explains, "then have a glass of whiskey. Then I would go to lunch. I would never sleep more than a few hours, little naps. It is hard to sleep during a time of war. Even if my eyes were closed, I was alert. I slept with a loaded AK-47 on one side, a .38 on the other. The safeties were always off."

Do I know of the death houses, he asks. "It would take a

book to do the death houses. After all, I know where six hundred bodies are buried in safe houses in Juárez. There is one death house they have never revealed that I know has fifty-six bodies. Just as there is a rancho where the officials say they found two bodies but I know that rancho has thirty-two corpses. If the police really investigated they would find bodies. But obviously, you cannot trust the police."

He especially wants to know what I know about the two death houses uncovered last winter. I say one had nine bodies, the other thirty-six.

No, no, he insists, the second one had thirty-eight, two of them women.

He carefully draws me the layout of this second death house. One of the women, he notes, was killed for speaking too much. The other was a mistake. These do happen, though the bosses never admit to it.

But he keeps returning to the death house with the thirty-eight bodies. It has memories for him.

I remember standing on the quiet dirt street as the authorities made a show of digging up the dead. Half a mile away was a hospital where some machine-gunned people were taken that spring, but the killers followed and killed them in the emergency room. Shot their kinfolk in the waiting room also.

"The narcos," he wants me to understand, "have informants in the DEA and the FBI. They work until they are useless. Then they are killed."

As for those who inform *to* the FBI and DEA, they "die ugly."

He explains.

"They were brought handcuffed behind the back to the death house where they found thirty-six bodies," he rolls on. "A T-shirt was soaked with gasoline and put on their backs, lit, and then after a while pulled from their backs. The skin came off with it. Both men made sounds like cattle being killed. They were injected with a drug so they would not lose consciousness. Then they put alcohol on their testicles and lit them. They jumped so high—they were handcuffed and still I never saw people jump so high."

We are slipping now, all the masks have fallen to the floor. The veteran, the professional *sicario*, is walking me through a key assignment he completed.

"Their backs were like leather and did not bleed. They put plastic bags on their heads to smother them and then revived them with alcohol under their noses.

"All they ever said to us was, 'We will see you in hell.'

"This went on for three days. They smelled terrible because of the burns. They brought in a doctor to keep reviving them. They wanted them to live one more day. After a while they defecated blood. They shoved broomsticks up their asses.

"The second day a person came and told them, 'I warned you this was going to happen.'

"They said, 'Kill us.'

"The guys lived three days. The doctor kept injecting them to keep them alive and he had to work hard. Eventually they died of the torture.

"They never asked God for help. They just kept saying, 'We will see you in hell.'

"I buried them with their faces down and poured on a whole lot of lime."

He is excited. It is all back.

He can feel the shovel in his hand.

HE IS CALM NOW. He is revisiting this evil time, he says, simply for my benefit. He takes his various drawings—how to do a hit, where some people were buried in a death house—looks at the green schematics he has created, and then slowly tears them into little squares until the torn heap can never be reconstructed.

Until late 2006, he worked all over Mexico for different groups, and the various organizations generally got along. There were small moments, such as when others tried to take over Juárez and it was necessary to necklace them. But his life in the main was calm. So calm he did not need to know who he really worked for.

"I received orders from two people. They ran me. I never knew which cartel I worked for. Now there is Vicente Carrillo against Chapo Guzmán"—that is, Joaquin Guzmán Loera, head of Mexico's largest cartel. "But I never met any bosses, so when the war started around 2006, I did not know which one I did the killing for. And orders could cross from one group to another. I am living in a cell and I simply take orders. In thirty minutes in Juárez, sixty well-trained and heavily armed men can assemble in thirty cars and circulate as a show of force.

"Then, at my level, we began to get orders to kill each other."

He is kidnapped but let go after an hour. This unsettles him, and he begins to think about escaping his life. But that is not a simple matter, since if you leave you are murdered. As the war escalates, he begins to distance himself from people he knows and works with. He tries to fade away. By this time, a third of the people he knows have been killed—"they were seen as useless and then killed."

He doesn't know the boss, he is still not even sure who his boss is. He drinks at home. The streets are too dangerous. New people arrive and he does not know them. He is not safe.

So he flees.

He confides in a friend. Who betrays him.

He pauses at this point. He knows he is guilty of a fatal error. He has violated a fundamental rule: you can be betrayed only by someone you trust. So you survive by trusting no one. Still, there is this shred of humanity in all of us, and in the end we feel the need to trust someone, to call someone friend, to share feelings with others. And this need is fatal. It is the very need he has exploited for years, the need he used when he put people in the police car and told them they would be all right if they cooperated, would be back with their families in no time if they were calm. And by God, they did trust him and rode across Mexico, went through checkpoints and said nothing, never told a single soul they had been kidnapped. They would trust him as they were tortured in the safe houses. They would help mop the floors, clean up the vomit and blood. They would compose songs. They would trust him right up to that instant when he strangled them.

So his friend gives him up. He is taken at 10:00 P.M., and this time he is held until 3:00 A.M.

But something has changed within him. And some things have not changed. Four men take him to a safe house. They remove all of his clothing but his shorts. They take pool balls in their hands and beat him.

But he can tell they are amateurs. They do not even handcuff him, and this is disturbing to him. He is the captive of third-raters. As they beat him, he prays and prays and prays. He also laughs because he is appalled by their incompetence. They have not bound him and their blows do not disable him. He sizes them up and in his mind plans how he will kill them, one, two, three, four, just like that.

And at the same moment, he is praying to God to help him so that he will not kill them, so that he can stop his life of murder. As he sits in the room, sipping coffee and recalling this moment, his face comes alive. He is passionate now. He is approaching the very moment of his salvation. Some people pretend to accept Christ, he says, but at that moment he could feel total acceptance fill his body. He could feel peace.

They point rifles at him. He cannot stop laughing.

"I was afraid," he explains. "I realized I would have to kill them all."

Two of the armed men left. One other guy went to the bathroom. He looks at the remaining captor.

"The guy says, 'I don't have a problem with you. Once, you told me to be careful or they would kill me. You did me a favor.'

"So, I am praying to God, help me! I don't want to kill these people. And I know I can do it rapidly.

"The guy turns his back on me and says, 'Get out, go.'"

He opens the door and runs without his shoes or clothes.

HIS FACE IS STERN NOW. He has come to the place, the very moment that has permitted him to recount the kidnappings, the tortures, the killings. He is selling and what he is selling is God. He is believing, and what he believes based on his own life is that anyone can be redeemed. And that it is possible to leave the organization and survive.

His thoughts are a jumble as he speaks. He is telling of his salvation, and yet he feels the tug of his killings. He feels the pride in being feared. Back at the beginning, when he first started with the state police, that was when Oropeza, the doctor and newspaper columnist, was killed. And Oropeza's killers, he now recalls, were his mentors, his teachers. He remembers that after the murder, the state government announced a big investigation to get the killers. And one of them, a fellow cop, stayed at his own police station until the noise quieted and the charade ended.

He is excited now; he is living in his past.

"The only reason I am here is God saved me. I repented. After all these years I am talking to you. I am having to relive things that are dead to me. I don't want to be part of this life. I don't want to know the news. You must write this so that other *sicarios* know it is possible to leave. They must know God can help them. They are not monsters. They have been trained like special forces in the Army. But they never realize they have been trained to serve the devil.

"Imagine being nineteen and being able to call up a plane. I liked the power. I never realized until God talked to me that I could get out. Still, when God frees me, I remain a wolf. I can't become a lamb. I remain a terrible person, but now I have God on my side."

He stares at me as I write in a black notebook.

His body seems to loom over the table.

This is the point in all stories where everyone discovers who they really are.

He says, "I have now relived something I should never have opened up. Are you the medium to reach others? I prayed to God asking what I should do. And you are the answer. You are going to write this story because God has a purpose in you writing this story.

"God has given you this mission.

"No one will understand this story except those who have been in the life. And God will tell you how to write this story."

Then we embrace and pray. I can feel his hand on my shoulder probing, seeking the power of the Lord in me.

I have my work to do now.

And so we go our separate ways.

In the parking lot he moves with ease, in a state of grace. The sun blazes, the sky aches blue. Life feels good. His eyes relax and he laughs. And then I see him memorize my license plate in a quick and practiced glance. He has told me he is bathed in the blood of the lamb, but his eyes remain those of the wolf.

CHARLES BOWDEN *is the author of twenty-three books, including* A Shadow in the City: Confessions of an Undercover Drug Warrior; Down by the River: Drugs, Money, Murder, and Family; Juarez: The Laboratory of Our Future; Blood Orchid: An Unnatural History of America; *and* Exodus, *with photographer Julian Cardona.* Inferno, *with photographer Michael Berman, was a finalist for the Orion*

Book of the Year for 2007. His most recent book is Murder City: Ciudad Juárez and the Global Economy's New Killing Fields.

Bowden is a correspondent for GQ magazine, and his work has appeared in Harper's, Mother Jones, National Geographic, *and* Esquire. *He is a Pulitzer Prize nominee and winner of the Lannan Literary Award for Nonfiction and the Sidney Hillman Foundation Award.*

Permissions

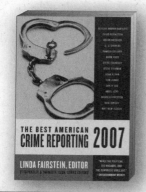